Miranda Glover has written and edited numerous non-fiction titles on art, food and design. Her début novel, *Masterpiece*, was shortlisted for the Pendleton May First Novel Award 2005.

Miranda is married to a photographer and they have two children.

Also by Miranda Glover

MASTERPIECE

and published by Bantam Books

SOULMATES

Miranda Glover

BANTAM BOOKS

LONDON · TORONTO · SYDNEY · AUCKLAND · JOHANNESBURG

TRANSWORLD PUBLISHERS
61–63 Uxbridge Road, London W5 5SA
A Random House Group Company
www.rbooks.co.uk

SOULMATES
A BANTAM BOOK: 9780553817645

First published in Great Britain
in 2007 by Bantam Press
a division of Transworld Publishers
Bantam edition published 2008

Addresses for Random House Group Ltd companies outside the UK
can be found at: www.randomhouse.co.uk
The Random House Group Ltd Reg. No. 954009

The Random House Group Limited supports The Forest Stewardship Council
(FSC), the leading international forest certification organisation.
All our titles that are printed on Greenpeace approved FSC certified paper
carry the FSC logo. Our paper procurement policy can be found at:
www.randomhouse.co.uk/environment

Typeset in 11/14pt Goudy by
Kestrel Data, Exeter, Devon.
Printed in the UK by
CPI Cox & Wyman, Reading, RG1 8EX.

2 4 6 8 10 9 7 5 3 1

This book is dedicated to my mother
– and my daughter

Prologue

We all have stories to tell, stories about our lives, the lives we remember living, the things we remember seeing or think we saw. This is a story about love, the lack of love and the search for truth. It's a story about a girl called Emi, a girl called Polly, and it's a story about the woman who made them, a woman called Sarah, who gave them all she could. As we begin, Emi and Polly are stuck in the middle of their tale, but already the beginning's starting to fade, the details to blur.

Have you ever lost someone? A young child, say, in a supermarket, or a friend at a festival, when the crowd's shoved you in one direction, them in another? It's like dropping a Disprin in water. Your insides fizz, your brain hisses then blurs as it reaches for rewind, struggling to recapture the last few frames, to work out where they've gone. Your fear soon accelerates from mild concern to complete panic – then you catch a glimpse of the child's red raincoat swishing past the aisle, or that familiar hand raised above the swaying crowd, waving only at you; and as quickly as it came, the terror subsides and your brain resettles, just as the water in that Disprin glass clears. Regardless, your relief is tinged with a bitter taste and you can't help but take little sips for the rest of the day. By morning, however, the memory's gone, its insignificance re-asserted.

Now just imagine, if you dare, how it feels when the red coat doesn't swish, the hand isn't raised and the water in the glass doesn't clear. Instead the bitter taste remains, that panic stays, as deafening white noise, and your sleep fails to come easily, if at all. Time passes, and then, well, in Polly's case, suddenly it's a whole year on and still there's been no red coat, no reassuring wave. Polly's replayed the moment so many times in her mind it's almost not her own any more – a fiction, a story someone else told her, one she's simply recounting, artfully, of course, as befits her profession, like all the other stories she's reported, like something she didn't ever experience for herself; that last glimpse she had of Emi, before she closed the blind. In fact you could say that, for Polly, Emi's going has become the stuff of modern myth.

But this is just an episode, a chapter in a story that began long before Emi went away. The first chapter really began at that moment, nearly thirty years ago, when Sarah first knew there was going to be a story to be told.

1

It's the tinkle of the running tap that stirs her from sleep. Sarah Leto opens her eyes then closes them again. Her husband Peter's in the bathroom and now he's humming as he shaves. The sounds are routine, familiar, something known. Until recently she's found them reassuring; positive measures of the security she's discovered inside her fledgling marriage. However, in the past few days she's felt a new, slow stirring of unease. It's lying in a well, deep inside her. This morning it's tugging, pulling upwards, into her throat. And there's a black smudge inside her brain, too; nebulous, like a thundercloud, amassing electricity as it grows. Her skin feels cold and clammy and her insides twist in a spasm. She rolls over and reaches for the plastic bowl secreted beneath her side of the bed, then retches bile into it. She pushes the bowl back, takes a tiny sip of water from her glass, then lies back, curls up and closes her eyes again as she hears Peter come back into the room. He bends over her quietly.

'Goodbye, darling,' he whispers, before turning to head out into the dark November morning.

Initially it had been strange, this shift in their

relationship from the professional to the personal. They had met, only a year and a half before, through work. Sarah was a receptionist at Peter's firm; it was her first job out of college, a stopgap while she tried to fathom what she wanted to do next. Peter was a senior manager. He was ten years older, seemed mature, in control, and their relationship had definitely begun on his instigation. He had sent Sarah endless memos, inviting her to lunch, and finally she had succumbed. It hadn't been 'love at first sight'; in fact, if she were honest, Sarah had found Peter's early displays of interest in her flattering rather than heart-fluttering. She'd never had a clear sense of falling in love. But she respected Peter and wanted the security he could offer – her past was a wrapped package, signed and sealed, her parents distant and self-involved. Inevitably they had been delighted by the news. Sarah had never exactly felt excluded by them, but their role in her life had always been compartmentalized. She had come late, an only child, and had boarded, from eleven. They weren't overtly affectionate, and there had never been much physical display of love. She remembers the school holidays, the endless trips abroad, the silent frustrations on her parents' brows at having to 'bring Sarah along' on their tours. Her father was a conductor, her mother a cellist. Their work was pure, focused and artistic. She had never displayed signs of their talents, had never felt so much a part of their world as a responsibility they shared. And now here she was, twenty-three years old, a parcel passed from parents to husband, and starting her own family, too. When she'd told them of her impending marriage, she'd thought she saw a momentary expression of relief pass between her father and mother, like an implicit code, the silent message understood. They were relieved; their job had successfully been concluded. For Sarah it was as if she had embarked upon an unplanned flight that carried her smoothly between the office and the church, while she stared passively down on to the foreign landscape below, a landscape she knew she would never explore.

Since then, Peter has become a director and she is his wife, no longer taking the tube into work to answer his phone, but lying in his bed, expecting his first child. Her parents would be expecting her to be pregnant now – it would come as no surprise, be weighed in as another measure of their own parenting success. It was the way it was supposed to work. But as she lies in her bed, feeling the churn of the sea inside her, she knows it's not what she wants – not what she wants at all.

For distraction she switches on the radio and listens to the early morning news. Jim Callaghan is to receive loans of 3,000 million pounds to support sterling, the newsreader says. Who would have believed it? The UK, in 1976, with a begging bowl to hand. She should call her father; he would have something to say about it, even all the way from America – he always did.

Six months later and the sky seems too bright, too celebratory. The heat is intense. Everyone keeps saying it will be remembered, this long hot summer of '77. Peter helps his wife out of the house and into the cab, his face grey with anxiety, as Sarah winces with the pain of another contraction.

'Not supposed to take you really,' admonishes the

cabbie, before winking at Peter and firmly shutting the door behind them. 'I hope she doesn't have it on the floor.'

'Them, not it,' Peter mumbles, trying to affect a smile.

As the cab heads off down the Edgware Road, destination St Mary's, Paddington, Sarah moans quietly and his arm tightens around her.

Two days pass, two days of what feels to Peter and to Sarah like physical and emotional carnage. The process is horrifying to them both, the pain, the bestial cries that Sarah emits, like a wounded animal incapable of helping herself through the pain – and then all the blood. Somewhere in the dark folds of the first night, a child is born; a small, flailing, female infant, bloodied and mottled, and she is placed gently on her mother's breast, where she immediately twists her tight face around towards the bared nipple and begins to suck. Moments later, the daughter is moved away and a needle is placed in Sarah's lower back. She feels her body numb as the bed is wheeled hurriedly down a grey corridor into a room of green-masked people and bright ceiling lights. Then her eyes close and Sarah falls asleep.

The first child they name Artemis, after the Greek goddess, the goddess of the moon, the protector of small children, of wild animals. There is something cool and opalescent about this tiny girl who can't settle, who is restless and hungry, particularly during the hours of darkness. She seems slightly desperate, sucking frantically for sustenance, and her pale, translucent skin seems to shine, to emit its own natural luminosity. The second they name Polly, after Artemis's twin, the Greek god Apollo. She comes into the world as the sun pierces the night sky red and Sarah sleeps her dreamless sleep. She's even tinier than her sister, has struggled inside Sarah's contracting womb along with Artemis, but unlike her older twin did not need to fight her way down the birth canal, instead was lifted gently out of her mother's body by a glad-eyed surgeon, straight into the willing arms of her father. Peter feels something more than the tiny weight of his second child when he first holds her in his arms; he feels an almighty surge of perfect love.

After ten days Sarah and Artemis are allowed home. Polly's still lying, test-baby-like, inside her incubator, being fed through tubes, an oxygen supply over her mouth and nose. Peter visits her every evening, but her main care is handed to the nurses, who fall in love with this extra-ordinarily calm, bright-eyed child who seems not to mind the constant light shining upon her, the noise of the other babies crying, the endless interruptions to her sleep.

'She's as good as gold,' they remark. 'As sunny as they come.'

Polly stays at St Mary's for five more weeks, in the air-conditioned whir, her body rapidly gaining weight and her lungs absorbing all the extra oxygen she needs. Peter visits nightly and calms his daughter, while Sarah stays at home in the stifling heat, nursing her older twin.

Artemis still won't settle and puts on little weight. Sarah doesn't tell anyone but she's terrified of this newborn infant lying in her arms. She's so frightened of her that she can't even seem to put her down. If she just lies there, cradling her gingerly, she thinks, then she won't be able to hurt her, drop her or smother her. So she keeps to her bed, to her bedroom. When Peter is there, or the midwife, who continues to visit weekly, she tries to appear content, as a new mother is meant to be. But inside her brain the black cloud feels fit to burst.

'Are you really all right, darling? You seem so pale,' Peter enquires – at least twice a day. He can sense the emotions that weigh Sarah down, but she's terrified of confessing to them.

'I'm fine, just tired,' she reassures him, with a too-wide smile, but she knows she makes her husband anxious, that he is hard to convince.

Sarah hardly visits Polly in hospital, makes apology that she is too weak, that it is too hot to take 'Emi', as they have now taken to calling Artemis, out, that she needs to catch up on sleep, to prepare for having the two of them home. Outside in Alma Square preparations are being made for the Silver Jubilee. Their clutch of narrow, hidden streets on the edge of St John's Wood is to host its own party. Red, white and blue bunting criss-crosses the road, fluttering in the breeze. Sarah quietly watches it all go up from her bedroom window, with Emi in her arms. But she doesn't venture out. On the day of the party it drizzles and Sarah says she thinks it best to keep Emi inside. Peter and their neighbour, Carol, head off to the Mall, to watch the Queen pass by in her golden carriage. Peter says he'll come back via St Mary's, to give Polly her four o'clock feed. Sarah nods and smiles. To her growing relief it seems that Peter likes being Polly's primary carer. After each visit he comes home glowing and he fills her in on their second twin's progress. Polly, it seems, is a happy, hungry baby.

She's feeding from a bottle regularly now, sleeping soundly in between. Soon the doctors think she'll need the milk thickened, perhaps with rice, to sate her growing hunger. Sarah looks down at Emi with her own internal, growing dread. The child she is nurturing is doing less well in her own mother's arms. Despite the heat, she feels a stirring of something cold and thin, like the cut of a knife, inside her and holds on to the baby more tightly.

2

The Friday before it happened was ostensibly a Friday like any other – the kind of day when you only think in the future tense, contemplating what the weekend holds in store. Emi was at work, finishing off a document for her boss, James, when Will rang. Usually when a marriage broke down the respective parties slunk off to lick their wounds with someone else. With Will and Emi it wasn't quite working out that way. Even after six months his natural inclination was to call her daily. Emi had tried to remain understanding – she felt that their undoing was of her making – but her patience was beginning to wear thin. After all, they were both still only twenty-nine years old; there was plenty of time to start again.

'What's up, Will?' she asked, failing to mask her irritation.

'Polly says you've always done this, ever since you were small – sulked, I mean,' he retorted. 'You've got to find a way to stop it.'

Emi chewed her bottom lip and hit 'save' on the computer screen. More and more frequently his jibes came laced with Polly's opinion as ally.

'Why were you two talking?' she finally enquired, coolly.

'I asked her advice.'

'Again.'

'Emi.'

'When did you see her?'

Will's pause was a split second too long.

'What exactly is going on between you two?' she demanded, the words escaping from her lips before she could consider their consequences. The very idea of Will and Polly forming an emotional alliance unnerved her; they were supposed to exist on opposite sides of her; that was the way it had always worked. But now she'd mooted the idea, it sprang into life like a jack from its box. There was something between them, something precious, something growing; Emi could sense it. She felt her stomach churn. Polly had been seeing Will with increasing regularity since Emi had asked him to leave. Whenever she'd expressed curiosity before, Will said that Polly was helping him cope, and when she had questioned Polly she'd reasoned that Will was in a mess and needed her support. And they both asked: what the hell had Emi done? To further ignite her suspicions, Will's only response now was to mutter an expletive and throw down the phone.

Until their split, Polly had always shunned Will, had shown complete disinterest in him. Conversely their mother, Sarah, had loved him like a son; she had welcomed Will into their family at a time when Polly had chosen to distance herself. It was almost beyond Emi's imaginings that Polly could now discover an interest in him for herself. The idea disgruntled her on many levels.

With men Polly had earned a reputation for being dangerous, cold and uncaring. She disposed of her boy-friends with a dispassion that Emi worried verged on the pathological. Over the past decade it had become a pattern. She knew Will could take care of himself, but he was no competition for her sister. Nobody was. And in any respect, this wasn't her only concern. The idea of them together, well, it felt perverse – a miscarriage of their shared nature.

As she sat thinking about it, James, her boss, wandered in, affecting indifference. She tried to focus back on her work as he took a file from the cabinet next to the window and glanced through its contents, whistling under his breath. Emi had worked for him for five years now. It was a significant job, although many would suggest, and had, that it was beneath her. It was true that she'd passed her bar exams, but had opted for a role behind the scenes. She didn't feel at ease in the theatre of the courtroom, it projected too much limelight on her retiring sensibility, but she liked the security this job provided and she knew she did it well.

Finally James turned and looked over his shoulder at her.

'Do you want to come for a drink after work, Emi?' he asked, casually. 'An American friend of mine's in town. She's launching a book.'

Emi knew that James had just overheard her latest spat with Will; that he was trying to be kind. She returned his gaze silently. James was forty-five, married, with four young kids; they lived in the country with their mother, Annabel, and he commuted from their flat in London at weekends. He was solid, generous and paternal – to a degree. Polly had often teased her about James, about Emi's and his professional 'friendship', and she'd always been irritated by her sister's lewd suggestions. They made Emi feel . . . irreverent. Unlike Polly, she'd never known how to do 'men' and flirting. She'd hate to feel that their relationship was based on unclear grounds. Hence she generally avoided socializing with him when Annabel wasn't in town.

'Come on,' he urged now, fixing her in the eye. 'You might even enjoy it.'

Emi couldn't think of an excuse because there wasn't one. He might just be right, she decided, maybe for once she needed to lose herself in the company of strangers.

'Great,' she replied. 'I'd love to.'

'Clare Smart has a reputation for writing sharp literary gems, short novellas with tight casts and psychological dilemmas that push her characters to their emotional limits,' James informed Emi studiously as they walked the short distance to the Ludgate Hotel.

'I know,' Emi replied, glancing at him sideways. 'I read her last one.'

James tried to cover his surprise and Emi laughed. She'd read it in Ibiza the previous summer. Will and she had gone to a favourite old haunt in a vain attempt to recapture the spirit of their premarital relationship. The holiday hadn't worked and she'd hidden inside the book's pages to avoid his incessant cross-examinations. She was tired of his over-analysis, his insistence on improving things, on getting life right, both in their domestic arena and through his political activism, too. In fact, she had finally informed him, she realized that their marriage had been a dreadful mistake. They were both still young, she had reasoned. There was still plenty of time for them both to start anew. Clare's book was called *Leya's Hour*, and Emi recalled feeling in tune with her style. There was something dry at the core of it, as if the prose was being forced to run over a parched stream.

She'd imagined the writer to be as tight and brittle as her writing, but the woman now greeting them was extremely voluptuous, with bottle-enhanced chestnut hair. Emi was taken aback by James's overt display of affection towards her, too, and as they embraced she wondered briefly at the history of their friendship. And then she realized that Clare was beaming at her expectantly; that she must have missed an introduction, and she took the author's proffered hand.

'I'm so pleased you came. You must both join me for dinner afterwards,' Clare now urged, glancing between them both. 'We're going to my favourite Indian restaurant and we have so much to catch up on.'

Emi sensed that Clare was intrigued by her, was wondering at the nature of her own relationship with James. She'd like to have cleared up the confusion by refusing the invitation, but before she got a chance, James had already accepted for them both. For the next hour, therefore, she found herself shadowing him as he manoeuvred his way around the book launch and traded business. James specialized in media law and there was always someone at a London party with something to ask him, or information to share. She tried to listen attentively. James had given her leeway since her break-up from Will and she didn't mind working this subtle form of overtime. It wasn't long before the room began to empty and Clare gestured to them that it was time to go.

Emi had never noticed Clare's chosen restaurant before, even though it was right around the corner from James's chambers and she must have passed it a thousand times. It was tiny and gem-like and inside the colourful tables were full of chattering diners, the air heavy with the sweet, sharp scent of aniseed and frying spices. A waiter led them down a narrow staircase to a second dining-room, crammed with more tables. Only theirs, in the far corner, was almost empty, set decorously with golden-rimmed goblets and plates. Only one person was already seated at its far side.

'Kalle, when did you arrive?' Clare cried with delight, taking hold of the new guest's hands across the table.

The man stood up awkwardly as she turned to introduce him.

'Kalle Strand and I taught together at Columbia,' she enthused. 'He's one of Scandinavia's most celebrated psychologists – and authors, too, of course.'

'Just not in translation yet,' the man answered with a gauche jerk of his shoulders. He was tall and wore a heavy-knit navy blue jumper. It struck Emi because it was so out of place here and yet evidently in keeping with his character. He was of indeterminate age, with thick unruly grey hair and looked as if he spent a lot of time outdoors. She didn't recognize his name and was immediately concerned that her ignorance of his work could prove embarrassing, hoping silently that she wouldn't be seated too close to him. However, Clare was now inviting her to take a chair directly opposite Kalle and next to James, who seemed to sense her discomfort and patted her arm kindly as they took their seats, murmuring reassurances in her ear.

The table soon began to fill up and the group seated to her right engaged Emi's attentions. They included an attractive couple called Lucy and Nile Somerton. She recognized them as architects who ran one of London's most successful young firms; Blairites with a portfolio of celebrity clients.

'Haven't we met before? Aren't you Polly Leto?' Nile Somerton asked her enthusiastically as he took his seat.

Emi smiled politely.

'Easy mistake,' she replied. 'I'm her twin sister.'

The words came out parrot fashion. She'd used them every day since she'd first learned to speak.

In all there were sixteen people at the dinner and their acquaintance with one another formed a chain around the table. The company energetically swapped news and shared stories as they began to eat from plates now piled high with exotic Asian hors d'oeuvres. Only two or three of the guests were Londoners; the rest had flown in from across Europe or from North America for the party. Evidently Clare commanded great loyalty. Soon the conversation split into three natural parties and Emi found herself drawn in with the architects, another writer and a professor of theology from Penn State University. They were charming and inclusive; but Emi remained un-forthcoming throughout the meal. She recognized the signs, it had happened before: a greyness, like a low front in the weather, was gradually seeping into her veins.

Kalle Strand was quiet, too, but unlike her, his natural reserve seemed born of innate self-confidence. He listened, absorbing the flow of information from the table, and when he did occasionally interject, the circle around him, particularly Clare and James, seemed to listen with heightened attention. During the main course Emi found her concentration on the discussion to her right wavering as her ear repeatedly wandered towards their discourse. Clare was now talking about her new novel, whose main theme, she was saying, was the part fate played in her characters' actions.

'You don't really believe one can alter one's destiny?' she heard Kalle ask her, a touch playfully.

'Of course I do,' Clare admonished with a throaty chuckle. 'Every decision a character makes affects the path they follow next.'

'Affects, perhaps, but I believe that their essential characters – and therefore choices – are pre-ordained,' he replied. 'Although, I do concede, none of us is exempt from cruel turns of fate.'

James and Clare looked across the table at one another and began to laugh, collusively.

'I can't have a sensible conversation when you guys get together,' Kalle chided, sitting back in his chair with a defeated smile. He was right. Clare was already reliving some past adventure while James leant forwards proprietorially and poured her more wine. For want of engagement, Kalle's focus shifted and he caught Emi's eye.

'What do you think, Emi? Could you alter the shape of your future?' he asked playfully.

'I'd like to try,' she replied, instinctively, then felt colour smarting her cheeks.

'How would you go about it?' he asked, his eyes narrowing with interest.

'Maybe just by walking out of my life, you know, by reinventing myself,' Emi said.

It wasn't a concept that she had ever conjured with before, and she wasn't sure where the idea came from. But it was too late to retract her statement now – Kalle Strand's interest had evidently quickened. He was regarding her inquisitively. His eyes were beautiful, she realized, stormy grey, like refracted light on a winter sea. She felt her blush deepen and averted her gaze.

'I don't believe anyone can truly reinvent themselves,' he was replying, meanwhile. 'Only we mad writers and the ancient gods can rewrite the paths of the characters we create.'

'I'm not so sure,' contradicted Emi, surprised to find her confidence building as her blush diminished. 'Perhaps some of us are living the wrong lives.'

Kalle's insistent gaze suddenly felt intrusive and Emi looked down at her hands.

'Kalle, when can we look forward to your next book?'

James's slurring words interrupted them and Emi wasn't sure if she was relieved or disappointed, then realized that she felt both. Kalle leant back and put his napkin down.

'I'm struggling,' he confessed. 'I've got what you English call "the block".'

As the two men began to talk again, Emi excused herself

and made for the Ladies. Did she really mean what she'd just said? Was she really that disillusioned with her lot? Did she really want to walk away from it all? She felt febrile and was tempted to slip off, to go home, but James had been so well-meaning tonight that she knew she owed it to him to see the last moments of the evening through. When she left the Ladies, she encountered Kalle heading towards her along the narrow corridor. He smiled and moved to one side to let her pass, but as she did so he touched her arm lightly and she hesitated.

'Would you really try it?' he asked her quietly.

'Sorry?'

'Changing.'

Emi paused; she felt put on the line. But, curiously, with this stranger she found she was unable to lie.

'Maybe,' she replied slowly. 'After all, sometimes I don't think I'd have anything to lose.'

Kalle glanced pointedly at her wedding ring and then back up at her face.

'That's a shame,' he said.

Emi shrugged, her embarrassment growing yet again. Why did he make her feel so exposed?

'Maybe we could talk about it more some time?' he added with a generous smile.

She floundered. This man was a psychologist, she thought; did he want to see her in a professional or a personal capacity? Either way, as Kalle retrieved a pen from his pocket Emi found herself giving him her number. In an unexpected touch, he scribbled the digits on to the inside of his left wrist.

'I'll call,' he said, resolutely.

Emi nodded and made her way back to the table. A few moments later, when Kalle reappeared, he stood directly behind her chair and made his apologies to Clare before quickly bidding a general farewell to the rest of the party. She felt deflated by his sudden departure; for a moment back there Will and Polly had completely evaporated from her mind.

James had definitely had too much to drink and was loquacious on the way home, reliving the evening in its every detail, enthusing particularly over how much he loved Clare – as a friend, of course. When the cab got to Emi's flat in Blenheim Crescent he jumped out and held the door open for her. It was late, the street was empty, and as he engulfed her in an alcohol-infused hug Emi suddenly felt small and lonely. For a brief moment she contemplated inviting him in for a coffee – so that she didn't have to go into the flat alone, to think about Polly and Will, to replay her strange conversation with Kalle Strand – but she checked herself, and was about to thank him when he pulled her closer and began to kiss her, quite forcefully, on the lips. It was the final straw. With some force, Emi pushed James away, then she turned and fled.

28

3

Polly lay under a fluffy white duvet in her king-size bed, her dark head propped up on a mountain of pillows, and gazed out at the early morning sunshine glinting tantalizingly over the dome of St Paul's. It was why she had bought this tiny Bermondsey flat: for the view. She had known at the time that the space had been compromised, that a fat-fisted developer had ensured that every ounce of profit was eked out of 'remoulding' this old wharf. But to Polly the pokiness inside was worth it for the space outside her windows. From her bedroom she could see all the way from Tower Bridge in the east to the Houses of Parliament in the west, the city laid out before her like a gargantuan feast waiting to be devoured. And devour it she was attempting to do, bit by bit. She made a living by reporting on the goings-on in the city and she loved looking out over it, across the past stories that had made their way to her daily broadcasts. Bermondsey was a contradiction, a part of 'original' London that had recently been renewed; it was a place where Polly could begin again, without her history snapping at her heels. Where Emi was, across the river, in Holland Park, you couldn't breathe in or out without a memory tugging at you, pulling you back. Even the porter in Emi's mansion block was tied to their past.

Her mobile started to ring, breaking Polly's morning reverie. She rescued it from the folds of the duvet and checked the number before picking up, dreading that it might be the studio begging overtime. To her relief, it was only Will.

'She's going fucking crazy,' he stated without preamble. 'She wants us to keep away from one another.'

Polly laughed. This was just the latest in a line of complaints that Emi had hurled their way.

'Well, that's just silly,' she told him. 'I'll have a word with her. We're meeting tonight, to go to that reunion thing.'

'What's that?'

'Oh, one of our old school friends, Helen, is turning thirty. She's in town for the weekend and she's hosting a dinner party for her old gang.'

'Emi'll hate that,' Will replied definitively and then he sighed. 'She hates looking back.'

Suddenly he sounded fragile, defeated. Without Emi he really seemed to have lost his way. Will was living in Clerkenwell, looking after his older brother Tom's flat while he in turn was working in the US for a year. It was just over the river from Polly's, and to the left a bit, in another newly developed, trendy part of town. It was a great flat and practical for his job, too. From there he could walk to his university department off Goodge Street in less than half an hour. Nevertheless, Will hadn't seemed able to settle since Emi had kicked him out. Polly felt sorry for him. She understood that weekends were probably the worst time.

'What are you doing today?' she found herself asking, more gently.

'I'm giving a talk this afternoon,' he replied, his tone lightening. 'Do you fancy coming along?'

Polly hesitated.

'I'll buy you coffee first,' he said.

Will showed up an hour later and sat huffing and puffing over the *Weekend Guardian* as Polly took a shower. When she emerged he was deeply ensconced, his biro scrawling notes in the margin, his eyebrows knitted together. Then he looked up at her.

'It's appalling, you know. Iraq had the best national health service in the Middle East before the war. Now a quarter of its kids are suffering from malnutrition.'

Polly sat on the arm of the sofa. 'Are you suggesting Saddam should have stayed?'

'That question is precisely why you need to come to my talk.'

She laughed. 'All right, all right, I'll come,' she conceded. 'But I need to be back by six.'

Will and Polly headed out into the winter sunshine, catching a croissant and a latte along the way. They walked in wide strides along Jubilee Walk, across Blackfriars Bridge and then on down the Embankment, enjoying each other's energy, their shared day out with a mission to fulfil. Will's passion was infectious. He was a crusader through and through, always tenacious and often a touch angry. Paradoxically, Polly felt that she'd only got to know him since he and Emi broke up. Before that there had never seemed to be the opportunity. He'd always been on the other side of Emi – the other side from her. She wasn't going to give up on him just because Emi had, however. After all, she reasoned as they picked up speed, he and Emi were all the family she had left in the world.

Will had always been politically motivated and had remained independent, on the fringes, ever since his undergraduate days with Emi at Sussex University. He was never content to sit on the sidelines; he was always organizing a demonstration, marching somewhere, or planning a protest against some injustice in the world. Nowadays his academic career focused on political statistics, and it balanced his activism well, each naturally fuelling the other. Emi had once complained to Polly that Will expended all his energies on global affairs; that there wasn't any space left for the minutiae, from which Polly understood that she had really meant for her. Polly, in turn, often wondered why Emi hadn't embraced Will's campaigns more actively, become a part of them herself. He had always championed significant causes with a wide reach, with global significance. She could have made a role for herself within it all. It would have made more sense than floundering around with that creep of a barrister, James. Will's latest fixation was 'Blair's war' in Iraq, as he called it. And you could see that it had fired him up more than anything he'd ever encountered before.

Will became increasingly quiet as they headed further west, his mind no doubt turned to the impending talk. As they threaded their way up Tottenham Court Road he turned and threw Polly a capricious smile, then took hold of her hand and led her lightly, quickly, through the crowds. Why, Polly wondered, had Emi let him go – and why was she now so keen to keep them apart? What was it she thought they'd discover? Something about her, or something about themselves?

As children Polly and Emi had learnt to coexist through veils of tears and intentional offers of misinformation about the goings-on in their interior worlds. They had guarded their secrets and desires from one another with rings of steel, secrets surrounded by electric fences. It was normal sibling stuff, the only way they knew to find emotional independence from one another when everyone around them was so busy remarking on their similarities. Sometimes, when there was nowhere else to go, their secrets had been forced to become lies. In adulthood it seemed a hard habit to break. Even so, Emi's im-penetrability over her break-up with Will was the most intense closure Polly had ever encountered from her twin. It was as if something inside Emi had snapped.

They passed up on to the crowd-free Euston Road now and Will let go of Polly's hand. For a brief moment she felt deflated.

'We're here,' he stated, pausing on the pavement and nodding with an uneasy grin up a stone stairwell to a pair of swinging doors.

'After you,' she smiled, and followed him up.

The large hall was jammed with students. Many signalled or waved as they spotted Will ambling towards the podium, Polly by his side.

'Final-year students hoping for firsts,' he murmured self-deprecatingly.

Polly had a feeling there was more to it than that, that he had a reputation of which she had never really been aware, of which Emi had never boasted. It was an eye-opener, seeing him here. Will led her to a reserved seat in the front row before heading off to wait by the stage. He was on third, and as she glanced at the programme she noted that he was the main speaker of the afternoon. When he finally mounted the podium he met thunderous applause then hushed concentration, and soon she understood why. Effortlessly and without papers to prompt him, Will's argument twisted and turned around the globe, cherry-picking leaders to bring to book about the crisis in the Middle East, plucking jaw-dropping facts and figures apparently from thin air, before returning to London for a warning about the threat of home-grown terrorism and ethnic separatism. She watched as he acknowledged the audience's positive response with a modest smile, then she saw him looking furtively towards her. She raised her hands and clapped harder.

'I'm off to the pub with my old cronies to shoot the political breeze.' Will grinned afterwards. 'Do you want to come along?'

Polly shook her head. 'I have to go,' she reminded him. 'I'm seeing Emi, remember? Best not mention to her that I came.'

'Whatever,' Will replied, raising his eyes to the sky.

Polly and Emi had been part of a tight-knit group of friends at school, and Polly had been looking forward to Helen's birthday for weeks. Although they'd kept in touch on an individual basis, this would be the first time they'd all got back together for more than ten years. Helen was over from her home in Frankfurt for the weekend and was hosting the dinner at her husband's elegant company flat in the heart of Kensington. Schoolgirl shrieks were already filling the air. Everyone looked the same yet slightly remoulded, some of their features softened, others hardened, with time. The effect was bizarre to Polly; some of the girls who had been the most beautiful at seventeen had lost their glow, while others, like Helen, who ostensibly had been the ugly duckling of the group, had learned to glide. Only Emi was yet to arrive. Soon the women were flick-flacking their words over one another; keen to mark the lost years, to cement the cracks that had created a momentary distance between them all. Despite herself, Polly felt a touch anxious for her sister and glanced intermittently towards the door. When Emi finally arrived she seemed a little nervous. She refused a drink, apologizing quietly to Helen that she'd been 'taking medication'. Helen looked enquiringly at Polly, who in turn glanced at Emi. 'It's nothing major,' Emi added nonchalantly. 'I just can't mix the pills with alcohol.'

The atmosphere among the rest of them was festive. It was only two weeks before Christmas and as they drank and ate, the rest of the women chattered inexhaustibly, hardly pausing for air. It felt special to Polly, being there with their old friends, and she tried to ignore her sister's dark mood. Of them all Polly was the one who, on a professional level at least, had achieved the most. Her news reporting had just about given her B-celebrity status in London and she couldn't help but enjoy the special attention it was affording her here. Everyone was intrigued by life behind the cameras.

After the meal, Helen lifted a glass. 'To absent friends,' she said.

There was a momentary pause and the air suddenly felt loaded. Everyone knew that one of the old crowd was missing, that one of them was gone.

'Yes, to Marie,' Emi added plainly, and for a moment there was a silence, then everyone got to their feet to raise their glasses sombrely.

'To Marie,' they all agreed.

But it was too late. Emi's bland pronouncement had succeeded in killing the atmosphere. Most of them had been there, that day at Hampstead Ladies' Pond fourteen years ago when Marie had swum out to her death. It was a shame to bring it up so literally now, when they'd been on such a high. Helen's subtle reference was adequate, would have left the air fresh. Marie's death had disturbed the balance between them back then and it was doing so again now.

In the pause that ensued, Emi gestured that she was ready to leave.

'I'll come too,' Polly stated.

'But you're heading east,' Emi objected.

'No problem, I'll put it on account,' Polly replied, determinedly.

As they got their coats from the lobby Polly could hear somebody putting music on and the sound of more bottles being opened. Without them the atmosphere was already picking up a beat.

'Now we're back in touch, you must come and stay with me in Germany,' Helen urged as she led them to the door. Polly was enthusiastic, but Emi remained silent and Polly felt her irritation begin to rise.

'Will you come too, please?' Helen asked, pointedly turning to Emi. She'd always been careful, Polly remembered now, not to leave Emi out. 'It would be so wonderful for me to show you where I live.'

'You know what they say,' Emi replied, with forced good humour. 'Two's company, three's a crowd.'

For a moment Helen looked taken aback, but quickly recovered her composure.

'Well then, we'll have to arrange a separate weekend, just for you and me,' she smiled.

'What has got into you, Emi?' Polly demanded as they got into the cab.

'Into me?' Emi retorted. 'Maybe you should ask yourself the same question.'

'Is this about Will? Because if so it's just silly.'

Emi said nothing, just looked out of the window.

'He rang me this morning,' Polly continued, knowing that now she had started, she couldn't let the issue drop. 'You told him that you don't want us to see each other. I mean, honestly, Emi, that's ridiculous. He's my brother-in-law, after all.'

'Was,' Emi replied. 'Remember, I'm divorcing him.'

Emi sounded strange, her voice disengaged, her tone unusually cold and dispassionate. It made Polly feel uneasy. They sat in silence as the cab drove them through Hyde Park and along the Bayswater Road into Notting Hill.

'Can I come up for a coffee?' she asked, as they arrived outside Emi's flat. They had to talk about this, she determined, to try to clear the air.

'I'm tired,' Emi replied unapologetically, reaching for the door. 'I need to go to bed.'

'What's the prescription you're taking, Emi? You are all right, aren't you?' Polly asked quickly, keen for reassurance.

'Oh, they're just sleeping pills,' Emi replied, dismissively. 'I've had terrible insomnia.'

'Emi, we've really got to talk – about Will,' Polly pleaded, but Emi shook her head.

'I'm done with talking about Will. It's over between us,' she replied. 'He needs to understand that and move on – and so, apparently, do you. I'm really sorry but I don't love him. I got it wrong. And so did he. There's nothing more to say.'

Polly felt the urge to respond, to guard her corner.

'Whatever you say, he's still my brother-in-law, our family,' she tried. 'And we haven't got much of that left.'

Emi got out of the cab.

'I just need a break from him. Maybe I need to get away,' she said, leaning back into the cab to look at Polly. 'And I have to say, I never thought you two would become allies.'

Before Polly could reply, Emi had turned and was walking away. Polly asked the driver to wait as she watched her sister enter the mansion block. Moments later the kitchen light on the first floor went on. Then Polly spied Emi peering out at her before dropping the blind.

4

'Have you ever wondered what it would be like to walk out on your life?' Sarah asks her neighbour, Carol, casually one day as they sit together in her garden. Carol had come round at eleven and encouraged Sarah to go for a walk with her by the canal with the children. It's the first day of spring, early April and unseasonably warm, and now they are back at Carol's house sitting on a pair of old faded green Regent's Park deckchairs that Carol has recently bought at Camden Lock. For once both twins are sleeping, stretched out in their matching Silver Cross prams, beneath the weeping willow tree. They're nearly too big for them already; they'll soon be leaving their cribs for a bed. Sarah wonders about timings: nearly two, was that about right? She would ask her mother, but she's on another tour in North America and will be away for months. Last time she'd spoken to her parents they'd said they were considering moving over there permanently; her father was a staunch Labour man, and there was talk of a Conservative government coming in. He said he couldn't bear the Tories' glib disregard for the arts; that he would rather conduct in the land of the free. Her mother said they wanted to buy a house, somewhere in Maine. Sarah had told Peter of their plans at the weekend. She thought he might feel sorry for her, 'losing' her parents in this way, but instead he was more interested in discussing the political shift that had brought their decision on.

'A woman grocer pounding on the door of Number Ten,' he had chortled with mirth. 'Who would ever have believed it?'

Sarah wanted to have a view, to care about it, to feel proud or fearful of Margaret Thatcher, of her set hair-dos, her sharp blue suits, of her meteoric rise. But she didn't have a feeling one way or the other. She almost asks Carol what she thinks about the impending elections, about the twins and their cots, too, but she stops herself. For one thing she knows Carol is an old-fashioned liberal, and for another, since the tragic death of her husband a few years before, she has remained both single and childless. She makes a mental note to ask the doctor, next time he calls to see her – when to change their sleeping arrangements, that is – she really doesn't know.

'What exactly do you mean?' Carol asks. 'Just leave?'

Sarah takes a moment to get back to where they were, then remembers what she's asked, about walking out on her life. She almost wishes she hadn't raised the subject, hadn't confessed to the thought. But it's too late to go back now.

'Yes, to leave the house, shut the door behind you and not look back,' she ventures, aware of her words quickening.

'Well, I suppose it's something people often do when they're depressed, or when they feel surplus to the

40

requirements of those around them, or when they've done something that, at that moment, seems irreversible, something bad or just plain stupid,' Carol replies slowly, then affects a light laugh. 'I've never felt that way; I suppose I must be lucky.'

Sarah looks wan. She has hardly left the house since the girls were born. She's nodding, her eyes closed to the sunshine that is warming the features of both their faces.

'It's something you might dream of doing, on those days when you feel a bit fed up, I suppose,' Carol adds, feebly. 'But of course there are always responsibilities, like the girls, that stop you.'

Sarah opens her eyes suddenly and shades them with a hand. She's becoming slightly flushed, perhaps from the walk, the fresh air. When she speaks, however, there's an unnatural excitement in her tone, a continuing acceleration of her words.

'Exactly, you'd only do it if you felt you were not quite leading the life you were meant to lead, that you're not quite inhabiting the right skin, the right place in the world, but something stops you, be it duty, fear – or just plain common sense. I'm sure for those who go there's rarely a single reason, but a series of disappointments, maybe over years, followed by a trigger, a person or situation that's given them the momentum to take the plunge, out there, into the unknown. Don't you think?'

Sarah feels guilty. She knows she is willing Carol to say something encouraging, to sanction her considering this course of action, but she can tell that her friend feels out of her depth.

'All this talk,' Carol answers with a nervous laugh,

getting up and smoothing her skirt with her hands. 'It's making me thirsty. I think I'll go and get us something to drink.'

When she returns a few moments later Sarah's deckchair is empty. Carol glances across at the prams, expecting to see her neighbour bending over the children, checking their well-being. But she isn't there either. She puts down her tray and runs towards the twins. Each is still sleeping, quietly, in the shade. She turns and hurries back towards the house, calling Sarah's name, but there is no response. Maybe she's gone to the loo, she thinks, desperately, but inside the house Sarah is nowhere to be found. Carol runs to the front door and opens it, looks up and down the street. She's just in time to see the back of Sarah's crimson dress swinging around the corner, away from them all. She thinks fast. What to do? Leave the girls and run after her? No, no, she can't do that; she must put them first. That's the difference, mentally, she realizes: she's capable of making rational choices, but Sarah, oh poor Sarah; she knows that her friend is lost, has been lost for months – for longer, in fact, since the girls arrived. She thinks for a moment. Peter had given her his telephone number at his office, 'just as a precaution', he had said. She had understood the implication: it had felt like a responsibility, a bond of trust, and she had liked it – until now. But he was too far away to be of immediate help. Instead she grabs the phone and calls the police. They promise to send out a patrol car, to do all they can to locate Sarah. Meantime, Carol paces the garden helplessly. The twins continue to sleep, oblivious to the unfolding drama. The sun has moved slightly in the sky and now Polly's face is in its full glare. Carol pushes her pram closer to Emi's in the shade.

No more than fifteen minutes have passed when there's a knock at the door. Outside there are two policewomen, one either side of Sarah. There's a sheen of perspiration across her face and she has a faraway look in her eyes.

'She was down by the canal,' one of the officers says.

'Please,' she whispers to Carol as they cross the threshold. 'Don't tell Peter.'

5

The next day was Sunday. In the afternoon Emi sat alone on a bench outside Tate Modern, her face catching the weak rays of the winter sunshine. She'd been there for hours, just sitting, waiting and watching. And now she'd got what she'd come for. At last everything had become clear and finally it was time to leave. She got up and moved quickly, away from the gallery, along the narrow, winding streets of old Southwark, between decrepit rail sidings and cave-like stores used for scruffy MOT garages and a-tenner-a-day parking lots; past the covert entrance to an ominously silent 'Boys Boxing Club'; then on along a soulless stretch of Southwark Street to the tube. She descended hurriedly into the system and slipped on to a waiting carriage. The doors snapped closed; she sat down, shut her eyes and counted stops in the dark. She'd come south this morning with a somewhat confused mission; to confront Polly, or to apologize, or to try to talk things through, but fate had taken her on a different path, and instead she'd found herself spending the day alone, lost in her own contemplations. And now it was too late, for talking, for reconciliation. The realization made her feel curiously light-headed, as if she'd become a vacuum inside her own skin.

Back at Blenheim Crescent she paced around the flat, finding it impossible to settle. Eventually she went into the kitchen, opened the fridge and began to eat rapidly, selecting items at random – low-fat rhubarb yoghurt, duck and orange pâté, apple juice, Cheddar cheese, cold chicken, a carton of double cream spooned straight from the tub. Then she cleaned the fridge out and switched it off. Minutes later she headed for the bathroom and forced herself to throw all the food back up. Her eyes watered and her stomach ached. She brushed her teeth and took a long shower in an attempt to rinse her skin and her mind clear. Finally she sat down in front of the mirror and slowly examined her face, pulling her skin taut with her fingers and scrutinizing every line, every pore.

Next Emi returned to the kitchen, where she scrubbed the work surfaces until they gleamed, emptied the bins and took the rubbish out. Then she washed the floors, moving with increasing urgency from room to room, sterilizing everything inside the flat, removing every last speck of Will and their lives from its surfaces, reducing their shared world to its spiritless component parts, without their touch or breath upon it any more; erasing his presence and hers from what essentially had really been her mother's home all along, rubbing their memories out. They had moved in after Sarah died, but she knew they'd never managed to imprint themselves, that this had always remained her mother's domain, a place where they had merely coexisted for a while. It was proving simple to wipe the slate clean.

In the bedroom she folded and tidied away her clothes.

Then she sat down on the bed and switched on the TV as Polly appeared on her regular 6.15 slot.

'*This latest assault occurred in a side alley while afternoon shoppers passed by, only metres away. Police are appealing to anyone . . .*'

It always fascinated her to watch her twin, she could see how similar they looked and sounded when Polly was on screen, how alike, superficially, they still were. Polly was wearing the same cord jacket and faded jeans as the last time Emi had seen her, she observed. She must have rushed to the scene to file her report, a little late, a little flustered, perhaps. She looked at her sister's composed face. There are so many hidden lines in any story, she thought.

When Polly was done Emi switched off the TV, closed the curtains and got into bed. It was already ink-dark outside, midwinter, the darkest time. She flicked a sleeping pill from the bottle on her bedside table into her hand and looked for water, but in her determination to clear everything away she'd removed the glass. Did she have the energy to get up for another? She swallowed it dry, then held the bottle up to the lamplight and observed the remaining pills inside, tipped another tablet out and rolled it over her palm. It looked so small and pure, like a pearl; it was hard to imagine that it could be deadly. She poured the rest of the pills on to the bedcover and counted them – sixteen in all, enough to do the job, resolutely. She lined them up before her and lay back, her head heavy against the pillow. These actions reminded her of something; a memory, just beyond her reach. There were two of them, but there should only be one. Polly had always been tougher, the stronger half. There was no space left for Emi to inhabit. She was suffocating. When she tried to think back she realized that there was no reason and no definition left. She picked up another pill, settled it on her tongue, and swallowed. She really would need water, she decided, in order to take the rest. In her mind's eye she saw her mother's concerned face as she pushed the covers back and swung her legs around.

At that moment the telephone rang. Its bell seemed amplified, more shrill and insistent than usual. For once Emi had not switched the answering machine on. She looked down at the sheets, at the line of white pills lying there, felt curiously caught out, like a child spotted in a corner shop, stealing sweets, and grabbed the receiver to block its sound.

'Hello?' she enquired, instinctively.

'Hi, Emi,' the voice said.

'Hi,' she replied, feigning recognition, her heart thumping loudly in her chest.

'I'm leaving London tomorrow,' the voice continued. 'I wonder, could we have dinner tonight?'

At once Friday came back to her and Emi knew that it was Kalle Strand on the line. The realization startled her into a ready, if monosyllabic acceptance. She listened as he suggested a place and a time, later that evening, an Italian café someone had recommended, around the corner from his Bloomsbury hotel, near King's Cross. Emi pushed the bedcovers back and allowed the pills to scatter across the bare floorboards, like beads from a broken string. She left them where they fell and went to take another shower.

At ten to eight she was being driven in a cab towards King's Cross, past the prostitutes hanging out by the corner of the station, past the drug dealers huddled outside the amusement arcades; London's disingenuous laid open to public gaze. She couldn't help but feel compelled by these sorry people – by their outsiderness, their slow, implicit sadness. Maybe once they had been like her, she mused, as safe as houses, and then, snap! – something had tipped them over the edge, sent them reeling to the other side, to a place where she felt, deep down, that maybe she'd been heading for a while. She turned and watched them disappear from view as the cab journeyed on, up the Pentonville Road and finally left into Northdown Street. Stillness had settled over the surface of the city like a cloak and nothing here stirred.

The restaurant was halfway up the empty road, with pretty, flapping red awnings and an oval lamp glowing on a wrought-iron stand. She paid the cab and hesitated on the pavement, wondering if she should go back home. She felt woozy from the pills she had so recently swallowed. Would he be able to tell? She glanced gingerly in through the window. Cheery red and white checked tablecloths adorned a dozen empty tables, each topped with a candle melted into a wine bottle, dispensing a cheap, flickering light. Kalle was the only customer, sitting towards the back of the restaurant, and he immediately caught sight of her gazing in; he raised a hand in welcome and she knew it was already too late to run away. She pushed the door open and headed in, moving purposefully towards him now.

'You came,' he said with a mild expression of triumph, or was it surprise?

Emi didn't answer; she felt exposed, because now she

was there, with him, she knew that there was no going back – although from what, she wasn't quite sure.

'You sounded reticent,' he added as if by way of explanation.

'Something . . .' Emi paused, wondering how to explain; she wasn't even clear in her own mind about the last twenty-four hours, about the way it had worked. It all felt hazy. 'Something had just happened, when you called. But it's unimportant now,' she ventured.

Kalle didn't press her to explain, but gestured to the chair opposite his and smiled. A waitress was already hovering. The girl was young and slim, with fine red lips and a coil of long, dark hair, like an oiled rope; evidently Italian, perhaps the daughter of the *patron*. She handed them menus. Emi's stomach still felt tender. She hardly felt like eating, drinking – or even breathing.

'Red?' he asked and she nodded, pulled her mother's red mohair shawl tighter around her shoulders, then tried to think of something to say. She always wore the shawl when she was nervous; it was like a comfort blanket, making Sarah seem close by. She found Kalle compelling – but she seemed for the moment to have lost the power of words. Polly would know, she thought, how to get to the next moment without faltering. She thought of her last night, the queen bee among their old friends, everyone hanging on to her last syllable, entranced by her glossy wit, which had sent its own sparkling sheen across the evening.

When the wine came, it was accompanied by a bowl of shiny black olives and some pale, sesame-dotted grissini. She picked one up and took a small bite as Kalle poured them both wine and water. Her mouth felt parched. She sipped the water, then took a glug of the wine to steady her nerves as together they surveyed the menus. Emi ordered a dish but as soon as the menus were removed she couldn't remember what she'd chosen.

'Did you just come to London for Clare's party?' she asked, finally.

'No,' Kalle replied calmly, sitting back in his chair and surveying her mildly. 'I mainly came to attend a lecture held by my wife.'

Emi felt a jolt of emotion. It sank and settled in the pit of her stomach.

'She's a molecular biologist,' he continued. 'Involved in the latest stem cell research, funded by a biotech company here. She was giving a talk about the latest developments in her program. I came, ostensibly, to help look after our daughter, Lotta, who is six. We were supposed to travel back together tomorrow afternoon, but now she and Lotta have decided to stay on, to see some old friends.'

The mention of a wife was disappointing, and a daughter felt complicated, but she still wanted to know more; in fact, Emi realized, she wanted – no, needed – to know everything there was to know about this foreign man.

'And you?'

He smiled, a touch guardedly.

'I like to support Stephanie, especially if she needs me there to look after Lotta, but I draw the line at passing my leisure time in her company – we separated, eighteen months ago.'

Emi tried to look sorry.

'We're lucky, it's perfectly amicable now,' he added. 'And her studies still fascinate me. They inform my own

50

research into the latest genetic advances, the latest learning about our DNA, the way our characters may be defined by it.'

'Defined?'

'Let me give you a simple example,' he offered, evidently pleased to move the topic on. 'We have far more genes in common, say, with the common fly or the earthworm than any scientist ever previously conceived. Indeed, the genes for laying down the body plan of a fruit fly turn out to have precise counterparts in a mouse – or, more significantly, a man. So similar are they, in fact, that the human version of one can even be substituted for its fly counterpart.' As he was speaking the food arrived but Kalle ignored it, so intent was he on his explication. 'Even more surprising is the discovery that the genes flies use for learning and memory are also duplicated in people – identical!' He faltered as he looked down at his food. He seemed surprised it was there. 'Heh, I'm sorry. When I get on to this subject, I easily get carried away.'

Emi laughed as Kalle picked up his fork and expertly twisted a long strand of spaghetti around it. She guessed that he did most things well. She took a sip of the smooth Chianti and felt herself relax, then looked down at her lasagne and played with her fork.

'If memory has a genetic link,' she asked presently, 'does that imply that the types of genes we inherit influence our ability to remember things?'

'It's a good question,' he answered contemplatively, fork held mid-air, 'but I'm afraid I don't know the answer. There's so much scientists don't yet know. Memories tend to be strongest when they evoke high emotion: elation,

51

temerity, shock or fear; and conversely, when we're depressed, we tend to lose the ability to remember details, it gets harder to move on from the general recollection to specific events. We do know, however, that a whole new map of the human being is being drawn up, one that puts our genes at the heart not only of our physical, but also our mental, make-up.'

'Are you implying that personality is genetic?'

'You've just hit on my particular area of interest,' he replied with a grin. 'Experiences and our particular memories of them define our identities – but our genes may also have an influence. What I want to know is, to what degree? Do we have happy genes, worry genes, neurotic genes? Do we learn behaviour or are we born with it? Where's the balance?'

'I wish I knew,' Emi replied, her thoughts turning once more to Polly. Would she, could she, have betrayed Polly if the tables had been turned, could she have fallen in love with Polly's husband? She didn't think so – and yet, why not? To all intents and purposes, Polly and she were genetically the same.

'Now we have actual chains of information to play with,' Kalle elucidated. 'As well as complex equations to deconstruct, however intricate they prove to be. The order in which the genes on our chromosomes can be imprinted inside a human is multiple, and any change in their ordering, it seems, may alter personality traits.'

'Now you've got me.'

'I'm sorry, it's not so simple.' Kalle's words had slowed. He had put his fork down and was observing her with critical concern. 'But, Emi, this isn't what I called you to talk about. After Friday I haven't been able to stop thinking about our conversation. I can't decide if you were being provocative, playful, or plain honest. What you said is a serious confession of defeat.'

She was shocked by his candour and felt the muscles in her throat contract.

'I did mean it,' she replied, her words suddenly sounding hard to her ears. 'If anything, I'm even more convinced now that it's time to change, to move on.'

'What about James? You seemed close, some might say intimate. Is your marriage really over?'

Emi hesitated momentarily, then burst out laughing, suddenly conscious that Kalle really knew absolutely nothing about her, nothing at all.

'James is my boss, not my husband. And I did mean what I said on Friday, I really would like to disappear, to start again. In fact, today I feel as if I don't have much choice.'

Emi was surprised at the conviction that had entered her tone, and by the quickening of her speech, too. Her words seemed to be leapfrogging over one another in an effort to get out. She no longer felt sick. If anything she felt light-headed, a touch inebriated. She lifted her glass and took another large sip.

'It's impossible.'

'Not for me.'

'Where would you go?'

'Anywhere. What's Stockholm like?'

Kalle appeared taken aback, but then he laughed too – involuntarily, she guessed. She got the feeling that he wasn't easily caught off guard, but her words had managed to derail him, at least for a moment.

'Well, it's not like London. It's a small, intimate city surrounded by more than ten thousand islands and a lot of water. It's straddled by hundreds of bridges; it's really light in the summer, really dark in the winter. It's culturally and ethnically less complex than London, but of course no less intellectually refined for that.'

'I'm sure. Everything here's so big, so loud, so complicated.'

'Relationships are complicated wherever you have them,' he replied.

'Tell me about Lotta,' she ventured, heading, she hoped, for safer water. It was her turn to be surprised, as she noted a fleeting shadow cross his brow.

'To be honest, I think it's because of her that I'm finding it so hard to get my current book finished,' he replied. 'It's hard to combine my clinical work with my writing as it is. Somehow, since our separation, I seem to have lost the writing time. I work three days a week, in Stockholm's biggest research hospital. The rest of the time I'm supposed to be writing my next book. I have her every other week, and I love it when she's there – but she engulfs me. She's at kindergarten some of the time. It has occurred to me, maybe I could get someone to look after her when I work, but it takes time to know these things and to be sure. One-to-one care outside school time is always best – my research has shown me this and I can't ignore my findings for my own flesh and blood.'

He pulled out his wallet, opened it and handed Emi a passport-sized portrait of a little girl with the whitest hair she'd ever seen, the palest skin, the bluest eyes. She looked as pure as fresh, poured milk.

'She's beautiful,' she told him – and fragile, she thought.

'She's the most important thing in my life,' he replied with a mix of pride and, she sensed, fear, as he took the picture back.

They ate for a while in silence; Kalle contemplative, Emi feeling woozy. She knew that she shouldn't have mixed alcohol with the sleeping pills, that it was a foolish mistake. She liked Kalle, she decided; she liked him a lot. He seemed strong, grown up, in control. It made her feel safe, as perhaps Will had done – at least until Sarah had died, and everything between them had changed.

'Why are you called Emi?' he asked, presently.

'It's short for Artemis. My mother was keen on mythology,' she replied, cautiously.

'Was?'

'She died, nearly three years ago.'

'Now it's my turn to be sorry.'

'Me too.'

'So she believed in fate as well?'

'I guess so,' Emi answered, finding it hard to suppress a smile. 'She'd say you were sent to me for a reason.'

'Go on.'

'She'd say I should try to find out your value and take full advantage of it.'

'And what do you think, Emi?'

She paused, feeling a little dizzy, and took a drink of water. Frankly, what did she have to lose? If Kalle hadn't called . . .

'Maybe you're my conduit for change,' she replied, slowly, aware that her words were beginning to slur. 'You walked into my life and made me see my predicament.

And here you are again now, just when I need you to be, waiting for something to happen, uncertain of what it might be.'

She took another sip of wine, amazed at her own boldness; she wasn't usually this forward, rarely took unnecessary risks. Kalle refilled her glass, then his own. He was struggling to keep up, she thought – and giggled.

'And what do you think that might be? I have to confess, I hadn't thought that far,' he said, affecting laughter, but she could see that she had unsettled him.

'I have no idea. Maybe I need to sleep on it.'

Emi knew that she wasn't going to last much longer. She was beginning to feel quite sick. She excused herself and went to the Ladies; she had to steady herself as she got up and as she sat on the loo her head was swimming. When she got back to the table Kalle was already paying the bill. They left the restaurant together and headed towards King's Cross. The fresh air went some way towards clearing her head, but she knew she needed to get home, to go to bed, before she keeled over. They stepped up to the taxi rank and waited in line.

'There is one more thing, Emi, before you go,' Kalle said. 'The discussion we had the other night, I meant my words. I don't believe any one of us can really change, we always carry our history into our future. I don't believe for a moment that you'll be able to leave your past behind, or that you can alter your essential nature. When you're least expecting it, it will creep up behind you and shout boo!'

'I know,' she replied, leaning forward and kissing him on the cheek. 'But I could always try.'

A cab pulled up and Kalle opened the door for her. Then he handed her his card through the open window.

'If you ever want to call me, please do,' he said. 'And if you ever want to visit Stockholm, I'd love to show you my city. I'd love you to come and stay.'

'When do you head back?'

'BA from Heathrow, tomorrow at five,' he told her, a touch regretfully, she gauged.

She felt disappointed, too. Back there it had felt like the start of something, and if only she didn't feel so wretched, perhaps it could have gone further. But right now, all she could think about was going to bed.

'I'd like that,' she said.

He smiled and held up a hand in farewell as the cab pulled away.

6

On Monday afternoon Polly was standing on a railway siding outside Dagenham, amid the mayhem of emergency services, when Will rang her. It was only four minutes till live and she was preparing to report on a recent train crash. She only answered because it was him, and after the weekend that had just passed, she had the feeling that it might be important.

'You're not going to believe this,' he began.

'What's Emi done now?' she asked.

'James got an email from her this morning,' he replied. 'She's gone and resigned.'

'Resigned?'

'Yep, with no explanation. I've tried calling her, but she's not answering the phone.'

Polly's mind briefly referenced Emi's mild threat to take a break, but she was surprised it was so soon, and so dramatic.

'I'll try to ring her later,' she promised.

There was a fireman with a stretcher, now two ambulance men and a black plastic body bag, and they were gesturing for her to move to one side.

'Oh, shit,' she said. 'Will, I'll call, I promise. But now I've really got to go.'

By the time Polly got home it had gone midnight and she'd forgotten to call Emi. The train story had become major league. There'd been some runaway calves on the track and the driver had braked too late. Two carriages had jack-knifed across rain-spattered fields, passengers tossed like scarecrows into the winter set-aside. There had been news flashes and updates to present all evening, and the mortality figures were rising. It was London's worst rail incident since Paddington. Polly took a shower, letting the water flood over her, trying to wash the news out. For all the pictures the public saw there were always a lot more, and sometimes they stuck, gave her nightmares. That night was a case in point. There'd been a baby on the train; it had been found half buried in a field, clothes shredded from its tiny pale form. The image was blocking the way for her to see forwards from the day. She scrubbed at her body and washed shampoo through her hair, then brushed her teeth till they frothed in the shower's cascade. Eventually she emerged, cleansed but not cured – and exhausted, too. She got straight into bed and was already on the edge of sleep when Will rang again.

'Why didn't you call her?' he demanded. 'I'm sick with worry.'

'Haven't you been watching the news?' she asked. 'I had more critical things to do.'

'I'm sorry,' he replied. 'I have been watching. The NUTD are up in arms. The signals weren't checked, cutbacks. Someone's head's going to roll.'

'Someone's already did,' Polly answered, coldly. 'I saw it, on the track. And by the way, it wasn't a signal failure, it was a cow.'

'Shit.'

'Exactly.'

'I'm really sorry,' he said, sheepishly. 'Are you OK, Pol?'

'Yeah, yeah, just knackered.'

'It's just I can't call her again,' he continued, ever tenacious. 'She obviously doesn't . . .'

'All right, all right,' Polly interjected. 'I'll do it now.'

'And if she doesn't answer, you will go over, won't you, and check that she's OK?'

Polly knew that Emi always left the answering machine on at home, even when she was there, that she hated picking up the phone. But when she dialled Emi's number now it simply rang and rang. The same was true of her mobile. These details made her curious, if not concerned. True to her word, however, twenty minutes later she found herself up again, hurriedly dressed, and driving west. She knew her sister was absent as soon as she entered the flat. It wasn't that anything was out of place; in fact, it was because it was not. There was no food in the cupboards, no laundry in the basket, no cup in the sink. She thought briefly back to her own place, the unmade bed she had crawled out of this morning and back into tonight, the dirty washing-up left over from last night. The weekend had been so intense it had wiped her out, and by nine she'd been beyond domestic chores. And today, with the train crash, the endless reports, the updates, there'd been no time to catch up.

She looked around some more, moving from the kitchen

to the sitting room. Emi had always been fanatically tidy, methodical; you could hardly feel her presence over their mother's at all. She glanced out of the bay window. This was Ladbroke Grove, but the Holland Park end of it, a place of increasing wealth, flanked on one side by Portobello market, on the other by rows of pastel-painted millionaire mansions. She remembered Sarah saying the flat felt 'appropriate' for a single woman of late middle age: respectable, well-proportioned – and very safe. It was one of the few blocks in the area that was still serviced by a porter, too, and she'd liked the daily contact. Little did she know she'd invested in a goldmine. In the ten years since she'd made the purchase its value had risen threefold. When she became ill they'd paid for a nurse to live there with her, twenty-four hours a day, until she was too ill even for that, and then Sarah had been moved to the Victorian hospice at St Charles's Hospital, just up the road.

When Sarah died, Will and Emi had moved straight into Blenheim Crescent. Polly hadn't wanted to live in this part of town, it was too far from work and she already had her own place. And, unlike Polly, Emi didn't seem to mind sleeping alongside such melancholy memories. To begin with, Polly had been both surprised and irritated that they hadn't felt the urge to change a thing. She'd assumed that they'd redecorate, replace the chintz with something more modern, try to imprint themselves on the flat, or at least to contemporize it, and a couple of months later, one Sunday afternoon, she had told Emi so. She could see her twin now, standing quietly by the bay window, arms folded across a cream cheesecloth top, some typically horrid hippy thing that Polly wouldn't have been seen dead in, holding a cup of tea in her left hand and with deep-seated obstinacy etched into her brow. If Polly shut her eyes tightly enough, she could even hear her voice.

'Changes would be superficial,' Emi had remarked coolly. 'They wouldn't erase Mum from my memory, or enable me to move on more readily from her death, if that's what you mean.' Then she'd turned from Polly to look out on to the gardens, before adding, 'Anyway, we like this old-fashioned stuff. We bought most of it with Mum. I'm not interested in your trendy minimalism.'

The backhand blow had been wounding. It still hurt now to think about it. Polly understood the inference, that she was unlike them, that she was too easily influenced, too thick-skinned to understand the subtlety of Emi's – or their mother's – ways. To a degree Emi was right: she couldn't comprehend her sister's obstinacy in the face of her urging. Polly would have wanted to mark the sad shift in their circumstance with a change in colours, a rearrangement of the furniture and new pictures on the walls. But now, three years on, as she sat there alone, she at last understood that there was something deep-rooted and reassuring about her sister's inaction in the resulting continuity here. It almost doesn't matter which of us is there, which is not, she thought. We're all players in the same drama, a drama that someone else has always been directing. No amount of redecorating could change that – or lift the depressing mood of the place. The sterility she felt reminded her of Emi's room the day before they had set off from their childhood home in Alma Place for their respective universities; more than a decade ago, now. Emi

62

had boxed everything up, emptied her room, even stripped her bed. Polly recalled that Sarah had been quite upset, as if Emi's attempt at leaving home so completely had been intended as a personal rebuff. For her part, Polly had just packed stuff for the term, leaving everything else where it belonged: in her room – clothes in the drawers, make-up on the dressing table, posters on the walls.

These thoughts brought her back to the present, and she had an idea. She wandered back into the bedroom and pulled back the covers of Emi's bed. Sure enough, just as back then, Emi had stripped it bare. The predictability of the act made her want to laugh aloud, but then a single pill rolled from beneath the bedcover and her curiosity rose. She leant down, glanced quickly across the dark, polished floorboards, spied it and flicked it up into her palm; a small, round, bright white pill. She slipped it into her pocket, then, sitting down on the upturned bedclothes, lifted the receiver of her mother's old Bakelite phone and dialled Will's number.

'What do you mean she's gone?' Despite his annoyance, Will failed to mask his anxiety.

'Holiday, escape, weekend away, I don't know, but she's definitely taken off. Not with much stuff, so I guess she'll be back in a few days. Kind of weird, kind of typical. In some ways I reckon it's been on the cards for months. James has always been too keen on her, she didn't like it; and to be frank, I don't think the law's ever really been her bag.'

'What shall we do?'

'Will, I'm totally bushed,' she replied. 'Maybe she'll call us in the morning.'

He didn't answer.

'Are you OK, Will?'

'I'm restless. I'm annoyed and if I'm honest, I'm really a bit worried. She's been so out of sorts. It makes me think of Sarah.'

Polly immediately felt guilty. It hadn't occurred to her that Emi's going away could signify anything more than her need for a brief escape. Maybe he was over-reacting, but the mention of Sarah triggered a deep, nervous tension that was now tugging at her insides.

'Why don't you come over?' she asked, gently.

'To Blenheim Crescent?' He sounded surprised.

'Don't be ridiculous,' she replied. 'I'll be back home in half an hour.'

When Polly got back to Bermondsey, Will was already leaning against the wall by her intercom, waiting, and he grinned with evident relief when he saw her. Despite herself, she responded in kind.

'Come on,' she sighed. 'I think we could both do with a drink.'

They headed up the clinical stairwell together.

'When Emi first kicked you out I was amazed that you called me,' she said as she turned the key. She could see him now, that first time, six months earlier, hangdog, affronted and dismayed, standing on that same threshold, suitcase of unfolded, rapidly packed clothes in one hand, essential lever-arch files in the other. His brother, Tom, was already away in the US and their parents lived in York. He said he couldn't think where else to go. Luckily Tom had since agreed to Will flat-sitting for the year.

'What made you think of that?' he asked, as she stood to one side to let him in before her.

She closed the door as he headed on into the sitting-room.

'Just now it occurred to me, that she's almost forcing us upon one another,' she reasoned, projecting her voice to ensure he heard her as she unbuttoned her coat and hung it up in the narrow hallway, slipped off her shoes, feet bare beneath. 'With Tom away, she knew you'd have to come here. And now, well, she says she doesn't want us to see one another, but then she goes and does a disappearing act. I wonder if it's deliberate. If, despite her vociferous objections, what she really wants is to force us into one another's realms.'

Polly was moving through to join him now. Will was leaning out of the window, smoking a cigarette, looking out at the Thames swirling beneath them in the dark. She poured them both whisky, neat, then headed over to stand next to him.

'That's a bit harsh,' he said, taking a glass and blowing smoke into the breeze. Polly didn't reply; just watched as the Thames rose with winter rain, buckets of it, spilling from the sky now, sloshing into the river's murky depths.

Later, as she finally lay in bed, Polly realized that she liked the sense of Will in the flat, sleeping at an angle along her too-short sofa. Increasingly his presence made her feel better, not about anything in particular, just in a well-being kind of a way. She'd first begun to notice his impact a couple of months after he and Emi had broken up; the way that, after he'd called by or phoned her, she'd feel calmer than she had in years. It wasn't like her to be able to relax that easily. She'd always been flippety-jib, as her parents would tease; on the move, restless, looking for something new to do. Emi had always been better at being on her own, had always been more placid, more watchful, more sedentary. But since Will had started hanging out with Polly time seemed to have slowed down for her. She often found herself taking longer breaths in and out, enjoying moments that passed when he was with her without particular purpose, without her even really noticing them slipping by.

In all the years that Will had been with Emi, Polly had blanked him out. She had been in her first year at Edinburgh when Emi had first brought him home. It was before their father had died, just after he had moved to Montpellier to live with his French mistress, Brigitte. Will had seemed to be part of the new package; had practically swung in through the doors of Sarah's new flat in Blenheim Crescent along with New Labour. She could see him in her mind's eye now, diligently painting their mother's sitting-room duck-egg blue, with paint spatters in his long, dark hair and wondered why, from the start, she'd given him the label of *persona non grata*. She supposed that she'd been unexpectedly wary of the new order – both politically and personally. Both heralded an uncertain era in their lives. They'd all wanted this new government; but when she'd got off the train at King's Cross that spring day and had seen the billboards, plastered with those gargantuan, smiling faces of Blair and Brown, the country's new super-team, the city had suddenly felt foreign, the public and her private landscapes running on an unfamiliar track. Her father no longer lived here, the house in Alma Place was sold – and there was a new prime minister in Number Ten. It all seemed to have happened at once, without her. And to top it all, when she got to Blenheim Crescent, there was Will, alongside Emi, helping Sarah to alter the fabric of their lives, their history piled up in the hallway in cardboard boxes. She'd felt like an outsider to it all, that first weekend. By contrast, Will, it seemed, had already 'moved in'. She hadn't felt jealous exactly, more disoriented, unsure of the way it was all meant to work now. As soon as she could, without truly offending Sarah, she had scuttled off back to Edinburgh. The weekend had triggered a pattern of active disengagement that had lasted, she now knew, until Sarah died.

'What's your plan, today?' she asked Will in the morning as she put on her coat. It was 7 a.m. and he was still half asleep on the sofa. She could taste the whisky on her tongue and her eyes were aching from lack of sleep. She needed to get back to the studios, however, to see how things had gone overnight.

'I need to get my post from college, see Ralph . . .'

'What are you guys planning this time?'

Will sat up and stretched. 'Just a little pre-Christmas reminder of affairs in Iraq, for the late-night partying people of London,' he replied enigmatically. 'Something real to think about as they fall into bed after their office parties on the last night of "term".'

'Go on.'

'We're going to carry torches of fire from Hyde Park to Trafalgar Square, one for each suicide bomb that's exploded since the war began, then we'll have an all-night vigil.'

'Sounds like one for me to report on.'

'Great.'

She could sense that something else was on Will's mind, and of course she knew what it was.

'And what else?'

'I thought I might head over to Blenheim Crescent, to check up on Emi.'

Polly was looking out of the window as she drew on her gloves. It was still pouring with rain. She thought of the derailed train, those poor people, their lives destroyed, the living and the dead.

'I think you might be wasting your time,' she replied. 'She'll call when she's ready.'

She had a new feeling this morning, that Emi wouldn't be back for a while. She gazed out over the Thames. Seagulls were swooping in and pecking at the scum that had settled on plastic bags and around bottles bobbing in the rising tide along the bank. A bus was stationary in the middle of London Bridge and behind it traffic was building, choking its way back as far as Blackfriars. She watched as a train slipped along one fork of criss-crossing tracks, its destination the grey terraces of eastern suburbia.

'I'll need my umbrella,' she said, too brightly, turning back to Will. 'It's going to be a shitty day.'

7

'These should help,' says Carol, handing Sarah an unlabelled white box and avoiding eye contact. 'But, really, you should come and see Mr Kapoor for yourself.'

Sarah shakes her head vigorously as she pulls out the first row of pills, extracts two and swallows them with water.

'I know I should, but it's simply that I can't,' she says. 'Really, Carol, I can't leave the house.'

The pills help. Even though they make her more sluggish, they also make Sarah less anxious and prone to better, deeper sleep. After a couple of months she takes Carol's advice and visits the Harley Street consultant for herself. The clinic is discreet and the bills are paid in cash. Peter need never know. He mustn't know. She'll be better now. It's essential that she holds it together, for his and – more importantly – for the children's sake.

Carol never refers to Sarah's brief 'escapade' – and the twins grow quickly. Peter comes and goes, keeping an increasingly wide berth. When the children are three he suggests that they hire an au pair. To begin with Sarah finds the intrusion into her personal space difficult to handle, but she doesn't have the energy to disagree – and then she gets used to it, at a very low level even becomes reliant upon these girls, as the public face of the family. She likes to read, to embroider, to stay in her room. If she's honest, she still finds the outside world a little frightening. Wide-open spaces make her agoraphobic. More often than not, it's Chloe, then Lena, then the next au pair and the next who push the children in their buggies to the park, who collect them from nursery, who go with them to buy their first school shoes. It's Sarah who sits at home, who bathes them, reads to them, soothes them to sleep, sews the name labels into their Aertex collars, helps them with their letters, their spelling lists. She is the homemaker, in what she nearly convinces herself is a normal home. She's always there for the children; she never leaves them, or goes anywhere non-essential. She adores them, does her best. There's a certain equilibrium in the house, rarely the sound of fighting, often of laughter.

And so these early years pass in a curious fug. When she tries to look back, even a few months at a time, the details are indistinct; there's no real need to invite strangers in, or to leave St John's Wood, to head further afield, which is just as well, since recently London has become victim to race riots, as, in her father's words, 'the disenfranchised black underclass' protest on the streets of Brixton, to the south of the city. When Sarah speaks of it to him on the phone, he takes on an 'I told you so' air as he maligns Tory policy, berating the inevitable widening economic gap between the rich and the poor. Maggie's been in power for two years, and already it's true, there are signs of an increased social breakdown. Polly and Emi are like two halves of a whole and they are blissfully unaware of the riots, the tempestuous world just a few miles outside their home, outside one another. They live in a mirror world of giving and taking, of eating and sleeping. Now they're getting past infancy, Sarah can relax a little, they almost take care of themselves, although she notes that Emi tends to stick closer to her than Polly does; that she always needs to know where Sarah is in the house. Sometimes she feels almost normal, forgets the anxiety that lurks somewhere beneath her skin.

'When are you next coming to see us?' she asks her parents repeatedly, but the answer is always the same, that they have such a 'pressurized schedule' it's hard to know when they'll get a break. They usually make it over once a year, but these past twelve months have been particularly intense.

'But we'd like you to bring the twins, maybe for Christmas?' her father ventures. This year the girls are turning four. 'We would pay the fares.'

He says he's working with one of New York's most celebrated contemporary composers, and her mother will play at Carnegie Hall over New Year. They'd love for her to be there, to come and watch. Sarah hesitates. She doesn't want to confess it to him, but she doesn't feel resilient enough to take to the skies.

'I'll talk to Peter,' she ventures, vaguely, but inevitably she never follows the conversation up and another Christmas comes and goes with only brown parcels making the transatlantic trip to her parents on the other side of the world.

Peter's business is getting busier, his workload increasing,

71

and he has to travel to Paris with increasing regularity, staying away for a night or two at a time. And when he isn't abroad, he often returns home from the office after the girls have gone to sleep. But in the mornings he always rises early and gets them up, gives them their breakfast. Often Emi clambers back upstairs and into bed with Sarah, while Peter and Polly snuggle on the sofa to read a book before Sarah brings Emi down again and he heads off to the office.

Sarah knows she should get out more, perhaps take up an interest, try to meet new friends, that to Peter she must appear to be becoming increasingly dull. But she's afraid to upset her status quo, afraid she might not be able to cope. She prefers to stay at home, with the girls. Carol visits regularly and together they often walk through Regent's Park to feed the ducks, pushing the double buggy, pausing to watch the world go by. Alternatively, they go up to Primrose Hill for apple cake at a small Polish deli, run by efficient young girls whose sullen demeanour belies an unusual depth of generosity. They always give the twins extra cake, extra-frothy hot chocolate. Afterwards, they all walk up to the top of Primrose Hill and they can see the whole of London spread out before them like a tantalizing gift, waiting to be opened, its contents explored. Carol always takes a deep breath, her eyes shining as she observes 'our wonderful city', and Polly seems to follow suit, shading her eyes with a hand as Carol points out the key landmarks to her: Big Ben, St Paul's Cathedral. At these times Emi tends to run in circles around the top of the hill, lost in her own world, and seems less interested in the wide-open view. The intensity of the metropolis, the noise, the bustle, the traffic, the upsurge in violence south of the river, overwhelm Sarah, make her nervous. She rarely ventures further than this from home.

One day, Emi and Polly bring a dark fairytale book home from nursery school, about a black panther who prowls around a London garden and befriends the children who live in the house. Halfway through the story, Sarah puts the book down.

'That's exactly what it feels like!' she exclaims. 'It's as if that black panther is prowling through my mind.'

The girls glance up from the page at her quizzically and she falters.

'I'm sorry, my darlings,' she adds, brightly. 'I don't know what came over me!'

8

Emi woke up in the pitch dark. It took a moment for her to remember where she was, and how she'd got there. The last thirty-six hours seemed to have happened almost without her participation. Now it was Tuesday morning and she was a very long way from London. Her pulse quickened. What had she gone and done? She shut her eyes and tried to retrace the steps that had taken her from that little Italian café by King's Cross to this little single bed in a foreign city a long way from home.

When she'd got back from dinner with Kalle Strand on Sunday night she'd been violently sick before falling into bed. She had woken early on Monday morning with a crashing hangover and had immediately sat down to email James, initially to say that she was unwell, that she wouldn't be coming in. But as she looked at the screen, she'd realized that she couldn't go back there – not just then, but ever – and instead of pleading illness, she found herself emailing him a letter of resignation. Of course he'd assume that his behaviour on Friday night was to blame, but the reality was that it had had almost nothing to do with it, nothing at all.

All morning as she nursed her hangover Emi couldn't stop thinking about Kalle, about the fool she'd made of herself over dinner. She had felt so drunk, made such absurd claims. By lunchtime she knew that she had to see him, that she had to apologize before he left. She'd go to the airport, she decided, intercept him before he got on his plane. And then she'd take off – somewhere, anywhere. She might as well, she'd be at the airport, it was the perfect opportunity, she could just look at the board, choose a destination, buy a ticket and whoosh! she'd be gone.

She packed a small bag, took her passport, then went back into her mother's elegant drawing-room and logged on to her online bank account. She moved some of the money left to her by her mother from her savings to her current account, then paid off her credit cards and set up new direct debits for the flat's utility bills. One of the few benefits of having dead parents was a healthy bank balance. Now she would have the freedom, she realized, to take her time, wherever she went, to come back when she felt like it.

Once done, she closed down her laptop, then picked up a photograph on the mantelpiece of herself with Polly and their mother. Sarah had asked Will to take it on her fiftieth birthday. It had been late springtime. Sunlight was flooding through the open bay windows and just as he was about to click the shutter a butterfly had fluttered in and come between them and the lens. They'd all laughed and Will had clicked. In the picture they all appeared naturally, euphorically happy, and there it still was, the butterfly, artfully imprinted at its left top corner, like a motif. But as Will had remarked later, more significant than that was the apparently tight resemblance in the photograph between Emi and her mother. Inexplicably, in the picture they looked more alike than even she and Polly did. She stared now at Sarah's smooth, oval face, her fine, dark eyebrows and clear complexion, her deep-set brown eyes and lustrous dark hair. How could fate have taken such a cruel turn? How could she possibly have died so soon after this picture had caught her, apparently in the second prime of her life? Suddenly, Emi missed her mother with a pain so deep it numbed her heart.

'I'm sorry,' she whispered to her image. 'But I have to go away.'

Emi took the tube to the airport and found the check-in gate for the 5 p.m. flight to Stockholm. It was only three o'clock and she assumed Kalle would not arrive much before four. She sat on a bench, just as she had sat outside Tate Modern the day before, waiting and watching. As she contemplated her options, Emi watched the departures board. Where should she go? Somewhere warm appealed, perhaps Goa, or maybe Thailand – anywhere really would do. She had no feeling; she'd never done something this rash – or was it brave? – before. Frankly, after her plan to take those sleeping pills last night, she felt she had nothing to lose. The experience felt tantamount to giving her a get-out-of-jail-free card. For now the future felt like a blank, open page.

Eventually Kalle appeared, walking purposefully towards the bank of self-check-in machines opposite the BA desks. Emi hesitated, then moved towards him and touched him on the shoulder. Kalle turned quickly and saw her there.

For a split second he looked taken aback and then his face spread into a broad smile.

'I felt so ashamed of my behaviour last night,' she stuttered. 'I had to see you, before you left, to say sorry.'

Kalle glanced at his watch.

'Come on,' he said. 'We've got time for a quick coffee before I go.'

To her surprise he put his arm around her and together they headed towards one of the departure lounge cafés.

By the time they'd drunk their coffee, Emi had explained how she had taken sleeping pills before joining him for dinner, and that evidently they had mixed badly with the wine. She had also told him what she intended to do next, but not the reason why. Kalle sat very still, listening to her, his eyebrows creased in concentration, holding her hand in his, gently.

'Come with me to Stockholm, for a while,' he said resolutely, when she had finished. 'Until you feel clearer about your future plans. Then you can take off somewhere hotter, further afield.'

It was Emi's turn to be taken aback.

Kalle glanced, once more, at his watch.

'I hate to rush you, Emi, but you need to decide if you want to come, right now. We've only got ten minutes to check you in.'

He picked up his case and snapped it open. Emi sat watching him, wondering what to do, as he pulled some documents from his bag.

'What's that?' she asked.

'Well, I've got Stephanie's ticket here. It was non-refundable. Maybe you should use it.'

'But the name, it won't match my passport.'

Kalle grinned and held up a standard European passport. 'Are you as much of a risk-taker as you seem to be, Emi?' he asked, a touch playfully. 'I've got Stephanie's here. I intend to mail it to her from Stockholm tomorrow. You look pretty much the same.'

Emi picked up the passport and flicked to the image; certainly there was a resemblance between them, they had the same bobbed brown hair, dark eyes, oval faces, but Stephanie was a few years older than Emi, and definitely more stylish, too. Clearly a different person.

'They won't look, believe me,' Kalle said. 'They think they're looking, but they're not looking for us.'

Emi appraised Kalle for a split second. She felt compelled.

'I'll do it,' she said.

He was right about Customs; the comings and goings of a respectable Swedish couple were not on the guard's list of high-risk travellers and they made their way directly to the boarding gate, passing through security without a problem. And before she knew it they were sitting on the plane and she was on her way to Stockholm, the past dissolving rapidly in the jet-stream, the future hanging like a wisp of cloud in the darkening sky. At the pit of her stomach a pinhead of determination pricked and as Emi breathed outwards from it the air in her throat felt cool and pure. Presently the fasten-seatbelt sign lit up and the plane began its shuddering descent. At Stockholm International they walked for miles along polished wood floors to the customs. The official in the passport booth glanced

78

lingeringly at the photograph of Stephanie then up to fix Emi in the eye for another moment. Emi felt her heart lurch as she returned his gaze steadily. Then he smiled and handed her back Stephanie's passport. Kalle sure understood human psychology, she thought; for all his scrutiny the Customs officer hadn't been looking at her at all. Neither Kalle nor she spoke as they now made their way through, then left the airport. Guilt for her actions eluded her. All Emi felt was relief.

The cab swung them along an empty highway lined with flat, dark fields, on past forest-thickened suburbs and finally over a wide, jet-black estuary and on into the fairytale beauty of what Kalle told her quietly was Gamla Stan, Stockholm's medieval old town. Small bridges straddled the spits of water that spliced the city's streets, lamplight shimmering across its drifting surface. It was late, a Monday night, and the cobbled streets were all but empty. The cab took a sharp turn left, up over a wide stone bridge and then through an underpass before heading up a steep hill into an area called Sodermalm, or Soder, as Kalle informed her it was called by its inhabitants.

'I've lived here for the past ten years,' he added. 'It's the largest neighbourhood in Stockholm, and I think the nicest, almost its own town.'

The cab had bounced up a narrow, cobbled street, lined on one side with yolk-yellow town houses, on the other with two large, nondescript grey apartment blocks, and pulled up at the top, outside an imposing, cream-painted block of flats.

'At last, we're home,' he announced, with a slip of a grin.

It was splinter-dark; as they stepped from the cab Emi slid on the black ice, slick as granite above the cobbles, and Kalle caught her elbow to stop her from falling. It was bitterly cold. The street was called Fiskgartan, she noticed, and now they were heading for the doorway of number nine; an imposing oak and glass-panelled door surrounded by a large, carved stone portico, implying the wealth of its inhabitants, flowers engraved into the arch over their heads like offerings from the gods. On either side of the door two art-deco style nudes had been engraved, holding more wreaths of flowers above their heads. There were at least a dozen buzzers and Kalle quickly keyed in a code. They took the lift to the sixth and top floor, to a long corridor with four front doors, and Kalle unlocked number twenty-two.

'Come in,' he encouraged, allowing the door to swing open into a wide hall.

Emi moved ahead of him and dropped her small bag to the floor. She watched as he took off his coat and hung it on a hook next to a child's cherry-red anorak. Underneath he was wearing the oversized, navy blue woollen jumper. The sight of it made him seem more familiar, reassuring, something known. He moved ahead of her into the sitting-room, a rotunda with three floor-to-ceiling windows giving a panorama of the city. To one side was the vast sweep of the port and beyond it Gamla Stan; to the other a wood-covered island with a large building on its shoreline, designed in the shape of a boat. The other looked across to a large, leafy park and immense under-lit church.

'That,' he told her, pointing past the church, 'is where Lotta goes to kindergarten. She lives the other side of the park with Stephanie and over there, that island, Djurgarden, houses Skansen, a magical wildlife park. You take the boat here,' he pointed now to the port below them, lined with small white ferries, 'over to there. It's one of Lotta's favourite places – she's in love with the bears.'

The room was pale, with wooden floors, a long cream sofa and two brown leather reclining chairs. Six small etchings were hung tightly together along the main wall. She took a closer look. There was something humble yet artful about them, sensitive seascapes and images of smooth granite beaches, the edge of a forest dropping into shining water beneath a perfect moon.

'Do you like them?'

'It looks as if the liquid's floated across the paper without the artist's intervention,' she mused. She felt her eyes filling with tears at the beauty of the scenes, at the impact of the moment, here, with Kalle, in a foreign place, away from everything.

'Lars would love to hear you say that. He's my brother, a fine artist, one of Stockholm's best,' Kalle replied proudly, his tone becoming immensely warm. 'We share a house, on the northern tip of Skärgården – I mean the archipelago. He has a studio out on an island there, too, and this is what he makes. He has a belief in coincidence. And you're right, he tries to capture the traces left by man, consciously, or unconsciously.'

Kalle looked carefully at Emi. 'And he likes to observe the quietest things – he says they often have the greatest significance,' he added. 'Come on, you need to sleep.'

*   *   *

81

Emi followed Kalle along the corridor, past a bathroom, to a small, pale blue room with a single wooden bateau bed straddling its width. It was made up with crisp white linen covered with a thick beige horsehair rug. There was a small basin in the corner and she washed quickly before slipping between the cool sheets. She had left her pills behind, and worried, momentarily, that she wouldn't be able to sleep. A few minutes later, however, she had drifted away.

Now here she was, in the early morning, and the flat was quiet. She got out of bed and headed into the rotunda in her pyjamas to look out over the ever-dark city. Lights were still glowing from the nineteenth-century traders' mansions lining the north side of the harbour, their pale yellow façades subtly detectable in the continuing pitch. They were austere, detached buildings hooded with grey and green zinc-tiled roofs. At first it seemed that the city had forgotten to wake up, but as her eyes adjusted to the dark Emi noted a steady stream of bicycles and cars working their way through its streets. White ferryboats with their fog-lights on were chugging slowly in and out of the harbour too, leaving faint, frothing trails in their wake.

Hearing Kalle come into the room, she turned. He was dressed in a jacket, grey wool trousers and brogues. And he was carrying a tray of coffee. Today he looked different: taller, straighter and detached, a bit like the harbour buildings, she thought. He hadn't belonged in London. Perhaps that had been his initial appeal. Here she could see him in context and he slid into his real world like a piece of jigsaw into a puzzle. She felt embarrassed, standing there, dishevelled in her nightclothes.

'How did you sleep?' he asked, with a smile.

'Well,' she confessed. 'Surprisingly well.'

He put the tray down and they both turned to gaze at the dark city, spread out beneath them.

'I'd love to show you around today, but I'm afraid the hospital beckons. Are you brave enough to go out there alone?'

A pale light was gradually seeping into the thinning sky and a slight sun was skimming the surface of the surrounding sea.

'I can't wait,' she replied.

'Perhaps you could do a little shopping, orientate yourself. Stockholm's not so big. I'll give you a street map, and then you can follow your senses. If you head south there are great stores, cafés, or you could head to Katarinahissen – it's an outdoor lift that takes you down into the centre. You'll be close to the water, the museums – and,' he paused, unable to suppress a slight smirk, 'the other tourists.'

Emi winced. 'I'm not a tourist,' she replied. 'Remember, I'm an escapee.'

Kalle laughed. 'Oh, and could you get some groceries?' he asked, handing her two 500-kronor notes.

After he'd gone Emi looked out of the rotunda at the ferryboats, lights off now. They were streaming steadily out of the harbour, following one another like sheep along invisible fault lines. Although she couldn't see it, she sensed the emptiness of what lay outside the harbour. She imagined the view from above, a toy town of building blocks, man's insignificant efforts against the sweeping gulf of the island-dotted sea. She glanced back at Lars's ethereal prints; surprised by how utterly they compelled her. Their small scale belied the magnitude of their subject; like slim, sharp glimpses into the vast, undeniable edge of it all.

The previous night Kalle had shown her only the tiny kitchen, sitting-room and guest bathroom. Lotta's presence was clearly apparent in the colourful plastic bath toys, the Barbie-doll electric toothbrush and pink towels hanging neatly from the heated rail. There was a door leading to Lotta's room, next to her own, then a metal curved stairwell leading up to Kalle's floor above. She pushed Lotta's door ajar now and glanced inside. The wooden slatted blind was pulled down, the cream curtains half closed. The room retained a quiet calm, like a silk cocoon spun for perpetual infant slumber. A pretty patchwork quilt depicting a white unicorn in front of a fairytale castle hugged the child-size bed. From the wall above it hung an old-fashioned clock, delicately moulded from clay and painted in pastel hues, with little sculpted mice scrabbling merrily around the perimeter of the face. Next to the bed a yolk-yellow wooden doll's house sat on a pine chest of drawers and there was a large, cream fur rug in the middle of the floor. Along the wall were three shelves of neatly lined books, and below them one of little hand-painted wooden dolls and animals. The room smelt sweet and slightly fecund, like forest fern, and it carried with it a muted tone, a thick, deep silence, reinforced by the double-glazed windows that blocked out the surrounding sounds of the city. She pulled the door to. It contained the world of childhood, one with which she had not recently engaged, and witnessing it as a bystander made her acutely aware that she'd spent the last decade solely in the company of adults, that she'd all but forgotten childish things. When she tried to think back to her own infancy it had all become a curious blur.

Outside, the air bit with cold. Emi realized as she walked that she had lost her mother's mohair shawl in London, the night when she had met Kalle. Its disappearance felt like a symbol, a severing of ties. Sarah had bought it in Rome, the year before she died. She'd seemed extremely happy back then, Emi contemplated now, as if she'd finally found a way out of her melancholy. She thought about Sarah as she wandered down the cobbled lane and through Mosebacke Torg, a small, pretty square with a theatre dominating its north side. A sign for Katarinahissen directed her across it. In the middle there was a statue, next to a green wooden telephone-box. Its subject was unusual and she stopped to observe it: a life-size white marble depiction of two conjoined, naked women, one with her arms in the air above her head, the other trying to wrench herself away. The title was readily translatable: *The Sisters*. It sent a cold sensation down her back. She looked at the phone-box. Maybe she should call Polly? It might be better. But she couldn't do it, something held her back. Later, she thought. I'll do it later.

Emi walked on, following the signs, until she found a wide wire fence-enclosed walkway between high buildings. At the end there was a tiny old-fashioned lift. Its metal gates opened as she arrived and a hand gestured for her to enter.

'*Tio kronor, tak*,' the small, ageing lift operator said, clicking the gate shut behind her. 'That's ten crowns, please,' he added immediately, when he registered her confusion.

Emi took one of her two 500-crown notes from her pocket but he lifted a hand in protest.

'Next time,' he said, with a smile.

As the lift creaked and cranked downwards the port came into focus, the colours and sounds of the city intensifying. Within a minute she was at ground level. Emi thanked him and headed out across the bridge, ready to absorb this water-filled city.

There were more cyclists than cars in the streets and people walking decisively at a pace, heads down, collars turned up against the cold; women in big furry boots beneath long leather and suede coats, their sleek silvery blonde hair unfurling from beneath Russian-style fur hats, their fine lips pursed in pale faces, large dark shades masking the expressions in their eyes. It was something she hadn't counted on – the harshness of the weather here. Emi had always felt the cold and now it was seeping into her bones like a disease. She wandered around the port in a daze, watching people queuing for ferries, or heading with clear intent for meetings, others wandering towards the shops or museums. Soon she found herself back at the edge of the cobbled old town and dived into a café. It was as warm as the inside of a glove, with the comforting scent of cinnamon and ginger permeating the air. On the counter there was a line of little red painted horses – or maybe reindeer, like those she had seen back in Lotta's bedroom. She asked for a coffee and to her relief the waitress answered her in accent-free English.

Next Emi made her way through the old town. It was full of little boutiques, restaurants and tourist shops. There was a bookshop and in its window she spied a pile of small, colourful diaries. She entered and picked one up, a paperback-sized white leather-bound book with gold-leaf edging. She ran her palm over one of its cool, blank pages. It felt precious, something with a spirit and small enough to carry with her every day. Her thoughts were drawn to the journals she'd written for years as a teenager, with a commitment that had surprised even herself. When she'd left home for university the diaries hadn't seemed necessary any more. She'd packed away the volumes containing years' worth of her life in an old leather case she'd bought at Portobello market and left them at the family home, along with many of the memories they contained. Thinking back to them now, she wondered how much of the detail she'd remember, or agree with, if she were to turn back the pages. Right now her adolescence felt like nothing more than a smudge of charcoal on a grey page. Maybe, with this New Year, it was time to start a new one, with a blank future, wide open. Who knew where it would lead her? She headed for the counter to pay.

When she left the shop it was nearly one o'clock and Stockholm's workers had taken to the streets in hordes. They were heading in and out of the countless restaurants and coffee shops now serving lunch. She decided to make her way back to the relative safety of Soder. A colourless gloom was spreading over the city like a watery but sincere threat. She walked quickly, freezing cold now, and took the lift back up, this time paying the already familiar operator with the correct change. He thanked her with a smile. Then she headed across the square, passing the sculpture of the sisters without hesitation, without looking at it, realizing there was no way she would be calling Polly today. She'd wait a while; Polly probably wouldn't even have noticed Emi's absence yet, she reasoned. Emi still had time to think things through, time to make decisions – although suddenly she knew one certainty: she wasn't going back. She made her way to Kalle's apartment block with growing haste, then hesitated outside to look at her watch. It wasn't yet two, but the sky had already bruised, was darkening again.

She wandered on past Katarina Kyrka, an imposing, neoclassical church painted mustard-yellow, mimicked in Lotta's doll's house and in many of the medieval buildings around Gamla Stan. All the doors were closed and the high, plain-glass windows were dark. There was something gloomy and disheartening about it, she thought, as she hurried across the large, dusky park and on to a wider main thoroughfare lined with regular shops. She spied a supermarket on the corner and went inside. Cajsa Warg was in fact more of a classy, upmarket deli. She pushed a trolley past rows of artfully packaged fresh fish and meat, sauces and relishes, arranged in softly humming refrigerated units. Kondillscreme, Romsas, Basilikacreme, she read, picking up one pot after another, then putting them back, uncertain of their contents. She chose more familiar vegetables, fruit, some salmon fillets and then cartons of what she guessed were yoghurt and milk; took some aïoli and finally bought freshly baked rye bread and a packet of saltless butter, paying the young cashier tentatively. It was still only a quarter to three but she headed back through the church gardens in near pitch darkness. It would still be light in London. She thought of James receiving her email of resignation. It was already too late, for everything, she decided. There was no going back.

Kalle was clearly tired when he got home and Emi cooked him supper. While they ate she retraced her footsteps around the city for him in words and he listened attentively. The atmosphere between them was calm and quiet, undemanding. He was evidently pleased with the food she'd bought and prepared, and, when she slid it from her bag, he inadvertently mimicked her earlier gesture as he ran his palm across one of the cool, white pages of her new diary.

'What a wonderful idea,' he said, then closed it and held it between his hands, looking across at her contemplatively. 'It seems you've been under the weather, Emi,' he began, picking his words cautiously, she thought, like blackberries from a bush, careful to avoid any hidden thorns. 'A diary is a fine place to work out what it is you think you've lost and what it is you think you need to find.'

She nodded as she took it back from him, but didn't trust herself to speak. There were lots of things – and people – that she felt she'd lost, or maybe not lost, simply allowed to let go. But what did she need to find? That was a far harder question to answer.

'Thank you, for having me,' she ventured.

'You are welcome,' he replied with a grin.

Later that night, lying in her bed, Emi picked up her diary. She opened the first page, hesitated, then began to write.

'*Stockholm's cold, dark, fathomless, with endless streams out to a wide-open sea. It feels like a mirror to my mind. I'm numbed by the climate and by what I've done, by what I nearly did. Yet I feel neither guilt nor fear. I feel as if I'm sleep-walking; I feel as light as air.*'

She paused. She guessed it didn't matter if her words made any sense. It was only a start, and only for her eyes to read. But even so, it was hard to be absolutely honest, to be clear. Her teenage diary had been a literal retelling of facts, a way to document her adolescent moments of external being. This needed to be something else, an attempt to reveal what lay within. She tried another paragraph, a different tack – an observation.

'*There was a statue. Something drew me towards it. Ironically, it was of two naked women, standing back to back, struggling to pull apart. It made me think of Polly. I nearly called but in my mind I keep seeing that last look in her eyes, and I can't, I just can't. I need to forget, just for a while.*'

Emi shut the book. Her eyelids were heavy; she couldn't stay awake any longer. She switched off the light and fell into another deep, dreamless sleep. She woke early once again, to a continuing, solid darkness.

9

With Christmas drawing closer, Polly found her workload intensifying, and Will became equally preoccupied with the plans for his impending peace rally. There wasn't a lot of time to worry about Emi, but when eight days had gone and there was still no sign of her they were both forced to acknowledge a deeper stirring of concern. However much they tried to convince themselves that she had taken a holiday, her lengthening silence was definitely uncharacteristic; she'd never really been one to venture far from home. They'd called around her friends but no one had heard from her. They agreed that, if she hadn't shown up by Christmas Eve, they would tell the police. 'It'll be more than two weeks by then,' Polly rationalized. 'Too long for a regular package to the sun.'

In the meantime they both called the flat daily and otherwise tried to concentrate on their work. On the day of Will's rally Polly was on an early shift, and after work she made her way down Oxford Street. She had planned to meet a cameraman at the rally at nine. Christmas trees twinkled in every window and the lights on Regent Street seemed brighter, more garish than ever before. She wove her way through the crowds in the West End, searching for presents. She wanted to buy Will something significant, something with which to say thank you, for being her brother-in-law, for being her friend. In the end she chose a silver 'peace' ring they'd seen a few nights before in the window of a trendy store in Carnaby Street. Then she looked for a gift for Emi. She was still convinced that she'd show up in time for Christmas. They'd never spent one apart before. But as she wandered from shop to shop, she had no clear notion of what to get her. This surprised her, rendered her hollow for a moment. She recognized in her indecision a distancing caused by Emi herself, by her silence, her determination not to allow Polly in on her thoughts or, indeed, her recent plans.

Finally, just off New Bond Street, she spied a tiny, ruby red, cut-glass perfume bottle glinting in the window of an antiques shop. It was shaped like a large lozenge and had a pretty, intricately engraved silver top. It had been flicked open to display the small glass stopper inside. Emi wore a ruby and diamond ring that had been their mother's and it made Polly think of it; it seemed to fit. She entered the hushed store and asked the tight-faced assistant if she might take a closer look. He nodded judiciously, then fetched the bottle with white-gloved hands and placed it gently on a velvet cloth for Polly to observe.

'May I touch it?' she asked.

He nodded curtly and lifted it into her waiting palm. When she held the bottle she knew that it was the perfect gift for Emi. It felt cool and surprisingly heavy and it fitted inside her closing hand like something discreet, like a valuable secret.

'Early Victorian,' confided the assistant. 'Very rare.'

Polly paid for the bottle, then headed to an old-fashioned perfumery on the edge of Soho and asked the ageing French patron to create her sister a unique scent to fill it. He asked Polly to describe Emi's temperament and when she faltered, he smiled.

'It's hard to describe the people we know best, impossible to be objective about their characters,' he philosophized, disappearing for a moment behind the counter.

He reappeared with a piece of hardboard covered with tiny squares of colour. 'Maybe you could recognize aspects of your sister through these,' he suggested. 'See if you can choose four and we'll go from there.'

Polly glanced over the myriad options. He was right. Suddenly she could visualize Emi as a series of colours, no, not even colours, but hues. She saw great sheets of them, billowing in the wind; cornflower blue blended with an inch of dawn light to match her ephemeral ways; bruised purple tinged with burnt orange to denote her spiky sensitivity and, above all, dove grey, the tone of her everyday geniality, her placidness and apparent lack of emotional extremes. This was the aspect of Emi's character that she'd always wrestled with the most, and her own inability to dig her spade into the fine sand dunes of her twin's mind.

'Interesting,' mused the perfumer, as she showed him her choices. 'Come back tomorrow. I will have created the perfect scent for your sister.'

Back outside on the corner of the street, carol singers rang out traditional hymns and the sweet, ashy scent of chestnuts permeated the cold air. Polly hurried now, keen

93

to get home, to put her presents away, then to get dressed up in thicker layers, ready to head back to Hyde Park for nine o'clock. In contrast to the general feeling of goodwill around the city, the anti-war coalition had geared up for its midnight vigil, and as the week had passed the number of attendees had rapidly grown.

Before she got to them Polly saw the glow of torches, the smoke from the flames causing a gauzy smog to rise in the light above the protesters' heads. It was creating a warm glow across the group, circling it in an unexpectedly atmospheric halo of light. They were gathered on the St James's Park side of Hyde Park Corner. Policemen on horses were already there, keeping the crowd back from the busy road. She immediately spotted Will standing on some crates with a loudspeaker in his hand. She hadn't seen him for days and felt her mood lifting. He was informing the group of their planned route up the Mall and then on into Trafalgar Square, and soon they were on their way. Polly hooked up with her appointed cameraman and they moved alongside the protesters, filming their progress, as they chanted, 'No more war! Out with Bush! Down with Blair!', their blazing torches held high. Once in the square, speaker after speaker stood up on a small, erected podium and voiced their protest to the crowds; others handed out leaflets to the stream of festive revellers, who paused to gawp before passing on by. When Will got up to speak he gained a rousing round of applause. The atmosphere was charged but peaceful and the night was crisp and cold. Polly stayed until one in the morning, mingling with the crowds, and before she left, she made her way to Will.

'Well done,' she said, giving him a hug.

He grinned, evidently pleased with the way things had gone.

'What time are you heading home?' she asked.

'Around eight,' he replied. 'But Tom's back for Christmas so I'll be kipping on the sofa.'

'If you want a good day's sleep,' she said, 'I'll be at work. You're welcome to the flat.'

Polly woke in the morning to the sound of Will on the buzzer. Beneath his fatigue she sensed his exhilaration. By the time she headed off for work he was already in her bed falling into a deep, day-long slumber.

Later, Polly played through the edit of her report one last time.

'*In Trafalgar Square last night hundreds of protesters staged a torchlight vigil for the victims of the Iraq war . . .*'

It had taken her most of the day to get it just right; it mattered that she didn't disappoint Will. She waited as Nick agreed the running order; she expected the story to take the main slot, but at the last moment he replaced it with a light-hearted piece she'd filmed yesterday, on '*The bling-bling of Santa's Christmas grotto, the biggest, most brash ever in Harrods department store*'.

She stormed into his office and demanded an explanation. Nick looked sheepish and she knew immediately that there was no point in arguing with him, that the order had come from a higher level. She grabbed her bag and headed home angry and dismayed. To her relief, Will was still there.

'Fucking typical dumbing-down,' he said dismissively, with a wry smile. 'I don't know why you're so surprised.'

'I don't want to let you down,' Polly said, surprised at how emotional she was feeling.

Will looked at her, quizzically. 'You could never do that,' he replied. 'Have you heard from Emi?'

Polly shook her head. She'd been trying not to think about it but now tears were filling her eyes.

'Don't you think we ought to call the police?' he murmured.

'Not yet,' she replied, her dread rising. 'I'll know there's something wrong if she isn't in touch by Christmas Day. We've always spent it together. Let's wait until then.'

Will looked concerned but didn't disagree.

10

Outwardly Emi and Polly are peas in a pod, but there's something about the girls that is distinctive, at least to Sarah: it's their scent. She's most aware of it when she reads to them on her bed at night. Emi smells like her to such a degree that when she puts her face to her daughter's hair and breathes in there is almost no perfume, no distinct scent there at all. But when she holds Polly close it's different, fecund, foreign. She would never tell anyone about this but the truth of the matter goes further. Although superficially they are identical, in her disposition Polly is easy-going; her mouth stretches wider than Emi's when she smiles, her lips are warmer and her eyes dance brighter. She is much more relaxed in her own body, too. At lunchtime when the children habitually sit together for half an hour in front of the television to watch *Play School*, Polly's arms and legs are always askew and she twists a curl in her hair in a lazy, easy way. Her skin is warmer than Emi's too; it seems, at times, impermeable, denser. She almost always feels toasty warm – as if she's just got out of bed. Emi's skin is cooler; her hands and feet are often really cold, like Sarah's own. Emi always tucks her legs up underneath her body when she watches TV, holds herself in, and folds her arms – and she chews constantly at her bottom lip.

Emi will often bring her books and colouring pens and lie on her mother's bedroom floor, playing, singing, chatting to her, while Sarah embroiders or reads. Conversely, increasingly Polly inhabits the whole house, leaving her things scattered wherever they fall. She's fascinated by outsiders, is always the first to befriend the latest au pair, to want to hear stories about their worlds. She's quick to learn the lyrics of songs; the latest girl has introduced her to pop music, and, much against her better judgement, even to Sarah Polly's juvenile renditions of the latest chart toppers are really very funny. And she's an avid storyteller, too, always inventing other worlds for Emi and herself to inhabit. It's almost as if she doesn't need Sarah at all. Conversely, Sarah always knows when Peter is home by the shrieks of delight that Polly emits as she hurls herself down the stairs into his welcoming embrace. There is a bond between them that is special, different; one that she knows neither she nor Emi shares with Peter. Emi loves her father too, but she tends to hang back, waiting for him to come and get her, to pick her up and hold her to him. And often Emi has a distant look in her eyes, as if she's searching for something, someone or somewhere else.

Peter and Sarah appear to have organized their lives to run in parallel lines – and parallel universes, perhaps. When their eyes meet there is no line of enquiry, no desire, on either side, to know what lies behind their expressions. When the family sit together in front of the television to watch the wedding of Prince Charles to Lady Di, she feels an affinity with the young princess. When Diana looks at her older husband, there is no passion in her eyes.

For her part, Sarah is afraid to allow Peter into the gloom that nestles beneath the surface of her drug-elevated state, and for his part, it would seem that Peter would rather skim the surface than confront the underlying confusions that plague his wife's inner life. It wouldn't work but for Carol, who is always there, holding the fort, ready and willing to help keep them all on track. She seems to enjoy the engagement and Peter tries to ensure that she feels appreciated. For her part, without realizing it, Sarah's dependency upon her friend grows as the years pass by.

11

Five days have passed since I arrived in Stockholm and with every hour I feel calmer, more at ease, less concerned about what I have left behind. When Kalle has been at work I've wandered around, absorbing this beautiful winter city, trying to fathom a future plan, to work out what I want to do next, whether or not I should go home, stay here, or head somewhere new. And when he's been free Kalle and I have talked and talked and eaten and drunk wine and talked some more. Even so, I haven't mentioned Polly to him, or her relationship with Will. Something is holding me back from complete disclosure. I guess I just don't want to 'share' any of this with him. I want to keep Kalle's world completely separate. I feel as if he's allowing me time to breathe freely without any pressure from him to become emotionally engaged, and yet what I really want is for him to hold out his hand, to take mine, to draw me closer.

Tonight, after we'd eaten, he asked me what I thought I might want to do next. I shrugged my shoulders.

'I know I need to leave, before Lotta gets back,' I replied. 'But I can't tell you what a cathartic time I've had here. I want to thank you, so very, very much.'

'Why don't you stay?' he asked gently.

'Stay?' I replied, confused.

How could I? It would be such an imposition – and he hardly knew me. We had talked, it was true, but I had yet to mention Polly or Will; I had intentionally played those cards very close to my chest. For now I just wanted to feel singular, for him to know me only as me, not as the twin sister of the 'real thing'.

'You could help me with Lotta,' he suggested. 'You remember, I said I was thinking about it, how to find her one-to-one care. And it seems to me, fate has brought you to me.'

I couldn't help but laugh. 'I didn't think you believed in fate.'

'Maybe you're changing my perspective,' he laughed, too. 'Go on. Don't think of it as a job, think of it as a helping hand, from a friend in need.'

'But I have no experience with children and I speak no Swedish.'

'Well, for one you wouldn't need to worry about Lotta's Swedish. Stephanie's half-American. We speak English at home.'

I thought for a moment. It did seem that fate had brought me to Kalle, had brought me here. For once I had hardly even tried to intervene, to control it.

'You've been under the weather, Emi. Lots of things could help you to feel better,' he continued, earnestly. 'Walking, swimming, laughing, taking piano lessons, playing foolish games with Lotta. And, hopefully, absorbing a new place could be its own tonic, too.'

I paused for a moment, took a deep breath. 'OK,' I said. 'I'll give it a go.'

So I haven't packed my bags and taken to the skies. Instead, this afternoon I sat and waited nervously as I heard the sound of the key in the door, of laughter entering the flat. I looked out at the harbour lights and listened to Lotta hanging up her coat, unbuckling her school shoes and slipping on her soft suede slippers, chattering all the while to Kalle in burbling Swedish. Then, in a rush that felt like a breeze entering the room, she was there, presenting herself before me with her hands hooked behind her back, her cheeks flushed with soft pink circles that animated her otherwise alabaster skin. I was struck by how tiny and fine-boned she looked, standing there in her knee-length red tartan dress, an impish, inviting grin displaying two gaps in the top row of her teeth and her long, ivory hair swinging in two tusk-like plaits down the sides of her face.

'*Hej*!' she said brightly, fidgeting nervously with the pleats in her dress.

'*Hej*,' I replied, a touch nervous, too.

Lotta hesitated for a moment, then skipped the two steps that separated us and placed her small hands inside my own. Lotta's felt reassuring, trusting and warm. 'Welcome to Stockholm,' she pronounced, fixing me with Kalle's sea-grey eyes. 'Papa's really happy you've come.'

I smiled, relieved. How could I have forgotten? Lotta spoke perfect American English – like her mother, of course.

*   *   *

102

During tea Lotta relived her visit to London, her attentions predominantly fixed on her father, every now and then glancing sideways at me with a sweet smile. She'd seen the Changing of the Guard, had taken a trip on a big red bus through Trafalgar Square. 'And we took a spotty boat, too,' she added, with growing enthusiasm, 'to a kids' museum called the Tat!'

'Tate,' I corrected, and immediately recollected the previous Sunday when I too had been there, sitting outside the Turbine Hall in the winter sun. I tried to imagine the little girl and her mother passing by me, even possibly sitting next to me on the bench. So many people had wandered before me, but I remembered none of their faces; I'd been lost inside my own daydream. But with Lotta here, suddenly I felt jolted awake. She'd already left the Tate story behind, and was now at London Zoo with a monkey which, she explained, had pointed and chattered at her. At this she leapt up and started mimicking it, dancing around the table with her tongue pressing out her bottom lip.

'I think the meal's over,' laughed Kalle, grabbing his daughter with a roar and carrying her off, giggling, to her bath.

I'd forgotten what it was like, this abandonment of order that comes in through the door with a child. I looked around at Lotta's scattered belongings, causing chaos in her wake. As I collected them up I thought how, for her, each new moment was like the next segment of a peeled orange, waiting to be devoured and enjoyed for all its fresh, sharp flavour. I could hear this manifest itself in her actions now, squealing at the first touch of her toes in the

103

steaming hot water, laughing as Kalle poured the bath foam, shrieking at the growing mountain of sparkling froth. Next I listened as she grumbled at Kalle's firm hands wrapping her in a warm towel, rubbing her small frame dry. I moved tentatively to the open bathroom door. Neither Kalle nor Lotta noticed me there. She was tiptoeing up high to reach the basin, squeezing the toothpaste on to her brush with her tongue sticking slightly out, touching her top lip, in intense concentration. Kalle looked happy, watching as she switched on the button and the brush whirred. At last they turned and saw me. Lotta giggled and scooted bare-bodied past me into her room. Kalle winked at me and followed her. I continued to observe them as Lotta put on her pyjamas and wriggled down into her bed, complaining with a glance up towards me of the 'freezing sheets'. Kalle sat next to her on the bed and opened a large, illustrated book. I whispered goodnight and Lotta sat forwards, beckoning me over. I entered the room and kissed the little girl's soft, warm cheek, then left the two of them to their story. As I passed her room minutes later, the light was off and I heard her whisper, 'Goodnight, Papa. I love you more than air.'

I'm trying to force my memory back, to myself at Lotta's age. But I can't think of a single moment in detail – simply the sensation of being there, in the bathwater, for example, with Polly, splashing and playing. Polly had not been like a separate entity in those early days, she'd been more like an extension of myself. I'd been conscious of my mother's shadowiness, my father's absences, but they hadn't mattered so much as had Polly. We'd been so close that we'd hardly been conscious of a separateness between us – in fact we had been like one entity split in two halves, a machine that worked its own cogs and wheels with little need for outside intervention. When, I wondered, had that begun to change?

This morning Kalle and I took Lotta to kindergarten together, so that in future I would know the way. She ran ahead of us in the lamplight and we followed behind.

'This darkness takes some getting used to,' I confessed.

'As long as you don't get SAD. So many people here do.' He laughed, a touch self-consciously. 'The darkness makes them suicidal.'

I felt myself blush at the thought of my sleeping pills and for a moment was glad of the natural shadows generated by this dusky dawn.

We walked down a narrow, cobbled street and through an innocuous green wooden door to enter the kindergarten. On the other side, the world of childhood rang out boldly in the large garden, which was full of colourful apparatus, a jungle scene covering the inner walls. A Christmas tree had been erected and its garish lights were twinkling. Lotta yelped with excitement as she spotted it and gestured impatiently for us to follow her inside. In the cloakroom we were met by a hubbub of children changing their boots for indoor shoes, unbuttoning coats and hanging up bags. Lotta quickly began organizing herself for the day as Kalle introduced me to Johanna, her teacher, a woman of about my own age with short spiky blonde hair, wearing a stripy sweatshirt, trainers and low-slung jeans. My experience of school had been nothing like this; our prep school in London had been a place of uniform, decorum and privilege, reinforced by traditional Victorian classrooms kitted out with old-fashioned wooden desks and straight-backed chairs. Here there wasn't a desk in sight; rather, a series of small interconnecting rooms, furnished with low, colourful Formica-topped tables loaded with activities.

'We encourage the children to explore the world through play,' Johanna explained, as if registering my preconceptions. 'There's no formal teaching until they turn seven. We try to empower them to make their own creative choices, to explore their own developing minds.'

A little boy was tugging at the teacher's arm. Johanna smiled, and instead of reprimanding him for interrupting, she turned to give the child her full attention. He pleaded with her in Swedish and pointed at his feet.

'Excuse me, he wants me to help tie his shoes,' she explained apologetically, as she bent down.

I turned and said goodbye to Lotta, who was already immersed in the contents of a tray of tiny wooden reindeer, then Kalle and I left, the green door swinging firmly shut behind us. I agreed to collect her at two.

'Are you sure it's OK?' he asked, anxiously.

'Of course. It's why I'm here,' I replied.

He looked relieved. 'Thank you, Emi,' he added. 'For everything.'

I felt myself blushing for the second time in the day. 'It's nothing,' I said. 'I am so happy to be here.'

He hugged me briefly, then turned and hurried away to catch his bus to work.

*　　*　　*

I walked back down to the old town, determined to buy a present for Lotta. On my first day here I had passed numerous stores selling rag dolls of a little girl with freckles and russet red hair, pulled into two cranky plaits. She was wearing a pinafore over her dress and pointy witch's shoes. She seemed to be the city's talisman, her face appearing in every other window I passed. It was reassuring that this seemed to be a place that so readily accommodated childhood. I went into an old-fashioned toyshop, full to splitting with dolls and books, and picked one up. The text was in Swedish but as I flicked through the pages I got the gist of the story. The child's name was Pippi Longstrump, which I guessed from her attire translated to Pippi Longstocking. She wore mismatched stripy stockings under her threadbare clothes and lived alone in a pink painted wooden house with a spotted white horse and a pet monkey. Everything she did appeared to be upside down – she sat on the table and ate her food off her chair, she put the washing out to dry when it was raining and she didn't appear to go to school. In the story a little boy and girl from the neighbouring house became entranced with Pippi. Every morning they entered her unconventional world to gawp at her antics. She in turn shook them from their bourgeois existence.

I decided to buy the large rag doll and a copy of the book. Maybe Lotta could help me to read the story in Swedish – then to translate it into English, too. It would be a start, something for us to share in.

Lotta was tired when I picked her up from school, and told me that she wanted to go home and watch TV. We snuggled up together on the sofa under a rug and as she dozed my thoughts turned, yet again, to home, to Polly and to Will. A week had now passed. Would they be worrying about me yet or simply still assume I'd just gone away for a break? Would James have called to let them know I'd resigned? Maybe they had no idea that I'd even gone. Maybe they'd assumed I was just lying low. Lotta stirred, looked up at me, anxiously.

'*Vad har hänt?*' she murmured, then smiled sleepily at my look of confusion. 'Are you OK, Emi? You're trembling.'

She was looking up at me with an endearing depth of concern.

'I'm fine,' I replied gently, touched by her intuition. 'But, you know, I think I need a haircut.'

She leapt up from the sofa, suddenly wide awake.

'Mama goes to a place near my playground,' she enthused. 'Can I play there first?'

Lotta ran up and down the little rickety bridge, clambered on to the red and green wobbly reindeer and pushed it back and forth rigorously, then sped up and down the slide, switching between humming and silence as her tongue tipped her top lip in concentration. I sat and watched her display of self-containment and thought back to the previous evening, to her ability to hold relatively im-pressive adult conversation for someone so small, her ability to communicate in subtle ways, with a smile, a flicker of her intuitive eyes, or with a quick gesture of her hand.

Soon she'd had enough and directed me to her mother's salon. Luckily they weren't busy. While the hairdresser was working her magic, we read *Pippi Longstocking* and Lotta played happily with her new friend, the Pippi rag doll. Then the hairdresser unveiled my hair from the silver foils.

'You look Swedish!' Lotta exclaimed with a twirl. 'I like it – you are like my big sister!'

It was true. With my new bleach-blonde hair, my skin appeared paler, my eyes more blue.

When we got home I prepared her tea while Lotta drew pictures of my transformation from 'English girl to Swedish sister', humming all the while under her breath. Kalle and Stephanie entered this scene together half an hour later. I heard their voices in the hall before they came into the room. I had my back to the door, pouring tea into a pot, when I sensed them come in. I turned to see Kalle about to make an introduction; but then he faltered.

'Wow!' he exclaimed.

Meantime Lotta jumped from her chair and flung her arms around her mother, who was still standing in the doorway, coat on, watching me nonchalantly, her long, dark hair curling softly down her back. She looks different from her passport photo, evidently a few years older, and totally unlike Lotta, who truly is the spit of her father. Before anyone had a chance to say anything more, Lotta was rattling off a story in her spinning Swedish burble and I deduced she was telling her parents about our day. Then everyone was laughing and looking at me and evidently admiring my hair, so I joined in, turning full circle for them to see the whole effect, catching Kalle's eye as I did so. He had a quizzical expression in his eyes but a smile on his lips and he held out his hands to steady me.

'It's nice,' he said, mildly. 'Now you look like you really belong here, in Stockholm. You look like one of us.'

Stephanie disentwined herself from Lotta, moved towards me and firmly shook my hand.

'One of them, he means! I'll never be a true Stockholmer, there's too much California in my blood. Welcome to Soder, none the less. I hope you have enough time to study as well as to look after Lotta. It will be a great help.' She glanced back at Kalle. 'For us both.'

Stephanie's around forty, extremely well composed, pretty in an angular, quiet way, and she has an unswerving, steady expression that implies sure-footedness. She's analytical, too; I felt her scrutinizing me with her scientific mind as she stood there smiling, her dark eyes remaining blank, and suddenly I felt a touch embarrassed by the adolescent style of my hair and found my hand reaching up to touch it, thinking as I did so that Polly would never lose her composure so easily.

'I like it,' she said, too readily in tune with my thoughts.

Lotta sat on her mother's lap, and during tea Stephanie filled me in on her routine with great efficiency and attention to detail: the days she has Lotta, the days that Kalle does, the schedules they follow, the classes Lotta takes outside school hours – swimming, ballet. I wrote a few details down as Kalle drank his tea, smiling wryly. Then he slunk off to his study. Stephanie glanced up once to ensure he was gone, then confided, 'He's fantastic, a brilliant father. But, my God, when Kalle has his teeth into a project things start to go a little haywire. He'll become forgetful, not take the right clothes to school for Lotta's swimming and so on. He has a book to finish by next winter, which means he'll begin to disappear into his work after Christmas, to his desk, head down at his computer.'

I tried to look sympathetic.

'I'm just warning you,' she continued, 'because it'll be then that Lotta will really need the extra help. I'm amazed he's found you – normally these things fall to me. But it seems the perfect arrangement.'

I looked into her expectant face. She was pleased, no doubt, that Kalle had found help, but I wondered if she was at all suspicious of the method, or simply slightly annoyed that he'd gone and hired someone before she had had a chance to interview them for herself. Evidently she was used to taking control. This little chat was her way of redressing the balance and I respected her for it.

She glanced at her watch. 'I'm afraid I need to go,' she said. 'I'm due to meet a friend at the theatre.'

The initiation seemed to be over. Kalle appeared to wish her farewell and they moved together to the hall. I watched from the open door as he leaned forward to kiss her goodbye. At the last moment she turned her face so his lips met her hair.

Lotta ran after them to give her mother a hug, then turned to me. 'Now, can you help me have my bath, Emi?' she implored.

I peered at this awkward triangular family from the doorway. Stephanie raised a hand in farewell and Kalle shut the door behind her. I was relieved; it was time to get back to childish things.

12

On Christmas Eve Polly woke to an insipid dawn un-wrapping itself slowly over London. Emi had been gone for exactly two weeks now and she had a hunch that her twin was going to tip back up today, just in the nick of time for Christmas. Last night Will had stayed over again. Tom and his new American girlfriend were here for the whole of Christmas. Will had told Polly that he felt uncomfortable invading their love-nest. Polly had laughed and had encouraged him to stay with her until New Year. She'd even contemplated clearing out the spare room so he could move in properly for a while, but so far he'd protested, assuring her that in the new year he'd go back to Tom's and start looking for his own place to rent, too. She left him sleeping on the sofa and let herself out of her flat quietly; she determined to head over to Blenheim Crescent, maybe to surprise a jetlagged Emi on her return home, to tell her that Will was at her flat, before Emi found out for herself, a way of damage limitation. The protest report had been her last until the new year. She herself was now on holiday. She'd intended to plan her own trip abroad, but hadn't got around to booking anything and now she was feeling a new, rising uncertainty. After all, if Emi wasn't there, what would she – they – do next?

Antonio, the porter, smiled and raised his cap as she let herself into the foyer.

'Hello, Polly. When is Emi expected home?' he asked cheerily.

'I'm really not sure,' Polly replied, with a smile. Inwardly her heart sank as she collected Emi's post and made her way up the stairs, then let herself into their mother's old apartment. She put on the kettle and searched the cupboards for instant coffee, made a cup and began to drink it black. Next she wandered into the sitting-room and sat down in the floral armchair where, increasingly, as she became ill, their mother had used to sit. She picked up the picture of herself, Emi and Sarah, taken, she recalled, by Will on Sarah's fiftieth birthday. She scrutinized the image. She could remember the day as if it were last week. She'd broken up with her latest, fleeting new boyfriend and had arrived distressed and in need of attention, but as soon as she'd seen Will and her mother arranging flowers and taking photographs together she had felt superfluous and unneeded. She thought about Will now and couldn't find a way to connect the person of that time with the one still asleep, this morning, in her flat.

She put the photo down and idly picked up the pile of post she'd brought up with her from the foyer. Then she had an idea: Emi's most recent bank statements were bound to provide her with clues to her sister's travel plans. There were three, sitting before her. With rising expectation she opened the first and glanced quickly down the list of transactions; but it was simply a utilities account detailing direct debits for the flat. The only unusual aspect was that there had been a frenzy of activity the day before Emi had gone away, in which she had set up new annual direct debits to all the utilities companies. This suggested housekeeping of the highest order, even by Emi's exacting standards. She ripped the second statement open now, with rising curiosity: it was a Visa bill. Again, the outstanding balance had been paid in full, the day before Emi went away. And since then she had not used the card. Finally Polly opened the third statement, revealing the details of her sister's day-to-day account. To her surprise, she now found that her hands were shaking. She blinked before allowing her eyes to focus on the details. And suddenly she knew that something had gone terribly wrong. The last transaction on the account had been made the night of Helen's dinner party: Polly remembered how Emi had asked the cab to pull over at a hole-in-the-wall. 'I need fifty quid,' she had said, as she nipped out to withdraw some money. Since then the account had not been accessed. It seemed that, for the past two weeks, Emi had been living on thin air.

London was quiet and empty. Polly and Will drove to Paddington Green police station without encountering a single jam. Neither spoke during the journey, and, in her mind, Polly kept replaying the last time she had seen Emi, turning it over and over, trying to see it in a different way, to spot the clues she had missed the first time, when Emi had actually been there, glancing at her from the kitchen window, before pulling down the blind. She could visualize her earlier in the evening, too, physically, sitting opposite her at Helen's, through the flickering candlelight, her face wan, her thoughts just out of reach. But try as she might, she was incapable of taking the next step forwards, into Emi's future, into this new unknown.

At the station they were directed to a large, characterless waiting-room dominated by a false Christmas tree sitting in a grey bucket of sand, evidently more usually utilized as an ashtray than a plantpot holder. They were given a numbered ticket and finally asked to fill in a missing person's form. Another hour passed before they got an interview with a junior officer, who seemed bored before they even began.

'What was particularly unusual at the flat?' he asked, without feeling.

'It's as if she's gone on a trip, but forgotten to take her make-up or clothes,' Polly answered. 'Oh, and the fridge was empty. Also, she hasn't accessed her bank accounts since she left.'

'Had she switched it off?'

'Excuse me?'

'The fridge,' said the officer.

Polly nodded; he appeared to think for a moment, then nodded gravely and wrote something down on his pad in very small writing that she couldn't read upside down. She guessed that it said, 'Suspicious action, fridge off,' but discovered months later that he'd actually written, 'Appears suspect has gone away by choice without alerting family members of her plans.'

'We don't open files on missing adults unless there is a

specific cause for concern – like emotional vulnerability, a disability or something to suggest a violent struggle before they went away. In this instance, I can't see that any of these factors apply,' he said. 'But we will check her phone line, for any signs of unusual activity.'

Will and Polly remained silent.

'People are within their rights to take off, if that's what they decide to do. If you haven't heard from her in a couple of weeks, come back in and we'll take another look at the detail,' he added, without apology.

Polly looked at him, then at Will. Will looked at the officer, who raised his eyebrows and gave them a curt nod, clearly implying that the meeting was concluded.

'It's fucking ridiculous,' Will raged, as they left the station. 'Two more weeks? It's fucking criminal. Anything could have happened to her, anything at all.'

'Everyone's too busy buying their Christmas turkey to worry about some girl who's taken off on a jolly,' Polly replied, trying to sound lighthearted.

'Do you think she's doing this intentionally, to give us a fright?' he demanded.

'I don't know. I don't see why, Will,' Polly replied, trying desperately to reduce the fear.

'So if she's OK, why the fuck hasn't she rung?' he retorted.

Throughout the Christmas break Polly and Will sat at Polly's flat and waited, sleeping only intermittently, before waking and sitting and waiting some more, watching the phone, their gifts to one another and to Emi left unopened on the coffee table before them. Eventually, on Boxing

Day evening, Will handed his present to Polly with a half-smile.

'Happy Christmas, and thank you for having me,' he ventured, and she affected a smile as she picked up her own present and handed it to him.

'You know I like it when you're here; you can stay as long as you like.'

They opened their packages simultaneously. Each had bought the other the same ring; they'd remarked on them in Carnaby Street, a few days before. Now they had an identical pair. The coincidence broke the tension and Will laughed, but now the atmosphere was loaded in a different way. Polly felt something stir and forced the feeling away as they both slipped them on. Meanwhile Emi's presents remained unopened on the table between them.

13

Recently Sarah and Peter have taken to sleeping in separate bedrooms. When he's at home he's been coming to bed later and later, telling her that he didn't want to disturb her sleep, that it seemed easier to make the spare room his own. She hadn't protested, and now six months have passed. The children will be six next birthday. When will they start to see that their parents' marriage has already ended, in everything but name? Sarah doesn't know what to do about it. When she thinks of change she feels a knot of anxiety tighten inside her. But when she thinks of the current paralysis, she also knows that it can't stay this way for ever.

There are nights when she contemplates erasing herself – not often, but occasionally – when she steps outside herself and looks back into the silent hell she's created for Peter, for herself and for the twins. Maybe it really would be better for them all, she thinks, if she simply vanished into thin air.

In the summer Carol introduces her to a woman called Hera; she has a daughter the same age as Polly and Emi.

Sarah has seen her pass by, a glamorous vision in Lycra, with long, curling blonde hair. Marie and Hera live in a dishevelled Georgian house just around the corner, and her husband is conspicuous by his absence. The twins become regular visitors to the house; they seem to love being there, running wild around the large garden, playing games up and down the stairs.

'Did you know that Hera teaches yoga classes, in her basement?' Carol says to Sarah one day. 'Maybe you should go along. I think you'd enjoy it.'

'I'm not sure,' Sarah replies. 'When does she take them?'

'Friday nights,' Carol tells her. 'She asked if I'd like to go, but it really isn't my cup of tea.'

'I couldn't,' Sarah says. 'I never know what time Peter will be home, and it's the au pair's night off.'

'I'll look after the girls while you go,' Carol offers. 'Just till Peter gets back. Go on, it will do you good.'

The following Friday Sarah finds herself heading for Hera's. She's been to the house before, to drop off or pick up the twins when they've been to play with Marie, of course, but she's never ventured beyond the kitchen, just off the hallway. She's been fascinated by Hera for a while, by her . . . her independence, her modern ways, she supposes she would call it. Her home is full of paintings and piles of magazines and cut flowers in large porcelain vases. There's always the sound of music playing from somewhere just out of reach, and windows flung open on to a large walled garden, overflowing with blowsy plants, and a hammock, she notices today, strung between two trees. She can just make out Marie's foot, hanging over the edge, and a pair of arms, holding a book.

Hera used to be a professional dancer, has been in West End shows, the twins had boasted, and now teaches dance, just up the road at Swiss Cottage. Sarah and Carol both assume that she used to be married to a producer, or a director, but there's something about her that discourages intimacy, shies from enquiry, shuns disclosure.

'You came!' Hera cries, as she opens the door and sees Sarah there. 'Really, I'm so pleased. Come on down, we're just getting the mats out.'

Nervously, Sarah follows Hera to the surprisingly capacious basement, where all the interior walls have been removed to provide a studio space, with steps leading up and out on to the garden at one end. There are candles lit, the very light scent of incense permeates the still air and a tape is playing some kind of ambient music, the like of which Sarah has never heard before. Two other women, whom Sarah does not recognize, are in the process of removing their tracksuits and sitting down, one on each of the four mats laid out in a line before a long, glass mirror. Hera introduces them all to her by name. Sarah says hello but feels too self-conscious to remember any of them. She is terrified yet fascinated in equal measure by this other world, just down the road from her own so private home.

'Close your eyes,' Hera murmurs, once they are all ready. 'Meditation helps to clarify memories . . . emptying out the detritus . . . keeps your mind organized . . . your thoughts healthy . . .'

Sarah finds herself losing a sense of place and time and is amazed at how tranquil she feels an hour and a half later when it is over. She walks home slowly, feeling lighter than before. Peter is back from work now and he and Carol are sitting in the kitchen, eating pasta. The atmosphere is cheerful and Peter's opened a bottle of claret.

'I've got the twins to bed,' Carol says, as she helps Sarah to a bowl and Peter pours her a glass of wine. Sarah feels her spirits rise as she tells them all about the class. They both seem really pleased and encourage her to go again. And she does. She begins to look forward to her weekly class; she finds it empowering to go out alone, to do something just for herself. And, God bless her, Carol appears more than happy to come over and hold the fort.

14

Stephanie and her boyfriend Marcus have gone to Thailand for Christmas and yesterday Lotta arrived to stay with 'us' for ten days. Stephanie only mentioned the trip to Kalle a few days ago; she said it was a 'last-minute' thing and would he mind having Lotta. I don't know him well enough yet to be sure, but when he came home and told me, I felt his despair at Stephanie, perhaps for leaving her plans so late, or perhaps for having made them at all. He told me in London that he was over her, but since I've been here I've sensed a deep remorse in Kalle and I'm not so sure I believe him any more. I don't feel I can ask him about her; our own circumstance feels too artificial, too unclear. Not only am I working for him now, but I'm also living in his home and observing the ins and outs of the most intimate relationships in his life. To make matters more complicated, I still don't feel ready to tell him anything about the relationships that I've left behind. Where could we possibly go from here?

Regardless of these insurmountable differences, we seem to be getting more and more relaxed in each other's company. We often spend the evenings together, quietly, sitting reading, or watching the fire. My silence used to drive Will mad. But Kalle seems to enjoy these moments, often asks me to come and sit with him, rarely retires to his rooms above the living-room. He regularly asks me if there's anything I need; I want to say, 'You! I want you!' but of course I can't. Instead I say, 'What more could I ask for?' and each time he smiles. To all intents and purposes, my response is true. He's taken me away from my nightmare, given me a roof over my head, a wonderful child to care for and, since I've been caring for Lotta, regular money to spend. I have a purpose, and the chance of a fresh start. Today I could even imagine what it would be like if we were a real family unit. The three of us spent this morning decorating an elegant fir tree with white lights and silver baubles in front of the rotunda windows, then went shopping for food at an exquisite covered market, to the west of the city. As we walked there, Kalle had his arm linked through Lotta's on one side, and halfway there he suddenly took hold of mine on the other and we walked the rest of the way all linked together. I felt a rise of euphoria inside me, as if I had found a place to belong.

When we arrived at the market, Kalle enthusiastically purchased all the provisions we would need to prepare a traditional Christmas meal, explaining all the while what each ingredient was and why we would need it. Then, this evening, he showed me how to prepare classic Swedish Christmas dishes: *julskinka* – baked ham coated with mustard and breadcrumbs; *lutfisk* – dried fish steeped in lye with mustard sauce; and, along with Lotta, a rather disgusting, glutinous rice porridge to put out tomorrow for '*tomte*', the folklore figure who, she informed me with utmost seriousness, 'looks after the house'.

Now it's eleven o'clock and we've all retired to bed. Tomorrow will be Christmas Eve, the main festival day here in Sweden. Back home everyone will still be rushing around, preparing for Christmas. I know it's then that Polly will realize something really has gone awry. I've never spent a Christmas Day without her, and for the past few years Will has invariably been there, too. If I don't call, they'll really know that there's trouble afoot. I wonder what they'll do to console one another? I wonder how far it's already gone – too far, perhaps, to pull back? Part of me wants to know, another part just wants to block it out and a third part wishes them well. But no part of me wants to call. I have less than two days to go, but so far none of the digits on my hands is prepared to key their numbers, or to write to them with reassurances of my well-being. Don't try to get me to explain; I have no words to describe the depth of my reticence. It has a stranglehold over me as hard as steel.

I know I'm hiding behind all that is new, behind my rapidly growing emotional allegiance to Kalle – and to Lotta, too. They make me feel alive, needed, useful. Lotta is complicated, curious, fascinating. One moment she's being this little six-year-old kid, lost in the world of play, the next she's asking direct, but complicated questions that seem far too old for her years, catching me off guard and making me acutely aware of both her and my own vulnerabilities. For example, earlier today, when we were cooking, Kalle went to answer the phone and Lotta was standing on a stool in her pink apron stirring a cake mixture. I caught her sticking her finger in it and I laughed. She smirked at me and jumped down from the stool, flinging her arms around my waist.

'Did you live with your mama and papa when you were a little kid?' she asked, suddenly serious.

I paused. The immediate answer that sprang to mind was yes, but actually, I knew that that was not strictly true.

'Some of the time,' I confessed. 'But my dad was away a lot.'

Then, as she stood there, hugging my legs, I could see Peter. In my mind he seemed permanently to have a suitcase in his hand.

'You see far more of your papa than I saw of mine,' I added, stroking the top of her head, suddenly morose.

Lotta looked up at me, nodded purposefully, then let go, got back on to the stool and began to stir the mix again.

'Papa lives in a grown-up flat, Mama and I live in a family flat,' she mused, 'but with you here this is beginning to feel more like a family flat, too.'

Before he put Lotta to bed tonight Kalle promised that he would take us to Skansen before New Year, to introduce me to all their favourite animals at the zoo. 'It's magical at Christmas, lit up with festive lights,' he said.

Before I had a chance to respond, Lotta was interjecting.

'Sometimes I wonder who really is in the zoo. I look through the glass at the animals and they look back at me. I think they are in a cage and maybe they think I am. Funny, huh?'

'Maybe the world is one big zoo,' Kalle answered, picking his daughter up tenderly and hugging her to him. 'And we all live in it together.'

I watched as Lotta quietly looked away across his shoulder, past our newly erected, glinting tree and out over the shimmering city. Her expression reminded me of the fragility in her spirit that I'd detected in the photo of her that Kalle had shown me back in London, the first time I'd seen her face.

After breakfast today Kalle left the table, 'to check something in his office', before we set off for our planned visit to Skansen. But he didn't reappear for more than two hours. Lotta was very forgiving, joking kindly that her papa was 'a mad professor'. The more time I spend with him the more aware I'm becoming that, just as Stephanie said, beneath his professional veneer he really is quite absent-minded, a bit of a dreamer, readily distracted by his thoughts.

While we waited, Lotta suggested we do some work on her imaginary kingdom and got out her 'work book'. I was intrigued. It was a large hardbacked volume and she told me that she tries to make drawings and write in it every day. Since she'd been staying, she said, she hadn't had time to fill it in. She let me take a look inside. The pages were covered with lovely naïve pictures and passages of pretend writing in myriad felt-pen colours. She explained enthusiastically that she had created her own kingdom of fairies and princesses, dragons and demons, goodies and baddies, some with their heads chopped off, others in sweet embraces or handing one another flowers or gifts.

'Let me read you one of my stories,' she said keenly, then sat down on the floor opposite me with a serious air. I could see that the words were not written on the page, rather that she was drawing directly from her imagination.

'Little Milla woke up in her princess bed and looked out of the castle window,' she began. 'It was very dark and the sky was angry and noisy with a wild wind. Something moved in the bushes. She grabbed her pet mouse, Kingston, and together they flew out of the window and towards the garden. Suddenly it was very cold and she shivered. Kingston took her hand and together they crept up towards the bush. Milla was very frightened. She looked back towards the castle but now all the lights were out and she knew that the King and the Queen, who were her mum and dad, were at a banquet at the next-door kingdom and that she was really all alone apart from Kingston. She followed him into the bushes and suddenly a little black monster with blue, fiery eyes blew smoke into their faces and grabbed Kingston. Luckily Kingston had magic powers and ripped off the monster's arms and legs and then bit off his head and then pulled his eyes out and then dug a hole and buried him. Then Milla heard a voice calling her name. She turned around to see her papa standing there with his arms open wide. She ran into them and she was saved and happy and he said he would take her to her ballet lesson as a treat later today but that now it was time to go back to bed. When she woke up Kingston was fast asleep in her bed and Papa told her it had all been nothing but a bad dream, but Milla knew that it was real because in his paw Kingston was still holding some black fur that had belonged to the monster.'

'Gosh,' I said, and Lotta jumped up and clambered on to my knees.

'Look!' she exclaimed. 'Let me show you the pictures.'

When Kalle finally re-emerged, he found the two of us working away at the kitchen table on a new series of drawings of Milla and Kingston that covered a dozen pieces of paper. He was mortified when he realized his misdemeanour, grabbed Lotta in a bear hug, apologized over and over to me, then ordered us both to 'grab your coats right away'. Before we knew it, we were practically running to catch the lift down to the port.

The ferry ride across the mist-enshrined harbour was mysterious and exhilarating, and as soon as we got to the zoo I understood immediately why Lotta loved it so much, with its mix of fantastic, historic houses and large open-air animal enclosures, where wolves, elks and – in the summer – the now elusive bears were able to roam. We had a mesmeric day, wandering around happily together, the air sharp and bright and cold on our faces, our hands deep inside our coat pockets, scarves wound around our necks; searching hard inside the enclosures for elks, drinking steaming hot chocolate, laughing and laughing and laughing some more.

Just before we set off for home, Kalle caught my eye as my face lit up at the antics of a group of otters, swimming in and out of their little pool of water.

'Thank you,' I whispered.

Lotta was distracted, kneeling down to watch the otters through a low glass wall.

'You already seem happier,' he observed, gently. I nodded, suddenly embarrassed. 'But one thing worries me.

Do you really not want to call your family, to wish them a happy Christmas?'

'The whole thing here,' I replied, avoiding the issue, 'the city, you, Lotta – it's amazing. And I really do love the zoo.'

'Next time you see reindeer, I hope it's back in the wild, in the forest,' Kalle answered. 'But are you sure – about your family? Won't they be sick with worry?'

My insides were twisting. As each day passes, the idea of phoning Polly has become further out of my reach.

'Maybe tomorrow,' I ventured, but Kalle didn't respond, just eyed me, curiously, for a moment, before turning back to Lotta.

'Come on, *solwhen*,' he said. 'It's getting cold. I think it's time to head home.'

15

In London, a ghostly week passed for Polly and Will, a week when the city seemed to have closed down, the streets echoing with the memories of a year passing them all by, a week with no substance, no permanence, no sense of the present, or, in their case, the future; a week when Emi did not call. They spent the time in limbo, either sitting at home, surfing the TV channels and trying not to watch the phone, or wandering the city like sleepwalkers, gazing around at strangers for a glimpse of the girl whom they were beginning to feel they had lost, whom they were beginning to understand they had allowed to slip, silently, through their careless hands. As they walked, or sat silently together in cafés, nursing cups of tea, they watched buses passing them by, glanced into the steamed-up windows for a face, a single face. But everywhere they looked, all they met were the curious expressions of strangers wondering why these two silent wanderers were gazing at them. Nowhere in the city did they sense the trace or the scent of Emi. Polly was starting to realize that Will had been right all along. Emi had vanished and she wasn't coming back. If it hadn't been Christmas, perhaps

Polly would have been able to delude herself for longer, to believe that her twin had simply taken off on a wild, unplanned trip. But she couldn't allow herself the privilege of delusion, not now that Emi had allowed Christmas to pass without a postcard, a text or a call. Something was evidently very seriously wrong; something had happened to Emi.

The New Year dawned with a call, but it was not from Emi, it was from Paddington Green.

'We don't have any leads,' the officer on the line said, 'but we'd like you to come in to file a further report.'

Together Will and Polly returned to the police station. This time, to their astonishment, they were led directly up some clinical stairs to a small office where a man sat behind a desk, chewing gum. His white shirt was yellowing at the collar. It was undone to his neck, displaying a few salt-and-pepper curls of hair against pale flesh. His sleeves were rolled up and his thickset forearms looked fit for a fight. His face was round and he had full, soft lips, but his small dark eyes were shrewd and they darted between Will and Polly like minnows while his hands rolled and tapped the briefing papers on his desk. He made Polly feel nervous; guilty even.

'My name is Richardson,' he stated plainly. 'And what I want to know is: who saw Emi last?'

'Me,' Polly replied, equally plainly.

'How did she seem?'

'Very depressed.'

His small, dark eyes glanced up and stuck to hers like glue. 'Do you know why?'

Polly hesitated for a moment and glanced towards Will.

'Well, our marriage was failing,' he murmured.

'Was there a third party?'

'Sorry?'

'Someone else involved, a lover?'

'No, no,' Polly said, too quickly, perhaps. 'At least, not as far as Will or I were aware.'

Will was looking hangdog, his eyes watching his fiddling hands.

'Do you think Emi might have had a secret life? A ghost in her closet?'

Polly shook her head slowly and Will shrugged.

'Had she ever run away before?'

'No.'

'Tried to commit suicide?'

Polly thought of the pill that had rolled from beneath her sister's bedcovers, the lack of medicine in her bathroom cabinet, and found herself divulging these details – apart from anything else, it implied vulnerability and she wanted the police to open a case file. She had intentionally avoided mentioning these facts to Will before now. She had convinced herself that they were insignificant and knew they would worry him, but as she described them to Officer Richardson their importance seemed to increase. She dared not look at Will.

'Is there any history of mental illness in the family?' Richardson asked, much more gently now.

'No,' said Polly. 'I mean, well . . .' Her voice trailed off.

Richardson watched Polly and waited as, uncharacteristically, she found herself fumbling for words.

'Polly and Emi's mother Sarah sometimes got a bit low, but it was nothing serious, nothing ever diagnosed,' Will interjected as Polly found tears welling in her eyes. He moved his hand on top of hers, squeezed it. Richardson glanced at the gesture, then handed Polly a box of tissues from his desk.

'Did Emi have any known friends in the King's Cross area?'

The question seemed incongruous, plucked out of thin air, and neither understood the link. Polly thought hard; Camden, maybe, Islington, yes, and Bloomsbury too. But King's Cross, which was caught between these other, smarter districts, was not the kind of place where any of them hung out; it was a no-man's-land, full of commuters by day, pimps and dealers by night. What was his point?

'The reason we called you in,' he stated, 'is that we've checked Emi's home line. There was a call made to her number on Sunday evening, the day before she resigned, at around six forty-five. The odd thing is, it was from a phone-box, outside King's Cross station. And before you ask, no, there isn't any CCTV footage. Maybe it was from a friend, recently arrived by train? From Edinburgh, Newcastle, perhaps?'

They both shook their heads. Ironically, Edinburgh was Polly's old turf, and Newcastle was their father's – his random choice of towns seemed an unfortunate coincidence. Apart from that, Emi had no link with either.

'What can we do to help find out who it was?' Will asked.

'There isn't much you can do, except pass her picture around the station, among the locals, the commuters, you know, see if anyone recognizes her, remembers anything. And you should get Emi's disappearance registered with all the agencies, get her details on to their missing persons websites. You'll need a recent photo, biographical notes. In the meantime, remain vigilant, call friends regularly, get the word out that she's gone away, listen out for clues. And remember, the chances are she's fine, that she'll be back before you know it.'

Afterwards they sat over bitter black coffee in a Lebanese café on the Edgware Road. Polly's left leg was shaking, bumping up and down of its own volition under the table. Will put his hand on to it to steady it, and left it there.

'Why didn't you tell me about the pill?' he ventured presently.

'I didn't want to alarm you,' she replied humbly. 'I thought it was my over-active imagination.'

They continued to drink their coffee in silence. Then all of a sudden Will looked up at Polly.

'Do you think she's dead?' he whispered.

Polly couldn't speak; she shook her head emphatically, although, truthfully, inside she had no feeling, one way or the other, no idea. But she felt, as Emi's identical twin, that she ought to know, that she ought to have a feeling, a sense of it. Her leg shook harder.

'We're going to find her, Pol,' Will added emphatically, pulling his chair close to hers. 'I don't hold out much hope of that Richardson guy – for him Emi's just another statistic. He must hear cases every day; you only need to look on the Internet to see the missing millions, girls disappeared in the back of sex traffickers' vans, run away from wife-batterers, bad debts, miserable marriages. But none of those things have happened to Emi. It seems she's just got herself in a bit of a fix. If we're going to find her, it's going to be up to us.'

'What about the call from King's Cross? It's weird,' she interjected. Her voice seemed to be as lost as Emi; she couldn't speak any louder than a whisper.

'No idea, but I can't imagine Emi knowing anyone there, unless, of course, Richardson's right, and it was someone who'd just arrived in the capital. If it was, then King's Cross itself isn't the clue. I guess we can look at timetables for around that time, but I can't think of anyone she knew from up north. Can you?'

Polly shook her head.

'We'll have to talk to locals, commuters, get her name about. I'll get a website going; we'll have to plan a strategy.'

Polly had heard Will speaking like this before; the strange thing was that this time the subject was not an atrocity against human rights, or an illegal war – it was her sister, her twin sister, her vanished sister, her missing sister. The words sounded foreign, tasted as bitter as the coffee on her tongue. But she knew that he was right, that if they were to find her it was going to be up to them. She thought about her job. She had to return to work tomorrow. How was she going to manage? She felt out of her depth for the first time in her life. She'd just have to find a way to turn Emi into news. It was a way to regain control. Her thoughts turned to her producer.

'I guess I'll go and see Nick,' she said, 'and beg for a slot.'

She looked up and fixed Will in the eye. As he returned her gaze he took his hand from her leg and they sat, watching one another, in silence. It was as if, for the past three weeks, they had been engaged in a choreographed dance, aware of one another's every move, determined not to stop the flow of each other's individual movements, yet trying, until now, to keep a perfect distance, not to touch.

16

Peter's company has relocated its sales and marketing division to Newcastle and he heads up there most Tuesday mornings, then arrives back home on Friday evening, in time for Sarah's yoga, for their weekends as a family, with the girls. And so they have fallen, almost without planning it, into a new routine, of sorts. For Sarah it is a relief not to have to try, not to have to pretend. But she notes that Polly seems more restless than usual during her father's absences, prowling around the house like a caged animal, her attention span reduced. When Emi comes into her room, Sarah calls Polly to follow, but often she elects to stay away, playing on her own or with their current au pair, Madeline. Time is going so fast, thinks Sarah, and in some respects she and Peter are missing it all. The twins will be eight next birthday and her memory of the details of their young lives is already indistinct. It must be the pills, she thinks. Nevertheless she daren't stop taking them, fears the consequences far too much.

One day, Sarah gets a call from the school asking her to come in and discuss her children's progress. As usual,

Peter is away on business, so she forces herself to attend alone.

'Emi and Polly are both progressing well,' the teacher says, with a bright smile, 'but we do worry a little about Emi. She doesn't seem to have found her own friend, or group of friends, yet. Polly, on the other hand, is very popular, often the centre of attention, gregarious and communicative. Emi tends to follow after Polly, struggles to break free from the allure of her sister.'

Sarah feels a wrench inside. Emi is 'hers' and is the one who is failing. She wants to protect her from the world, wants to put her arms around her daughter, to tell her that it's all right, but she knows she can't.

'We're trying to separate the twins in the classroom, to ensure that Emi isn't too often' – at this the teacher pauses, as if searching carefully for a word that will not offend – 'in the shade,' she says finally.

Sarah talks to Peter about the discussion when he comes home at the weekend.

'You need to relax with Emi a little, let her go a bit,' he says.

The comment feels like a personal slight. Sarah pretends not to understand, but underneath she knows that he has a point, that she is overly protective of Emi because she seems more vulnerable than Polly. And sometimes Sarah worries that Polly doesn't like her, that she has somehow absorbed Peter's growing disdain towards her. Because, although he doesn't say a word, Sarah's beginning to appreciate that, on some very profound level Peter has given up on her, that he is just biding his time. But until what, or when, she can't be sure.

*   *   *

Madeline is a gentle Paris girl in her early twenties who has studied music at the Sorbonne. She offers to teach the twins to play the piano, which has sat unused since they bought it three years previously. Polly delights in her newfound activity, spends hours on end practising her scales with Madeline at her side. Conversely, Emi displays no interest in the piano at all, and after the first few sessions elects not to continue to practise.

As a child, she remembers feeling equally uninterested in her parents' great passion. Recently she finds herself thinking more and more often of them, of their protracted absences, of her sense of displacement in infancy, her feelings of raftlessness as a child. She never had a place she could call home; they were always on the move and, even now, it feels as if their absence is finite. Her parents call faithfully, once a week, to see how the girls are; her mother grows more distant with every conversation, while her father engages in an active discourse of desensitization with Sarah, readily referencing current affairs in England as his point of departure from the domestic, from any discussion of how his daughter really feels; this week his call is about the IRA bomb that nearly killed Margaret Thatcher in Brighton, how close a shave it was, and how Sarah must be diligent, with the children.

'We've already made alterations,' she reassures him. 'Madeline is not to use the tube, and she walks the children to school, rather than taking the bus, just in case the IRA choose to strike at the heart of the capital, to attack the general public.'

'That sounds wise,' he replies, then falters before adding, 'Your mother can't come to the phone today, I'm afraid. She's taken to her bed. There seems to be something wrong with her hands.'

Sarah feels white panic.

'Should I come?' she asks.

'No, no, dear, you stay there and look after the twins,' he replies. 'It's the darn cold here, in Maine; the winters are harsh and she seems to have some form of arthritis. It means she can't play her cello at the moment, which, as you know, makes her cranky. We'll visit you in the spring, when she's feeling better.'

Sarah feels nervous and guilty in equal measure. She ought to go and visit her mother; it is unlike her to be under the weather. And the word arthritis makes her sound old; she can only be, she has to think for a moment, sixty-three. She has a sinking feeling, but she's nervous of flying and doesn't want to leave the girls, so she agrees with her father and hopes for the best. Part of her wonders what would happen if she had to go and leave them with Peter; wonders, if she did, whether she'd ever come back.

She'd never really do it – leave them – of course. She would hate to disrupt the world that she and Peter have created for their daughters. She fears that if she did mess it up, perhaps in adult life they'd follow in her own footsteps, into equally unhappy marriages, in order to find some kind of stability, something permanent. If they stayed as they were, as a whole, albeit discordant, unit, even with Peter's weekly absences, she convinces herself that surely it would follow that the twins' foundations would feel far more secure than her own ever did? Her absolute priority remains the well-being of her daughters, and for as long as she can manage to retain the status quo, she realizes that she will – pretty much at any cost to herself.

The call comes a few weeks later, that her mother has 'taken a turn for the worse'. Sarah's father sounds strange, as if he is hiding something from her. She asks for a prognosis.

'They think she has Alzheimer's disease,' he says quietly. Evidently it has been hard for him to use the words.

'We'll come, straight away,' says Sarah.

'I think you should be prepared,' he continues, bewilderment entering his tone. 'She may not know who you are.'

Before Sarah calls Peter, she goes to see Carol, who says she will come and stay, that between them she and Madeline will care for the twins. Peter's surprisingly gentle and supportive, and books them on a business class flight to Boston without a moment's hesitation. It's a new feeling, being away with him, without the children and, with the help of Mr Kapoor, she makes it to America in a woozy haze.

Her father collects them from the airport. She is shocked by the way he looks and feels, downcast, bony and fragile. They drive out of Boston on the turnpike and he chats about the worries in the world with affected good humour. They head directly to the care home. It is a large colonial house on the outskirts of the city with rolling lawns and wide-arching sprinklers, ensuring the grass stays a perfectly even evergreen. The staff share a measured walk, and their heads bow at the same slight angle as if in perpetual apology; their mouths set in a regular, muscle-tightened line, neither up, nor down. A pretty young nurse is called to take them to Sarah's mother, who is sitting in a wicker chair in the shade of a large cedar tree, a newspaper propped on her knee. Sarah can hardly bear to look at this old lady. She wonders where the years went, why her mother has never needed her. It's already too late to ask. Her mother's looking curiously at Sarah and then towards her father for help.

'Who are they? What do they want?' she asks, her voice altered, harsh and yet a touch fearful, too.

'Don't worry,' murmurs Sarah's father, crouching down with difficulty and putting a trembling arm around his wife's shoulder. He looks defeated, his posture curved, his sense of himself imploded, crushed in. He glances back up at his daughter and Sarah looks down at her dad. 'She often gets confused in the afternoons,' he apologizes.

When he stands up, Sarah's mother's eyes look down blankly at her paper. Her father catches Sarah's eye and smiles stoically but a single tear rolls down his cheek. She takes a tissue from her sleeve and dabs at it, tenderly, then puts her arms around him.

'I can't bear it,' he whispers as they walk back together across the grass, Peter following behind. 'I won't know how to live without her.'

Sarah and Peter stay for a week and they all visit her mother every day. But there really seems little point. The disease has struck her unusually hard and fast, and evidently she already has no recollection of who her daughter is. The visits are excruciatingly painful for them both. At last, to Sarah's relief, it is time to leave.

Her father drives them to the airport, and when they arrive he heads for the boot of the car and opens it up. Inside there is a large black instrument case. It is stickered with tickets to every corner of the globe. He takes it out gently and hands it to his daughter.

'She would want you to have it, for the girls,' he says, resolutely.

Sarah takes the cello, the heart of her mother's life, and Peter balances it on top of the luggage trolley.

'Why don't you bring her home, Dad?' she asks, as he embraces her goodbye, but he shakes his head sadly.

'It's already too late,' he replies. 'And we're safe here. We know our ways.'

Halfway through the flight Sarah turns and glances at her husband. He is reading the *Spectator* and drinking a whisky on the rocks. She thought he liked it with water. She realizes she doesn't know Peter any more; that maybe she never did. Being with him is like being with a stranger, someone whom she perhaps met once, a long time ago, at a party, talked to, even exchanged an unexpected intimacy with, before saying goodbye. Meeting him again now, so to speak, away from home, like this, she realizes that they have nothing left to talk about, nothing at all. Not even her mother, or the twins. Their life together feels like a receding memory, their present already part of their past. Regardless, Peter is a decent, dutiful man; he treats her with great gentleness, like a precious, porcelain doll. She senses that he knows if he lets her fall from his hands she might smash to smithereens.

17

This morning the night's residue darkness felt heavy, like drugged lids drooped over the city, their linings made moist by the sea mists that had descended with yesterday's premature dusk. It muffled all sharp sounds and muted all tones, like a local anaesthetic. I found it impossible to raise myself; instead I just lay in bed and thought about Lotta's leaving us, yesterday afternoon.

Christmas has whizzed past us, and now the new year has arrived. One moment she was there, filling the flat with the sound of laughter, with energy and mischief, and the next Stephanie had arrived, glowing and tanned, and had scooped up her daughter, taken her off, almost without a backwards glance, without enquiry into our previous two weeks, without a thank you. After they'd gone, Kalle took himself directly to his office and began tapping away at his computer keys. He stayed there all evening. We spent the holidays in a whirlwind of playing, drawing, cooking, reading, exploring the city, using the whole of Stockholm as our playground. We took boats across the harbour, went to the children's boat museum, the modern art gallery. Kalle was euphoric with his daughter around; it was a playful time, a time to laugh and look forward to the next immediate activity, a time to enjoy being, not thinking, too much, about Will or Polly, about their concerns for my safety, which must, by now, be growing by the day. I feel paralysed with regard to them, and as each day passes I'm finding it harder to call.

I finally dragged myself out of bed and made my way to the kitchen, where Kalle was already up and dressed, sipping his coffee and reading the paper.

'It's horrible without her,' I mumbled, reaching for the pot.

He didn't speak, shrugged and attempted a smile, then took another sip of his coffee.

'Last year must have been ghastly, when they first went away.'

He put down his cup and surveyed me, seriously. 'Of course you're right, but I'm getting used to it now. And with you here, it feels so much better. Thank you, Emi, for everything.' He looked back down at his paper before adding, 'Particularly for your gift of empathy.'

No one had ever called me empathetic before; sullen, yes, introverted, yes, shy, yes. Empathetic? Never – Polly perhaps, but never me.

'And to cheer us up, I have a suggestion. Lars has invited us to Solgläntan, next weekend, to celebrate his birthday.'

'Solgläntan?'

I met his eye. Kalle's expression had completely altered: it was bright with anticipation.

'Sorry – that's our house, on the island. He's been out hunting, wants to make venison and juniper casserole. It's an old family recipe. Lotta will still be with Stephanie. What do you think?'

I felt my mood lift in tune with his.

'Will we be able to visit his studio?'

I had looked at Lars's etchings at least ten times a day since I'd arrived.

Kalle knew so and chuckled. 'If you're lucky. But it's two hundred metres off the main island,' he cautioned. 'We won't be able to row out there in this weather, but we could always skate.'

'Are you serious?'

'I've been doing it since I was a child,' he confided, with a boyish grin. 'Don't worry: if you're too afraid, I can always carry you across on my back.'

I felt restless all week. Kalle had gone back to work and I had no Lotta to care for. Time alone wasn't easy for me to manage. My mind fixed on my past preoccupations and I couldn't shift London from my thoughts. I spent the time wandering, sitting in cafés, people-watching, then coming back to the flat to cook for Kalle. I looked forward to his return with excessive anticipation; it was the only value in my day.

Tonight when he arrived home snow began to fall. We watched it together from the rotunda windows, swirls of thick flakes cascading from the sky like goose feathers from a giant pillow, split and shaken of its load into the wind. A light emanated upwards from the city's streets into the enveloping sky, a glow pure and fine. It felt like a miraculous moment shared; I wanted to turn and hold him, for him to hold me, but I have no idea if he feels the same

146

way, or, if he does, how we get from the place we're in now to the next. I couldn't bear to instigate intimacy and then be rejected – because I know that then I would have to go. And where would I end up? The idea frightens me too much to contemplate for more than a moment at a time.

In the light of morning Stockholm had dressed in an extra winter layer; a luxurious cloak of white hugging itself around the body of the city like a second skin – a thick cover that Kalle told me is unlikely to lift now until spring. When he went to work, I went out walking, keen to observe the spectacle of this glowing winter city. It was such a dramatic change, so exquisitely beautiful, that I wanted to shriek with delight: evidently it was nothing new to anyone but me. The resident Stockholmers had grown skis beneath their feet, were carrying snow-picks in their hands. Their faces had disappeared beneath layers of lambswool and cashmere. Snowploughs had appeared on the trains' bumpers, ice-cutters on the prows of the boats. I bought myself a thick, long padded coat and a pair of boots, then slowly made my way home.

Kalle appeared back early, just after me, with two bagfuls of groceries and bread, he informed me, triumphantly, purchased from the best bakery in Stockholm. In his hand he shook the keys to a four-wheel-drive he had hired for the journey to Linanas, the island that was home to Solgläntan.

'We need a good vehicle to get there in this,' he added, glancing pointedly at Lars's prints. 'The cottage really is far out – but we have to get there, we can't miss Lars's birthday, whatever the weather. We can't leave him to celebrate alone.'

We headed out of the city in the early dark, one link in a chain of head- and tail-lights illuminating the pure, shining snow that covered the lay-bys, flat fields and forests on either side. Soon the traffic thinned until ours was the only car making its slow trail through an increasingly remote terrain. An indirect light was being thrown up from the snowy landscape, dissolving into a grey mist that drifted into a black sky pricked with shining stars, like silver studs on a silk cushion cover. Kalle put on a CD, given to him, he said, by a couple of his students who busk on the streets of Stockholm, one with a key harp and the other a cello. The music swung seamlessly between the uplifting and the deeply melancholic and I found my mind fixing on a single image of Polly, playing our grandmother's cello. It was one of the few contexts, I realized, in which she was ever completely content. I held the image behind my closing eyes and as I drifted to sleep Kalle drove us deeper into the wilderness.

I awoke to Kalle shaking my shoulder, gently. We had stopped and someone was outside the car, shining a large, round torch in at my window, momentarily blinding me.

'We're here,' Kalle said.

I peered out at the man, thickly clad in a long, dark coat and fur hat, a scarf wound around his face, as Kalle got out of the car and they hugged like big grizzly bears in the dark. Then Lars pushed a gate open and Kalle got back into the car. We inched slowly up the snowy driveway as Lars shut the gate behind us and followed on foot.

'It's really cold up here tonight,' Kalle observed, happily, 'but the sky's clear. Once we're through the forest you'll be able to see the moon.'

The lane petered out and moments later the car came to a halt on a scrubby promontory next to a large, rust-coloured barn. Kalle switched off the engine and the car's lights.

As I opened the door, sharp, cool air pinched my senses, revitalized me, and I felt my excitement stir. Reassuringly, Kalle took my arm, to steady me.

'Be careful as you get out, it's really slippery,' he warned.

We moved away from the car, and as my eyes adjusted to the dark I saw that the forest that lay to three sides of us was tipped with white above deep, dark fern. Ahead and slightly below us was a large, imposing yellow house. A glow emanated from the back porch and before it there was an enclosed veranda with steps leading down to the garden, which in turn sloped towards the moonlit sea. I gazed out over a silver pathway that crossed its rippling surface, towards a scrubby island, just detectable further out into the water.

'Is Lars's studio there?' I whispered.

'Yep, and here's the man himself,' Kalle replied with enthusiasm as his brother approached, torch now off, its help no longer needed.

He patted me on the back, with glove-clad hands.

'Welcome to paradise,' he exclaimed. 'Come on, let's get you guys inside by the fire.'

We entered the house through a small cloakroom that led on to a larger, square formal hall, with a wide, wooden staircase to the right and double doors to the other side. A dozen or so fine, porcelain-white deer skulls hung in spectral rows along the walls. Lars caught my eye fixing on them.

'Hunting trophies from our ancestors,' he informed me, with a capricious smile.

The brothers were slipping their feet into sheepskin slippers waiting by the back door, and Lars opened a cupboard under the stairs, rooted about and found me a smaller pair.

'We all use these when we're here, and they get better with age,' he said with a slight chuckle. His natural joviality immediately put me at ease. As I slipped off my shoes and put the soft slippers on, I wondered if they had belonged to Stephanie. A large, very fluffy white dog suddenly appeared out of nowhere and scampered in after us, ran round and round us in circles, then jumped up at me with surprising force.

'*Ner*, Bosse!' Lars commanded.

Immediately the dog slumped down and I laughed and knelt to pat its soft coat. It rolled on to its back and put its paws in the air.

'Good! You like dogs,' exclaimed Lars, patting his knee. Bosse responded to his master's call and followed through the double doors. With a wry smile, Kalle indicated to me to follow. A fire in a wood-burning stove in one corner was heating the space. Even so, after the warmth of the car, the large room felt edged with ice.

'The house was built by our great-grandfather in 1899,' said Kalle, proudly. 'It's one of the oldest "summer houses" in the area. We inherited it from our father five years ago. He's built a newer house in the southern archipelago, near our mother's family, a place of greater comfort for their retirement.'

'And left us with his old wreck!' interjected Lars, beckoning me closer to the fire.

It was true that the house was in need of some redecoration – the chalky white paint peeling from the walls and damp stains on the ceilings – but a wreck? If so, I'd never seen such a majestic one. The living-room was wide and split by two arches; on one side to a dining area, to the other an internal deck, or summer room, with large windows that must look out over the sea. The dark-stained floorboards were polished smooth; but in areas the varnish had disintegrated, and the natural wood underneath was pale and rough. The furniture appeared ancient – other than for the deep, plush cream sofa on which I was sitting. A collection of art-deco style chairs with heart-shaped motifs cut from the straight backs was arranged in a square, with a card table in the middle; and two white, wooden rocking-chairs with high-arched arms were positioned either side of the fire. There was also an old white wooden grandfather clock – which appeared not to be ticking. Lars followed my gaze.

'No, that gave up the ghost with our grandfather,' he admitted, with an impish grin that reminded me of Lotta. 'But it doesn't matter: here you'll quickly learn to tell the time by the light of the sun and the moon. Now,' he clapped his hands together, 'although it's not my birthday until tomorrow, I feel we should welcome you with a schnapps.'

Kalle raised his hands in the air despairingly and Lars

chuckled as he headed through an open door from the dining area into the kitchen, Bosse following faithfully at his heels. As I watched, it occurred to me that he was like a less refined version of his brother, stouter, less athletic and with a distinctly ruddier complexion. His hair was greying and curly, like Kalle's, but far more unruly. I assumed that he was the older of the two. Tonight he was wearing a pair of old, faded brown cords, a thick, cream wool jumper with a hole in its left elbow, and walked, if I wasn't mistaken, with a very slight limp. Kalle glanced at me.

'He's a character, a true personality, should I say – and one of the kindest people you're likely to meet while you stay in Sweden, apart from Lotta, of course.'

'I hope you're right about that,' I found myself replying. 'I worry that one day she'll detect my lack of expertise with children and punish me for it.'

Kalle looked startled, and then began to laugh as Lars reappeared with a tray now laden with a long-necked, deep blue bottle, glasses and small plates of salmon and potato salad, piled on top of brown rye bread.

'What's so funny?'

'Emi's afraid that Lotta might be cruel to her.'

Lars put the tray down gingerly on a rickety wooden table, then set himself down rather heavily beside me.

'Lotta? Be unkind? She wouldn't know how, it's not in her nature,' he confided with a wink. 'It's her father you need to watch.'

He handed us each a drink from the tray. 'Here now, have some schnapps, and welcome to our little house by the sea. Let me tell you all about it.'

We chinked our glasses, then the two men held their heads back and swallowed the clear, throat-burning liquid in one. I took a small sip, and then another, immediately recognizing its key value – to warm your insides against the cold. Lars handed us both a plate of food, poured us all some more schnapps, and as we ate, he set forth on his tale, his tone confiding, his pace slow.

'More than a hundred years ago a man came to our island from Linanas. He arrived by sailing boat from Stockholm, a trip that took two days. The man had a map; he knew where he was heading. At the time there was no bridge connecting this final spit of land to the mainland, as there is now. It was midsummer and he sailed into the natural harbour in the dazzling sun of high noon. Then he anchored his boat, took off his clothes and swam ashore with a fishing rod and a bundle of clothes tied to his back. The summer had begun warm, and when he climbed ashore his body dried quickly. He dressed, then clambered up the ancient, ice-polished granite rock face that slipped from the land into the sea, and then on along the edge of the forest until he reached the end. Beyond the coastline he could see a small island, covered in trees, and beyond that the wide, crystal Gulf of Bothnia. The man spent the afternoon wandering along the coastline, through the deep flower-filled meadows and the airy forests, watching the light dance on the surface of the water between the pine and silver birch trees. Sea eagles and honey buzzards circled in the sky, and he heard the clickety-clacketing of roe-deer hooves on the granite outcrops that littered the forest floor behind him. Otherwise it was very quiet – no one had built here yet, and he had the distinct feeling he was the only human being to have set foot on the land for a very long time.

'As the evening approached he felt hungry and cast his fishing rod, readily hooking a Baltic herring, a summer delicacy famous in the restaurants of Stockholm. He relished the act of roasting the fresh fish himself on an open fire, made with kindling from the beech trees that hugged the shoreline. He ate it in thick, fleshy pieces from the bone, and drank water from a stream he'd found deep in the heart of the woods, then lay down and closed his eyes against the bright night and slept soundly until early morning. When he awoke the sun had already risen high in the sky and he took his clothes off once more and swam in the brackish sea. Then he explored a little further. He found himself wandering through two wide prairies, filled with . . .' Lars paused, looking towards Kalle for help . . . '*nastrot?*'

'Orchids, wild orchids,' Kalle informed him quietly.

'Wild orchids, and daisies, mayweed and St John's wort, butterflies dancing above them in the shimmering sunshine, and he knew, at that moment, that he had found paradise. Then he moved through a small wood, his heart and his pace quickening. Something, call it instinct, was drawing him on, drawing him out, further around the coastline, towards his unplanned but now imperative destination. What he found startled him, even within so much beauty. The staggering delight of the meadow into which he now emerged was beyond his wildest imaginings; it was pierced by the sunlight, filled with rare wild flowers and commanded views over a small bay, a place to moor a boat – twenty boats. And beyond that a view over the sea that was as limitless as the wonders of life. "I will build a house here," he said to himself. He repeated the words, over and over, louder and louder each time, as if he wanted the whole world to know of his plans, until he was near dancing a jig. He turned round in circles, his hands held high in the air – in the manner his great-great-grandson, Kalle, often mimics today.'

'Go on,' Kalle chided. 'Finish the story.'

'Christa was a trader from Stockholm who had made his money bringing spices from India and Malaya to these northern shores. Now he brought building materials and tools – along with his two younger brothers – to this edge of nowhere, and they began to dig foundations. For ten summers the three young men toiled, until finally the work was completed. They had built an extraordinarily modern house, a statement that would become a standard to follow for those who, over the following decades, traced their trail out and began to build their own summer houses on the thousands of surrounding islands. The middle brother, Johann, was an artist, and he designed all the original furniture in the house. Due to the cold climate, the pieces have hardly warped with time. Then Christa brought his wife, Amalia, and their young family out from Stockholm for the first time. She was an haute-bourgeoise woman, one of the city's élite – her father was a politician, her mother a great beauty known to all in Stockholm society. If they had been born British, I guess they would have been termed aristocratic.'

Lars paused, leant forwards and refilled his glass, took a large sip, then settled back against his cushion.

'By all accounts, Amalia loathed sailing and complained bitterly of all the summers that Christa had chosen to spend not with her but building the mythical summer house, which had become nothing but a symbol of his absence and the loneliness of her childbearing years. For their first family voyage, Christa and his brothers chartered an impressive sailing boat, and they set off from Stockholm early one fine June day. In all, they comprised eight adults and twelve children. In her arms, Amalia carried their fourth child, Jonas, who, at the time, was only three months old. The trip was a great success, the archipelago was kind and it took only six hours for them to make their journey from Lindingo to Linanas and then on, around the peninsula into the harbour.

'As they turned into our bay the house stood proudly before them on the promontory. The sun was still shining brightly, even though it was now the middle of the evening, and they sank the anchor in a trail of silver light that bounced towards them from the open sea. It was then, as the children jumped up and down with unrestrained excitement and Amalia stood dazed at the sheer magnificence of her husband's achievement, that fate took its cruel turn. Christa was tying the boat's ropes, lost his footing and fell overboard. As his body hit the surface of the sea, his skull smashed on a boulder lurking beneath the waterline. Amalia heard the crack, then the splash, and turned her gaze just in time to see her husband drown in a pool of shimmering scarlet. Without even setting foot on dry land, Amalia ordered the boat to return directly to Stockholm, the body of her beloved now stowed aboard.

'Amalia never once returned to the summer house. And

it wasn't for more than twenty years that any of her offspring ventured back either. But then came Jonas. Although he'd been witness to his father's tragic demise, he'd been too young to remember it. He, like his father before him, had been born with the spirit of the sea in his blood, and when he was old enough, he took a boat and made his own trip back out. Over the intervening years his uncles and cousins had enjoyed the privilege of summers at the house but now it was time for him to reclaim the property and its land. Over time the cousins who loved it there most erected their own properties in the vicinity, and they all summered here until they grew too old to make the journey any more. Then their children took over the reins, then their children's children, and now, at last, it has become our destiny.'

Lars sat back, sipped more of his schnapps and sighed.

'Fate, destiny, what a mystic you've become, my dear brother,' Kalle teased, sitting down next to him now so that the three of us were nestled in a row, watching the fire smouldering in the stove.

'You and your science,' Lars retorted. 'You know, most of what you learn from your books and studies is simply common sense. If you listened harder to the natural world you'd discover the same fundamental truths about life that you learn from your academic tomes. In the end, like Christa and Jonas, our senses will lead us where we know we should go. We all carry with us the patterns passed on to us from our forebears. We have no choice but to follow them. And we all already know that our characters are set in the womb – just look at us!'

He glanced across at Kalle with affection. 'You wait,

157

Emi, until I show you a picture of Christa.' He nudged me kindly. 'He's his great-grandfather reincarnated.'

'Really?'

'Absolutely – what do you think, Emi? Do we need to be blinded with science to discover our true natures? Or can we rely on instinct?'

'Well, I think instinct, or perhaps you'd call it fate, has brought me here tonight.'

Lars nodded enthusiastically, then his expression turned to enquiry.

'Why are you called Emi? It's a name I haven't heard before. Is it a derivative of Emily?'

'No.' I hesitated. I didn't want to elucidate – the subject had nigh-on inevitable consequences – but I couldn't see an obvious way around it without appearing rude. I was warming to Lars, too. Like his brother, I was fast becoming aware that his manner stimulated confession.

'Artemis,' I said, quietly.

'Artemis? So you're named after the goddess of the hunt,' Lars said, heaving himself up and looking down at me, with his hands on his hips. He appeared inordinately pleased with this discovery, threw his head back and roared with laughter.

'I'm afraid, Emi, you therefore have no excuses, none at all. Tomorrow we'll be seizing our rifles and heading for the woods.'

I glanced nervously towards Kalle for help. He grinned.

'It's roe-hunting season, and we own the licence to the land. It's part of our responsibility, as landowners, to protect the forests from over-infestation with these roguish wild beasts,' said Lars.

'Come on, Emi, it's a new experience,' Kalle coaxed. Evidently he was amused by my silent reaction. 'I'll stay here and write, and when you've got your beast you can come back and tell me all about it.'

The brothers began to pour more schnapps but I put my hand over my glass and pleaded fatigue. So Lars showed me up to this small, bare, blue room where, for the past hour, I have been sitting, huddled under a bundle of mismatched linen and rough woollen rugs, to write all of this down, lest I forget my first impressions of this magical place, or Lars's extraordinary tale. The blackness here saturates everything, like a permanent dye. Already I love it: it seems to permeate all my senses – and block out my own memories.

In the morning I woke to the sound of Lars singing and tramping around below in the dark, Bosse barking excitedly at his owner's merriment. When I came downstairs Kalle was already sitting in the kitchen at a table covered with a blue and white checked cloth, drinking tea. It was just getting light. Mist was hanging over the water below us, the coastline clearly edged in white; even the trees were petrified and static with snow, icicles hanging from their branches, glinting in the late-rising sun. As I glanced down across the empty bay I wondered where it was, the rock that had stolen Christa's life away.

Lars appeared from the hallway.

'*Hej*, Emi!' he said.

'Good morning,' I replied.

'We'll set off in about ten minutes,' he added enthusiastically. 'Have you ever used a rifle?'

I shook my head. I'd always been averse to physical acts

of violence. As a child, I'd even found it impossible to fight off Polly's attacks – she was always far happier to throw a punch, pinch my arm, inflict a Chinese burn, or land me a sideways kick if a disagreement got out of hand. I didn't like the idea of hurting, let alone killing, a wild animal, a roe deer: it sounded too poetic, too beautiful.

'I don't think I've ever even held one,' I admitted, sheepishly. 'And I'm not sure I could shoot anything if I did.'

'Artemis, Artemis,' he teased. 'You evidently need to get in touch with your inner self.'

We trudged out of the house, Bosse rushing ahead, his white fur a natural winter camouflage, as Kalle waved to us from the sitting-room window. The sun had risen now but the sky was almost as white as the snow beneath our feet and the air was static with cold. We soon turned off into the forest, where the canopy had hindered the snow's progress, leaving a more mixed palette of greens and browns, punctuated by patches of white. Our feet crunched and crackled beneath us.

'How much do you know about your goddess, Artemis?' Lars asked presently. I had had a feeling the subject was going to come back up.

'Very little,' I lied, hoping to dispel his interest.

'I love the myths,' Lars answered wistfully. 'Their implicit messages, the way they link us with the ancients, with more mystical times. I often use them in my work, you know.'

'How so?'

'By implication, the sense of a story once told, half

forgotten, the play of memory, half-recollections. Hopefully one day I'll be able to show you some of my paintings; maybe they could explain it better for themselves.'

'I saw your etchings at Kalle's flat,' I confessed. 'They're wonderful.'

Lars looked pleased.

'Well, in that case, I promise, later, or tomorrow, or next time you come, even, to take you over to the studio. Lotta loves it there, too. She likes to draw with my chalks while I work. Sometimes we spend the whole day over there together, then we take a swim to get the pastel dust off us. In the summer, of course!'

'You are very fond of her, aren't you?' I said.

'Of course, she's wonderful. If I ever have kids, I want them to be like Lotta. And if I don't – well, I'll always have my beautiful niece.'

'She's very lucky to have you and Kalle. Most kids don't have one father who loves them so much – it's as if she has two.'

'Did *you*? I mean, have a loving father?'

I faltered. I don't know why I'd said that about fathers. Had Peter loved us? I guessed so, but I had always been wary of him. Stuff had happened, he was so often away, I had sensed there were other women, other affairs, outside the home. In fact, if I can bear to think back, I knew so. And I had lived with our mother's quiet disappointments, always present, like a dank vapour that saturated everything, as deep as the darkness at night here.

'It's not that he didn't love us,' I replied, finally. 'Rather that he was often absent, spent most of our childhood preoccupied with his work, with other things.'

161

'And now?'

'Oh, now, well, he died, you see,' I said, finding my voice trailing off.

Fortunately, Lars's attention had suddenly shifted elsewhere. Bosse had stopped, stock-still, too, wagging his tail energetically but not making a sound. Lars held my arm and we paused – we had come quite a way and were now in the depths of the forest. Other than for the occasional cracking of a branch overloaded with snow, or the soft thud of it falling to the ground, everything was very still, very, very quiet.

'There must be deer – Bosse always knows,' he whispered, carefully lifting his rifle from his back and positioning it before his eye, finger suddenly to the trigger. He moved the barrel in a slow semicircle around us, searching for his target.

We stayed, silently, for what seemed an age, our breath sounding thick and heavy, emitting white clouds of vapour into the air. Then there was a small movement in the bushes, some way away to the right, and I turned my head. I saw it, for the briefest of moments, the frame of a small, chestnut-coloured faun, its head turned, staring back at me. I felt prickles down my spine as it appeared to trap my focus in the white of its eye. Then it darted away, quickly, into the undergrowth, and vanished.

'It was over there, it's gone,' I whispered. 'Over there.'

But Lars only shook his head slowly and continued to watch the middle distance, gun still poised.

'No,' he whispered back slowly. 'Look over here. The herd.'

My eyes shifted to Lars's line of vision. Through the

trees, in a huddle, I suddenly saw them. The deer were scrabbling in the undergrowth for winter food – berries, I guessed. There must have been at least five, but it was hard to tell because they were moving together, as one. The males' antlers clicked as they nudged at the ground, their earth-brown bodies almost indistinct against the undergrowth.

'I can't shoot at a group,' Lars whispered. 'It's no good if you can't isolate one from the rest. And that's Bosse's job.'

He took a whistle from his pocket and held it between his teeth. Then he raised the shotgun again and gave a very short, shrill blow. Bosse leapt as if sprung from a box towards the deer, and they in turn looked up, startled, then began to disperse.

'Don't!'

I found my voice at last and grabbed at Lars's arm. He held the gun firm for a moment, then allowed it to drop to his side. The deer had gone, the dog following after them, barking excitedly, and he turned to face me.

'I couldn't anyway – they were too close together,' he reassured me with a characteristic smile.

We wandered back home quietly. As we approached Lars pointed out the smoke rising in grey curls from the sauna. Kalle appeared from it, welcomed us home and urged me to go straight in. It wasn't yet three, but already the day was darkening and I was suddenly very cold, so I took his advice. An oil burner filled the tiny room with a flickering light and threw out the sweet, sharp essence of eucalyptus. As I lay there, absorbing the dry heat, I retraced Lars's and my earlier footsteps through the snow, trying to imprint them, to ensure the memory remained clear. I had loved it out there, almost more than anything I had ever experienced. I couldn't explain why – but something about the whiteness, the silence, the deer had entranced me. I had presupposed a dislike of hunting, but had found the experience exhilarating. I had felt safe enough with Lars even to enjoy the element of danger. I wondered how often I'd rejected the prospect of a turn in my life due to an inbuilt reticence to try new things, an instinctive aversion to risk; Mum had always been cautious, wary of the outside world. I remembered a time in Regent's Park when we were children. It was 'Asia Day', and elephants to ride had been brought in for the festival. Polly was desperate to have a go, but I remember sensing my mother's fear of the beasts and hung back with her as Polly clambered aboard. I remember her waving, grinning wildly back at us as she ambled off. The sauna, like my memories, was suddenly stifling. I pulled the towels up around me then headed back out into the dark and the cold to take a shower.

'This is the sixth day Lars has been in residence,' Kalle told me later, as we stood chopping shallots, braising the venison, in preparation for his brother's birthday meal. 'It takes that long for the walls to start breathing again after a spell of ice.'

I was surprised that for once I wasn't feeling cold; the sauna had warmed me right through. Inadvertently I thought yet again of my mother, of her ever-cold hands. I wondered if she had ever taken a sauna. I knew, instinctively, that she would have loved it.

The meal began with Kalle's own home-cured gravadlax,

followed by the steaming-hot venison casserole, tasting woody and sharp. It was sweetened, he informed me collusively, with juniper berries and bay. Lars sat at the head of the table, Kalle and I on either side of him, the casserole between us, ladled into our warmed white bowls. A bottle of claret glinted in the candlelight on the table.

'I think it's time for a toast,' Kalle suggested presently, and raised his glass.

'To my brother, my best friend, and story-teller beyond compare. Happy birthday, Lars.'

'We need to get going,' Kalle apologized at breakfast this morning. 'The forecast is bad.'

I was happy to head back into town. I'd gone to bed before Lars and Kalle again last night, intent on writing my diary, and I could hear them laughing as they moved around in the kitchen below me. After a while I realized I needed the loo; the problem here is that the only one is outside, by the sauna – the house has no bathroom, only a single running tap, as is standard in these traditional summer homes. Eventually I forced myself back up out of the now-warm sheets into the icy room, slipped on the sheepskin slippers, then began to make my way down the stairs. Halfway, however, I heard my name, and paused. The men were evidently washing up from dinner, and the kitchen door was ajar. I listened, surprised to realize that they were still speaking in English.

'It's different,' I heard Kalle say.

'But since Steph, I haven't seen you like this,' Lars replied. 'She's special. How did you guys meet? She's so quiet it's hard to know what she's thinking, but I like her, instinctively – and I always rely on instinct. It's as if she's carrying some big secret. But she's got you attracted like the moth to her flame.'

Kalle laughed. 'I can't help it. She's had a bad time, like me, a separation. She just needed a break. And she's going to help me with Lotta.'

'Did you need a smokescreen?'

'It just worked out that way.'

'Where did you meet her?'

'She was at a party in London, you know, for Clare's new book.'

There was silence.

'Clare asked after you,' said Kalle.

The silence continued. Then I heard the clatter of a plate.

'Why don't you call her, Lars? She'd like to come to see you. She loves it here. Maybe it's time.'

Still there was no reply.

'You wouldn't need to commit to anything. Clare knows what happened, how hard it's been for you to come to terms with your loss. There would be no expectation. But you never know, you might enjoy seeing one another again.'

There was another silence, then the clink of cutlery being put into a drawer.

'Did she get on with Emi?' Lars asked.

'I think they hardly exchanged a word. Emi was very withdrawn, she hardly spoke to a soul.'

'She still is,' Lars replied, contemplatively.

'She's coming out of herself. She intrigues me. I want to see what lies beneath. I'm going to study her.'

I heard Lars guffaw.

'For once in your life, Kalle, just follow your instincts, not your science. Don't analyse it too much, you'll kill the spirit.'

'Like I did with Stephanie?'

'I think you were both responsible for the breakdown. After all, it wasn't you who slept with your colleague,' said Lars.

'It was just as much my fault. I get so wound up with my research. I blocked her and Lotta out.'

'Don't do the same with Emi. You'll lose her, too. She's like an angel landed . . .'

At that moment Bosse pushed the kitchen door open and bounced up towards me, beginning to yap. I made a noise welcoming him, and continued down the stairs at a pace, just in time to see Kalle's face appear around the door, looking slightly abashed.

'I just woke up,' I said, blearily, before he had a chance to ask. 'I need the loo. What's the time?'

'It's already gone two,' he informed me, relief spreading across his brow. 'Come on. I'll get you a torch.'

In the cold light of day my fear at the consequences of this conversation had not abated. What did he mean, study me? And if Kalle brought Clare out here, if she came to see Lars, then I'd have to accept that my cover would be blown, too. She would surely have heard from James about my disappearance, and she would tell Lars. It was inevitable. And as soon as I knew my whereabouts might be discovered, I realized that it was the last thing I wanted in the world. However cruel it might seem, I just didn't want Will and Polly to know where I was. I felt I had started on a new path and I couldn't turn back until I had completed it. But I couldn't voice my concerns to Kalle without alerting him to the fact that I'd been eavesdropping – and therefore that I'd also heard him say that he found me 'intriguing'. The word was embedded in my mind. The slow, quiet growth of our relationship had felt comfortable, unconstructed, and I certainly didn't want to raise it as a topic for discussion. I was fascinated by the implication that Lars had suffered some kind of tragedy in his life, however, and guessed that it must have been in relation to a woman. As we left the island and drove towards the city, I raised the subject of his love life, hoping that, by one twist or two, it might lead us naturally to Clare.

'Lars had a long-term relationship,' Kalle began sadly. 'It was a terrible tragedy. Her name was Pauline – she was a painter, too. They were together for a good ten years but, a bit like Lars, she was eccentric, uneven. She would often disappear, for weeks at a time, into 'the wilderness', she used to say, to gather material for her work, then return without either the desire or the compunction to explain where she'd gone. Lars needs his own time to immerse himself in his work, too. I think it suited them both. Whenever Pauline was around their affair was tempestuous, and when she was away he produced his most intense creations. But then, three years ago, she took off on one of her adventures and didn't come back. For the first few weeks Lars wasn't concerned. After all, for her the irregular behaviour was regular. Then he got a telephone call from the Danish police. Her body had been washed up on a southern shore. It seemed there was nothing sinister about it, just a simple swimming accident, that's all. She'd hired a small fishing hut in a cove for three months, and when Lars went to collect her things, signs of intense creativity abounded – there was a series of half-completed collages that used shingle and shells from the sea. And on the beach they found her book, her sandals, her towel.'

The story was disquieting, in more ways than one. Pauline's disappearance seemed suddenly like my own recent escape – and thinking how Lars must have felt made me feel creeping guilt for what I was doing to Polly and Will. And then the drowning, too; it took me way, way back to our childhood, to the tragedy surrounding my friend Marie.

'He spent the next year at the island, and we hardly saw one another,' Kalle continued. 'He didn't encourage visits, just worked – and worked out his grief in the only way he knows: through his art and his hunting, his engagement with the canvas and the natural world. That's why it's still so important for me to come back and see him as much as I can, particularly around birthdays. It's an excuse to check up on him, to make sure he's surviving OK.'

'To me he seemed well,' I said.

'This year we had a very warm summer. I brought Lotta out to stay. Lars would eat with us, then retire. But on the fourth day Lotta asked to go with him, to the studio. They took bread and smoked salmon and a bottle of homemade cordial and rowed out. They were gone all day. Eventually I swam out there to see that Lotta was OK – after all, she was only four years old. I thought she would have got bored by now and was surprised she hadn't wanted to return. I found her asleep on Lars's lap on a deckchair in the garden, her legs spattered with a rainbow of paint colours, her pale hair speckled with it, too. Her head was resting on his chest, and they were soaking up the last of the day's warm sun. Lars was sitting quietly, and as I approached I became aware that tears were rolling down his paint-spattered cheeks. That, to me, seemed to be the turning point. Once he had started to cry he could begin to heal. And you're right, thankfully, he almost seems back to his pre-Pauline ways now; his natural lightness of spirit has found a crack in the defences and forced its way back to the surface. This weekend, especially, I must say, he seemed content. He evidently liked you too.'

'Are you sure her death wasn't sinister?'

Drowning, from my own experience, wasn't always so clearly an accident. Marie's death had occurred when we were all sixteen. We had all been there – it was one of those adolescent 'accidents' when no one was really thinking straight. In many ways I think we were mutually culpable. Polly and I had almost willed it to happen, and Hera, Marie's mother, had been asleep on the grass. The memories made me feel nauseous: they were too wrapped up with other things, our father's infidelity, everything. I hadn't swum since. This weekend I'd heard of two other deaths by water – first Christa's, now Pauline's. I noted that when Kalle and Lars spoke about either of them they both employed a matter-of-fact tone, as if the passing of a life was a tragedy to accept and move on from – philosophically speaking. They made me aware that, where my own 'losses' were concerned, I had never learned how to do that. It was true that, since our mother had died,

Marie's ghost had stopped haunting me. I had simply switched off emotionally, feeling nothing, not grief, not happiness, not anything at all. No wonder I couldn't make a marriage to Will work. Now, here, something about this place, Kalle and Lotta, was waking me back up.

'In the end it's easier to find solace in the assumption that she drowned by accident,' Kalle answered, slowly.

'What do you mean?' I retorted, falteringly.

'Pauline,' he replied, his eyebrows knitting at my confusion, his face still focused forwards, on the darkening road ahead. 'But the book she left, I don't know, maybe it contained a hidden message. The essays were entitled *Further Studies in Sanity and Madness*, by R. D. Laing. I'd given it to her the previous year as a present.'

The clouds above the city looked fit to burst. As we entered the city a flurry of snowflakes was falling, in vast, poetic swirls. It was too late to try to move the conversation round to Lars's relationship with Clare, yet I was pleased that Kalle had trusted me enough to tell me about his brother's dreadful tragedy.

'It's going to be a harsh winter,' Kalle said, turning to me now with a reassuring smile. 'You're lucky – you're going to experience Sweden at its most extreme.'

18

Scissors was reassuringly mundane, slotted between a newsagent and a greengrocer up the Finchley Road. Inside, perfumed bleach clogged the air and the drone of whirring hairdryers was whisked into a frothy base of Radio One. They had both had their hair cut here as teenagers, Polly and Emi, in the time before things changed, before they grew up, during all those years when they'd done everything together. It was routine, thought-blocking. When she'd got her first month's salary, however, Polly had switched to an upmarket stylist on New Bond Street. To Polly the change had felt like success, but Emi had always stuck with Linda. Going back now felt reassuring, like a homecoming of sorts. There was familiarity here and a sense of Emi, of a time before everything had changed. When Linda saw her coming through the door she rushed towards Polly and gave her a maternal hug. Then she pulled back and searched her face for clues. You have to admire her resolve, thought Polly, L'Oréal blonde with a Rimmel peach complexion and Dior mauve eyes. But for all her efforts even Linda couldn't escape the passage of time. She was beginning to look weathered.

'Can I put up this poster?' Polly asked, her voice trembling.

Linda nodded firmly. Will had had the leaflets printed showing Emi's moon-like face for a 'hand-out' session around King's Cross, and over the previous few days they'd spent hours there, talking to passers-by, sticking up posters, loitering around by the phone-box where the mystery call had been made – all to no avail. Now they were taking them further afield – anywhere people might recognize Emi. It was only the third week in January but already it felt to Polly and Will as if they were looking for a needle in a haystack. After endless consultations Polly had finally been given the go-ahead to run a report on Emi's disappearance. And that was why she was here now. She'd grudgingly agreed to a re-enactment of her twin's last known moments to add 'dramatic tension' to the tale. Will had not liked the idea, but Polly had persuaded him that desperate situations demanded desperate measures.

'Now, what can I do with your hair, lovey?' Linda asked, once the poster had been stuck firmly to the glass inside the front door.

'I want you to cut it as if I were Emi,' Polly replied calmly. 'I need to look exactly the same.'

Linda nodded decisively but avoided Polly's eyes as she worked, her glossed lips pursed in a straight, determined line, polished nails flashing red as her fingers move quickly and efficiently through Polly's changing hair. Half an hour later the blow-dryer had been turned on and Polly's new style began to emerge. One by one the other stylists stopped working and made their way over to watch the transformation. As she looked out through the mirror, she met four pairs of sad eyes gazing back at her. It was only then that she looked objectively at herself. And what she saw gave her nearly as much of a start as it had everyone else. She looked more like Emi than even she could have believed possible. It wasn't only the short auburn bob that now framed her face, but something much more profound in her own expression that had changed since Emi had gone away; something she hadn't been aware of until now. There was an unfamiliar, haunted look in Polly's eyes, a look she now recognized had been a permanent feature of Emi's face. She blinked and glanced away as Linda swept her shoulders with a clothesbrush. Then she paid, thanked Linda and texted Will that she was ready to go.

Soon he pulled up outside in his clapped-out old car. She hopped in and he pulled straight off, just managing to make his way through the changing traffic lights as they turned to amber, then accelerating round St John's Wood roundabout and on towards Regent's Park. Generally he wasn't an aggressive driver, never trying to beat the queues. Today, however, he focused entirely on getting there first. Eventually they came to an inevitable halt behind a queue of cars vying to get on to the Marylebone Road. Only now did he turn his head slowly and give her his full attention.

'Weird shit,' he commented, blankly.

Polly moved an arm and placed it gently around the back of his seat, just touching his right shoulder.

'Don't worry, Will, you'll get used to it,' she tried, but he didn't respond, and when they arrived at Polly's Will left the car idling as she got out, then apologized that he had a research paper to finish and swung off towards his brother's place, the car picking up speed as it left her behind.

They filmed the re-enactment the following day. When Polly arrived there was a hush as the crew took in her new look. They all knew Emi and were evidently moved by Polly's perfect mimicry. She'd been to the flat and picked up the clothes Emi had been wearing the night before she disappeared, too. It was ironic, she thought. They had spent their lives dressing and behaving as differently as they could. Reversing the principle felt perverse, an imposition on Emi's space. Polly joked that even she would have trouble telling herself and Emi apart, but no one laughed. It was a strange feeling to Polly, being felt sorry for. It hadn't ever happened before and it made her uncomfortable. She'd never been, nor wanted to feel, the victim in life. Some people enjoyed that role, it encouraged others to look out for them – in fact, she thought, Emi had always needed someone, had had Sarah, and then Will; Sarah herself had had their father, even her friend Carol. Polly had always been keen to look out for herself.

Polly'd been reporting on London news for five years now, and standing in front of a camera was second nature to her. But she soon discovered that it was different when she was acting – and when the report was so personal, too. The film began with a shot of her, as Emi, leaving her flat to go to Helen's dinner party, then forwarded to her returning to Blenheim Crescent with Polly at 1 a.m. the following morning. Afterwards the crew filmed a short interview in the street outside the flat. It took four attempts before Polly felt they'd got the message right. In the end, she used a reluctant Will as an interviewee and together they built up a picture of her sister. Polly attempted to play down her twindom and play up pictures of Emi as she'd looked in the days before she disappeared. Now Polly had cut her hair it was eerily difficult to tell the reporter apart from the photographs they displayed on screen. There was something particularly unusual about Emi and Polly – a characteristic that their mother shared. Most people wouldn't have noticed it, unless they looked very carefully. But Will had spotted it through the lens of his camera at Sarah's fiftieth birthday party: they all had perfectly parallel features.

'That's what makes you all so compelling, so beautiful,' she remembered him saying as he clicked the shutter.

When the filming was finished, Polly and the crew headed back to the studio but Will rushed off, apologizing that he still had to complete his paper. Polly felt thrown off course, raftless. No one had ever made her feel like this before – apart from Peter, that was. Her father's protracted absences had made her ache in the same way that Will's every departure from her side seemed to do now. She tried to push her anxieties to one side as she went through the rushes with Nick. The report was to be aired the following evening, during the prime slot at six fifteen.

When she got home there was an overtly apologetic message from Will on her answering machine, saying he had promised his fellow lecturer Ralph that he'd write a lecture on 'The West's hypocrisy over nuclear proliferation in Iran' in time for a class the following afternoon. She hesitated for a moment, then called him back.

'How's it going?' she asked.

'Reagan's policy in Iran in the eighties was fucking sickening,' Will remonstrated, his voice rich with anger and frustration.

Polly felt confused. Her brain was fuzzing; the image of herself, as Emi on film, was still embedded in the forefront of her mind. How could he focus on anything else?

'Pol?'

'Sorry, yes, I'm sorry, I'm sure you're right, but all I can think about at the moment is Emi,' she spluttered. She felt desperate. 'She can't have just disappeared; life doesn't work like that, not unless you're caught up in some horrible war or a tsunami, or a terror attack. But none of those things has happened to Emi. I'm sure of it. She's chosen to go away, she must have done. It's too much of a coincidence, what she said to me, about needing a break. What I don't understand is where or why.'

There was a pause on the line.

'I'm sorry, I guess my work's my means of escape,' Will finally replied. 'I found today a bit too . . . raw. I hope you're right, about her choosing to leave. I just feel blank about it, numbed. I haven't got a feeling about where she is or how she got there. But I'll get this lecture written, then get our webpage set up tonight, before the broadcast goes out tomorrow. I promise. Then we'll get together, talk it through again, and go down to King's Cross with some more leaflets, OK?'

19

Carol wakes to the sound of urgent tapping on her front door. She glances at the clock; it's a quarter to one in the morning.

'Peter?' she whispers. But when she glances through the grill she sees the young, peaky face of Jeanne, Sarah's latest French au pair, on the other side and unlocks all the bolts quickly.

'It's Sarah,' the girl says, thickly. 'She's on the floor, I think she took something.'

Carol doesn't bother to put on her dressing-gown, simply runs, barefoot, with Jeanne across their shared front path and into Sarah's house. She finds her friend slumped half on, half off her bed. There is an empty bottle of sleeping pills on the floor. She feels Sarah's pulse, which, though weak, is regular. She tries, to no avail, to wake her, then calls an ambulance.

Peter is, in fact, still in Newcastle. He comes home the following morning and takes control, thanking Carol and chivvying her off. Uncharacteristically, she gets the feeling he finds her involvement with this crisis intrusive, as if she's bringing the truth through the door with her and he doesn't want to see it. Luckily the twins seem blissfully unaware of the depths into which their mother's condition has slipped. And, as with the first time, all those years before in their Silver Cross prams, they both sleep through the drama.

The next morning their father tells the girls that, sadly, their grandmother has died and that their mother has taken the news rather badly. They are going to stay with their friend Marie for a few days. The girls are concerned by their mother's absence, and saddened by the news, but they didn't know their grandmother very well, and soon they are feeling better again, looking forward to their weekend away with Marie. They love her mother, Hera – she's 'foreign' to them, exotic; she's bright and funny, always laughing. The twins are ten now, confident enough for sleepovers, and they love being in her bright, colourful house.

Their absence gives Sarah the chance to recover from her shock and Peter takes a week off work to support her. They all go to Boston for the funeral. On the way there she keeps apologizing to Peter; she says she has no idea what came over her, it just seemed she needed to punish herself, for not having been there when her mother needed her, for shying away, for being weak and afraid. In response, Peter shakes his head despairingly.

'What about us?' he asks, under his breath, glancing at their daughters, sitting together, reading two copies of the same book, across the aisle. 'And if not me, what about the girls? What would they have gained?'

*   *   *

Sarah's father remains stoic and dignified throughout the ordeal of his wife's funeral. Sarah feels absolutely nothing; numbed by the shock, and perhaps the Valium she swallows before the service takes place.

'Will you cope?' she asks him before they leave.

'I don't know,' her father replies, frankly.

'It's early days,' she tries.

'It will always be early days,' he says, despairingly. 'She was my life.'

'Oh, Dad.'

'It's OK,' he says. 'I simply have no expectations left.'

When they return she watches Peter as he tries to work his way around her, to avoid focusing on the critical issue. As much as she might like to help him draw conclusions, Sarah can't. Nevertheless, this drama is a wake-up call for them both, and silently they acknowledge the fact. It's taken years to come. Peter calls on their medical insurance and finds Sarah a new doctor who prescribes different drugs. And then he promises not to go away so frequently, to try to help her get really better this time.

20

This morning the sun didn't seem able to raise itself fully from its winter slumber, shafting only its lowest, weakest rays over the winter city. Lotta slept late, and as Kalle and I sat eating breakfast, he pulled a sheaf of notes from his case.

'I give them to all my undergraduate students,' he said, enthusiastically. 'They introduce behavioural genetic research, and general child psychology, too. I thought you might find them interesting – both for you personally, and for your relationship with Lotta. Don't worry if some of it goes over your head, or seems boring – just skip to the next part.'

I was pleased he had given the notes to me and packed them in my bag. After dropping off Lotta, I began to wander again, determined to find a cosy café to sit and read in. I followed my senses without clear direction; back past the church and its dark, granite gravestones, then left through the playground, the swings swaying emptily in the rising breeze. I turned right past a school and heard a child's raised voice, followed by a wave of laughter lifting and falling. Now I was moving on down Nytorgsgatan, a long, characterless street flanked by insurance companies, banks and estate agents. And then, suddenly, I was in a different kind of world, an enclave in the city, a park surrounded by colourful cafés and junk shops, art galleries and small boutiques, and there was a large café on the corner.

Glancing in through the slightly fogged windows, I could see mismatched sixties furniture, red, amber and green circular 'traffic' lights flashing on and off slowly by the bar, and large, speckled old mirrors reflecting people seated at tables all over the large room. They were reading newspapers and sipping long coffees served in tall glasses. I pushed the door open, entered the warm space, removed my coat and sat down at a corner table. A young waiter, dressed in sloppy jeans and sporting a beard and sideburns like the latest fashion accessories, approached me slowly and offered me a lazy, appraising smile, along with the menu.

'You need to try a blueberry muffin,' he stated nonchalantly in English, a Californian drawl almost masking his Swedish accent. 'They're still warm.'

I couldn't help but smile and agree, and as he wandered away I found myself pulling Kalle's papers from my bag. I settled back and began to read. The first chapter referenced early childhood and the way it impacts upon our later personality's development. I was just becoming immersed when the waiter returned with a glass of frothing coffee, a glass of water, and the promised muffin.

'Studying?' he asked, with an easy confidence, as he placed them before me.

'Kind of,' I replied, glancing back down at the papers. 'Behavioural genetics.'

'Wow, that sounds kind of cool,' he said, straightening up and stroking his beard.

He hesitated, and I considered engaging him in further conversation, but I had just come upon an extraordinary section and determinedly looked back down at the papers.

'Don't let me intrude any further,' he smiled, turning slowly and moving away.

Recent research programmes have found that the relationship between the primary carer and the infant, especially in its first year after birth, has a direct impact on the formation of the baby's brain [Kalle had written]. *Therefore, a loving and attentive parent can stimulate the development of a social brain, the pre-frontal cortex, a part of the brain that develops almost entirely postnatally. There, the key emotional responses such as empathy, self-restraint, and the ability to pick up on non-verbal cues are organized – the neurological rules according to which we will govern the rest of our lives.*

Also, a baby's stress response – the production of the hormone cortisol by the hypothalamus – is set like a thermostat, usually within the first six months of life. Babies cannot regulate cortisol production at birth, but they learn to do so through repeated experiences of being comforted when distressed. If a caregiver expresses resentment or hostility towards a crying baby, or leaves him distressed for longer than he can bear, the brain becomes flooded with cortisol and will go on to over- or under-produce the hormone in future stressful situations. Excess cortisol production is linked to depression and insecurity. Too little can result in aggression and detachment.

Curiously, I realized that my heart was thumping in my chest. Depression? Detachment? I put the paper down and tried to project myself into the scenario. Surely Polly and I, as babies, had been treated the same way? And yet I recognized many of these characteristics as if they were my own. I tried to think back, to test the premise. I knew that Polly had been in an incubator to begin with, that I had received the greater share of maternal love. If anything, therefore, I guessed I should have been the one with the more 'social' brain. But that was definitely not the case; it was as if the roles had been reversed and I had always thought of myself as the 'second twin' even though I knew, essentially, that I had been born first. I read on, my interest growing. What kind of start had I really had? Could our genes and subsequent nurture at least partially be to blame for the paradoxes between my identical twin and myself? I thought momentarily about Polly and her relationship with our father, then of mine with our mother. I could see myself, as a child, lying alone on the rough carpet of their bedroom floor, drawing and writing. And then I looked up and saw my mother, reclining on the bed, staring vacantly at the ceiling. Where had Polly been?

'That paper is recent research by a psychotherapist called Sue Gerhard,' Kalle informed me at dinner. 'It follows on from the twentieth-century work of British psychiatrist John Bowlby. He argued that maternal deprivation during the formative first three years of a child's life would cause irreparable scarring of babies' "psychic tissue", and that they would go on to become inadequate parents themselves.'

'Do psychologists still believe that today?' I enquired.

Kalle shook his head. 'It's generally recognized that genetic make-up and the wider environment have their part to play, too; and that children are influenced not only by their primary carer, but also by their wider set of relations and their peers – particularly, Gerhard would say, their peers. What is so interesting to me, however, is her assessment of the neuro-scientific development of the post-natal brain.'

I creased my brow and Kalle laughed.

'You see, it implies that emotional intelligence is nurtured post- as well as pre-birth, that the trigger for a balance of cortisol inside the developing brain is human love.'

'And how so before?' I asked.

Kalle clapped his hands together, apparently delighted by my question.

'I'll see what I can find for you to read. It's all to do with the pre-natal environment, both the effect of the mother's moods and even the levels of protein that a foetus receives. You know, it's been proven that the level of protein received in the womb can even differ between one identical twin and another, perhaps affecting their resulting personalities. I'll dig out some reports: it makes fascinating reading.'

Unbeknown to Kalle, he was getting too close to the nub of the matter. I looked away.

'Are you OK, Emi?' he asked. '*Hej*, what did I say?'

'It's nothing,' I lied, smiling weakly through my glass of wine.

21

'Look at this one,' said Polly, tossing a letter across the desk at Will. 'I think it's a bit creepy.'

They were sitting together in their 'campaign HQ'. Nick had sorted it out for them at the TV-channel offices – a small anteroom off one of the corridors that had been empty for years. It smelt of dust, stale cigarettes and empty cardboard boxes. Now it was crammed with files, boxes of envelopes, a photocopier, a computer and a telephone. The contents of this letter were similar to so many of the others Will had been receiving since that first broadcast, invitations to meet women – and also some men – offering a shoulder to cry on. There was something sad and similar about these missives – they were rarely emails – often handwritten in blue biro, always in a lonely, backward-arching style, the serifs curled up under the lines, like unborn foetuses.

Will glanced at the letter, grimaced, then screwed it up and chucked it in the bin. It was already ten in the evening. They often ended up here after work now; it was the only time they both had to do this job – and tonight, while Polly opened post Will had been ploughing through the latest glut of emails that had flooded in over the past week, looking for clues. London's public had been moved by this tale of separated twins. Money had been arriving, too, pound coins wrapped in paper inside envelopes, cheques for tens, even occasionally hundreds of pounds. People wanted to do something to help Will and Polly in their search for Emi, but so far it seemed to be making no difference at all. Initially they used the cash to print and distribute more professional posters of her face all over the capital, and to place Missing ads in national newspapers. They chose a happy, smiling photograph of Emi that, ironically, Will had taken on their wedding day, but all their efforts had met with a cold silence. The phone rang now and Will picked it up. He nodded and frowned, agreed, arranged a time, then asked the caller to hold and looked across at Polly.

'It's the *London Evening News*,' he said. 'They want to know if they can help us.'

Two days later a double-page spread appeared in the paper, describing Will and Polly's plight. This in turn triggered national interest, but still no news was forthcoming.

'It's like the start of a Grimm's fairy tale,' Polly said to Will gloomily, 'with everyone holding their breath for a grisly ending.'

But as the weeks turned into the second month and still there was no sight or sound of Emi, both of them feared that the media would begin to lose interest, that the story, like the weather, would start to grow cold. Sure enough, on a bitter, mid-February day, Nick called Polly in for a meeting. She assumed that they had come to the end of the road.

'Don't worry,' he reassured her. 'No one's suggesting we drop the campaign, but it needs to enter a new phase, one that can take us longer term, keep a steady momentum and, you know, same old, same old, retain the interest of the public if, that is, time were to, you know, move on without Emi showing up. Perhaps you and Will could try to come up with a mini-series about Emi's life, about twins, genetics and nurture, to keep the viewers focused? It could have all sorts of spin-offs. We're prepared to take you off all other reports for the meantime, while you get this planned and running.'

Polly was surprised to realize that she felt optimistic for the first time in weeks. She knew that there was only so much time and attention an undeveloping story could sustain. Nick was right, of course, that she needed to find a new 'creative angle'. It was supposed to be what she knew best – spinning stories like a spider spins its web. She and Will had already managed to ensnare the public, but now they had them trapped they needed to hold on to their interest – until someone spotted Emi – because, she told herself, over and over, eventually someone must.

'Thank you,' she managed to say, falteringly. 'I'll do my best.'

'First report would air a week today,' he replied, with a reassuring smile.

After the meeting Polly went back to her office and reread her planned script for her next report.

According to Home Office statistics about two hundred and

ten thousand people are reported missing in the UK each year. The vast majority return safe and sound within seventy-two hours but, distressingly for those of us left behind, thousands of others do not. State agencies such as the police do not look for missing adults other than in the case of vulnerability or crime. Of course adults are within their rights to start again, to go somewhere new, but it doesn't make it any easier for those of us who have to face each new day worrying where our loved ones have gone. Charities such as the National Missing Persons Helpline fill the gap left by the state services. I went to meet them to discuss Emi's case and that of other missing people like her . . .

Vulnerability. The word played over and over in her mind. Emi hadn't been vulnerable in an obvious way; but the longer she'd been absent, the more clearly Polly sensed her fragility, a fragility that she didn't share. It was beginning to unnerve her, that Emi and she were so different in this respect. After all, genetically they were the same. She wondered how she was going to satisfy Nick's request for a deeper, or should it be broader, approach to her reports about Emi. There were two ways to go. She could either begin to review other cases, turning her stories into a general campaign to reunite the missing with the missed, or she could go into a more detailed assessment of Emi's case – but what exactly would that mean? Raking up the leaves of their past and seeing what lay beneath? She wasn't sure how useful that would be. One of the women at the Missing Persons Helpline had said something today, however, that had stuck. *'When people go missing like this, there's usually a clear reason; either something has been building up for years, then a trigger sets off the emotion to leave; or*

189

something happens to them in the twenty-four hours leading up to the disappearance. Perhaps one way to approach Emi's case would be to look at the two scenarios, and see if you can piece events together that would guide you to her.'

She left the studio and started to walk, heading west, trying to clear her head, trying to think. Over the past couple of weeks the frost between her and Will had begun to thaw, and they had grown accustomed to spending all their non-working hours together, at the campaign office, or walking long distances, traversing the city on foot, wherever they needed to go, an unsettled pair, more at ease in transit than when sitting still. There were things to distract them that way; buskers, street sleepers, snippets of other people's conversations, a reminder of other lives going on around them, normal lives not paralysed by fear or grief. Plus, of course, although neither of them ever confessed to the thought, there was always the slight chance that among the anonymous crowds they might just spot Emi, the real Emi, not one of Polly's increasingly common false sightings. It was always worth a second glance, always worth being alert to the possibility. Polly often thought she saw her twin – in the gesture of a hand, the turn of a head – and the sightings made her feel increasingly febrile, disconnected.

Unusually tonight, Polly was walking alone. Will was giving another speech, this time on the 'facts and figures' behind the US 'phoney war' in Iraq. He'd told her on the phone this afternoon that 'There are already up to forty-three thousand reported civilian deaths in Iraq, but the real figures could be four times as high . . .' Each time he fed her such facts she felt a pang of guilt for her concern over Emi; one disappearance against a country of loss seemed fatuous, and yet it wasn't just a figure – for her Emi's disappearance amounted to a world of loss, for with her disappearance it felt as if she had lost a part of herself, too, as if a part of her had also vanished, dissipated like steam into the vapid air.

She decided to make her way to Will's meeting, which was taking place in the same lecture hall as the first one she had attended, back in December, on the very day, she suddenly realized, that she had last seen Emi. Everything had been so different back then. As she got closer to the Euston Road, however, she realized that she would pass King's Cross and, at the last moment re-routed. She and Will hadn't been back to the area for a month, not since that first broadcast. Will didn't feel at ease there; he was convinced the bogus call had been a coincidence or a mistake. He had urged Polly to keep away from the area, too.

By the time she arrived at the station it was nearly nine o'clock. She glanced about her. It was quiet now – the commuters had all gone and the night trade was yet to pick up steam. She wandered aimlessly, glancing furtively into strangers' faces, looking for a hint, allowing them to look back at her too, in the hope that her features might trigger a memory of Emi, but it was hopeless and all the faces remained blank. Eventually she headed up York Way, intent on circling the insalubrious back entrance to the station. It was dark and shadowy and suddenly she felt slightly nervous. She was just under halfway up the road when she decided to head back. But as she was turning she heard a voice behind her, calling from the shadows.

'Are ye lost?'

She swivelled around to see a girl stepping out of the gloom. For a moment she was afraid.

'I've spotted ye around before,' the girl continued curiously. She had a sandpaper Glaswegian accent. 'Are ye a copper?'

'No, no, I'm looking for someone – my sister,' Polly offered, tentatively.

The girl stepped forward, so now they were standing face to face in the lamplight. She appeared to be around the same age as Polly and Emi and, like them, was slightly taller than average, with similar dark brown hair but a far skinnier, malnourished frame. It was hard to tell if she was pretty; she had masked her looks with iridescent green eye make-up, false eyelashes and scarlet lipstick. She looked theatrical, like a tropical bird or, indeed, a tragic circus clown.

'What's her name? Mine's Kaz, by the way.'

'Emi,' said Polly, her voice suddenly sounding thin and weak.

'Aha,' said the girl, contemplatively. 'When did she go?'

'A couple of weeks before Christmas.'

Kaz glanced around, left and right. 'Och, ye must be dead worried. It's quiet tonight. Come on, do you fancy a cup of tea?'

Polly hesitated, suspicious for a moment, then nodded, suddenly overcome with emotion. She felt foolish as tears started rolling down her face. It was freezing cold, too; a mean February wind was coursing along this dark corridor of a street, between dark warehouse buildings. It took a lot for Polly to feel the cold, but now she started to shiver uncontrollably. Kaz was wearing a thin sheepskin coat over purple knee-high PVC boots. She placed a bony arm around Polly's shoulder and strangely Polly didn't feel the urge to shrug her off; she understood, instinctively, that the gesture was meant in kindness.

'Come on, hen,' Kaz said. 'It's ne' so bad. She'll show up when she's ready.'

Together they headed for a small neon-lit café on the other side of the street, where Kaz was evidently known to the Middle Eastern man standing behind the counter.

'Regular?' he asked and she signalled for two.

They sat down in a corner next to an electrical heater and Kaz took off her coat. Underneath she was wearing a lime green PVC T-shirt, with no bra. Her scrawny arms were studded with needle marks and bruises in varying shades of brown, yellow and green. She lit a cigarette as the owner brought them the teas but no bill.

'Tell us about your sister,' she suggested now, keenly, fixing Polly in the eye, her pupils bright and tight. Polly looked back at Kaz and wondered why she cared; maybe, she thought, she just needed the distraction.

'It seems I've lost the ability to know her at all,' she began, falteringly. 'I can't understand her motivation and I have no idea where she could have gone. None at all.'

'Go on, tell me it all. Tell me her story,' Kaz urged, kindly.

It was now that Polly recognized it: a look of empathy. Of course Kaz in her own way must, like Emi, be both missing and missed. Once she must have been someone else, somewhere else, perhaps even carrying a different name. In Polly's search, this lost girl had recognized something of herself. She tried to resurrect Emi more clearly in her mind, to visualize her, make her tangible again.

'Well, for a start she's my identical twin, and when I say identical, I mean exactly the same,' she began, tentatively. 'When she disappeared, though, I realized I hadn't really known her for years. You'd think, sharing the same genes, we'd run our lives along parallel lines, but for me and Emi, it didn't go like that.'

She opened her eyes and was touched to see that Kaz had stubbed out her cigarette and was leaning forwards, hands under her chin, concentrating hard.

'Why do you think she's gone? Was it drugs, boyfriend trouble, money?'

'No, it was because of me.'

As she said it, Polly knew instinctively that she was right and the words started to pour from her, fast and with utter conviction.

'She couldn't stand it, the way I was. My life was busy, on a roll. She was retreating, depressed, impossible to talk to. Her marriage had failed . . . she was in a corner. And I should have known how to pull her back out, but I was too bloody self-obsessed to see it, to try and help her, until it was too late and she'd gone.'

'You're quite hard on yourself,' Kaz said, taking a sip of her coffee, then lighting another cigarette. 'Why do you feel so guilty about her? Emi's the one who's walked away, not you.'

Polly saw Will in her mind's eye and tried to push the image away.

'I guess I feel guilty for not anticipating this, for not being aware of a danger brooding somewhere on her horizon line.'

'There's something else,' surmised Kaz, knowingly. 'Tell me, what happened, just before she left? There's always something, a wee trigger.'

Kaz looked bold yet vulnerable, as if she'd seen it all, yet essentially, deep inside, had managed, miraculously, to remain completely innocent. The combination made her seem unshockable. What was the harm? Suddenly Polly felt desperate to confess, to tell someone, anyone, her deepest, darkest secret.

'Nothing had happened beforehand, nothing at all. It's now, since she's gone, that I've seen the truth, but a truth Emi couldn't have known – because I didn't know it myself back then.'

'What truth?'

Polly took a deep breath.

'That I'm in love with Will.'

'Who's Will?'

'Will is Emi's husband,' she said.

Polly was right. Kaz's expression didn't shift to judgement. She imbibed Polly's story along with the caffeine and nicotine, nonchalantly accepting its combined, bitter flavour, as if she swallowed a similar tale every day.

'I'm in love with her husband,' Polly repeated, more clearly. Now it was out she knew it was true and she felt both fearful and relieved.

'Maybe she didn't know that. Maybe she just wanted a fresh start,' Kaz replied. 'It's her right, you know. If you can't find her, maybe it's because she doesn't want you to.

You could spend years searching, or you could get on with your own life, with Will, and wait for her to come back, when she wants to.'

'But what if something's happened to her? What if she's in trouble?'

'Is that what you think?'

Polly shook her head as someone entered the café, and Kaz glanced up furtively through her false eyelashes and sighed. Polly turned to see two short, sturdy men standing in the doorway, one black, the other white. The white one gestured to Kaz.

'Time's up,' she said with an apologetic smile. 'I need to make some money to pay for my,' she glanced down at her forearms, 'medicine. I'll look out for Emi, I'm usually on the strip. I take them under the arches,' she paused as she got up, put on her jacket, 'for my special kind of service. What exactly did you say she looks like?'

Polly wondered how much of her story Kaz had taken in. Maybe she was too high to listen; perhaps Polly's words had evaporated into the air, without really being heard. It didn't matter. She felt better for her confession, either way.

'Me,' said Polly. 'She looks exactly like me.'

Kaz laughed. 'Of course, ye said, she's your twin.'

The other man at the door hissed at her now.

'All right, all right, I'm coming,' she admonished, then looked down once more towards Polly. 'You'll spot me, I always wear this coat and my purple boots,' she confided, opening and shutting her jacket swiftly. 'Oh! And my narcotic-coloured tops.' She looked to the men and raised her eyebrows. 'It gets them going.'

She moved quickly now, to join her keepers. Then the door swung shut behind them and she was gone.

Polly didn't mention her encounter with Kaz to Will – she knew that he would disapprove of her hanging around at King's Cross in the first place and she didn't want to reveal the contents of the conversation, either. She also reflected that, however wise Kaz's advice might be, that Emi would come back when she was ready, she wouldn't give up her search for her sister. Over the following days she tried to work out how to turn her tale into an ongoing drama that would continue to interest her viewers. She wondered about biography, whether she should go for the highly personal and tell a tale of a twin growing up and losing her way. But maybe that was too close to the bone. She suggested this approach to Will. He looked wary.

'I think we should be careful we don't just become the new reality TV show,' he said.

'You know, we could use memorabilia, tell the story of a regular girl from birth to disappearance. It might be interesting,' she urged.

'What, start with the fact that being born second made her feel like the shadow of her identical twin? Are you sure that's what you want to reveal? After all, that, to Emi, would no doubt be what she would call "the start",' he retorted.

'Why ever would she say that?' Polly asked, genuinely confused.

Will seemed uncomfortable, put on the spot. 'Because it was how she felt,' he replied.

'But she came first, you do know that, don't you?'

By his expression, Polly knew that he didn't – that for some reason Emi had lied. She'd heard the story of their birth so many times it had almost taken on fictional qualities, but she also knew that the facts were accurate.

'Mum went into labour, four weeks early, and Emi was born first, after a protracted and difficult birth,' she told him, urgently. It was suddenly essential that he understood. 'She weighed only four and a half pounds but could breathe unaided. I got stuck in the birth canal, and Mum was rushed into theatre for a Caesarean to extract me – very clearly the second twin. I was put in an incubator and I couldn't breathe on my own for weeks. I was in hospital for two months, while Emi went straight home. Mum cared for her alone – I was looked after by the nurses – and Dad. You know, I wasn't even breastfed. Emi got all that maternal sustenance to herself – she was hardly deprived.'

As she'd been talking Will's expression had shifted from the cynical to the acutely interested. 'And Sarah, how much time did she spend with you at the hospital?' he enquired.

Polly's eyes clouded. Of course she didn't remember the details, but later, much later, when her mother was dying, she recalled having had a frank conversation with Carol, at her mother's bedside. Polly had said that she felt an emotional distance from Sarah, a lack of instinctive intimacy. Carol had been silent for a while. Then she had told Polly how Sarah had been knocked out by the pregnancy and by the birth of her daughters. She had explained that after the birth Sarah had been listless, that Polly had been in hospital for weeks and Emi had been brought home. Sarah had breastfed her, but Polly recalled

Carol adding that she had shown little affection towards Emi, no real interest or emotional attachment. Peter, on the other hand, had fallen head over heels in love with Polly and had spent every possible hour with her at the hospital. When he brought her home, he fed her himself, with milk – Carol had paused, smiling affectionately at the memory – enriched with honey and rice.

Polly repeated these details to Will now, adding that apparently she had been a hungry baby and had demanded double portions. She had eaten and slept well from the moment she had worked out how to breathe, so long as there was music playing and a nightlight was left on. She had needed less attention than Emi and Sarah had become increasingly depressed as Emi struggled to put on weight, or to learn to settle. A dependency quickly formed between Emi and Sarah, but Carol had said that it wasn't necessarily a healthy one for Emi.

Polly remembered now that she had wanted to ask Carol more, that she had sensed she had further stories to tell, but at that moment Sarah had stirred in her bed and their attention had shifted to her needs. Three years had since passed. Perhaps it was time to carry on the conversation. Carol was the only person left who had known Emi and Polly since their infancy, she had been a loyal friend, almost like an aunt to the girls. She'd helped Sarah to move out of the family home when the separation from Peter had finally happened – along with Will and Emi – she remembered, a touch guiltily. Polly herself had kept away, had found the whole separation too upsetting to confront. Carol had been devastated by the news of Emi's disappearance and still called regularly.

'I need to call Carol,' she told Will.

'Why?'

'She understood how it was, but there was something she nearly said, when Mum was dying, about me, about my relationship with her, but in the end we didn't get to it.'

She reached for the phone now and, without hesitating, called the number from memory.

'Are you sure?' Will asked, as the phone began to ring. 'You're turfing up the past, it's not always helpful.'

Polly shook her head, and as soon as Carol heard Polly's voice she urged her to come over, as soon as she could. 'We'll talk,' she promised.

Polly hadn't been back to Alma Place for years, and as she knocked on Carol's door the following morning she tried to prevent her eyes wandering to the next porch along, to their own old childhood home. It was impossible to believe that, of the four of them, she might be the only one still standing. Their neighbour's house felt like a museum piece to her now, and going there was like stepping back in time. Nothing inside, apart from Carol, seemed to have changed. As Polly looked at the woman on the threshold, however, she saw the lines around her eyes that marked the passing of the years that her mother had not had – and for a moment could see how Sarah would look now, if only she had survived.

She hesitated before following her hostess through the fading grandeur of her wide hallway and on into the sitting-room, filled with clunking colonial furniture that she knew Carol had inherited from her diplomat father. It was sad, she thought, that she'd never met anyone new to share it all with. She'd lost her husband very young; he'd been a pilot in the RAF, it had been an accident. She had never remarried, was a staunch Catholic. She had almost 'adopted' Sarah and the twins as her good cause. What had been in it for her? What was her payback? She could have been pretty, Polly realized suddenly.

They sat together and Polly explained falteringly the reason for her visit. Carol seemed nervous as she began to pick up the threads of a conversation the two of them had begun more than three years earlier. Her brow knitted as she crossed and uncrossed her small, blue-veined hands. But then she looked up, determination tightening the pupils of her pale green eyes, and fixed them on Polly sternly.

'When the two of you were eighteen months old your mother got very ill. She had a nervous breakdown. She tried . . . It was so long ago, I wonder what the point is now. Perhaps your father should have told you before.'

Polly moved to sit down next to her and took one of the older woman's hands in her own. It was cold, and the skin felt polished and tight around her knuckles. Carol turned and put her other hand on top.

'And then later it happened again. She fell apart. You were ten; it was in the night. Jeanne appeared at my door, in a panic. She said your mother was unconscious. She had been prescribed sleeping pills. I'm afraid she had swallowed the lot. She was lying on the floor in the bedroom in a long white nightdress and you and Emi were fast asleep, doors closed.'

As Polly listened she felt a growing dread. The story shocked her, but it seemed remote, almost like fiction, something of which she had no personal recall. But there was an element to it that carried a ghastly, present resonance. She couldn't help but think about the pill she had found among the bedclothes when she had gone searching for Emi on the night she had disappeared.

'It took a massive toll on your father and, inevitably, on the relationship between the two of them,' Carol continued. 'He tried, but there was no love reciprocated. It was as if Sarah had lost the knack. In the end the inevitable consequence was their divorce. It wasn't Sarah's fault, and it wasn't your father's either. He was so like you, Polly, a kind, loving man. They just couldn't work it out.'

Polly observed her curiously. Carol had been Sarah's ally – hadn't she? She didn't know why, but she didn't like the way Carol was talking about her father. It felt too knowing. She thought back to the funeral; how Carol had taken Sarah's place. It had almost suited her; she had nothing else, after all. Polly had always thought that Peter had rather despised Carol and yet she was speaking of him now with unbridled affection. It was peculiar.

'But Sarah seemed so much happier afterwards, when they were apart. She called the years with Dad her misery years.' Polly reasoned, slowly. 'If it was depression, how come breaking up with him eradicated it?'

Carol shook her head authoritatively and squeezed Polly's hands. A warmth was spreading between their fingers that almost felt like trust.

'It wasn't just the separation that helped her. Don't you remember? She'd been getting better for years, was happier, with her studying, everything. I think taking lithium was the trigger. It took time, but it was like a huge weight lifting from your mother's shoulders. She felt balanced, happier, more at ease with herself and the world. Just look around Blenheim Crescent and you can feel it, see it. And then, of course, she met Louis . . .'

'Louis?'

Carol hesitated, as if wondering whether she was going too far.

'She had a relationship towards the end, with a decent, loving man. He was very gentle with Sarah, very kind. He helped her work out what triggered her mood swings; he helped her, I suppose you would say, "manage them" better. He taught her not to be afraid of large spaces, for example. They used to walk his dog around Kensington Gardens. And then she stopped taking the pills.'

'What happened between them?'

Polly wanted to know and yet felt uneasy, as if she was invading her mother's private affairs, her adult life, a place naturally barred from the children, whatever their age.

'She kept him to herself.' Carol smiled. 'It was a very private affair; he was still there, you know, to the last. Do you remember when we went to Rome? That was after Louis had entered her life. I can't tell you, Polly, it was as if she had regained everything that the depression had looted from her for all those years – she was all light and music, laughter and joy – in fact, I remember thinking how like you she suddenly seemed – so much fun and *joie de vivre*. We giggled like teenagers all weekend, at everything, the coins in the Trevi fountain, the flirtatious waiter at the restaurant. She was so alive, Polly, just as she had been before you were born. It was wonderful.'

Polly couldn't speak. She felt overwhelmed with sadness,

happiness and, most of all, loss. She was pleased to think of Sarah with a lover, of her becoming free of her dark spirits, too. She wished she'd got to know her again, better, but she'd been too self-absorbed, too wrapped up in her own burgeoning career at the time to be interested. She couldn't, however, agree with Carol's sense that Blenheim Crescent was a physical manifestation of her mother's late change of heart.

'To me it felt as if the residual vapours of Mum's depression followed her in through the door of that flat, and saturated everything,' she confided sadly. 'Most significantly, transferring its powers to Emi once Mum's spirit had moved on.'

To her surprise, when she got back home Will was waiting for her.

'I thought you might need me,' he said.

Polly threw caution to the winds, moved into his arms and closed her eyes. She could feel his heart beating fast against her shirt and then she could feel her own, matching its rhythm, coming into line.

'Did you see it in Emi, the same malaise that Mum always had?' she asked him.

'Of course, but I never saw it as a depressive quality, more a subtlety of nature with Emi – that is, until Sarah died. It seems to me that it was then that she became more prone to mood swings, to high highs and low lows. In many ways she was much more fun, more appealing that way. It was as if our relationship moved up, or was it down a gear? I don't know.'

'I can feel it now, like a wall of water, pushing me there,

to the other side of myself, the side where Emi and Sarah found it easier to stray. The side, maybe, where you existed for Emi – and now, perhaps, are starting to exist for me.'

'Shh,' Will admonished. 'Emi could be happy, you know, in a quiet way, but she lacked your natural exuberance. Don't let that go because of this, Polly. It's what makes you beautiful.'

'It's weird, the way that Carol talks about them, with such authority, with such apparent knowing. I can't really explain it, but it's as if she was in love with them both.'

'Everyone needs to feel loved,' Will whispered.

Polly didn't want to spoil this moment between them. It felt wrong, stolen, but she was too tired, too needing of Will, to pull away. Carol's needs, her own, Will's; they were all so complicated, she thought, so bound up with Sarah, with Emi, with Peter. They were all part of the same ever-turning wheel; a wheel that right now was heading downhill, gathering speed, out of control.

22

For their thirteenth birthdays Sarah and Peter give Emi and Polly fifty pounds each. It's quite a significant sum of money and they sit around the breakfast table discussing options.

'It's about responsibility,' Peter explains. 'Now you are teenagers' – at this the girls catch one another's eyes furtively; Peter determines to retain a serious air and ignores the look – 'you must start making your own decisions about your finances. See this not as a test, but an opportunity.'

Sarah sits and watches quietly from her side of the breakfast table, thinking that Peter sounds as if he is conducting a business negotiation, that he is foreign to her, someone from the outside. However, she also has to pinch herself that these two beautiful, apparently identical beings are the children she gave birth to. They are already becoming young women, with thick, dark, lustrous hair, like hers, she supposes, and clear, pale skin; Peter's bright blue eyes. She glances between them. It is extraordinary to her how two such perfect, monozygotic twins can behave so differently, in every way. At this moment Polly is looking gleeful, as if she's just been given a get-out-of-jail-free card, and is flicking her five ten-pound notes through her fingers in an excessive display of excitement. Conversely, Emi is eyeing her stash thoughtfully. It lies on the table before her and she hasn't touched it yet. Instead she's chewing her bottom lip in quiet contemplation.

'I know what I want,' says Polly, definitively, 'at least with ten pounds of it.'

Peter laughs heartily and puts his arm around Polly's shoulders. 'Well, then, perhaps you could lend me the rest – I've got my eye on a horse in the three-fifteen.'

Soon after breakfast Emi and Polly slope up to their bedrooms. Peter and Sarah hear a giggle, then one door opens and another one shuts.

'There must be a summit meeting going on,' says Peter, and Sarah smiles as she clears the plates. Today everything feels different – normal – as if they are just another ordinary family enjoying the start of their shared weekend.

When they reappear the twins announce that they want to go to Oxford Street – but not together. Emi will go with her friend Helen, and Polly plans to take her trip with Hera's daughter, Marie. Peter and Sarah send silent messages between their eyes, then Sarah nods in slow agreement.

'You are to stick together, are not to talk to strangers and you must be home by five,' officiates Peter.

Once they're gone, Sarah and Peter sit quietly in the sitting-room reading and Sarah feels a certain contentment, as if they might, at last, be turning a corner. It's three years since her breakdown, since she took the sleeping pills, and these days she wonders what on earth possessed her to do such a thing. Her mother's death had come as a shock, both to her and to her now-ailing father, but to consider suicide? It was impossible to imagine. She can't put herself back into those shoes, rather fears them from a distance, like invisible shackles, a silent threat existing just beyond her reach. She has new drugs that make her less woozy, and she doesn't feel nearly so erratic as she has in the past. This afternoon she takes the opportunity of the girls' absence to present her idea to Peter, of them all taking a holiday together, as a family.

'Perhaps we could go somewhere abroad,' she ventures, her confidence growing with every word. 'To a Greek island, or a villa in Majorca? I feel as if I might be able to manage a flight.'

The merest hint of a shadow crosses Peter's brow, then he smiles and reaches forward to take the brochures from her proffered hand. She watches her husband sitting calmly, flicking through the pages now, but that briefest moment of hesitation has forced a sudden spiralling of her mood. Who is she – are they – trying to fool? Peter's naturally a kind man, has never tried to make her feel guilty for her acute lows, but she knows, deep down, that he has never managed, or even actively tried, to engage with her problems either, always preferring to keep his distance rather than confront her mental instability, to try to put sticking plasters over the wounds rather than attempt to deal with the underlying issues. And although he's here now, sitting opposite her, she thinks, apparently enjoying a normal Saturday afternoon in the company of his family, she suddenly knows, clearly and irrevocably, that he does not love her, that at best he suffers her, and only intermittently at that, for the sake of the twins. If she is honest, she knows that the way he has coped with the situation is by making another separate, private life for himself, somewhere else. She's never felt the right to challenge Peter as to his whereabouts when he goes away, has always felt his absences were essentially of her making, and is fairly clear – and accepting – that her husband must have had affairs. Until now she hasn't blamed him, has only blamed herself. But as she sits there, watching him, she wonders if he has not, after all, been utterly selfish really, managing to create a world where he can justify both having his cake and eating it. She feels a well of loneliness swirl inside her. She's still only thirty-six years old. Maybe there could be another future for them both, apart? Peter glances up at her from his brochure, conscious of her quiet scrutiny.

'What?' he asks, smiling a touch teasingly.

He evidently feels on safe ground, she thinks, and it's suddenly on the tip of her tongue to ask Peter who he is in love with. She doesn't know where this certitude has come from. But instinctively she can tell that her summation is correct, that there is a new woman, and she is something far more to Peter than any of the others have been.

But at that moment the door opens; it's Polly, back first. She looks bright-eyed and bushy-tailed, charges up to her room and slams her door shut. They both laugh. The moment for enquiry is gone. Minutes later Emi appears. For once she seems equally flushed by the excitement of the day and matches her sister's exuberance with a similar charge up to her bedroom to try on her purchases. It's only a moment later that they both hear the shriek.

'Bitch!'

The expletive is immediately followed by the sound of a scuffle and then an almighty crash from above. To Sarah's amazement, it's not Polly's voice but Emi's that has just filtered to the sitting-room. Both parents leap to their feet and run to the foot of the stairs. The girls are lying in a tangled heap on the landing above them. Polly is on top of Emi and she's got her pinned to the floor. Peter takes the stairs two at a time and wrenches them apart. Tears stain Emi's juvenile, mascara'd eyes, dripping down her cheeks, and tiny bubbles of blood are surfacing from a long scratch mark under her right eye. Polly is flushed red and daggers spark in her eyes.

'She must have heard me,' Emi gasps between sobs. 'I told Helen, and she just had to go and get the same.'

Peter stands back and he can't help but laugh. His two daughters are standing there, livid, each wearing exactly the same new emerald green dress. Sarah rushes up the stairs and without thinking puts her arms around Emi's shuddering shoulders. It is a mistake.

'You always take her side,' explodes Polly. 'I didn't know – we both saw it, in *Just Seventeen*. It's just coincidence, but Emi has to turn it into one of her bloody "poor old me" dramas.'

Before either parent can respond, she turns and stomps into her room, slamming the door.

There's silence on the stairs. It is the first time the twins have had such a physically vicious falling-out. They've always been protective of one another, until now, and the differences between them, her bright-eyed Polly and ethereal Emi, have always seemed to balance each other out. To date they've shared everything, toys, books, friends. But Sarah knows that this is the start of adolescence, in all its fragility, passion and searching for identity, and all the confusions it brings naturally with it are here compacted by their duality. She recognizes that this will not be the first or last time her daughters will fight one another for the centre ground.

Peter pats Emi's arm but Emi shrugs him off, then turns and flees to her own room, second door slamming. Peter raises his eyes at Sarah, helplessly.

'They're going to have to go through this,' she says.

He nods and begins to make his way back down the stairs.

As Sarah follows Peter, she knows that this is not their time for making significant decisions.

'Perhaps Crete would be a good choice,' she says brightly. 'Let's have another look at those brochures.'

Three years pass, calmly. Peter is like clockwork, leaving home every Tuesday morning, arriving back on Friday evening. Sometimes he is in the UK office in Newcastle, at others in the international HQ in Paris, depending on the nature of the work. It's convenient for them both; there is little tension, and no intimacy. The girls are growing fast, and seem to spend more and more time behind their own closed doors, separate, uncommunicative. They continue to do well at school and share the same group of friends, however, which Sarah finds reassuring; and although Emi is often the quieter of the two, she seems to command as much loyalty as her twin among their crowd. As Polly's interest in music blossoms, Emi becomes more studious. Their interest in their appearance continues to grow, and now the girls have completely different haircuts; Emi's is longer than Polly's – and, in their own words, they 'wouldn't be seen dead' wearing the same clothes. But they are still, essentially, dependent upon each other for reassurance, for their confidence with the outside world. They always check with one another that they 'look OK' before they leave the house, that they haven't made a mistake, that their juvenile attempt at applying lipstick is straight, that their eyeshadow is not too dark. As she watches her fiery Polly and ethereal Emi Sarah finds it hard not to smile; in some respects they are still so similar, despite themselves.

Of course this affected equilibrium can't last; it's as if the family has been anaesthetized, or put under a soporific spell. The eventual implosion begins with a bottle of champagne. It is spring. Emi and Polly have celebrated their sixteenth birthdays and have both been studying hard for their impending GCSE exams. Peter's about to go on a long-planned, two-week business trip to America. The day before he leaves, and to Sarah's great surprise, he comes home early from the office brandishing a bottle of Mumm.

'I want to toast our lovely daughters, my wonderful family,' he exclaims.

Peter's face is slightly flushed and he's speaking just a touch too loudly. His behaviour is out of character. It makes her nervous. She wonders if he's already been drinking as he goes to the kitchen with the girls, who are yelping with delight. Then she hears the cork popping.

When he returns from his trip Peter looks healthy, happy. Sarah asks few questions, welcomes him back with the twins by suggesting that they all go into Chinatown for a meal. She can see that Polly is positively delighted to see Peter and her face glows with the thrill of his presence. He is equally effusive, telling the twins jokes about President Clinton and his interns as he unloads gifts he's bought – perfume, jewellery – with, Sarah surmises, uncharacteristic, female acumen. By contrast, Emi seems more under-whelmed by her father's reappearance, is pale-faced and keeps her arm linked through her mother's as they wander down Shaftesbury Avenue, then on into the heart of Chinatown. Sarah understands Emi. She finds the chop-ping and changing in their lives difficult, from the three of them to the four and back again, endlessly. It doesn't suit her temperament, makes her feel less sure. Polly hates it, too, but for different reasons. When Peter is away she feels left on the outside. Sarah wonders who sat beside Peter on the aeroplane, whether or not they checked into the hotel as a married couple, in her or their name. Before he'd left on this trip he'd made another false promise, about their shared future, and yet here they are again. She wonders, but she also knows that frankly she doesn't care. Finally she's beginning to feel really very well. There's also been talk of 'cognitive therapy', which they say may be of some help. She's considering it, as an alternative; she's truly sick of taking pills to keep her straight. Sometimes she thinks she can feel them rattling through her veins. In her mind

Sarah's started planning for her own future, a big open page, blank but, for the first time in years, ready to be filled – when the time is right for the girls. She hasn't told Peter but she's considering going back to college: as her girls prepare for their first external exams; it seems ironic, at her age. She shares the idea with Carol and she detects a moment's doubt cross her friend's brow, a slight frown.

'I think you ought to consider it very carefully before committing to a serious course,' Carol warns, averting her gaze, fingering the tablecloth as she talks. 'The drugs have done wonders, but it would be a shame to spoil it now, by putting yourself under too much pressure.'

Sarah feels knocked back for a moment, but also a slight stirring of distrust at her friend's words; what are her motivations for wanting Sarah to stay 'down'?

When they get home, Peter retires to his office to work and Sarah sees the girls off to bed. Their exams are looming, they need to get their sleep. Then she goes to her bedroom. She opens the door, then stops and looks towards the bed, holding on to the door handle to steady herself. She feels her body swaying slightly. In her mind's eye Sarah sees a hundred snapshots: Peter bringing Polly home from hospital in her Moses basket, his blue eyes shining with pride; Peter laughing in the garden while their infants turn wonky cartwheels round and round him on the grass, giggling madly; Peter serious in his suit, briefcase in hand, looking down wearily at his wife lying incapacitated in their bed; Peter's absent eyes as he sits at the breakfast table telling her he's off to Newcastle, or America, on yet another business trip. And then Peter, only a fortnight ago, clutching champagne, urging her to try again, suggesting they focus on getting better together. She had believed . . . something – quite what she can't remember now. Because before her on the bed is the reality: her husband's suit jacket, abandoned only minutes earlier, and falling tantalizingly from the inside pocket a gold and amber necklace, half in, half out. It is not wrapped, it is not a gift, it is not intended for Sarah. It is a piece of jewellery discarded, then forgotten, in a hotel room, picked up by the lover who left the scene second, ready to be given back at the next rendezvous. Half in, half out. The phrase sticks. Sarah knows that this is the state of her marriage. Her dizziness is subsiding, and a stone-cold sensation is growing inside her, a sensation of stark disappointment, coupled with a new feeling – of injustice. He had not needed to raise the issue, to make a new commitment to anything, he hadn't for years and it wasn't expected. And yet she had half believed he meant it, had willed herself to. Which makes this turn-around all the more despicable. It's like a double deceit. At least before there had been an unspoken understanding between them that their marriage was nothing more than a smokescreen, essential for now, for the children's security, but his 'change of heart' had suggested other possibilities to Sarah that, to her amazement, she had been willing to consider – no, actively to embrace – even after all.

She's been so self-absorbed that she does not hear Peter ascending the stairs until he's standing behind her.

'Are you OK?' he breathes kindly, close to her now.

Sarah finds an unfamiliar energy rising within her and

she swings around to confront her husband face-on. He's looking bewildered and concerned and she wants to laugh at the sheer audacity of it. Instead she finds herself physically repelled, backing away from him, as he follows her into their room. Approaching the bed, she turns and scoops the necklace up and out of the pocket. It is a fragile, beautiful, sophisticated piece, a hundred gold strands plaited around at least a dozen amber stones; a rare thing of great beauty. There's something familiar about it – perhaps nothing more than the emotion it conjures.

'How could you?' she whispers, her voice hoarse.

Peter continues to look confused. He moves forward towards Sarah, holds out his hand to take the object. She spreads her fingers wide and stretches them towards him, but as Peter takes the necklace she finds her hand snatching shut. In Peter's hand is now one half, in hers the other.

'Where did you get it?' Peter asks, shaking his head in bewilderment.

For the first time in her marriage, Sarah's mirth knows no bound. Her characteristic discretion evaporates in the emotion of the moment and she finds herself screaming at Peter. She can't remember her words, or his in return, but what starts as a row over a necklace ends in Peter telling her that he really had hoped things could change, get better, but that this proves him utterly wrong. Now he's turned and left the room. She hears the sound of him descending the staircase, collecting his keys and his coat, then the front door closing gently behind him. Once he's gone Sarah sits down on the bed. Her wrath spent, she feels numb, her head filled with a white vacuum, and then she begins to cry; a river of salty tears. Hearing something move, a sound, she glances up to see the wide-eyed, pale faces of her two daughters peering anxiously at her from behind the door.

'I'm so sorry,' she says, as they move forward, apparently in unison, and join her on the bed. Emi puts her arm around her mother as Polly leans down and picks up the two parts of the now broken necklace from the floor.

23

For the past few days Lotta's had a cold that she seems incapable of shaking off and her pale skin has taken on an almost grey pallor. Really she should have had time off school, but Stephanie's been working on a paper for presentation in Chicago in two weeks' time, the last week of March, and has actively ignored the symptoms. When I got to school Lotta was waiting for me at the door. Her mother had dressed her in a pair of designer pink woollen trousers, a green angora wool jumper and an almost floor-length blue tweed coat. She was clutching her Pippi doll very tightly to her. Together they looked like tragic characters out of some kids' cartoon. I immediately realized something was wrong. The only hard and fast school rule is that the children are not allowed to bring their home toys into school.

As we wandered homeward I casually enquired why she had the doll.

'Johanna's allowed me to because Pippi's a magic doll who chases bad dreams away,' she informed me, with a sideways glance.

'I didn't know you were having bad dreams,' I said.

'It's only at Mama's,' she answered.

I was taken aback, but didn't push her to explain. I'm learning that often it's better to allow Lotta time to cogitate on her thoughts; generally she elucidates of her own accord, when she's ready. Instead I suggested a trip to Café String – fast becoming our usual haunt – for a hot chocolate and a cookie. To my relief she shrieked with delight at the idea, allowing Pippi to fall to her side, her woes forgotten.

'I saw someone just like you,' our usual bearded waiter exclaimed, as he approached the table, with more than a degree too much enthusiasm. 'An English girl, on the TV, when I was surfing channels after work last night. She's gone missing. Her sister's looking for her. It was so weird, you look so like her.'

Lotta was under the table, 'putting Pippi to bed', and, to my relief, was too busy chattering away to the rag doll to hear the waiter's words. I thought fast. Café String had become my sanctuary, the place I came to read Kalle's increasingly interesting notes that he had taken to passing to me on a weekly basis. And this waiter has been one of the key attractions; he's made me feel welcome, seems unperturbed when I sit for hours over a coffee, scrutinizing the papers before me. I didn't want to give up the café, but also I didn't want to confess to the truth. Right now he was holding my stare and I was finding it hard to reply.

'What's your name?' I ventured.

'Frank,' he said, and I almost laughed.

'What?' he smiled.

'It suits your disposition,' I said.

'I like your hair better this way,' he replied, standing back and appraising me 'frankly', thumbs in the belt-holds of his sloppy jeans.

I thought for a moment. I couldn't speak, felt sick.

'Everyone has a doppelgänger,' I tried, lamely.

'But not everyone has an identical twin, Emi,' he answered slowly, intentionally emphasizing my name.

At that moment Lotta's head popped up from the other side of the table. 'When are we going to get our cookies, Emi?' she whined, exaggerating the words and groaning. 'Pippi and I are starving.'

'So she knows your real name,' he said, then leant forward, his back to Lotta, for a moment.

'*Hej*, I'm sorry. I didn't mean to frighten you, really. It's your choice, Emi, we all have to make our way. I won't tell anyone, not a soul. So long as you keep coming in for your coffee – you promise?'

I nodded. I was thrown off course and yet relieved, not only that Frank had made his own promise, but also, strangely, that someone here knew my true story. Instinctively, I found I trusted him.

'You want your regular?' he asked.

I nodded again.

'It's on the house,' he said with a grin, turning lazily and wandering back towards the bar.

I felt in a mild panic for the rest of the day. The last thing I needed was to be the subject of a missing-person hunt. I should have known that Polly would turn my disappearance into a media fiasco – surely in her heart of hearts she must know why I've left the scene. What should I do? I want to talk to Kalle about it – and my anxieties regarding Lotta, too, but since our trip to see Lars he's become increasingly distant. Just as Stephanie predicted, he seems lost inside his own world. Meanwhile I'm getting richer by the week. Stephanie has compensated me admirably for all the extra hours I've been caring for Lotta, but I don't care about the money. I'm pleased to look after her. It's a distraction and is becoming an excuse for not working out what I'm going to do next with my life. I need to find a way to get back home before home comes to me, but I don't want to go. I don't want to leave Kalle and Lotta, Lars or the archipelago, behind. Lotta is alive, she makes me feel awake, makes me want to *be*, not to analyse. And I feel an affinity with her too – as if she's also lost out, needs rescuing. I'm worried, for example, that she's too accustomed to playing alone, that she seems to feel little need for the company of other children. She has a curious habit of talking about children as 'they' rather than 'we' and rarely mentions group activity at school. She generally calls the children to whom she refers by their whole name, which I find quite strange; for example, 'Carolina Petersson said she's going ice skating,' or 'Erik Hansen was naughty.' And I'm concerned by her comment about nightmares – maybe it's just a kid's intelligent method of getting her own way, to be allowed to take Pippi to school, but I'm not so sure.

Tomorrow we've been invited to a tea party at the school. Predictably neither Kalle nor Stephanie can take the time off work, so I've elected to go. Maybe it will be a chance for me to ask Johanna, 'off the record', about

Lotta's anxieties – meantime I'm afraid that it will be an opportunity for some other stranger to recognize me as that missing London girl.

When I arrived at the party, women were putting open salmon sandwiches and pretty little pink, yellow and white fairy cakes on trellis tables in the early spring sunshine. I felt self-conscious there – the only English person, the only non-parent or teacher, too. I loitered by the climbing frame, waiting for Lotta to appear. More and more mothers were arriving until the playground was full of chattering, pale-haired women and excited toddlers weaving in and out of their legs. I saw Johanna at the doorway, carrying a tray of cakes.

'Have you seen Lotta?' I asked, and she looked around curiously.

'I'll see if she's inside,' I said, and moved past her into the labyrinth of now-empty rooms.

I was just beginning to feel concerned by her apparent absence when I heard a stifled sob emanating from the Wendy house in the corner of the final playroom. I approached gingerly and peered through the window. Sure enough, Lotta was crouching in the corner, arms wrapped tightly around Pippi. She was wearing a pretty new white dress printed with huge blooming purple pansies and her hair was braided with deep purple ribbons.

'*Hej*, Lotta, come on,' I whispered.

The little girl glanced up, saw me and shook her head, sobbing some more. I opened the door and crawled inside. It smelt of plastic and chalk dust in the little room, and it was stiflingly hot. However, I crouched down next to her

222

and waited for a moment. Eventually she shuffled along and put her head against my chest.

'What happened?' I asked.

'Everyone else's mummy's come,' she said, chokingly. 'And they don't want to play with me.'

For a moment I felt angry with Stephanie for abandoning her child, but then I thought again. Essentially I know that she's dedicated to Lotta, that she adores her, and any blame I might wish to lay at her door was more for the evident impact her separation had had on Kalle than on their child. It was too easy, I knew, to criticize from the outside. No family was ever going to be perfect. My mother, I suddenly thought, had always been there, but that hadn't necessarily been a good thing either. Nevertheless, I felt Lotta's loneliness like an ache in my own heart. At least I have Polly, I thought, startled at my momentary sense of good fortune. Or did I? Had I completely destroyed our trust? Or had she? And had it already become too late ever to go back?

'Come on,' I told her. 'We can do this together.'

Lotta had tears trapped like tiny glistening pearls between her eyelashes and I took a tissue from my bag and wiped them away. Her face was hot and flushed and I stroked her cheeks with a single finger.

'Promise you won't leave me?' she said, suddenly, earnestly.

I smiled weakly but couldn't reply.

The party was in full swing when we got outside and the sunshine seemed even brighter. Everyone was holding hands in a circle, moving round and round, singing Swedish nursery rhymes. Suddenly enthusiastic, Lotta led me into the ring and the next half an hour passed in a rhythmic daze.

Afterwards I managed to find Johanna.

'Where was she?' she asked.

I glanced around. Finally Lotta had left my side and was climbing up the slide.

'Hiding in the Wendy house,' I admitted. 'She was crying. She wanted her mother.'

'She's very lucky to have you – she adores you,' Johanna answered quickly.

'I wasn't offended,' I replied. 'I know I can't replace her mother and that Stephanie loves her – but I do worry that she doesn't seem to have any friends.'

'She's a solitary child, it's true,' Johanna agreed. 'Sometimes I worry for her, but all kids are different and since you've been here I've noticed she's a lot calmer. We all need to take just one day at a time, don't you think?'

I felt a tugging at my sleeve and looked down to see Lotta there again.

'Can we go home now, please?' she asked, plainly.

I looked over to the slide to see three or four other children now climbing up and down it, just as Lotta had been, moments before. It seemed that their arrival had precipitated her desire to depart. I felt her isolation from them as if it were my own.

'Come on,' I said, reassuringly. 'Let's get your coat.'

After Kalle left for work this morning I noticed that he'd left his jacket on the kitchen chair. For the first time since I came here, I found myself drawn up the stairs to put it away. As I entered his bedroom I was struck by its bright simplicity; a double bed with two skylights above the pillows throwing Stockholm's sky in reflection on to the plain, white cotton sheets, a lovely, old-fashioned azure blue armchair in one corner, a small door leading to a shower room, and then, off to the right, another open door, leading to Kalle's office. I ventured inside to find a small, ascetic room, containing a desk with a laptop computer on it and bookshelves above. There was a small round window above the desk, too, like a porthole, and I leant forward to glance out. It was even higher up there than in the rotunda, with even more breathtaking views out across the city and beyond.

I glanced across the desk and saw a photograph propped up in front of a pile of books. It was of Lotta and me at Skansen, looking through the railings at the moose. I remember Kalle taking it, just after Christmas, when I'd only been here for a couple of weeks. I looked at ease, open and – dare I even think it – really happy. In fact, I realized, I looked just like Polly. The thought panicked me and I felt guilty for being up there. I moved swiftly now from Kalle's rooms, back down the curving staircase, and grabbed my coat and bag. It was time to be outside again, in the sudden spring weather, time to embrace the fresh air and the sunshine.

Last night Kalle came home with some further studies on the subject of twins. I went to Café String and spent the morning reading them. One, by Elizabeth Spitz, a researcher at the Université René Descartes in Paris, suggests '*that the number of membranes identical foetuses share*

225

depends on when exactly their single egg split into two embryos. If this divisional split occurred early (within four days after fertilization), then each twin grew to birth in its own little world. Each developed its own chorion, the outermost membrane, and its own amnion, the inner membrane that contains the amniotic fluid in which the foetus floats. If the cell division happened later (four to eight days after fertilization), each twin got its own amnion but shared a chorion. If the division happened later still (eight to ten days after conception), the two foetuses shared both chorion and amnion.'

The research fascinates me, and makes me wonder so much about Polly and me. Our personalities are made up of a number of factors: genetic, chemical, physical and environmental. The more I read, the more dissimilar we seem to be becoming, after all.

I think that at last I might be beginning to accept that Polly and I are two completely independent human beings, with different starts, even from the womb. Since birth our faces have caught different angles of the sun, and our experiences, although similar, have never been the same. Perhaps the fact that we have both loved Will is as much coincidence as fate. It makes it easier to digest, perhaps to accept.

I've spent my life trying to understand why I'm not like Polly, assuming that I should be and, if I'm completely honest, assuming that she must, deep down, think the same way as I do. But I'm beginning to see that I'm not like her, and she's not like me; that, essentially, I'm just like myself and nobody else. My mother keeps reappearing in my thoughts, however. I'm beginning to understand that she has had a greater impact on who I am than I have ever previously allowed myself to recognize. I have always compared myself with Polly but now I am beginning to see what Will always joked about – even in that photograph that he took of her and me – how much I look, and feel, far more like Sarah than my own twin. And when I think of Peter I also know that Polly and he, essentially and implicitly, were also the same. I keep thinking about him, about the way his absences used to make me feel, and how differently Polly reacted to them, too. If I'm honest, as a teenager, I used to dread his presence. By contrast, when he was away, I know that Polly hankered after him, would become melancholic and restless until he returned. I think it was because I sensed my mother's dread of him. She was my mood thermometer, and never Polly's. I fear I have also inherited the innate gloom that she used to feel – it often falls over me in waves. I know that Mum used to take anti-depressants, but in the end they only seemed to keep her moods at bay, they never eradicated them. She was either desperately low or oddly, plasticly euphoric, slightly wired. That is, until she left Dad. In fact there was a time in her forties when I really thought something in her had shifted. But that was nothing to do with drugs, it was to do with something inside her, in her relationships, her situation. She never told me if she had met someone, found someone to love, but I sensed her loneliness drifting away, effortlessly, like a summer breeze.

At her funeral there was a man. He stood quietly at the back of the church. When I acknowledged him he told me his name was Louis, but made no attempt to explain his connection. He had a kind, earnest face and I could see that my mother's death had affected him deeply. I said nothing then, but I knew that in her dying she had whispered his name.

When Kalle and I are together in the evenings, sitting quietly after supper in the rotunda, watching the city twinkling below us, or reading, or talking, always of small things, I feel my spirit ease, and I know that if I can be here, always, with him, that my own melancholy will in time begin to evaporate. He continues to treat me with the utmost gentleness, never prying into my past, never stepping too close. I know it's what I asked for, but now I'm beginning to feel undermined by my own lack of disclosure. Without knowledge of my history, I worry that for us there can't be a future. Kalle's lack of information about my world seems to negate my own enquiry into his. So we're coexisting in a semi-formal yet oddly intimate way. It's like a choreographed dance, both of us implicitly knowing the precise distance that we should keep, close yet not touching, knowing yet constantly in the dark.

Now I'm aware that they're actively looking for me, I sense it won't be long before my past catches hold of my coat-tails, just as Kalle warned me it would, all those months ago in that little Italian café. I should talk to him about my fears, but in truth I still can't bear for Kalle to know me as half of her.

24

The loft at Blenheim Crescent was a small, cramped, dark space above the hallway. It took a stepladder borrowed from Antonio, the porter, for Polly to get up inside. He stood below, whistling tunelessly between a wide gap in his teeth, watching as she clambered up. A number of tea-chests were tightly squeezed along the right side of the space. She recognized them and was clear about their contents; the flotsam and jetsam of her parents' shared life together, objects no one had wanted to use, but that neither of them had had the heart to throw away – an inscribed silver tray they'd received as a wedding present, Royal Doulton china that now seemed outmoded, a canteen of silver cutlery and the remnants of her mother's wedding trousseau. Polly had assumed that one day, when they both had family homes of their own, she and Emi would get them all down, pull straws for each item in turn, but it occurred to her, suddenly, that this moment might now never happen, perhaps there would be no reason to share, and she knew that she wouldn't want any of it, that it was all immaterial, that the most valuable mementoes of a life were those you stored within your own mind.

Along the other side of the space were more recent additions, Emi's 'stuff' from university, four neat boxes of files with her forward-arching handwriting scrawled along the spines and two faded old caramel-coloured leather suitcases. She recalled that Emi had bought them at Portobello Market, when they were about seventeen. Polly and her first boyfriend, Jake, had been with her. She could see Emi clearly now, as they arrived back outside the house in St John's Wood, her canvas satchel slung across her back, one case in each hand, the corners knocked and gnarled out of shape, the result of manhandling on someone else's transatlantic cruises, train journeys from London to Hastings for weekends by the sea. Peter and Sarah were standing there, and everyone but Emi had laughed at the cases' beaten-up state. Emi's reaction had been to scowl at each member of her family in turn as they stood around her, observing her purchases with increasingly wry smiles. 'What on earth did you get these two old dogs for?' Polly recalled her father asking Emi, before catching Polly's eye and winking.

'I love them,' Emi had interjected snipingly, glaring angrily between them, 'for what they represent – time passing, voyages to other places, the sense that they've already been somewhere else, had foreign experiences.'

Their father had laughed affectionately at Emi, his sky-blue eyes that matched theirs glinting in a ray of sunshine that suddenly passed straight through him like a bolt from the blue. 'I didn't mean to upset you, Em,' he cajoled, moving forward to put a protective arm around her, but it was already too late to make amends, too late for every-thing, and Emi had shrugged him away and flounced off up the stairs, dejected and forlorn, dragging the cases behind her as if her life depended on them.

Polly remembered how a couple of years later, when she was preparing to leave for college, Emi had spent hours in her room, door shut. It later transpired that she'd been storing all her childish things in those two leather suitcases, clearing her room so assiduously that when she left for Brighton there was very little of her left behind. It occurred to Polly as she sat in the eaves that perhaps Emi had recently done the same thing here, all over again, literally 'cleared out'. The clothes she had left behind bore little of her life in their creases and folds; unworn, they had quickly become nothing more than fabrics with no history. She recalled their mother having to rearrange the look on her face from one of absolute dejection to humble acquiescence when she'd walked in that day and seen the transformation of Emi's room, and realized what Emi had done. It was such a clean severing of the umbilical cord, so clinical and clear in its message.

By contrast Polly had taken what she thought she might need for Edinburgh and left everything else as it was, rock posters on the walls, make-up on the dressing table, books on the shelves, underwear in the drawers, to come back to in the holidays, when she knew she might well need some mollycoddling away from adult life. But both Polly and their mother understood why Emi had felt the need to clear out, knew that, like them all, she couldn't stand the house with the veneer of their family unit collapsing. A year later, Sarah was on her own and their father was in France. Snapping the locks of those old cases shut decisively, Emi had asked their mother if she could store them in the attic and Sarah had willingly agreed. Presumably she'd simply had them hoicked from the house in St John's Wood to Blenheim Crescent when she herself had finally moved on. But Polly wondered now, as she began, a touch guiltily, to tug the first one across the floor to the trapdoor, if Emi had opened them since. She lowered it down for Antonio to take. It was heavy, a dead weight. She followed the first with the second, then came back down herself and pulled the trapdoor shut.

Once she'd firmly closed and locked the door behind Antonio she sank down on the floor in the hall by the cases, eyeing them with suspicion. These were Emi's private affairs, things she'd never wanted to share with Polly, the items that marked the differences between them, the secret things of their adolescence. Polly had always envied Emi's measured management of her memories, but had never been disciplined, or needed, enough to hang on to such objects herself. Now she took a deep breath, wiped the dust from the lids of the cases and snapped the first one open. It was packed tight with an array of cardboard and decorated trinket boxes, tightly tied sheafs of handwritten letters in envelopes, and sleeves of developed photographs. She fingered the surface of the objects lightly, but none jumped at her as having a clue attached, or a useful story to tell. She clicked the other case's lid open next and pulled it back. On top a number of silk scarves were neatly folded. She remembered now that Emi had collected these old 1950s relics from Camden Market; she had liked the patterns, but had never worn them. Polly lifted them out

232

gingerly and underneath saw what she suddenly recognized she had been looking for all along. Five thick, hard-covered books were packed tightly underneath – Emi's diaries from her teens. She took out the first one and calculated backwards – Emi had written it when they were just thirteen years old. On the black cover the words 'KEEP OUT – ESPECIALLY POLLY AND MUM!!!!' were written in silver biro, in bold, childish capitals. She turned the book over. On the back Emi had doodled in the same silver pen, and had stuck little stars and red balloon stickers around her writing: 'Wham are cool. Rock-on! I hate school!!!' It was the language of early adolescence and for a moment Polly wanted to smile. She hesitated, then leant her back against the wall and with a nervous hand opened the journal.

New Year's Day
Welcome to the first day of the rest of my life!!! My new year's resolutions are:
>   *to write this diary every day – even on the most boring days (e.g. all the school ones!!!)*
>   *to be nicer to Polly (that's going to be hard)*
>   *to work harder at school (yuk)*
I think I can do the first one but the other two are going to be reeeeeeally tricky.
But first, let me introduce myself to you dear diary. My name is Emi Leto and I am thirteen and three-quarter years old.
Top Ten characters you will meet in my diary are:
>   *Mum: who can be a bit weird but who I love very much*
>   *Polly: who is my twin and a pain most of the time but who I also love (a bit, sometimes)*

Dad: who is away a lot and likes Polly better than me – but I love him anyway

Carol: Mum's best friend who sits in the kitchen nattering and drinking coffee a lot who I like a lot

MY friends:

Marie: who is a complete daredevil and sometimes thinks she is better friends with Polly but who right now is my best friend

Helen: who had a sleepover for New Year's last night (so coooooool and am I tired???!!!) who is kind of dorky but really nice, too

Jane: pretty and popular with the boys – Polly's best friend but still part of our gang

Lucy: another ace girlie in our gang

Jules: the final ace girlie in our gang

XXXO!!!!' I will always write his name in code so if Mum or Polly reads this they won't know who it is – I am in love with him and he goes to XXX????OOO school.

I think that's enough for today!! Byeeeeeee Lots of love, Emixxxx

Polly turned the page. The cases sat open, one on either side of her. She'd piled up Emi's five teenage diaries in date order on her knees. This was the first. She flicked forwards through the pages. Most of the entries were mundane, light-hearted, and often only contained a single paragraph: 'Got up, went to school, I HATE MATHS!! Got an A in English (oh wow what a thrill)' and so on; entries that reminded Polly more of how they all used to speak than of the particular details of their days. She was surprised by how little her own name appeared – weeks passed without her gaining so much as a mention. When she did, it was often so that Emi could voice a complaint, about the way Polly had treated her, or how hard-done-by Emi felt. The accusations were low-level, but even so, nearly twenty years later, Polly couldn't help but feel slightly hurt by her sister's apparently constant disdain for her twin. There seemed to be a trend emerging, one of frustration on Emi's part, at not being able to – she sat back against the wall and tried to work out what it was – keep up, she guessed. On reflection, she'd never previously considered this to be an issue. But then, perhaps, if she had been the one keeping up, there was no reason for her to have noticed Emi's struggles. At thirteen she knew one was totally self-obsessed, and unaware of the deeper emotions of others. Apart from where their parents were concerned, that is – on that front she and Emi had both been aware, perhaps too aware, of the troubles that lay ahead. Emi's way of coping with her worries had been, at least in this first diary, to vent her rage at their parents via occasional short sharp entries: *'Dad's away again and Mum's being all dark and broody – tried to talk to her, but sometimes I wonder what's the point? She's off in her own world.'* Polly tried to remember how she had coped. Whenever she had felt miserable, she had resorted to music. After an hour at the keys of the piano, or the strings of her cello, she generally felt soothed. More often than not, however, way back in 1991, it seemed Emi's focus was mainly on the standard monotony of school days: *'BORED BORED BORED – AND "XXXO!!!!" WASN'T EVEN AT THE BUS STOP'* was typical of the least descriptive entries, which filled many of the lines. Polly tried to think back to who the mystery boy filling Emi's waking and presumably sleeping hours might have been, but had a total lack of recall. What was most impressive about the diary was not what Emi had written, but how dedicated she had been to filling the pages. Every day was covered, not a single one left out. She talked of sleepovers, which Polly now recalled were the highlight of the year, and of the petty jealousies that occurred between them and the other girls in their 'gang'.

She skimmed the pages more and more quickly; there was evidently little about 1991 that was going to throw light on recent events, although that word 'character' did keep drifting through her mind. Even Kaz had said it: finding Emi was going to be easier if Polly could pinpoint why she might have left, her motivations – essentially what it was in her character that would have made her feel the need to go away. Eventually, certain there was nothing here to go on, she put the diary to one side and picked up the next but one: 1993 – the year they were fifteen, turning sixteen. Now possibly that would be a more interesting read, she thought; many things had happened during 1993, things she would never forget. But relevant? She couldn't imagine that they would hold the clue to the missing months that now informed her experience of Emi – how ironic, she considered, to go from such complete disclosure within these pages to her recent circumstance of absolutely none at all.

Polly was about to open the first page and begin to read when she noticed it was getting late. Instead, she shut the diary again and called Will. He was over at his brother's, having lunch. She told him what she was doing and that she wanted to bring the diaries home, to read through later tonight, but that she didn't want to be there with them alone. Will agreed to come over but she sensed that he found her sleuthing immoral, or at least unnecessary, and for a moment she was tempted to put the diaries in the case, to close the lid and slide them back up into their dark attic home. But something spurred her on; she needed to read about 1993. She wondered whether events that year had been the first 'crisis point' for Emi, when she had stopped knowing how to be contented, and equally when she, Polly, had perhaps discovered her own greater inner strength.

As she travelled back to Bermondsey Polly tried to see patterns in Emi's life and it occurred to her that, apart from her brief time in Brighton, until now Emi had always stayed very close to home. She'd never had the desire to travel, had married her friend from student days and stuck with a very small, local group of friends. She hadn't been brave. Polly had found it easier to meander – OK, only across the river, but in London that was like travelling to the other end of the universe. She hadn't needed to stay put and she had had the confidence to put herself on the line – both with her work and with her relationships. That was partly what made Emi's disappearance so alarming – how could someone who had practically clung on to the last remnants of a family life, even when all that was left were the bricks and mortar to hug, suddenly get up and go away, vanish into thin air? It was such an extreme act, one that she couldn't believe Emi, in a sane moment, would ever manage to undertake. It just wasn't in her nature.

*   *   *

Later Will and Polly lay fully dressed on her bed, heads propped up on a mountain of pillows, a pot of tea on the bedside table, the diaries spread out between them. The clocks had gone forward and the sun was still up, at eight. It felt as if a lid had been lifted off the city and for a moment Polly felt optimistic. With the summer might come new hope. She handed Will the volume for 1991 and she opened 1993. Will glanced over the pages quietly, and occasionally she heard him snigger.

'I love all her codes, to stop you from guessing names, even if you did read this stuff,' he murmured, 'and all this about you being so good at music and her being useless – you know, she's never got over that.'

'Really?'

'She's insanely jealous of your talent.'

'But she could've done it, too.'

'She was no good,' said Will.

'Crap,' replied Polly. 'She just didn't want to do anything I did. Have you read the stuff about clothes? About us choosing the same dress? We both went into town, I remember it as if it were yesterday. She went with Helen and I went with Marie. When we got home, we'd bought the same dress, exactly the same dress, from Miss Selfridge. She was livid. Even I knew that at the time; I didn't need to read her diary to be reminded. She thought I had been following her, had watched her buy it, then done the same, just to spite her. The truth was, we'd both seen that dress in *Just Seventeen*.'

Will raised his eyes.

'It's a magazine,' she continued. 'That very morning. It wasn't such a coincidence that we both wanted it so badly.

But somehow to Emi anything that we shared was a source of disdain. And she could always conjure a story to support her accusations. I tell you – I think one of my sister's greatest weaknesses is her over-active imagination. She's always been able to dream up a plot, a scheme, a reason that didn't previously exist for some extraordinary chain of events. Nothing in her world exists at face value.'

'And does it in yours, Polly? In any of ours?'

'There are limits,' Polly replied, 'to what one can actually read into a situation, and what one has to create to make a drama. She made the dramas, and, as you know, I like reporting on the facts.'

'And the music? What happened there?'

'When it came to piano, the fact that I did it meant that she would not. And the cello, well, she never even took a lesson. Mum brought it back from Boston – it was our grandmother's, very treasured and precious. Emi wouldn't touch it. So how could she know if she had any talent or not?'

Will seemed bemused, didn't reply, instead allowing his eyes to slip back down to the open page. Polly sat and watched him, fingering the pages of the diary that now lay open on her lap, but still she couldn't bring herself to read it.

'What's up?' asked Will, eventually, laying the volume to one side.

'Nineteen ninety-three is when Marie died,' she confessed. 'And when Mum and Dad split up for the first time. It was our *annus horribilis*. Whatever's written in here, I've got a feeling, is not going to be how I recall it. And I just don't know if I can cope with Emi's twisted fiction when it comes to such significant events. It's bad enough that she told you she was born second. But with this stuff, well, I'm not sure I want my memories reinvented by my missing sister. It might prove to be too much.'

'Who was Marie?' asked Will, curiously.

'Don't tell me she didn't even tell you about that?'

Will looked confused. Polly was genuinely shocked. It had been a seminal moment in their childhood. How could he have not known about it? She was beginning to realize that, however close Will and Emi had appeared to be, she had been far from transparent with him about her life, her past. If he didn't know about Marie, what did he know about Emi? Anything real at all?

'Go on, pass it here,' he demanded. Rolling over on to his stomach, he began to read.

'Oh dear,' he said, almost immediately.

'What?'

To her surprise, Polly saw that he was smirking. He turned the open diary round towards her, so displaying a defaced photo of Polly at sixteen, with arrows through her eyes and devil horns sticking out of her hair, the words 'I HATE POLLY' written in thick bold black letters around it. Polly knew she should see the humour in her sister's adolescent rivalry, but she couldn't. Essentially, she had thought their adolescence was happy, even though their parents' marriage had shown ever deeper signs of division as the years had passed by. There had been lots of good stuff going on, too, and they were both clearly loved by both parents, even if she had always found it easier to get on with their father and Emi with their mother. They hadn't had such a bad time. Nevertheless it seemed that Emi had been determined to paint a bleak picture.

'Sorry,' said Will, pulling a hangdog face, his head going back down to the page. Polly didn't answer, just lay back and waited patiently. He hadn't hit the summer months yet, and when he did, she knew that the smirk would be wiped off his face.

Sure enough, half an hour later Will's immersion was complete and the pages turned more slowly. His tea went cold, and as Polly and he sat in silence he absorbed a part of Emi's past that she didn't need to guess at and which she now understood that her sister had never shared, not with Will, not with anyone. They had hit on Emi's first psychological block. Evidently Emi had closed off this whole chapter in her life. Eventually he looked up at Polly with clear, bright eyes.

'I can't read this to you,' he said quietly. 'I think you need to read it for yourself. I don't know how you saw it, but Emi's painted a pretty vivid picture. It's like a fucking time-bomb – reading this makes everything clear. She was just waiting, for a moment, to go, to try it again, whether she knew it or not.'

'To do what?' enquired Polly sharply. She didn't know what he meant.

'To try and change things, to see if she could will life to be different. She used to talk about it sometimes, about how we could all alter our future, if we really wanted to. She even implied that our marriage was a twist of fate that she had forced, and that was why it failed. And now we're talking about it, I do remember a time, after university, when she said she'd thought about reinventing herself, you know, literally, walking out of her life and trying to become someone else – it was just after your father died – she was quite low. She said she'd always felt as if she lived on the edge, that she was like an aura that wasn't properly substantiated – that you had always been the complete one, the visceral one, with the anchor at your centre. She'd called herself a genetic drift – apparently that really is a scientific term, she'd looked it up. Thankfully at the time she didn't act on her impulses – and then time passed and it seemed we'd made it through. But this time, when she went crazy again, I was worried. It was like before, this cloying depression, accompanied by a slightly manic anxiety – and obsessive behaviour, too, if I'm honest. She kept tidying things up, putting them away in boxes, so neatly, as if they needed protecting, or were being packaged up to be moved to another place.'

'Like the diaries,' Polly interjected miserably. 'And Mum's flat.'

'This time, God alone knows what the consequences of her actions might be: last time it seems it was fatal.'

'What has she said in there?' Polly's words came out razor sharp and she wrenched the diary from Will's limp hands. It was getting cold and she felt frightened. She knew exactly what had happened, all those years before. Or at least she thought she did. What fictions had Emi managed to conjure up this time? She crawled under the duvet with her back to Will and opened it up.

In the two years that had passed since her 1991 diary, Emi's handwriting had become slightly more refined, and therefore easier to read. Hence Polly flicked quickly through the pages until she hit May. She knew that anything written before that date would be irrelevant. That time was before the trouble really kicked off. After all, Polly hadn't forgotten anything, either. She had just not seen the need to write all the gruesome details down. They were embedded in her mind like the words carved in Marie's tombstone; as clear as if they had happened yesterday. All she needed to do was close her eyes and she was back there. If she willed herself to be. But she had never seen the point, she'd learned that there was nothing to gain from so doing a long, long time ago. She had allowed herself to leave this behind, other than as a very sad memory. Why was Emi forcing it all back up to the surface? What was it she was supposed to see? Will sighed heavily and got up, headed into the kitchen with their cups and the teapot on the tray.

'Call me through when you're done,' she heard him say, drily.

May 1
There was a May Festival at school yesterday. Guess who was the May Queen? Surprise, surprise, my darling sister . . . mind you, it was more fun hanging out with Marie and Helen, while P had to sit on her silly throne with all those flowers in her hair. It's bank holiday tomorrow, so we all went back to Marie's for a sleepover. Hera is so cool – she dresses so trendily, buys all her clothes down Camden Lock, she says. Marie's so lucky. We talked about our mum, how sad she seems right now, and then Helen said something horrible, she said how she overheard her dad talking to her mum about our dad and how he had been

243

a bit 'lively', he said, at the School Fundraising Dinner last week, how he had had too much to drink and had pinched one of the waitress's bums. I don't think Polly heard – but it made me feel sick. Then everyone started talking about parents having sex and how disgusting the idea was, and then about affairs, and how Lucy's mum had had one for years before her parents split up and how she heard them doing it once, and how perhaps my dad was having an affair as he was away so much. I laughed along with everyone else, but inside I was feeling more and more sick at the idea of it. And then I couldn't sleep, even after everyone else did, and now it's around two a.m. and I just keep thinking that they're probably right – he goes away so much. I want to go home.

May 2

The more I think about it, the more I thought they ARE probably right, are trying to warn me, to help me to stop it from happening again. I'm sure it was well meant but how am I supposed to stop Dad? He's gone off to Newcastle again on business. I walked into Mum's bedroom and she was just sitting on the edge of the bed, with a tissue in her hand and I knew from the red rims around her eyes that she'd been crying. She didn't seem to see me come in and I stood watching her for ages before, suddenly, she seemed to wake up and saw me there. She appeared startled and then a watery smile passed her lips and she asked me what I wanted. I know what was happening. She was thinking about Dad and all his other women. P would never believe it, she thinks he's a saint.

May 11

This is so much a bad end to a bad weekend. Polly and I stayed over at Marie's so we could all go to the school disco together. XXX asked Polly to dance and I'm sure she kissed him although she denies it and says she doesn't fancy him anyway. Why does she always have to take everything from me? I hate her I hate her I hate her. And then, this is a major crisis and secret, PLEASE DON'T TELL ANYONE. When Dad came to pick us up Hera offered him a drink. We went back upstairs to pack our stuff, but I came back down to get my hairbrush from the kitchen and you won't believe it, but they were practically SNOGGING by the fridge. It was GROSS. I ran back upstairs, the door was open into Hera's room, so I crept in. There was an open jewellery box on the dressing table with tonnes of necklaces spilling out. I couldn't help it, I took one. PLEASE DEAR DIARY DON'T TELL ANYONE. It's really long, lots of gold threads plaited together with tiny amber stones threaded through them. I feel reaaallllly bad about it, but at the same time I HATE THEM for what they're doing. Dad has gone to America so at least I don't have to speak to him for at least two weeks.

May 28

Last night Dad got back from his trip to America, and we all went to Chinatown for supper. Mum was trying really hard but she seemed distant and not at all pleased to see him. I snuck into Mum and Dad's room when we got home and slipped Hera's necklace halfway into Dad's suit pocket which was lying on the bed. After Polly and I went to bed I heard arguing and then crying and shouting. Polly tiptoed into my room, 'What's going on?' she whispered. A few minutes later we heard Dad exclaim, 'For Christ's sake, Sarah, I can't stand much more of this. I know you're ill, and I try to understand, but this is MADNESS.' Then we heard him stomp down the stairs and the front door slam. We could hear Mum's muffled sobs from her room and so we both went to see what had happened. She was lying, face down on the bed, sobbing her heart out and on the floor by the bed was the necklace, broken in two pieces. Polly picked it up and looked at me quizzically. Mum just kept saying, 'I'm sorry, I'm sorry,' so I called Carol and she came round five minutes later. She told us to go back to bed. Part of me feels REALLY guilty about what's happened but at the same time I know their future needs to change.

May 30

When we woke up this morning, Polly came racing upstairs and told me that we were going to stay at Hera's again, for the WHOLE weekend, to give Mum some rest. P seemed soooo pleased and I have to admit that I am, too, although I am worried about Mum. Carol says she'll look after her and Dad's gone back to Newcastle. We are going to a school disco on Saturday and XXXO!!!! is going. Lucy's brother's in his class and she says he said he fancies me!!!!!!!!!!!!!!!!!!! If we stay at Marie's we'll be able to stay out late because she's so much more laid back than Mum and Dad, yippee. Suddenly I don't feel so fed up . . . Good night sleep well dear diary. I want to say sorry to Mum, but how can I? xxx

June 1

Carol's come to stay for a few days. Mum's very quiet and pale and just lies listlessly in her bed. She keeps saying, 'Sorry.' I feel for her so much, they can't really work out what's wrong, I think she's just sad because of Dad – and I understand why. He's calling every night, trying to be nice to me, but I don't want to be friends if he's having an affair with Hera. I haven't been talking to Marie at school and she seems quite upset, but what does she expect? Polly's being really quiet. She practised her cello for so long last night that I thought the strings might break.

June 3
Carol's put a TV in Mum's room and after school today we all sat together on her bed and watched Neighbours. It was really good fun and even Mum laughed a bit. Mum says Dad will be home at the weekend. It seems my plan hasn't worked after all.

June 4
Mum seems much better. We even went to Regent's Park for a walk after school and had a picnic in the Secret Garden. The weather is PERFECT – HOT AND SUNNY!!! Mum sat on the little bench under the pergola and Carol, Polly and I laid a big rug out on the lawn. Carol had gone to Waitrose up the Finchley Road and bought Spanish strawberries and clotted cream and cake, and sandwiches and it felt really nice and happy. But suddenly Mum said, 'I'm sorry for putting you all through my misery,' and then she started to cry and we all hugged her and then I started to cry too and Polly shot me such a look of disdain I felt really bad. Then she said she needed the loo and stomped off towards the café by the Rose Gardens. Why can't anything be normal?

June 6
We've been sent to Marie's again – can you believe it? And Dad and Mum seem much happier, too, which really upset me as I thought this necklace drama would bring his guilt to the

surface. Polly and I have decided to keep half the necklace each – as a tryst between us. It's the first time she's seemed to be on my side for ages. We both agree we have to protect Mum from Dad's philandering, HOWEVER, I didn't tell her that it was Marie's mum's necklace . . . and she now assumes it belonged to an unknown lover of Dad's too . . . I daren't tell her the truth.

June 8
Staying at Marie's. It's SOOOO hot – a heatwave. Tomorrow we're all going to the Hampstead Ladies' Pond for a swim, including Hera and Marie. Helen's come to sleepover, too, which is lucky because Marie and I are still not really talking although she's trying REALLLLY HARD to make friends. I have to admit, I'm finding it hard not to like her, because of all our gang, she's the one who I naturally get on with best. I wonder if she knows about her mum and my dad . . . bet she doesn't or she'd be finding it all as hard as me. I might tell her, tomorrow.

June 9
I can't write today. It's too TERRIBLE for words.

June 10
Marie's dead. That's all I can say.

June 11
I'm going to write it down.

On Sunday morning we got up and it was BAKING so we got our stuff together and our picnic and Hera, Marie, Polly, Jane, Helen and I went to the Ladies' Pond. We had a picnic and swam about in the shallows. Then Marie found a red ball under a weeping cherry tree. She, Polly and I were throwing it in and daring each other to swim out to get it, further each time. Helen and Jane were lying in the sun reading books and Hera had fallen asleep. There's a bit of the pond that's surrounded by overhanging boughs of late white cherry blossom. It's really pretty but very deep and dark and full of weed underneath. Polly threw the ball to me, then I threw it really hard, to Marie, but she missed and it floated out towards the tree. Marie hesitated and we all watched the ball floating further out. Then she grinned, turned and swam boldly out to retrieve it. I watched from the shore and Polly hung back in the shallows. Neither of us called out to Marie to turn around – Polly stared at me and I stared back at Polly, mute. With our eyes we gave our silent pact. Then we both turned and stared at Marie. We both knew it was a bit too far for either of us to swim. Suddenly Marie started splashing a lot, she was quite a way away. Part of me wanted her to carry on, to be in danger, to feel fear for all that had happened, for all her mum had done. And she did, she carried on, out. She went a little further and then she disappeared under the surface, like something had sucked her down. She reappeared for a moment and gasped for breath and I thought perhaps she was just tricking us, that it was a game, to frighten us. She was always quite daring, it was how she was. But then she went under again. We both stood watching, silently. It was like slow-motion, then there was nothing – just a red ball drifting silently on the silky smooth green surface of the water and the heat above us and a few bubbles and then Polly screaming and screaming and screaming and the next thing there was loads of action and lifeguards and stuff and then Marie was brought to the surface and pulled ashore but it was *already too late. IT WAS HORRIBLE. We killed her, we urged her out there, we knew it was unsafe. We wanted her to go, to take the punishment, for what Hera and Dad have done, and now it's happened and I know it's our fault. Nothing will ever be the same ever again.*

June 19
The coroner's report said ACCIDENTAL death. Ha. It's still so hot. Everyone at school's avoiding our eyes – I know they feel sorry for us. Hera's gone away. She's on Valium, I heard Carol say to Mum. I can't talk to anyone about what happened, ESPECIALLY NOT POLLY. It's tooooooooooo bad.

Polly dropped the diary on the bed. It was if she'd been reading her own history with the perspective skewed. In it she was a sideline player in a drama that, until now, had been her own. Only now did she see that maybe she and Emi had never really shared the centre ground. Emi had always been on the sidelines, like that day, when she didn't have her feet in the water. She had stolen that necklace – Polly had never known, had always misunderstood, as, she now saw, had Sarah. Their father must have been completely baffled. No wonder he left in such a rage. She felt a shred of anger towards Emi, but it quickly subsided. It was too late for that, too many years had since passed. It was an immature act, an emotional impulse made by a teenage girl, desperate to try to retain the status quo.

She flicked forwards through the pages. The diary continued, with regular reference to the tragedy, throughout the summer. She skim-read the later entries, feeling sick and disarmed by Emi's account of Marie's death. Strictly, what had happened at the pond was accurate, but Polly found Emi's sense of their apparently shared guilt over Marie's death baffling. Polly knew it had been an accident, that it was nothing more, nothing less. They didn't swim out to save Marie because . . . She tried to remember. Because it was too far and until she disappeared they didn't know she was drowning – did they? They couldn't have done, surely? She felt prickles of sweat shiver down her neck as her memory took her back to the day. The sun was beating harshly above their heads, the sky was cloudless, there was a blistering, unexpected heat. The water was soft, and had a nip to it, under the surface, but once you'd acclimatized it had felt OK. She remembered standing in the water, her toes being sucked at by the murky, soft mud. She was watching the tiny brown fish nibbling at her ankles beneath the flat, green surface, and then Marie threw the red ball at her and it had smashed through the water, refracting it into a thousand effervescent bubbles, sending the minnows darting to safety. Polly had grabbed the ball with a shriek and thrown it to Emi on the bank, then watched as Emi threw it out to Marie once more. The throw was a little hard, and a little off its target, too, and Marie had to swing round to watch it skim past her over the water, before it landed with a splosh and floated out towards the trees. Marie had laughed wickedly and turned swiftly to swim out after it. No one had either urged her on, or called her back. Polly had watched, calmly at first, then with a growing paralysis as she realized what was unfolding. She shouted out to Marie, but her mouth was dry and her words stuck to her tongue. Marie had disappeared. She glanced back at Emi, who looked like her own reflection, standing motionless on the bank; then Polly looked back at the water again, willing Marie to resurface. And then she started to scream.

There was a little brown package folded and taped into the back of the journal and as she'd been reading it Polly had been feeling it with growing interest. She knew instinctively now what lay within. She pulled the envelope off the paper and peeled back the tape. As anticipated, Emi's half of Hera's necklace slid out into her hand. She went to her own jewellery box and rifled around inside it. Underneath the main tray were old ring boxes and trinkets. Inside one, as anticipated, she found the other half. Will reappeared to discover Polly sitting on the edge of the bed, fiddling with the two halves of a chain, trying to link them back together again.

'Is this it?'

'Yep.'

He sat down close to her and took the two pieces, held them up to try to see the break.

'Emi had a vivid imagination,' he murmured. 'She thought she carried far more influence than she did.'

'She played with people, and in her own way she did affect their fate,' Polly replied, standing up. 'I can't stay inside. My head's all fuzzed up.'

'Polly, it's nearly midnight,' Will pleaded, looking up at her from the bed. It was so tempting to lie back down, next to Will. But Emi's diaries had made her anxious – perhaps this was exactly what Emi wanted to see happen. Perhaps she thought she could manipulate them, too.

Instead she put on her coat. 'I don't care, I need to get some air.'

Will got up with a groan and followed her out.

They turned right along the river path, past the closed restaurants and shops, as far as the Design Museum, its white walls lit up against the dark Thames, Polly mentally kneading the past over and over, back and forth in her mind, like dough.

'Maybe Dad did have an affair with Hera,' she reasoned. 'Maybe Emi was right about that. After all, she said she saw them kissing – before the necklace incident. Our parents broke up only a year or two after Marie died, and, you know, I did acknowledge then that he must have had affairs with other women. For a start, he already knew Brigitte. But I didn't blame him – more so I felt Mum had brought it on herself. She was always so downcast, I thought it must have been very hard for him to live with her.'

'I'm sure,' Will observed. 'When I think of the way Emi closed up, how impenetrable she was, towards the end, it makes me wonder, truthfully, how long I could have stood it. I know it was her decision, to separate, I mean, but to be honest, you can't live with a block of ice for ever. It would turn you insane. Your dad had just as much of a right to seek happiness as Sarah did.'

'And you do.'

'And Emi did.' Will paused and turned to Polly. 'And you, too, Polly.'

They'd stopped on a wharf. There was a distinctly salty scent of seaweed churning in the tide below them. It was pungent and slightly sickly – and it shook Polly's senses, made them react to a sensation outside herself. She thought about Will's words. Happiness – what was it? She'd always filled her time so completely that she had never had to stop and question what that word meant – or whether she was anywhere near attaining it for herself. As for Emi, her sister had always struggled to feel content; she'd had a closed demeanour – although some would call it mysterious, she guessed, moon-like, opalescent, shiny but cool, unlike her own fiery, emotional nature, outward and keen on disclosure. Until now, that was. Where her emotions towards Will were concerned she found herself remaining silent, particularly because, if she was scrupulously honest, she felt, at this moment, that her happiness depended utterly upon him.

'I hope what Emi's finding is happiness – or at least some kind of contentment,' she said, shifting the focus back to her sibling. 'Will, sometimes I worry that she's dead, but in my heart I'm sure she's alive. She's out there somewhere, searching for a better way. And I think she needed to. And do you know what? Suddenly I feel really sorry for her. I think I'm beginning to understand. And you know what, she's not the girl she once was to me any more. She'd become all shadowy and now she's becoming real – separate. Maybe, if it works out, it will have been for the best, for both of us. So long as the journey doesn't destroy her in the process.'

'Or you.'

Polly understood what Will meant. Emi's disappearance had caused a new melancholy to grow inside her, a searching in herself, a more serious contemplation of what it is to grasp the nettle, to work out what really counts. She saw her life, to date, as one immense, complex jigsaw puzzle. She could see all the pieces of her past now, as if they'd been scattered around her on the floor. She'd never questioned much before, had been too busy living, getting on, working, finding new lovers, hiding from her emotions, from Emi. It was time to piece them together, to see the picture more clearly and to make better sense of the future. It was time to take a more profound control of things. But the idea frightened her. She turned her focus from the river below and looked back up at Will. He was standing in the lamplight, which was illuminating his ever-serious face, his brow knitted in characteristic concentration. She knew that he was trying to help her, to understand it all. She couldn't help but love him, whether it was right or wrong; for his earnestness, his desire to see things right, for his patience and naturally quiet aura. She didn't know if this love was based on dependency, on grief or trauma, and if so, for how long the feeling would last. But for this moment, at least, it felt limitless.

'Come on,' he said, with a wide grin. 'Enough memory stalking. Let's get home. It's so late, and I'm tired.'

As they wandered back along the silent path, Polly's thoughts turned to Hera and her beautiful necklace. It was precious, and she must have missed it. She knew what she had to do next.

'I need to see Hera,' she confided. 'I want to return her necklace and I want to ask her about Marie, whether she blames us, and also I want to ask her about Dad.'

Will winced. 'It was a long time ago, Polly,' he said. 'Seeing Carol only stirred you up. Are you certain it's wise?'

25

Peter writes to Sarah from Newcastle; a calm letter, stating that the origin of the necklace is completely unknown to him, that her accusations with reference to it are unfounded, but that he has decided to spend a month working directly between Newcastle and Paris, all the same, so that they can both get some perspective, decide what's best. He doesn't deny having a lover – or even lovers – and Sarah feels certain that their relationship is finally closing down. The girls are absorbed in their exams, and after the initial tears, she feels better, stronger. She tells the twins that all marriages have their ups and downs, that their dad will be home soon, that he has an arduous schedule, that it is best for him to be absent for a while. He calls them every few days, and talks, mainly to Polly, but otherwise he stays away.

Once the exams are complete a blistering heat hits the capital and the girls spend their liberated early summer in the garden, hanging out with their friends in Regent's Park, or over at Hera's, with Marie. Hera's house has practically become their second home. The yoga classes have come and gone, and since then Sarah has had little to do with Hera, outside of scheduling their daughters' movements. It's not that she doesn't like her, but their worlds are too different, their outlook is not the same. From the outset there has been no space for a friendship to grow and neither has tried to bridge the invisible gap. On Marie's sixteenth birthday, the girls are invited for a sleepover and Hera has promised to take the entire gang of them swimming, at the Ladies' Pond on Hampstead Heath. Sarah enjoys the peace in the house; she's got all the brochures for courses at Birkbeck, the postgraduate university college off Tottenham Court Road. She wants to do something, she's not sure what. She decides to spend the Sunday afternoon in the garden, with a cup of jasmine tea, to go through the options, to consider her future. She's just settled down when the phone rings.

The next thing she knows, she's there, standing in the hall in her rose-patterned summer dress, holding the receiver. The atmosphere is still, and thick – oppressive, she thinks. It is the hottest day in June on record. The city is almost silent outside. No one is moving very far or very fast. There's a stasis in the air. Sarah doesn't want, indeed can't believe, what she's being told and she has to ask the voice to repeat what they've just said. There's been some kind of an accident, the voice is telling her. It's Marie. At the Ladies' Pond on Hampstead Heath. It doesn't sound as if it can be true. Can she come to the station, they ask. The twins are there and they need her to take them home.

'Of course, yes, yes,' she says.

But Sarah finds she can't make the distance from the telephone to the front door. However hard she tries, she can't get one foot to follow the other forwards. There's a sharp pain in her chest. It's too much for her to bear, and Peter's still away: Marie, drowned in front of the twins. If she shuts her eyes and breathes slowly, perhaps it will all go away.

Eventually Sarah does what she's always done in times of crisis. She calls Carol. Together they drive to Hampstead police station and collect Emi and Polly. There's been a heatwave for two weeks now, but the twins are ashen beneath their early summer tans. They're still wearing their bikinis, with shorts over the top, and flip-flops. Their fast-developing teenage bodies, narrow-hipped, flat-tummied, emerging breasts, look caught between childhood and the adult world and Sarah feels a surge of fear for them. Sixteen years old and experiencing this. It's too soon. It's too soon. On the journey home Emi keeps shuddering and moaning and curls up on the back seat, while Polly stares with blank eyes from the car window and doesn't speak. When they arrive in Alma Place, Carol calls Mr Kapoor, who arrives within the hour and gives them something to help them sleep.

The next two weeks pass in a hot, sticky summer haze. Peter comes home immediately, but he and Sarah circle one another widely, both focusing all their attention on the well-being of their daughters. The girls are both in a state of emotional shock, paralysed by what they've seen. Sarah surprises herself by coping far better than she feared she might in the first moments after the tragedy occurred, but even so she keeps away from the heart of the crisis, allowing Carol and Peter to help Hera with preparations for Marie's funeral, withdrawing from Peter each evening, behind her closed bedroom door. And with each day that passes she feels calmer and more watchful. There's no doubt that she and Peter have reached a silent agreement. Oddly, the idea that her marriage is over feels like a burden lifted.

Slowly but surely, the girls emerge from their shock and over the following days, in fits and starts, Polly tells Sarah and Peter about the accident. With each instalment, Emi sits next to her twin but adds nothing, no embellishment or point of view.

'We were playing with a red ball,' Polly explains, falteringly, eyes flicking to Emi for agreement, then back to Peter for reassurance, 'and then Marie swam out after it, too far, and she got caught in the reeds. Hera was asleep. Before anyone realized that Marie was struggling, it was already too late.'

Although there is no surface acrimony between her daughters, Sarah is suddenly conscious that Emi and Polly have learned a negative behavioural pattern from Peter and her, are playing a similar game, keeping each other at arm's length, doing everything in their power to avoid redress or confrontation. She wonders what Emi is really thinking. Usually she can tell. But this time, her daughter's closure is complete.

The funeral is so full of young people, music and flowers that it seems almost like a party. Hera is dressed in bright clothes, gives a most moving and uplifting eulogy to her daughter and asks the congregation to sing in celebration of Marie's brief life. Afterwards there is a wake at Hera's home.

'I'm so very, very sorry,' Sarah tells her, holding Hera's hands in hers as they are about to take their leave. 'And your eulogy was so perfect, I don't know how . . .'

'For the sake of your beautiful twins,' Hera interrupts before she has a chance to complete her sentence, 'for their future; it's even more important now.'

26

Lotta, Kalle and I arrived at Solgläntan this morning. We've come just for one night, a lightning visit. It feels like a homecoming, a moment outside things. When we arrived we headed straight for the forest, Lotta and the dog running ahead of us, Kalle on one side of me, Lars on the other. The clocks went back last night and the light felt new, piercing. The sun's rays were breaking between the trees, warming the air they touched, leaving the rest stone cold, like warm cross streams teasing an icy sea. The snow still lay compacted in patches on the forest floor. With the lengthening day, I felt a surge inside, felt my own darkness lift.

'Although Artemis was the goddess of the hunt, she was also a lover of nature,' exclaimed Lars, out of the blue. Kalle glanced sideways at me, and we both laughed. Characteristically, Lars ignored us, and carried on strolling – and talking.

'She would've felt at home here. You know we have a tradition, or should I say philosophy, in Sweden called *allemanstratten*. It means that anyone can roam anywhere, over field or through forest, pitch a tent, pick mushrooms or berries, gather wild flowers – so long as they respect the rights of others. She would have liked that. She was an unusual goddess in that she tried to befriend mortals.'

Kalle sighed audibly and I giggled some more.

'She was really on the lookout for them and their well-being. She carried a silver arrow with her, you know, that only killed with a painless death. She loved all things silver – had silver sandals, wore a silver robe.'

'As do I, whenever I get the chance!' I murmured and Kalle chuckled. Lars frowned between us both.

'That, Emi, as I'm sure my brother will agree, is because you carry her behavioural patterns,' he proclaimed, with fake authority. 'Now shush, let me finish. Artemis was a gentle goddess – she was more likely to offer her protection to wild animals than she was to slaughter them, particularly the very young. She clearly had a natural maternal instinct.'

'So no wonder, on our last visit, I tried to stop you from your cull,' I exclaimed.

'And no wonder you care so beautifully for Lotta,' Kalle added, quietly, so only I could hear.

Lars paused and looked up at the sky. 'I think I saw a buzzard,' he said.

As Kalle raised his binoculars I took a moment to consider his words. They flattered me. Recently I've read a number of studies that highlight the critical effect of good maternal nurturing, and I had begun to worry that if Mum was depressed after she had me, she had inadvertently caused my lack of emotional confidence.

'Artemis had a silver chariot in which she would ride across the sky and shoot her arrows of silver moonbeams down to the earth below,' Lars continued, cutting short my self-immersion.

'In fact, in many myths she comes across as a rather hapless fighter, one who would always rather stand down,' I interrupted. 'Unless she'd been ordered by Zeus, of course. Then she could very readily punish and, if necessary, kill.'

Lars stopped in his tracks, looked at me quizzically, then began to roar with laughter. Lotta ran back with Bosse to observe him curiously. He put an arm around her.

'So you have learnt about her after all,' he admonished. 'What more do you know?'

'Where should I begin?' I now replied, as we all turned and began our walk homewards. A wry smile had arrived on Kalle's lips and stuck there. In my childhood, Mum had read us the myths until they almost felt part of Polly's and my own past.

'Artemis is associated with three main characteristics: chastity, purity and possessiveness,' I explained slowly. 'She's also the goddess of many contradictions. At an early age – in one legend she was only three years old – she went to her father, Zeus, and asked him to grant her eternal virginity. She would punish any man who attempted to dishonour her in any form. In one legend, I remember, a mortal called Actaeon, while out hunting accidentally came upon Artemis and her nymphs, bathing naked in a secluded pool. Artemis transformed him into a stag and set his own hounds on him. They chased and killed what they thought was another stag, but was in fact their master. In another legend, Orion tried to rape the goddess, so she killed him with her silver bow and arrows. Another tale tells how she conjured up a scorpion, which killed Orion and his dog. Orion became the constellation the Great Bear in the night sky.'

'And his dog became Sirius, the dog star,' interjected Lars, with evident delight.

I leant forwards and gave Bosse a pat.

'We must all beware the wrath of Artemis,' murmured Kalle, teasingly.

'I don't suppose by any chance you have a twin brother, named Apollo?' Lars now asked me, evidently warming further to the theme.

I found myself faltering. 'No, no, of course I don't,' I replied, anxious to sound light-hearted, but I knew that my words were spoken too quickly, that they were too fixed, had given something away.

After lunch, Lars and Lotta rowed over to the studio to 'do some painting'. I nearly asked to go, I still hadn't been there, but Kalle was staying behind and I was keen to spend time with him. We sat quietly and read on the jetty together. He seemed different, here again, back at home, more relaxed, less self-absorbed, and I sensed our intimacy growing. As the dusk fell and the air grew cold, he suggested we take a sauna.

'You caught Lars out back there,' he said, once we were settled on our benches in the flickering candlelight. 'Chastity, purity and possessiveness – would you say you share your goddess's traits?'

His tone seemed a touch flirtatious and I laughed.

'I guess I've only ever really had one relationship, and I don't let go easily,' I answered, truthfully. 'I find it hard to move on; you could call that possessiveness.'

For a while Kalle was silent. I guessed he was weighing up my words. I wondered how they made him feel – reassured or, conversely, nervous of me?

'Emi, I want to apologize for my introversion, for my distance. I struggle with the dark,' he said suddenly, earnestly.

'It's OK,' I ventured, but I know my tone was unconvincing.

'Also, Stephanie's and my divorce has come through, this week. I've been dreading it, the finality of it all. I loved her, you know. I wanted it to work.'

'I know how that feels,' I said, surprised at the depth of my sentiment.

'Disappointing,' he said.

'Yes – but at least we didn't have a child to fit into the equation.'

'You didn't?'

'Of course not.'

'I have wondered. I feel there's something you're not sharing with me, and it occurred to me that perhaps that was it.'

'No,' I answered, feeling my skin stinging with embarrassment. I was behaving so unfairly. But still I couldn't speak of her.

'Anyway, how could I ever regret Lotta?' he asked, breaking the silence for me.

'I didn't mean that,' I said.

'I know,' he answered. 'But of course it would be easier, different perhaps, if it weren't for her. In some ways, your coming has made the pain more acute, it makes me see how we could have been, as a family, how good it could have been, if only things had been different.'

The silence grew once more, and for a while I felt no need to break it and neither did he. I thought about Mum and Dad, about their shared life, and I wondered, if they had not had us, whether they would have persevered. I knew that the answer was no. I could understand why Kalle was so disoriented by his own failed marriage – he was a perfectionist: he didn't 'do' failure readily.

'If it's any consolation, I hated my parents' fake marriage,' I said. 'In fact, as a teenager I did my best to try to destroy it for them. But Mum was determined to stick it out, to the end. I guess Dad didn't have the heart to break it for her. I think it drove a wedge between my sister and me; one we've failed to fix, even after all these years. Eventually Lotta would hate you too, for sticking with it if it's broken.'

'How do you think she is?' he asked.

'OK, particularly this weekend,' I answered, carefully. 'But I think she may be missing Stephanie's input.'

'Stephanie's away more and more,' he agreed. 'And she and Marcus seem heavily immersed. I'm sorry, Emi, I'll try to work less. It's been an intense time. I don't quite know what I would have done without you.'

I didn't reply. I wasn't sure how to feel about his gratitude – was it for my relationship with him, or purely with Lotta?

'You are feeling OK, aren't you?' he asked now, more tentatively.

'As you say, perhaps just a little more of your time – I mean for Lotta, of course,' I replied, quietly. 'And of course, more light.'

'You've found the darkness hard, too, haven't you?'

'I didn't realize quite how hard until the light came back.'

'Next year we'll have to invest in some daylight bulbs for the apartment,' he said. 'That is, if you're still here.'

'Would you like me to be?'

Kalle sat up, pulled his towel around his waist and reached out his hand for mine.

'It's what I want more than anything else in the world,' he replied, holding my fingers firmly. 'But it won't work unless you reconcile yourself with your past and let me come closer.'

'I'm trying to work it all out, but so much seems confused, indistinct,' I answered, numbly.

'Trust me,' he said quietly. 'Empty it out.'

I didn't reply. My conscience cried out for me to tell Kalle about Polly, about my need to feel separate, to exist independently of her, to be seen for who I was, without her shadow. I feared Kalle's reaction. I knew he would be fascinated, that it would alter the way he perceived my character, and I held my tongue.

This morning we had to rise early to return to the city. Just before we left, Lars took me to one side.

'I'm coming to Stockholm in a month's time, to take you both out to the opera,' he enthused conspiratorially. 'It's Kalle's birthday. You must make Lotta promise not to spill the beans.'

'You sound happy,' I found myself saying.

There was a pause, and when he replied, he sounded surprised at the revelation.

267

'You know, Emi, you might just be right. I'm far out here and I haven't really seen anyone since you left before Christmas. But I've been working like a madman. I've got a whole new series of drawings. Yes, you're right, for the first time in months I'm feeling better than OK.'

27

Carol had Hera's number and her address but she sounded wary of giving them to Polly. She reasoned that Hera had moved years ago, soon after Marie died, in fact, out of London, back to Norfolk, where she had grown up – a long way from the scalding memories from which, no doubt, she had needed to flee. But Polly insisted, and soon she was calling Hera. The woman who picked up the phone feigned surprise, but needed no real reminder of who she was talking to. How could she ever forget? thought Polly. No doubt a part of her would always be stuck back there, at that precise moment, waking up in the harsh summer sunshine to find her daughter drowned. Hera sounded sad when Polly said she 'needed' to see her, but after a momentary pause she agreed to her coming to Norfolk, as if the call had been pending, like a debt that had been shelved but would always need, in the end, to be paid. Polly arranged to drive up with Will the following Sunday afternoon.

In the meantime she found herself unable to sleep. Memories of Marie's death resurfaced with all the misery and force of her friend's body being pulled from the pond in the heatwave of that summer day so many years before. She had managed to blank it out for years. She kept thinking of Emi's words – did they really will Marie to die? Could they – should they – have swum after her? Could they really influence each other's fate to such clearly destructive ends? Why had Polly not moved when she first recognized that Marie was struggling? Why had she not swum out to help her friend? What was it that had stopped her? Polly had never felt guilt about the tragedy before, but now culpability crawled over her skin like a stinging rash. Maybe, after all, Emi was right. And maybe it was the initial trigger in a chain that had now made Emi go away. Polly kept thinking back to that solitary white pill – and then to Carol's revelation of her mother's attempted suicide. Maybe Emi had carried the weight of guilt around with her for all these years and had finally decided to sacrifice herself in the name of it all? Maybe Sarah's depression had finally caught up with her sister, just as she, now, was finally catching up with Hera?

She voiced her fears to Will on the way to Norfolk but he shrugged the concept off.

'Maybe Marie and your mother are becoming good excuses for not blaming yourself, ourselves, for Emi's disappearance,' he suggested plainly, keeping his eyes firmly on the road ahead. 'Your digging around in the past might help you understand your sister better, but it won't necessarily give you the clue you need to her present whereabouts. Reading those diaries made me see what I think she's done. She's having another go at influencing the future, changing her – indeed all of our fates. I

270

recommend we try to live in the present, and let her get on with it. It's the safer way.'

Hera lived alone in a small white fisherman's cottage perched on the flats like a bird watching the skywide estuary. Gulls dipped and rose over a warm grey sky and the wind rushed through the seagrasses, spiking the low-lying waterways that seemed to seep too close to the house. It seemed strange to Polly that Hera would choose to live so close to water.

Will and Polly made their way up the narrow path, between high-growing deep purple lupins that seemed to lean forward to caress her bare arms as they passed. It was very still, very quiet. She knocked lightly on the red wooden door. The woman who opened it looked surprisingly youthful. Hera must be sixty, she calculated, but she was still slender, with sleek grey hair and marble-green eyes. She was wearing a white T-shirt with a butterfly emblem sewn on its front in silver sequins, three-quarter-length pale faded jeans and a pair of red flip-flops, toenails painted scarlet. She embraced Polly warmly as a look of deep-rooted emotion flushed across her face. Then she turned and took Will by the hand.

'It's so nice that you've both come,' she breathed. 'I'm sorry I hesitated on the phone, Polly, really, it's such a wonderful surprise.'

They followed Hera inside, moving quickly after her through a small, shadow-filled sitting-room, crowded with oil paintings of flowers, and shelves heaving with hardback books, then on into a boat-like galley kitchen. Hera moved ahead of them, outside into a small courtyard garden filled with pots of bright-coloured geraniums. Polly had been so caught up in the bleakness of her memories that the vivid colours and tones of Hera's life came as a shock to her – she had expected sobriety and instead was confronted with exuberance. It took her a minute to redress the imbalance in her mind.

Hera had evidently spent time and attention on the detail of preparing for her guests. There was a table in the middle of the small terrace and she'd placed a curvaceous glass jug of elderflower cordial and three ice-filled glasses on it. She'd filled a cerulean-glazed ceramic bowl with strawberries and placed it next to the jug. It all looked slightly staged, like a still life waiting to be painted. Hera offered Polly and Will a glass of elderflower and poured one for herself, as she enquired casually after Peter and Sarah. Polly took a sip of the cool nectar, then explained that they had both died, that Emi had gone away and they were searching for her. Before she could stop herself she'd blurted out the whole story – or at least the part about Marie's death, and her sister's very clear sense of their guilt, their culpability for it. She didn't mention the necklace – yet. Hera clasped her hands around her glass on the table, leaning forward and listening to Polly attentively. Will was sitting next to her, his arm placed casually around the back of her chair. When Polly had finished talking, Hera took another sip of her drink calmly, then stood up. She moved towards one of her pots, bent down and snapped the head of a dying pink geranium flower off the plant, then turned to look at Polly, twisting the stalk round and round in her fingers.

'Polly,' she began, with authority, as if talking to a young child of adult things. 'I want you to listen. I spent years blaming myself for Marie's death. I fell asleep that day, in the sun. It was so hot, such dreamy weather. You know I should have been watching her, all of you. It was my responsibility. You were still children. But as the years have passed I've come to accept that blame and guilt provide no solutions. They are soul-destroying emotions that only deepen the misery.'

She paused, her fingers inadvertently pulling the fragile, drying petals away from the flower in her hands, dropping them one by one on the terrace, around her bare toes. 'I'm to blame. I have to live with that – but I have to carry on, too, for her sake.'

Polly sat silently, digesting Hera's words. Despite the exuberance here, the colourful flowers, the bright house, the pain of Hera's loss was palpable. It throbbed just beneath the surface of her skin. Her expression was brightening now, however, as she mentioned the name of her daughter.

'Marie was a natural risk-taker,' she marvelled, 'and she loved a challenge. Do you know, when she was just seven she climbed up a ladder that was leaning against the greenhouse in my parents' garden, just near here, got up on to the roof, climbed over it, then fell off the other side. She was lucky not to break anything – that time. For some reason the scare taught her nothing. It was in her nature – to push things to the limit. She always did. Throwing that red ball out was metaphorically like throwing a red rag to a bull – maybe Emi knew that, but Marie should have known her own boundaries; they were always going to be tested – if not then, at another time. I suppose I'm guilty, in my own way, for encouraging her to push things, as I've always done in my own life. I've always sought out excitement, but luckily for me I found an outlet for my risk-taking early on, through dance. I often think that's my own salvation, that it kept me safe. Marie and I both take after my father – he was an intrepid explorer who didn't recognize his own limits, or if he did he chose to ignore them in the name of the thrill.'

Polly glanced at Will. His face was passive, blank. She sipped her elderflower cordial as Hera sat down and watched her in a lengthening silence. She couldn't think how to respond to this confession, to this brave woman's steady acknowledgement of her own guilt. Instead she pulled the small green velvet pouch she had brought with her from her bag and slid it across the table to Hera, who looked confused, then took it and emptied the contents into her waiting palm. When she saw what was there she looked truly startled.

'I'm so sorry,' Polly said, before Hera had a chance to ask. 'Emi stole it from your bedroom, all those years ago. She thought,' she faltered as Hera looked at her with growing enquiry tightening her eyes, 'she thought you were having an affair with our father.'

Hera hesitated, then began to laugh, hollowly, and shook her head as she dropped the necklace between one cupped hand and the other, backwards and forwards.

'Poor Emi, poor you. It wasn't the easiest of adolescences, was it? Your mother suffered so deeply when you were children, you know. And we all tried to help your father, with you two, to lend our support. But have an affair with him? It was never ever on the agenda, never. Of course, with Carol, well, that was different, but I suppose you all knew about that, you must have done, it was like a seam running through your parents' marriage; in some ways I always thought that it almost kept it together. It broke Carol's heart far more than your mother's when he ran off with that French woman, Brigitte . . .' She paused when she saw the look on Polly's face shift. 'Oh, dear . . .'

For the first time since they had arrived, Hera's eyes moved momentarily to fix on Will.

'I'm sorry,' said Polly, weakly. She felt stupid to have missed the clues, to have allowed herself to be sucked back in, after all this time.

'Don't be,' Hera replied. 'It was all a long time ago. I do hope you find Emi, and that when you do, you tell her that she was wrong, that none of us can control other people's lives, that the independent will is stronger, that people are not puppets. Maybe she's learnt that now. She can only try to control her own destiny – no one else's. And even then, fate will always play its part.'

'It seems to me that's precisely what she's trying to do,' added Polly, defeatedly.

'When she's found her own path, she'll find her way back to you,' said Hera, confidently. 'And in the meantime, don't let her absence destroy your present. It's all we have, the here and now, then the next here, the next now. Cherish your life, Polly, and you too, Will. Do it for yourselves – and do it for Marie.'

Will drove Polly back to London in silence. She felt slightly ashamed of herself, for having dredged the past back up, for disturbing Hera and her eternal grieving. She

275

was still shaking from the shock of Hera's revelation. Her father and Carol, together for all those years. She could hardly even bring herself to contemplate it. More duplicity. Maybe it was all set, deep within their genes.

The meeting, she realized, had been a gentle affirmation of all she had already known – and more. Hera had forgiven Polly and Emi years ago, whether they needed forgiveness or not. And she had done something else too – she had willed Polly to make a better go of things, in her daughter's name. The hard thing to know was what was making a go of it and what was taking what was not rightfully hers – like, for example, Emi's place in Will's affections. Maybe she and Emi had never been honest with each other, had spent their lives guarding their independence from one another so ferociously that they had been forced to become dishonest with themselves. It was like a habit, a serial denial of the truth, a way to get on in a world where two people were trying to inhabit a single space.

As they cruised closer to London, Will left his right hand on the wheel and held Polly's left one, which was lying limply in her lap. For just a moment, Polly followed Hera's advice, to live for the moment, and she squeezed Will's hand.

The next evening Polly and Will agreed to meet after work for a drink in Soho. She took a bus along the Embankment, alighting at Trafalgar Square. There were crowds of people milling about, sitting on the edges of the fountains, on the lions' manes, enjoying the early evening light. The sun was still high and the atmosphere was celebratory. As she zigzagged her way through them, her focus on the north side, she sensed a continuing presence close behind her. She glanced round. There was a man walking quite close behind, and as she looked at him, his pace slowed. She turned and continued to walk on. Presently, she stopped and turned again. Now the man had stopped, too. She looked at him enquiringly and he returned her gaze with a tentative smile. He was in his mid-forties, she guessed, well-dressed in a blue linen jacket and a crisp white shirt over dark jeans. He had quite a large frame and was tanned and handsome – in a rugged, unkempt way, with curly salt-and-pepper hair. There was something foreign about him and she assumed that he was lost, was looking for a theatre or a restaurant.

He stepped forward and held out a hand. She looked down at it but did not offer hers in return.

'Can I help you?' she asked.

'I didn't mean to frighten you,' he said, and she noticed that he had a soft, foreign accent she couldn't place. 'It's just I wanted to say how sorry I am, that Emi disappeared.'

For a moment Polly's heart sank. Was this one of the odd characters who had followed the story and wanted to be a part of it? And yet there was something about this man's tone that made her disbelieve her own premise.

'Go on,' she urged.

'Well,' he replied, glancing around, unexpectedly hesitant. 'It's just that I'm sure, I mean absolutely certain, that she's OK. You mustn't worry about Emi.'

Polly was suddenly gripped by a feeling that blended fear, nausea and anticipation.

'You know? Where she is?' she demanded, suddenly desperate.

But the man was backing away and she realized that he intended to retreat, to turn and leave her, standing there without a clue. She moved forward and grabbed hold of his sleeve. He turned back to her and she wondered, for a moment, if, after all, he was mad. But then she saw something else, a depth of kindness and pity in his eyes.

'Tell me, please,' she implored, her words trembling, but the stranger still shook his head.

'It's not my story to tell,' he replied quietly, then put his hand in his pocket and pulled something out. He moved it towards Polly's and slipped a small object inside hers. It was cold and smooth and round. She opened her palm and saw Emi's ruby and diamond ring sitting there. She turned it over in her hand, looked inside for the inscription; *PL-SL-AL-PL 1977*. It was the original; Peter had given it to Sarah when the twins were born and Sarah had left it to Emi in her will. Then she sensed an absence and jerked her head back up to demand more, but she was already too late, the man had gone, vanished into the swarming crowd.

Polly started to move, faster and faster, the ring held tight in her hand. She wove in and out of the tourists, up to St Martin-in-the-Fields and left into Leicester Square. She cut over Shaftesbury Avenue, ran a short way up Wardour Street, then turned left into Beak Street. Will was standing against a wall outside the bar where they had planned to meet, smoking. A look of anxiety flooded his features as he spotted her running manically towards him and then he held out his arms. All the emotion of the last few months had risen like a tide, broken its banks and was flooding from her. She shuddered and cried and couldn't speak. As people moved off the pavement and around them they threw Will accusing glances, assuming that he must be responsible for putting the girl in his arms into this state of total collapse. Eventually, when Polly had calmed down a bit, she handed him the ring.

'You have to tell me what's happened,' he ordered, turning it round and round. 'Let's go inside, get a drink.'

He led her in to the wine bar and ordered her a glass of wine, himself a beer. Between gulps, she told him about the foreign man in the square.

'Did you recognize anything about him?' Will asked.

'No. I'm certain I've never seen him before. But he was a kind person, he had a good spirit and I believe him. Emi's OK, she's really OK. But I still can't bear it. We need to find her. I have to know where she is. I can't explain, but without her, it's as if a part of me has vanished too. I can't be complete without her here.'

Polly felt tears rising in her eyes again. Will got up and took her by the hand. 'Come on,' he said gently. 'We need to eat.'

Together they headed for a cantonese restaurant on Wardour Street, with its plum-glazed ducks hanging upside down along the windows, like surreal New Year decorations in the sweet heat of early summer. Last time she'd been here, Polly recalled, had been years ago, with Emi and Peter and Sarah, before they took their GCSE exams. Peter had come back from a trip. Sarah had been distant, and she remembered feeling desperate to hold on to Peter, fearful that if she didn't make him aware of her devotion he might go away again, this time for good. Emi and Sarah had hung back, walking and talking together, but she had linked her arm through her father's and kept it there. He had been so funny and warm and loving and happy that night. He had bought them both perfume from America and it was in that gesture that she had suspected a new, prevalent female influence; the choice of scent was perfect, but it was unlike him to get right something so feminine. It seemed strange, tonight, that she was here again, but this time with Will, feeling equally anxious, and, suddenly, equally fearful of losing him. She desperately wanted Emi to resurface, but at the same time she knew that if she did, she'd have to let Will go.

The ground floor of the huge restaurant was crammed with diners. A small-framed Chinese waiter pointed and nodded efficiently towards the stairs to the first floor. Will continued to hold Polly's hand as they went into the cavernous canteen above, where all the large round tables were bustling with diners. It was as if, now they had touched one another, neither was willing, or able, to let go. Once seated, he placed an arm around her shoulders and pulled his chair in close to hers as they studied the menu together. They ordered duck with pancakes, then sat back and watched the other diners around their table while they waited for the food to arrive; a young Russian couple with their chairs turned at a right angle to the table, deep in intense conversation, a Chinese family of four, elbows forward, slurping noisily over large steaming bowls of glutinous stew.

When their food arrived Polly and Will concentrated on

the ritual of taking the hot steamed pancakes from the little lidded basket, smearing sweet sauce across them, adding the crispy flakes of meat, a few strips of cucumber and the finely sliced spring onions. Then they rolled them up to eat in two or three mouthfuls before repeating the process. They digested the food with a large pot of jasmine tea sipped from little Chinese plastic cups, which Polly refilled after each pancake. It was reassuringly noisy; the place was filled with post-theatre crowds and pre-party-goers. Polly watched the Russian couple leaning forward now over a shared plate of noodles, still talking intensely between their stringy mouthfuls. The air between them seemed fused, as fused as it suddenly seemed tonight between her and Will, but unlike theirs, the Russian couple's universe seemed complete, and she envied them. She could tell that their lives hadn't been damaged by a tragedy or a loss – yet. The *yet* stuck with her; she thought of Emi, of Sarah and Peter, all evaporated now. And then she thought of Kaz, lurking in the shadows at King's Cross – and finally she thought of the man in the square. All of them understood that life was fragile, that happiness was fleeting, that the best moments were often those already behind them, held in the past. One day, this innocent Russian couple, they would know it, too. No one was exempt. Will was looking at her, searching for reassurance in her wan face, and she saw his genuine concern, his love for her, and despite herself she smiled.

Presently they finished the food and for once she didn't fight Will for the bill, scribbled in biro by the waiter on their section of the white paper cloth. Again, as they left, she found his arm settling around her shoulders, and again she didn't shrug him off. They began their slow walk back to her place, heading first across Trafalgar Square, looking around them, but now the square was empty and of course there was no sign of the earlier messenger. They crossed over the bridge at Charing Cross, stepping down on to the South Bank in a steady silence. The theatres were long out and it was quiet now. Tonight, suddenly, everything was different. Tonight, for the first time since Emi had disappeared, Polly believed that her sister was alive. She also knew that, for the moment, at least, she didn't want to find her, and she didn't want Emi to see her and Will, as they were now, heading past Tate Modern together, under the lamplight shimmering over the calm Thames, holding hands. Just for tonight, she wanted to pretend that Emi didn't exist, that she and Will were just another normal couple, on their way home from a pleasant evening out together. On her finger, she was wearing Emi's ring. She knew that the stranger was honest and she determined to believe, at least for the moment, that Emi was OK, that there was nothing at all to worry about.

By the time they got back to the flat it had already past midnight.

'I'm thinking about going away for a while,' Will ventured in the darkness of her hallway. 'To get some distance from all of this.'

Polly felt her heart hammering in her chest. Why did he have to tell her this tonight? There was too much emotion swilling around them — maybe it was frightening him, maybe that was precisely why.

'A distance from what? When?' she mumbled.

'Ralph and I have been invited on a trip out to the Middle East, in August.'

She felt dizzy, blind panic, standing there in the dark, hearing Will breathe, fearing his absence, fearing his impending death in some war-torn state. 'Please,' she implored, her voice no more than a whisper, 'I couldn't bear it, if something else went wrong, if I lost you, too.'

As she spoke she moved towards Will and he towards her, and then she was back in his embrace and, without meaning to, they were kissing, at first tentatively, then with urgency, a deep need. Then his warm lips were kissing the nape of her neck, his hands moving up, forward, feeling her breasts through her shirt.

'Not here,' he murmured. 'Let's go to bed.'

Unlike Emi, Polly had slept with a lot of men. For every occasion that Emi had rebuffed the advances of strangers, or friends, acquaintances or colleagues, Polly, habitually, had seized them. It had been to do with her searching for something that clearly she hadn't, to date, been able to find. She knew the psychobabble, that she'd been searching for a replacement father figure, that Peter's absences during their childhood, followed by his untimely death, had left her depleted and unresolved, that in her lovers she had been looking to replace him, but recognizing the pattern hadn't made any difference to her behaviour, it was all she had come to know, familiar territory. She'd always had a desire to test the boundaries, too. She'd lost her virginity to a boy called Jake when she was seventeen. It had happened in her bedroom while Sarah and Emi earnestly studied together in her father's defunct office downstairs. It was the summer before uni; he'd played the sax. They used to jam together and then they'd fuck. It was marvellous while it lasted, though deep down she'd never really cared. But once she'd done it, she found she had an appetite to do it again, and again. She didn't cheat, or mess anyone around. She never, ever lied, or hung around when the chips were down, or tried to make an affair outlast its natural life cycle, she'd always been clear about that, with herself and with her boyfriends, that she wouldn't repeat her parents' habit of nearly a lifetime. Sarah and Peter's eventual break had alarmed her, more so because it happened at all than because of the simple fact of it; she had expected it for so long that when, in the end, they actually separated, Polly had found it almost impossible to believe, or, perhaps, emotionally, ever fully to acknowledge. If she were honest, she had almost willed them to break free of one another, ever since she could remember. She had found their pretence at a happy marriage insulting, offensive, and held the two of them mutually culpable for their insidious deceit. Or, if she were scrupulously honest about it, she had in fact found her mother's behaviour worse than her father's – a part of her had despised Sarah for her countless years of martyrdom, for her simpering passive aggression, her steadfast determination to see it out, at any price to them all. At least Peter had had the gumption to find himself a flat elsewhere, to take lovers, to try to find a modicum of happiness, a degree of satisfaction along the way.

But now, in her bed, as Will's mouth started to respond to hers again, his fingers, deftly, to peel back her clothes, his lips now to move down her throat, brush her nipples, pause, between them, then move to the right and take it between his teeth, to tease it, then begin to suck, his hand to move down, to skim her naked buttocks, to move urgently now between her thighs, Polly felt something new, something unlearned, unimagined. Before he entered her she was already travelling to a place she'd never been with any of her lovers, travelling through a sea of colours she'd never seen. She knew she was heading for unchartered waters, that they were dangerous, that they should be out of bounds. Her father and Carol, duplicity; her mother, too, with Louis. When did that start, and why had Carol felt the need to tell her? The patterns were repeating themselves, she was part of the deceit, she and Will. She knew this was the last moment she had to bale out, before it was too late, but she also knew that for this experience she would readily drown.

28

Since the month of total separation and Marie's death Peter has fallen back into their old routine, working away all week, home for the weekend, and Sarah finds herself studying for a diploma in the history of textile design. She's nearly forty-one years old and her daughters are now approaching their eighteenth birthdays. At last she can feel the stormclouds that have made her body their residence for so many years beginning to disperse.

The course includes a week's residency, in the summer holidays, at a country estate just outside London. Historically she would have asked Carol to come and stay, but since she began studying she has seen less of her old friend, feels as if, now she is becoming more independent, Carol reminds her of the darker years. Cognitive therapy has helped her recognize the triggers that bring her down, to avoid them, and sadly she realizes that Carol has become one of them. Instead she asks Peter, who readily agrees to stay at home and take care of their daughters while she is away. With a slight stirring of trepidation, she heads off.

The course is a revelation. There are other people out

there, with similar interests, people who know nothing about Sarah's life, about Peter, or the twins. She works hard, and although she attends the evening dinners, she feels extremely tired at the end of each day, so leaves as soon as the meal is over and heads to her little single bedroom overlooking formal gardens to the back of the house. There is a man on her course whose name is Louis, and after a couple of days she recognizes that he follows the same pattern as her. Evidently he finds it equally hard to fit into this group situation. She begins to look forward to seeing him, at breakfast, during their breaks. On the third afternoon they have free time. It's a beautiful day, and she and Louis take a walk around the gardens together. To begin with they talk about the course and their shared passion for medieval art, but soon the conversation moves to their personal lives. He is a lawyer, a divorcee, with a son in his early twenties, he tells her. Recently he has started to work only part-time, is thinking of taking early retirement, at fifty, of pursuing his love of art, of taking this course to the next level. He is funny and light-hearted and Sarah finds herself relaxing, enjoying his company, and discloses a few rare details.

'I have twin daughters,' she begins. 'Oh, and a failing marriage,' she adds, falteringly, looking out across the lawns.

When she gets home, Louis calls Sarah, asks if she would like to go to the cinema with him, there's a new film out that everyone's talking about, it's called *Pulp Fiction*. Louis is funny and persuasive, but even speaking to him from her home phone makes her feel heady with deceit and she rejects his invitation to meet, apologetically, yet firmly. When she puts the phone down, however, she realizes that she feels euphoric. That evening, one by one, she flushes away all her pills. And then she tries to put him to the back of her mind.

29

Spring has now snatched firm control of Stockholm. An acute sunshine glints tantalizingly on the water but still the air remains sharp and cold. It hits the back of your throat and tastes of salt, as if rolled in on a breeze from far out to sea. Everything seems quicker, the city moving at a faster pace, the streets full of noise; people chattering, car engines purring, birds screeching, bicycles rattling over the cobbled back streets. After school Lotta and I now often take the lift down to the port to wander around people-watching, or counting the quaint bird boxes that perch on top of signposts around the harbour, carved in the shapes of owls, egrets, seagulls. Stephanie's being far more attentive and it's making a difference, too. Lotta looks better and is calmer. She hasn't mentioned sleeplessness again, and Pippi is back to staying at home during the school day. Kalle's workload is still intensive; he keeps promising that by midsummer it will have abated, but I don't mind so much now; the atmosphere between us has changed. Still neither of us has made the distance across the physical divide, but since we talked about his divorce at Solgläntan, there's been a new, tacit understanding that, at our own pace, we are heading towards something more.

Lotta and I have decided to create a wall-hanging for Kalle's birthday, and today we went to Skansen to make sketches of our scene: Soder over the sea from the park, with our – or should I say their? – flat clearly visible on the far side of the harbour. Admittedly we've used artistic licence, and the rotunda stands out big and bold against the sky. I told Lotta that it's going to be what might be called a 'naïve' artwork and she keeps repeating the term, as if it holds great significance. I've located and bought a small loom to weave it on. I've surprised myself by remembering how to use it, and as my fingers and Lotta's interweave with the coloured silks, I remember, so clearly, how I used to do this with my mother as a child, my hands interleaved with hers.

We've finally finished the wall-hanging – just in time! Kalle's birthday is tomorrow. Lars will arrive at five and we're going to surprise Kalle when he returns from work with a birthday cake and tea, before taking Lotta home to Stephanie's and heading off to the opera. There's been a sense of anticipation in the air all day, and Lotta's worked with furious attention, evidently determined to finish the project, to get it just right. As I watch her I see her father's perfectionist trait, as if it has been handed directly down the line.

After school we set the table and put the candles on the cake. At ten to five there was a ring on the buzzer and Lars appeared. Lotta couldn't contain her excitement, dancing up and down in the hallway, waiting for the lift to come up from the ground floor. When the doors slid open she literally threw herself at his robust form. I was surprised to see that he was dressed in an old shabby coat that I recognized from one of our walks. His eyes were twinkling as he scooped her up, and I moved to one side as he clambered with her into the apartment. Then he put her down and gave me an equally exuberant bear hug.

'Where is he, then?' he demanded, looking into the rotunda. 'Don't tell me your papa is still at the office?'

Lotta giggled mischievously as Lars removed his coat to reveal flamboyant attire underneath; a turquoise shirt beneath a navy blue linen suit.

Kalle was suitably delighted to see Lars and was effusive in his praise of our picture. Lotta sat on his knee throughout the tea and blew out the candles on his cake for him. After we had dropped her at Stephanie's, we took a taxi to the opera house. All the way Kalle couldn't stop smiling, and as Lars jumped out of the cab first to pay the driver he turned and put his arm around my shoulders. 'You are wonderful,' he said, as if it was a surprise, even to himself. Before I could reply, he had got out of the car and moved around to open my door. Little red lanterns were hanging gaily at the entrance to the beautiful eighteenth-century opera house.

'They're lit to tell the world that the opera house is full,' he explained. 'Aren't we lucky to be going? Come, let's get in out of the cold and have a drink before it starts.'

The foyer was packed and we had to weave our way downstairs to the bar. As we approached it, Lars glanced back at us over his shoulder. 'And now for my next surprise!' he exclaimed. He had no idea how right he was. Turning and looking at us, from her bar stool, was an all too familiar face.

'Clare!' Kalle exclaimed.

Sure enough, Clare Smart now stepped down from the stool and moved forwards to embrace her old friend.

'Isn't he bad?' she said, turning to Lars with a wicked smile. 'Lars happened to call just as I was about to get on a plane to Denmark, can you believe? I have book signings to do all over. It was just one little hop and here I am!'

Her attention now shifted to me.

'Didn't we meet in London?' she asked, pleasantly.

I nodded, didn't trust myself to speak.

'I love your new hairstyle,' she added. 'It almost makes you look completely different.'

So she knew.

'I have ordered champagne. Come, we must make a toast,' Lars interrupted, blatantly unaware of the turmoil he was causing. 'To my brother's good fortune, his health and his birthday.'

I sat through the opera in a fug of anxiety. In the dark Kalle's hand found mine and he held on to it tightly. At the end of the first act, as the audience applauded, he leant forward.

'Emi, what's wrong?'

I was trembling.

'I don't want them to know where I am,' I mumbled. 'Inevitably, Clare will tell James.'

Kalle looked troubled.

'You mean you really haven't told anyone where you are?' he whispered.

I shook my head.

'What am I going to do?' I felt on the verge of tears.

Kalle hesitated as the theatre curtain reopened.

'We'll be fine,' he said reassuringly, as darkness fell over the audience once more. But he didn't sound convinced.

After the opera had finished, we went to eat at one of Stockholm's most traditional restaurants, the famous chandelier-filled Sturehof, where white-aproned waiters glided around with measured efficiency. Kalle and Lars ordered quickly, promising that tonight we would savour Sweden's best herring and wild boar. After more champagne, wine was ordered and Lars ensured that our glasses were refilled with increasing regularity. I couldn't think what else to do, so I glugged my drink and ate the delicacies in a faint attempt to disengage from the crisis that now lay before me.

Lars was on great form and regaled Clare with tales of his hunting exploits over the winter, and of the artworks he was in the process of completing.

'They're full of mysteries and myths,' he explained, enigmatically.

I could hardly listen, let alone speak, and Kalle avoided eye contact. Thankfully Clare filled every pause in the conversation. She informed us that her feet had hardly touched the ground since her last book was launched, that she'd been on endless aeroplanes, sleeping in countless soulless hotels. I watched as Lars listened to her, attentively, a touch uncertainly. The emotional tension that existed between them was clear. Finally, towards the end of the meal, Clare excused herself to visit the 'bath-room' and, taking the opportunity, I got up and followed her. She was standing by the basins, evidently waiting for me, and needed no preamble.

'You must know the commotion you've caused,' she began quietly. 'James is devastated. And your sister, well, apparently she's in a dreadful mess.'

'I can't . . .' I began, before the words seemed to dry out of their own volition, and fade away.

'I saw them, you know.'

'Will and Polly? Were they . . . together?'

She hesitated.

'James says rumours abound – all denied. But that Will seems never to leave her side. I have to tell them, you know that, don't you?' she added, quietly. 'James is my friend.'

'Please,' I implored. 'Please, don't.'

'I head to London, a week Tuesday,' she replied, evenly. 'Perhaps you and I can meet tomorrow, and have a proper chat? In the meantime, I promise, I won't say a word.'

'Not even to Lars?'

She looked incredulous. 'He doesn't know?'

I shook my head.

'And Kalle, surely he must know about Polly?'

Again I shook my head. I couldn't speak. Her expression changed to sympathy – pity, even.

'Come on,' she said, putting an arm through mine. 'I think we need to go slam some schnapps. Isn't that what they do here, when the chips are down?'

*   *   *

By the time we arrived home it had gone 3 a.m and we were all inebriated. Clare and Lars headed off in the cab to a hotel at which, apparently by coincidence, they had both elected to stay.

'I have great hopes!' Kalle laughed as we went inside.

I remained silent, relieved to at last be away from her. He didn't switch on the light, instead just swung around and held his arms open. I sank into them, relieved.

'It's going to be all right,' he whispered. 'Maybe it's time to let London know you're here. It's been a long time.'

'I don't want this to end,' I found myself replying.

'It doesn't need to,' he said. 'But we all have some talking to do.'

'I think it does,' I answered. 'It's all about to come tumbling down.'

'No, of course it's not. Can I sleep beside you tonight?' he whispered.

Kalle led me up the stairs to his bedroom. Quietly, slowly, he helped me to undress, then slid me between his sheets and sat down on the side of the bed.

Time dissolved, and when I resurfaced a bright dawn had pierced the sky above us. Kalle was still there next to me, in his boxers and T-shirt, sleeping soundly, but our bodies were not touching, indeed had not touched. My head was splitting, and when I sat up I felt incredibly sick. Those guys surely could drink. I crept from the bed, went downstairs, took a shower and tried to focus on my impending meeting with Clare. We'd arranged to see each other at Café String at midday. Maybe Kalle was right. If Polly had to know I was here, I reasoned, what difference would it make? At some point Kalle would have to know more about my past, particularly if . . . I could hardly allow myself to imagine a future with him. I wanted it so badly, but I knew, instinctively, that I had to allow it to follow its own natural, slowly emerging path. I wasn't prepared to break this spell, not now, possibly not ever. Without Polly around me, I also knew that I was finally learning to feel comfortable in my own skin. Still I had told Kalle nothing about Polly, and to him my ex-husband was nothing more than an abstract notion, with no name.

With these thoughts swimming through my head, I left Kalle sleeping and made my way to Café String. When I arrived Clare was already seated, by chance, at my favourite table. Frank was there, too, and when he saw me he came ambling over. Clare seemed surprised at the evident familiarity between us.

'Does he know?' she enquired, as he went to get me a coffee.

I nodded, defeatedly. I wondered if Clare's novelistic fascination with other people's complicated lives was ticking its way through the information, working out how it might be used in a future work of fiction, and realized that, at this juncture, honesty was probably the only sensible ploy.

'He saw Polly and Will talking about me on TV; confronted me about it. He's promised not to say anything and so far, so good. It's cemented our friendship.'

'Luckily for you, neither Lars nor Kalle are big TV fans,' she said.

I remained silent, waiting for Clare's next move as Frank brought our coffees.

'Lars tells me that you and Kalle are in love,' she ventured, boldly now, stirring hers slowly. 'Is that why you came here?'

'I came to recuperate, after a failed marriage.'

Clare was silent for a while. Finally she spoke.

'Don't you think your punishment of them is severe?'

My conscience was pricking but my resolve to make her understand tightened. Even so, I was surprised by my honesty.

'Polly and I, we swallowed one another whole,' I said. 'We needed to let our souls breathe, independently. I needed to evaporate, to give us both the chance of a new start. And that's what I'm getting, with Lotta, with Kalle. If my past creeps back into my present, I don't see how I can make an independent future.'

Clare looked pensive.

'You've taken hold of a new life, perhaps,' she replied. 'But at the expense of other people's. Polly, James and Will, they're paralysed by your disappearance. You haven't given them the chance to renew, you've just frozen them in the past, in the moment you left. If you think they can build futures from there, you're sorely misguided.'

I didn't speak; had nothing to say. We sat in silence for a while.

'OK,' she said finally, with a sigh. 'Here's the deal.'

'Deal?'

'Yes,' replied Clare, determinedly. 'I feel I have a moral responsibility to reassure these people who love you that you're OK. That doesn't, however, mean I need to divulge where you are, or to tell Lars and Kalle about the fiasco you've left in your wake back in London – I'll leave that to your conscience.' She sipped her coffee. 'It's your story, not mine. You need to give me the script and I'll take it there.'

A note? A letter? Saying what? I could tell I had no choice. Slowly, I took my diary and a pen from my bag, tore out a page and looked down at it. I'd been trying to make myself contact Polly for months but something – fear, stubbornness, paralysis, had stopped me. To my amazement, now I had no choice, I felt relieved.

So, as Clare sat, watching me patiently, I wrote Polly a note. Then I gave it to her, along with my sister's address. She placed it carefully between the leaves of her book and slipped it inside her bag.

30

Over the following weeks Polly felt disconnected from reality, separated from Emi, from the outside world, from everything but Will. She knew she should feel wrong about this, but she couldn't. She reasoned that Emi was definitely alive, out there somewhere, living her own life, and that no one else had ever made her feel this way. All her previous lovers had managed to do was empty her out. With Will she felt emotionally and physically filled up.

By day they both carried on with their normal lives, working hard, affecting distance, continuing their search for Emi, but at night they headed back to Polly's and hid inside one another's bodies, their lovemaking so intense that they started to lose a sense of where one of them ended and the other began. It was like a drug. They didn't voice it, but they knew that it was only when they united physically that Emi evaporated completely from their minds. And as May slipped imperceptibly into June, Will didn't mention going away again and Polly didn't dare mention it, either, because the idea of losing him was too frightening for her even to contemplate. All the while, their intimacy seemed to grow, to block out all other emotion.

'Just because you're identical doesn't mean you're the same,' he murmured one night, as they lay in the dark. 'And the more I get to know you the more I see it; you're like two halves of a walnut in its shell, imprinted in reverse on one another. Where Emi retires you strike out, where you laugh, she'll cry. When you sleep, she wakes. It's fascinating, extraordinary. And yet . . .'

'What?' Polly felt nervous, hardly wanted to know what he was about to say.

'You're reassuringly the same in ways I find hard to explain. Perhaps I could have loved Emi in the way that I'm beginning to love you, if only she had let me, but there was always something holding her back.'

'I don't understand, you're frightening me.'

Will was quiet for a while.

'Don't feel afraid, Polly. It's important that I try to explain.'

'What?'

'It would be easy to say that I've fallen in love with you because I can't have Emi, that you're a replacement. But it's not like that, not at all. And yet, of course, there are things I loved about Emi that I also love about you – things inevitably that you do share.'

'Like what?' Polly felt vulnerable, at a loss and very, very sad.

'I couldn't draw Emi out. With her I coexisted and, you know, I think I felt very protective of her, she was so kind, so fragile. In retrospect, you know, it was almost as if I treated her as one of my causes – and how patronizing is

300

that? I can see it now, and I feel guilty. It didn't help her, you know, to have me to rely on; if anything I think it lowered her self-esteem. I'm always so active, so focused, so involved. I guess I kept her in the shadows. Not that I ever meant to. No wonder she wanted to leave me. With you, it feels as if, when we're together, we're equal, and the whole world is at our feet. You know, she was right, it was a mistake, our marriage. In the end, ironically, of the two of us she was the bolder one, for recognizing it first and for being brave enough to step out. I've always been so hell-bent on making things work. We'd been friends for so long, I just couldn't believe we could fail, and I loved her, too, in a platonic way, I suppose. I think she always thought that she made our marriage happen, that it was her motivation. But I was equally culpable; we should never have gone over the line, and I should have known that after Sarah's death she was in no state to make rational decisions. In some respects, I think Emi forced our relationship with the very intention of seeing it self-destruct. We were never really together, sexually, not like you and I are; at least, before Sarah died, you know, and even afterwards we could never find . . .'

Will hesitated, but now that he'd started telling her, Polly needed to know it all, she needed him to go all the way.

'It's OK, tell me,' she said, although she hated his words. They stung like acid rain.

'It was as if Sarah's death changed something in Emi, made her want to push everything to the limits, regardless of the consequences. I think she couldn't see another way to break free from me. I think she knew Sarah loved me

301

and she wanted to honour her commitment to me as part of your family. We were holding each other back from having a relationship with anyone else, and yet we weren't really having one with each other. It's funny that you ask if you're Emi's replacement, because sometimes I used to think, with her, that I was simply yours – her soulmate, so to speak, because she didn't have you any more. She needed to have "another half" around. But she and I both knew in the end that that wasn't enough.'

'Thank you for trying to explain,' Polly whispered, holding him close. She listened as his breath evened out. At the moment he lost consciousness she knew that Emi would always be there, inside her and him, between them, that they were stealing moments, that their time was already running out, that inevitably it would have to pass, whether Emi ever came back, or not.

31

Over the summer of 1994 Polly has acquired a boyfriend and she emanates a glow that makes her beautiful. Jake is young, blond, dishevelled, smart – and he plays the saxophone, too. The teenagers lock themselves away for hours on end, 'playing records' and jamming along with their classical instruments in her room. With his arrival, music and laughter return to the home. Emi remains more reserved, as ever; she is quieter than Polly and studies frantically hard. Often Sarah and Emi sit together in the study that looks out over the back garden, working on their separate assignments but physically close together, for hours on end. These times remind Sarah of the years when the girls were young, when she would sit and embroider on her bed while Emi lay on the floor, drawing or colouring in her books – thinking back, during these times, Polly was often roaming elsewhere. Emi seems content when she's immersed in her schoolwork and Sarah finds herself working on her diploma with an equally intense endeavour. It's liberating to have something cerebral outside the family to work towards, but she also savours these last moments with Emi, she knows that time is running out, that soon the girls will be gone.

When she's not studying, Emi hangs out with her school friend, Helen. They both seem to spurn the advances of boys. They are the studious ones, the children for whom love may well come later, Sarah thinks. Occasionally Polly teases Emi for her shyness but it seems to Sarah that, since Marie's death, there is a deeper, more generous rapport between her twins again. Jake is good fun and Emi seems to enjoy his company, almost as much as Polly does. Often now there's a gang of teenagers hanging out in the house. They seem capable of passing endless hours together, slumped in front of the video, devouring endless plates of baked beans on toast, listening to gritty pop music. Emi is always included in the gang and Sarah is happy that the children use their home rather than the streets of London as their adolescent playground. She also likes the house to be full of noise. It makes her feel more alive again, and Peter's absences seem less acute when the house is filled with laughter.

For their eighteenth birthday the following spring, Peter buys the girls trips on the new Eurostar train, under the ocean to Paris, and Jake accompanies them. They all go to stay with their old, favoured au pair, Madeline, who is now a thirty-year-old woman with a lecturing post at the Paris Conservatoire. The twins arrive home scented, with a new sophistication in their stride, a knowledge of a foreign place away from London, away from her. For Sarah this voyage from her feels like their first step towards their departure from the family home.

The following months pass without further unwelcome or unsettling events. A levels come and go, and all the money that Peter has spent on the children's education is well rewarded when they both pass their exams with the same high grades. The twins spend hours studying the university prospectuses and, to Sarah's surprise, elect to go to opposite ends of the country for the next stage in their studies – Emi to Sussex to read Law, Polly to Edinburgh, for a degree in English and Drama. Somehow or other, Sarah thinks, they've all managed to make it through everything, pretty much intact.

The closer the date for the girls to leave for university comes, however, the more conscious Sarah becomes that time for her and Peter, for their charade, is running out. Since the necklace incident they have made a silent pact that their relationship is on hold. He spends the entire week away, at his flat in Newcastle, and returns at the weekends, predominantly to play golf and to see the girls. She's amazed that Emi and Polly have not questioned his recent prolonged absences more directly, that they have seemed so at ease with the growing distance that has evolved between their parents. They are so preoccupied with their studies, their friends, and in Polly's case, thankfully, she supposes, with Jake, that there hasn't been much time for them to focus on their parents' affairs.

One day, however, just a week before they are due to leave for university, Polly arrives home and announces bluntly to Sarah that she's broken up with Jake. 'Oh, darling, are you OK?' Sarah cries, rushing to her daughter's side, arms outstretched, ready to console her daughter's tender, broken heart. But, to Sarah's astonishment, Polly shrugs off the embrace and returns her look contemptuously.

'Of course I am. It was my choice,' she remarks coldly. 'There's no point pretending it could work with me in Scotland. When a relationship's over, you have to move on. No one benefits from prolonging the agony.'

Sarah feels as if Polly has slapped her in the face. She's confused by her daughter's dispassion in the face of her first love affair but also gets the underlying message: that the girls clearly understand their parents' affairs. She wants to mention Peter now, to talk it through, but before she gets the opportunity Polly has turned on her heels and headed upstairs. Moments later, she hears Emi shriek.

'Oh my God, how could you, Polly? Poor, poor Jake.'

It seems, if anything, that Emi is more devastated by her sister's actions than Polly is. For the rest of the week a summer frost hangs in the air between them all.

When Peter arrives home that Friday, Sarah tells him of Polly's break-up. If Sarah is not mistaken, she sees his eyes twinkle.

'She'll have plenty more fish to fry in Edinburgh before she finds the love of her life,' he laughs, dismissively. 'She's only eighteen, Sarah, after all.'

At that moment there is a ring at the front door. It is Carol. Sarah's beginning to feel guilty about her neighbour, about how little she seems to see her these days. When Peter opens the door she can hear them talking together in low tones and she catches only the tail end of their conversation.

'Yes, yes, tomorrow,' she hears Peter say.

They treat her like their shared patient; she thinks, I'll show them.

When Carol comes in Peter suggests that he take Polly

to Edinburgh, that perhaps Carol could accompany Sarah on her drive to Brighton with Emi. Sarah is left with no option but to agree.

The next day they pack up the cars and take the girls. It is a poignant trip and Sarah can hardly bear to look at Emi as she leaves her, waving them off anxiously from her halls of residence, set back from the main, modern campus in a dreary low-rise brick building. It is a drizzly day and Sussex University is bleak, like an open prison, she thinks.

Halfway home, Sarah practises on her friend.

'I'm going to ask Peter for a divorce,' she states, eyes fixed on the A23 ahead of her.

'Gosh,' Carol replies, 'are you absolutely sure?'

If she's not mistaken, Sarah sees Carol's cheeks flush.

When he gets back Sarah asks Peter to sit down. The house is so quiet it feels as if its spirit has drifted out of the door, along with the girls. Sarah knows that with their absence nothing is left here for her now. She tells him she has something she'd like to say.

'I'm ready,' she states, mimicking the dispassion to which Polly introduced her on announcing her separation from Jake, only a week before. 'I'd like a divorce.'

Peter hesitates momentarily but his expression doesn't change. Then he sits forward in his chair, clasps his hands together and tells Sarah all about his French mistress, Brigitte. He has known her for years, he says, since he started to work part-time in Paris. She's a widow with two adult children. She worked for the same company as Peter, as a marketing manager, but now she has moved to Montpellier, in the South of France. Their affair only

307

started in recent months, he says, but he feels certain that he would like to spend more time with her.

Sarah listens and watches Peter. She feels cold and unemotional and disinterested and reassured, all at the same time. She says nothing, simply nods and then asks him when he would like to leave.

32

We're streaming out of Stockholm harbour on the ferry to celebrate this, the dazzling light of midsummer. It's early morning and our little white boat's packed with energized weekenders, their bags bulging and their hampers packed. There's an air of hushed anticipation on board as people prepare for the long day's night, sharing plans as they drink their coffee in the tiny downstairs bar, or sitting up here, like me, outside on spray-softened wooden benches, watching as we leave the majestic metropolis behind. Already we're zigzagging our way between lush, green-forested islands dotted with pretty, freshly painted summer houses, nestled between the trees, stopping occasionally at tiny jetties to drop off handfuls of passengers into the waiting embrace of family or friends. Kalle and Lotta are standing together, leaning over the edge, his arms protectively around his daughter as the spray hits her face. I wish it were me, standing there in his arms with his face in my hair and his heart beating against my back.

'Coffee?' he mouths, and I nod as his face lights up with a smile. I am in love with this stranger with sea-grey eyes; I wonder if he knows. I watch as he heads down the steps now and Lotta comes to join me, sits with her head against my shoulder.

'Tomorrow we'll dress up and put flowers in our hair, then we'll dance and sing to the light,' she murmurs. 'In midwinter we celebrate the darkness – then we dress in white and sing the "Lucia". One day I hope to be Lucia herself. The sun and the moon, the light and the dark, that's our way.'

Now she's closed her eyes and is beginning to doze as we head for another jetty; to drop off a couple with their infant child in a pack on his father's back.

Kalle's returned with the coffee; he's trying to read over my shoulder. It's time to close my diary.

By the time we approached Lininas more than three hours had passed and Kalle, Lotta and I were the only passengers left on board the little boat. As we got closer to land we could see Lars standing at the end of the jetty, wearing a straw hat and a red T-shirt, with Bosse spinning round and round at his heels. Lotta ran along the gangplank first and leapt directly into his arms. By the time Kalle and I had unloaded our provisions and greeted Lars, the boat had already turned and was speeding its empty way back towards Stockholm. We loaded his old Saab, tucking Bosse and bags in the boot, and began the final leg of our journey. The countryside looked foreign to me without its blanket of white; the rolling meadows resplendent with wild flowers, the grassy prairies grazed by brown and white cows. Soon we moved on through more familiar territory, deep pine and silver birch forests, punctuated by rays of bright sunlight, and finally across 'our' small, wooden bridge over the Baltic sparkling below us, as Lotta shrieked and jumped up and down. At last we were back at Solgläntan, our own, far-out little piece of paradise.

As I got out of the car and stood looking over the sea, I realized that the ground felt incredibly steady beneath my feet – in fact, I felt as if I had 'landed'. I wondered if Lars would say that here in the land of *allemanstratten* ownership had no real hold, that it was the spirit that made the home. I've never felt this way before. Alma Place was my childhood home, but since then, I've never felt truly settled. Blenheim Crescent was always Mum's home, never mine. It was a place where she evidently felt she was meant to be. Will and I were always just passing through. While we lived there I felt damp with the emotion of the flat, and although I denied that Mum's spirit 'bothered' me there, I realized now that sleeping alongside my memories of her had saturated my spirit. Looking out on to the communal gardens made me claustrophobic, too; all those dark windows looking inwards, all those eyes, covertly watching the space between, a deep enclosure, with no routes out. Conversely, in her little modern flat in Bermondsey, looking over the swirling Thames, I recognized that Polly had found a place where she felt expansive and at ease. I wondered if Will felt the same way about it now. I could imagine him, spending hours staring out over the river, across the cityscape beyond. Like Polly he's always liked the bigger picture, the world outside the window.

Lotta and Lars had raced off towards the house with Bosse. I could hear them singing in Swedish, a long way away, and I watched as Kalle came to join me. I was staring down towards the little harbour, over the bobbing boats and the crystal-clear sea, to the spot where, decades earlier, Christa had lost his grip.

'Happy to be back?' he asked.

I nodded as we both turned at the sound of Lars calling to us in Swedish.

Kalle laughed. 'Lars wants us to bring the groceries up. Lotta's hungry.'

'What's all this with speaking Swedish?' I enquired, as we picked up the provisions and began to make our own way up to the house.

'It must be midsummer madness,' he replied. 'It's a very Swedish affair – maybe it even has an effect on our tongues.'

This evening we ate in the garden, the four of us sitting together on old wooden chairs in the ever-steady light, discussing plans for the next evening: the actual midsummer solstice, when all the islanders would descend upon us for a party, food and wine in hand. Eventually Lotta fell asleep in Kalle's arms. It was late but the sun was still remarkably bright in the sky. He took her gently up the stairs to bed.

'I'm going to spend July in the US, with Clare,' Lars informed us when he got back. 'We want to go whale-watching and then I plan to take off on an adventure.'

He was trying to sound casual, but the weight of his words was lost on neither of us. Since Pauline had died, the furthest Lars had ventured from his island was Stockholm. Evidently Clare was having a cathartic effect. Maybe in her own way, I considered, momentarily, she was helping us all. Something held me back from my belief, a shadow of doubt. She'd promised silence about Will and Polly to Lars and Kalle. Since our brief night together in Stockholm, the subject had not been raised again between Kalle and me. I wondered how much Lars really knew. I brushed my suspicions away.

'Just make sure you come back,' Kalle said, a touch paternally.

'Of course,' laughed Lars. 'I'll be here by the last week of August. You know I never miss the crayfish season.'

He got up and began clearing the table and I stood to help him, but Kalle put a hand on my arm. I sat back down as Lars disappeared into the house.

'I put Lotta in the blue room, your room,' he said quietly.

'Don't worry, I can share,' I said.

'Maybe with me?' he asked.

Kalle and I lay innocently together, but this time he held me as he slept. I was too enthralled, feeling him so close to me, to even want to close my eyes. In the end I rose, resigned to not sleeping in this high light. And now I'm writing this sitting on the balcony as the longest day of the year makes its clear, calm ascent. A light breeze is whispering its secrets to the trees and below me in the harbour the rigging is tinkling on Kalle's boat. I don't want to miss a single detail. Whatever the future holds I don't ever want to forget a thing.

As the evening approached, preparations for the party gathered momentum and guests from surrounding islands began to arrive. By nine o'clock around forty people had congregated, cramming the harbour with their tiny boats, then slowly carrying their vast quantities of food, beer and schnapps up the granite path to the house. The sky remained clear, the sun high above our heads, the house and gardens standing out against the forest like a sunlit stage. Lotta beckoned to me to come with her and we slipped away, heading through the wood, across the meadow, then on down to the spit of land that separates the island from Lars's studio.

We sat quietly together on the smooth granite beach and Lotta threw pebbles into the clear, cold water. I remembered Kalle describing her therapeutic effect on Lars last summer and I felt its impact upon me now. I empathized with her desire to escape for a moment from the crowd. I had felt nervous with all those unfamiliar people. I put my arm around her as we watched the eternal sunshine glinting like a million diamonds over the sea. The quiet hint of a moon was also rising, as little more than a mere gesture. When I looked down, Lotta had drifted off in my arms. A sprinkling of freckles dotted her nose and as I counted them a deep surge of affection rose inside me. And suddenly I thought of Polly, of how much she, too, would love it here. I knew that, like Kalle and Lotta, she would have no problem sleeping under this unremitting sun.

After a few minutes I heard the steady beat of music lifting and falling in the air. It was time to head back to the party before we were missed. However, I wasn't sure how I was going to carry Lotta across the meadow to the house; in sleep her weight seemed to have doubled. I was about to wake her from her midsummer reverie when I heard the sound of footsteps. Lars appeared from the forest path, carrying a large red wool rug.

'I guessed I'd find you here,' he murmured, as he took Lotta from me and wrapped her up in the blanket. 'It's good she's had a rest. The night's still very young.'

We left the beach together and wandered back across the meadow.

'We're ready to raise the *Majstång*,' he said, then chuckled quietly at my confusion. 'It's our maypole. It's traditional to raise it in the afternoon, but here we make our own rituals. Until recently the islanders here believed that plants and water had special healing powers during midsummer's night; evil spirits were said to be free, too, and they lit bonfires to protect themselves against their powers. We continue that tradition today. Parents would send their young girls to pick a bouquet of flowers, too, alone and in total silence; they'd include sea starwort, orphine, wild chives, tansy, mayweed, St John's wort and wood anemones. They believed that if they put the flowers under their pillow, the daughters would dream of their future husbands.'

Lotta stirred as we neared the house. The barbecue was being lit, Kalle behind it, apron on. He raised a fork in the air as he saw us approach. A bonfire was sparking and crackling a little further away, and the party was already in full swing. Lotta looked around, disoriented for a moment, then wriggled out of Lars's arms. Without a second's hesitation she ran to join the group of island children.

People started to form a large circle as others carried a

huge Celtic-style cross covered in green, coiled ivy and entwisted with pale blue flowers to the centre. The children reappeared with garlands in their hair and instinctively, it seemed, they all began to sing, children and adults alike, simultaneously moving forwards to raise the great pole. Once secured, they promenaded around the cross, singing some more. I felt an arm round my waist and turned to find Kalle by my side.

'Come on,' he said. 'We have to join in.'

The rest of the evening passed in a blur of dancing and singing and eating from the feast we'd laid out, a vast, traditional summer *smörgasbord* including salmon, meatballs, herring, new potatoes and fresh dill, cheese and wild strawberries. As the evening wore on, we drank and danced and sang and drank some more, until the sky flushed a deep lilac and I thought that finally darkness would descend. For half an hour a deepening, purple glow filled the air and then, almost immediately, a riotous dawn chorus began. Slowly the party made its way down to the sea. Kalle put his arm around me again as we all stood on the jetty and toasted the dawning of a new day. The sun seemed to have touched, then risen back up above, the horizon line without ever really disappearing at all.

Finally, people began to drift away. Lotta had fallen asleep on the white sofa in the sitting-room, and together Kalle and I took her upstairs. A small bunch of flowers had been placed on her pillow.

'Lars always picks them for her.' He grinned as he laid Lotta down.

*   *   *

When I woke, Kalle was fast asleep next to me, his body curled around mine, his left arm resting protectively across my waist. Lotta was snuggled in next to him, on the other side, clutching her posy of flowers. She was disturbed by my waking. Together we headed downstairs.

'Are you going to marry Papa?' she asked me, between mouthfuls of yoghurt.

'I don't know,' I replied, gently, trying not to smile.

'I'd like it,' she stated, and took another spoonful.

33

Polly was heading for the shower when she saw it; a flimsy white piece of paper, folded in three, slipped under the door. As she bent down she assumed it was from a neighbour, perhaps complaining, she thought, somewhat guiltily, about the noise she and Will had been making in the night. But as soon as she saw the writing she knew that she was looking at a message from Emi. Her knees gave way under her and she sank to the floor to read it.

Polly,
I know I should have written before but I couldn't find a way. I'm sorry but I had to escape. Will and I tried to make it work but there was something about us that was never quite right – something missing in me. And all the while the truth was staring us in the face, just none of us could see it – apart from Mum; you know, I think she did, but how could she ever have said? You and I are like two halves of a whole. I used to think that we must essentially be the same, that feeling unlike you meant that there was something wrong with me, but I'm beginning to understand that it's OK to be somebody else, somebody quieter, somebody less certain. You have the half that can work with

Will; the ease of being, the exuberance, the passion for that big bad world out there. You should love each other, it's your destiny. Please don't let your concerns for me stand in the way. When I'm strong enough, I promise I'll come back. So please stop worrying. I'm fine – almost happy, even.
Emi x

Polly's blood pulsated in her head. It had been so long coming, six months already, but the moment of absolute affirmation, that Emi was still alive, left her feeling unexpectedly deflated, angry too. It was pitiful, this artless, flimsy memo, scrawled, it seemed, hurriedly on a piece of paper torn from a pad, and not even sealed in an envelope. But it was definitely from Emi: there was no doubting that handwriting – or her turn of phrase. In some ways Polly realized it changed nothing, in other ways it changed everything. She thought of Will, and of Emi's willing for them to be together. But it was like the necklace, and it was like Marie. She thought again of Hera's words. Emi's will couldn't shape other people's emotions. It was as if she was stuck in some fictional, adolescent place where everything external was impacted by her own view. It might be true that she and Will loved one another. But how did Emi know? Did she know before she left? Before they did, even? And had Sarah really seen it, or was that just another of Emi's figments?

Polly read the note again and wondered what ramifications it might hold. For a start, she supposed, they would have to stop looking for Emi. They would have to learn patience, to allow her to find her own way back when she was ready; just as Kaz and Hera had said. But in another way, until they did find her, Polly knew that she wouldn't be able to resume her own life fully. She scrutinized the note once more. Of course Emi wasn't stupid. She'd left no clues. With a growing dread, she moved back into the bedroom and woke Will.

'I told you. We're behaving like pawns in one of Emi's games,' he said defeatedly, once he'd digested the contents of her note. 'It's as if she planned it all.'

'How did she know – before we did?' Polly asked him.

Will shook his head.

'I don't know, I don't understand. But I'll be damned if I'll let her destroy us now.'

34

'Darling, I've found a flat. I know it's a lot to ask but would you come and look at it with me?'

Sarah's tone contains a slightly nervous flutter, it's high-pitched and she's speaking a little bit too fast. Emi's standing in the corridor of her halls of residence on the shared payphone and her voice sounds echoey. Sarah can still hear as she puts her hand over the receiver and speaks in a half-whisper to someone next to her, about meeting in a minute in the union bar.

'Of course I will,' she replies. 'But have you asked Pol, too?'

Sarah pauses. 'She won't come from Edinburgh just to see a silly flat, but I'll ask her if you think I should.'

'No, no, don't worry.' Emi sounds guilty for having asked. 'Can I bring a friend along?' she adds, tentatively.

'Of course, darling, that would be lovely,' replies Sarah, relieved.

Emi and Will catch the train up to London together the next morning. They meet Sarah with a man from the local upmarket estate agent outside the appointed flat in

Blenheim Crescent. Sarah and Emi's eyes meet and Sarah sees a pang of sorrow for her, as she stands there, looking, she knows, so innocent and ageing at the same time, so expectant, with this hungry salesman who is certain to screw her on the price – unless Emi and her new friend can step in and negotiate on her behalf.

Sarah looks hopefully at this pair of young students, standing there gauchely in their faded 501s and black T-shirts, both with long dark hair, tied back. The roles are reversing, she realizes. Emi and Will seem streetwise, confident, and for a moment they look oddly alike, more alike even than perhaps she and her daughter do. The ties are loosening, she thinks, with a jolt – and where does that leave me?

'What are you studying?' she asks Will, as they follow the estate agent into the smart, quiet foyer. It's all so new to her, this stage in Emi's life, this flat-hunting lark, too. It's best to talk about something else.

'Politics, Arabic,' he replies earnestly. 'And European law,' he adds, with a wry smile. 'That's the boring but necessary bit.'

The agent is now opening the door to the flat – to her possible future, thinks Sarah. She returns Will's smile, thanking him and Emi for lending 'moral support'. And with that they all head inside.

The flat is on the crescent's west side. It's elegant and well-proportioned, Georgian, with wide rooms, high ceilings and narrow balconies to both aspects, one side on to the crescent and the other on to magical communal gardens, like a step through the looking-glass, Sarah thinks enthusiastically, a place from which to stand and watch other people's lives play out, down below in the gardens or up above, through the countless floor-to-ceiling drawing-room windows that glint tantalizingly during the day and, no doubt, light the sweep of the crescent's first floors at night.

Sarah is enamoured and soon it is hers. Will proves himself to be an anchor in the midst of the moving storm. He reads through all the paperwork for her – he's a confident negotiator for one so young and he successfully helps Sarah conduct the deal. Within four months she is in. And Will, in his own way, is in too. He's become part of their future. He has a share in it that is more than emotional. He's helped to carry the furniture and tea-chests up the stairs, he's painted the sitting-room duck-egg blue. He has brought a stepladder and dragged cases and trunks up into the attic space above the hall. He's even shared their first meal, a Thai takeaway that Carol brings over on the night Sarah moves in.

The flat soon becomes indulgently feminine. It smells of vanilla and star anise. She and Emi now spend countless Saturdays together, in Liberty's, at Portobello or her favourite, Alfie's antiques market, choosing fabrics, furniture. Sarah positively revels in her choices: Designers Guild curtains, pale rose carpets, a deep-seated chintz-covered armchair and an ornate gilt mirror to place above the Edwardian marble fireplace. She always has cut flowers throwing out their fresh scent across the threshold, too: they create 'eternal spring', she says, with a smile.

*   *   *

Polly comes down for the summer holidays and she and Emi stay together in the spare room. Polly passes few comments about the flat and she seems uninterested in their mother's newfound energy. She avoids time alone with Emi, too, as if she is determined not to discuss this turn of affairs, at all, on any level. Emi introduces Polly to Will but Polly looks at him through blank eyes and asks no questions. Emi knows better than to push her, but beneath the skin Polly's blatant negativity stirs a deep melancholy inside her. On the third morning, Polly suddenly announces she's going back to Edinburgh for the festival. Emi recognizes pain in Sarah's eyes and she tries to persuade Polly to stay longer.

'I'm going to help a friend with a comedy sketch,' she says, decisively. 'I promised.'

Before she leaves, however, Emi manages to persuade Polly to go back to Alfie's with her and Will to buy Sarah a joint moving-in present, something her mother had admired the last time they were there; a pair of art-nouveau table lamps, polished aluminium, back-arching female nudes, holding tinted opalescent glass lamps out before them in their long, slender arms. At the last moment, Polly says she'd prefer hers to have a tangerine-coloured lamp, and gets the dealer to switch it over; no longer an identical pair.

35

Every day now more mothers and children join us in our little park after school, their packed teas made. Lotta's making great progress; recently she's even been prepared to entertain a couple of playmates in the sandpit. They bring their buckets and spades and spend the otherwise empty sunshine hours between school and bedtime together, repeatedly filling and tipping out the golden grains, earnestly building castles, digging moats. The mothers either hide inside their downtime with eyes fixed on books, or seek out the company of others like them, congregating in groups of two or three, chatting or fussing around their toddlers while their older children play.

I'm isolated from the pack, the only foreigner, the only 'au pair' – and although they always bid me hello, these true Stockholm blondes don't invite me further in. So I tend to sit alone, sometimes reading, but often as I sit watching Lotta I find my thoughts turning not to Polly but to Mum. At last enough time seems to have passed for me to start to see her again, as she once was; a complete person, not the fading woman who lay so thin and agitated in that hospital bed towards the end. I'm reclaiming Sarah

Leto in visual snapshots, at different ages, from different angles, sometimes turning, bending, looking me straight in the eye. At other times I simply hear her voice; laughing, serious, serene or just plain sad. I'm finding a portrait of her, a fully evolved woman, with a history and a heart and a personality of her own: one outside me and Polly, and outside our father, too. I wonder more about the man called Louis whose name I heard her mention, about the part he played. I wonder if it was through him that she lost her melancholy, just as with Kalle I feel my own quietly slipping away. Regardless of the continuing uncertainty between us, I feel stronger, as if I'm finally letting go of my grief, being informed, not brought down, by her ethereal presence; stronger, and with her love, not her darkness, at my core.

Since midsummer Lotta's been staying, as Stephanie's gone away again. We have all returned, silently, to the way it was before; Kalle and I sleeping in our separate rooms, back to our daily routine as if midsummer were literally a dream. He's thrown himself back into his work and I wonder if Lotta's constant presence in the flat has gone some way to causing his recent retraction from me, but I don't know how to ask, to raise the subject. Kalle warned me, apologetically, that until the summer break in three weeks' time he was going to have to work ferociously hard, but that afterwards we could take off together to Solgläntan for the whole month of July. I, of course, am thrilled at the prospect. Lotta will be in America with Stephanie and Marcus for the summer vacation, and Lars is heading off with Clare. We will be completely alone. Even so, I can't help but feel that this is only part of the story, that Kalle is struggling emotionally with his divorce from Stephanie, with giving up his past, or, perhaps more so, his idea of what the future would be.

Over the past few days, Stockholm's experienced a frenzy of activity followed by a sudden stillness as people have taken to the boats and headed out to their summer houses to recuperate for the month. Now the city's filled with tourists swinging camera bags and gazing wide-eyed over bridges at the sparkling sea. Still I have heard nothing from Polly. I'm beginning to realize that Clare must have kept her promise, had not given her a hint or a clue as to my whereabouts, after all. I haven't heard a thing from her since she left and am finding it hard not to conjure a number of scenarios in my mind: Clare confiding in Will and Polly, giving them a detailed account of my life; Clare taking Polly to one side and explaining that I have fallen in love with Kalle; Clare urging them either to come or not to come and find me. The fact that I haven't heard from them since she took the note makes me wonder if perhaps they feel they already know enough, feel no need to look for me any more.

Now Clare and Lars have gone to the US and today Lotta flies out with Stephanie and Marcus. I am going to try to push them all from my mind for a month. Lotta won't be home now until September. Kalle's cleared all his clinical work and tomorrow morning at last it will be our turn to leave the city. A whole month at the summer house, just Kalle and me. I feel great, I feel ready, I feel certain that this is the moment, at last, that this will be our time.

*   *   *

We woke up this morning to gathering, granite-grey stormclouds and drove back out to Solgläntan in a rainstorm that washed away all idea of summer in its wake. Water cascaded in from the sea, roamed over the forests and through the meadows, gathering a pace as it swept away the wild flowers in its path. A sharp chill chased its tail. Now we're at the house and the atmosphere is dank and morose. Out to sea further rainclouds are preparing to sweep in from the east. Kalle's lit a fire and we're huddling by it, side by side on the sofa. He's reading as I write. The atmosphere between us is calm, yet expectant. I don't care about the weather, I don't care if it rains for ever; this is all that I want in the world.

Last night, without question, we slept together in Kalle's big old bed and he held me close to him, but again there was no further intimacy. I am afraid to push him over the line, I'm afraid to mess it up and yet for the first time the ambiguity between us is also making me uneasy; where are we going to go from here? When we got up the rain continued to fall and we took a long, quiet walk through the muddy forest in ankle-length raincoats, stopping occasionally to pick the bilberries that grow discreetly on the forest floor. Then we came home to dry out and eat lunch together on the little covered balcony, watching as the rain attempted to drench the sea an even deeper grey. I told Kalle I'd never seen rain like it and he laughed, promising me that there was nothing at all unusual in the weather.

'But it will change soon,' he added, reassuringly. 'It always does.'

'When I was a child . . .' I hesitated, but Kalle was watching me, urging me on with his eyes. 'My mother hated the rain. She said it drowned her spirit. And I knew what she meant. It always made me feel nervous and threatened. Whereas, curiously, my sister didn't seem to be bothered by it at all.' Finally, I'd said it.

It was the first time I'd mentioned 'a sister' since I arrived. I was amazed Kalle didn't pick up on it. Instead he enquired after my father, his view of inclement weather.

I thought for a moment. What had Peter thought about anything?

'I don't know the answer to that.'

'And now?'

'My father or the rain?' I laughed, despite myself.

'Both.'

'My father, well, he died, when we, I mean I, was twenty, so I guess he doesn't care one way or the other. And the rain here? Shall I be honest?'

Kalle nodded.

'It feels like a cleansing. I love our walks, I love the feeling of it soaking everything, drenching our skin.'

'And how about your sister? What would she think of it?'

Finally, I thought, he's come to it.

'I guess she'd hate it,' I replied. 'She's a sun-worshipper.'

'Tell me about her, tell me it all, Emi. What exactly did you run away from?'

I felt myself panicking. I'd just led Kalle to this moment, but now Polly was facing me head on, I realized that still I wasn't ready, I couldn't articulate it all.

'She's on the other side of me,' I said, weakly.

Kalle opened his mouth to speak, then thought better of it and simply looked away, out across the sea.

'Give me time and I'll take you there,' I added, but I'm not sure I sounded convinced.

Kalle's taken to swimming off the little jetty in the down-pours while I sit and watch him from under the sauna's eaves next to the pure white skull of a sharp-toothed pike, caught, he told me, by Lars when he was not a day over thirteen. Today he urged me to join him in the water.

'I don't swim,' I said.

'Don't or can't?' he teased.

I faltered, confused.

'Can't – I mean, don't,' I said, looking away from him and down at the spilling rain. In my mind I saw Marie's pretty face. Kalle surveyed me quizzically, then turned and dived off the jetty and began swimming out. He went further and further, until he'd become no more than a mere dot, way out in the sea. I waved my hands, helpless and anxious. At last he turned and began to swim back towards me.

'Did I frighten you?' he asked, as he finally climbed on to the jetty. I turned away, my eyes smarting with tears.

'I'm freezing,' he added, walking from me. 'I'm going to take a sauna.'

I didn't follow. Why is it all going so horribly wrong?

This morning I woke up and knew that something had changed, even before I opened my eyes. When I did I saw that sunshine was flooding over us through the windows. I shook Kalle awake and he smiled a big, open, wide smile.

'I told you it would all change,' he said.

We took Lars's little boat and rowed out past his studio. I craned my neck to see more. A jetty led to steps through gorse and a white wooden house, built at the top of a small mound, surrounded by decking. To the right of the house there was a copse and behind that the island petered out to the open sea.

'Maybe when he's back?' I ventured hopefully, and Kalle laughed.

'He's working on a very special project,' he said. 'You'll need to wait for an invitation.'

He fished from the side of the boat as I lay back blissfully and closed my eyes, letting the sun flood my inner lids orange. Everything seemed calm again. After a while he caught a shiny sea bass, and as it flipped and lurched in the base of the boat he rowed quickly back to the beach. Together we built a small fire and grilled our catch. Then, after eating the fresh white flakes of fish, we lay dozing in the gentle afternoon sun.

When we got back Kalle lit the sauna again and urged me to come and take a swim with him before using it. I could tell that this was becoming a psychological challenge that, for some reason, he was determined to win.

'After the sun, the sea on your skin is such a balm,' he enthused. 'You'll feel a million dollars.'

Still I shook my head.

To my surprise, Kalle shrugged his shoulders sulkily and wandered back up to the house, muttering something about 'making food'. I sat alone looking out into the cool, clear water. I've never talked about it, but since Marie's drowning I've not been back in the water. It's been a block for me; and a punishment of sorts, too, because before that fatal incident I'd always loved to swim. But I was beginning to realize that if I were to salvage something between Kalle and me, I had no choice; that I had to do it. Quickly I peeled off my clothes and stood naked, looking out across the sea. I knew if I could force myself to overcome this fear I'd be able to do anything – even, perhaps, to face Polly. First I dipped my toe into the water. It was freezing. I hesitated, then ran to the end of the little jetty, shut my eyes and jumped. The sea seemed to swallow me whole. I found myself submerged in a dark, ice-cold place. I resurfaced and struggled to find the slippery steps, hauled myself back out, relieved to find my feet back on dry land. Then I ran along the jetty and on into the safety and heat of the sauna.

A few moments later Kalle tapped on the door.

'Did you go in?' he asked nonchalantly, lying down on the opposite bench and closing his eyes.

'You know I did,' I said wearily. 'I could sense you watching me.'

Kalle was silent for a moment. 'I'm sorry,' he said. 'I couldn't help it. But are you OK? Something made you panic.'

'Bad memories,' I replied. 'It was an accident of sorts, when I was sixteen.' I paused as the memory came flooding back, then forced myself to elucidate. 'We were at the Ladies' Pond, in Hampstead; a group of us, including our friend Marie and her mum. It was very hot and Marie's mum had fallen asleep in the sun. Three of us, my sister, Marie and I, were playing with a ball in the water. I threw it out past Marie, too far out, into the weeds. I knew it was dangerous to swim out there, nevertheless, I willed her to go after it. In that moment, I felt furious with her for everything that was happening in my life; I willed the water to open up, to consume her – and it did.'

I also remember glancing over my shoulder, back towards Polly, although I didn't mention this to Kalle. She had stared back at me, the message clear, transparent; one thought, two minds. 'Sacrifice her,' it said. By the time we looked back at Marie she'd already disappeared from sight.

'It was my fault, our fault, that she drowned,' I added.

Kalle didn't speak for a while. 'You know, one of the common effects of depression is the inability to see outside yourself,' he finally replied, his voice taking on a certain, clinical air. 'To think that everything bad in the world that anyone else does, in relation to you, is of your own making, is your fault. But that is not the way that people, or the world, really work. Would you say that, naturally, Marie was a risk-taker?'

I immediately felt defensive.

'Yes, I guess so,' I said eventually.

'Try looking at it from a biological perspective. Some people have dopamine receptors that reduce the buzz they get from a regular level of risk. They will go to more extreme lengths than the ordinary person to gain that dopamine high. Perhaps Marie was one of those people? Perhaps that was why she swam out.'

'The novelty-seeking gene,' I murmured. 'I know, I've read about it, in some of your notes.'

'As the media call it, yes,' he replied. 'In your case, Emi, I'd hazard a guess that you were born with your dopamine receptors tuned in fairly high; that you sense danger, anxiety, very readily. And even when you take risks, like coming here, you handle the experience with immense caution. Maybe, as a result, you saw the danger coming for Marie before she did. That doesn't mean it was your fault that she drowned. Other genetic differences influence our attitude to risk, too. For example, the less monoamine oxidase we have in our brains, the more likely we are to crave excitement and to take greater risks to find it.'

'Today, when I got in the water, I felt as if I really was going to drown,' I confessed. 'I panicked. And then I thought of Marie. I could see her, being pulled from the weeds.'

'Don't you think, perhaps, that her mother should have been watching her? After all, you were only children. Maybe she was like her daughter, and was equally insensitive to the risk she was taking by falling asleep.'

'I guess so . . .' My words trailed off; I was lost in the science.

'There's something about you I can't put my finger on, Emi,' he murmured. 'You're so very afraid of articulating your emotions. I wonder who used to do it for you. Was it your mother – or your sister? Is she older? Maybe she was the one who carried you along.'

'Of course she didn't. No one did,' I retorted.

Something inside me had snapped. It was suddenly too hot in here, I couldn't breathe – I had to get out. He was going too far, too fast. I left the sauna, grabbed my clothes, and ran away from Kalle as I heard him calling for me to come back; and then I was inside the forest, moving fast, blind to the direction. My anger, I knew, was not at Kalle but at myself, for my inability to say what I meant.

Finally I slowed down, then stopped to put on my clothes. Then I headed towards the beach. Lars's rowing boat was tied up where Kalle and I had left it only hours before. I sat and watched the water for a while, wondering if Kalle would come to find me here, but when he didn't appear I got in and rowed myself over to the island, moored up and climbed ashore. Something was compelling me forwards, into Lars's studio, into his haven. I knew I was trespassing, but I also knew Lars would forgive me, that he would understand. I ventured up the stone steps between the gorse to the wooden house at the top. From the balcony I surveyed the dizzyingly expansive view out across the sea, turned golden by the setting sun. I felt as if I were on the top deck of a boat, setting sail in the midst of the ocean; another voyage into the unknown. I turned and peered in through the windows, then tried the door. It creaked open. An easel was standing in the middle of the room and shelves lined the walls, loaded with pots of paints, paper, jars of brushes. Drawings and paintings were pinned to the walls and hung too from clips hooked to wiring that stretched from corner to corner across the room. And on the far wall there was a noticeboard, covered with photographs and postcards. I took a closer look. Some were of Lotta, Kalle, one of Clare – and lots of pictures were of a woman I didn't recognize, a pretty woman with red hair and gooseberry green eyes, a young woman whom I guessed to be Pauline. There was also a copy of the same photo of Lotta and me that Kalle kept on his desk back in Stockholm.

The works clipped along the wires were semi-abstract

etchings, not seascapes but illustrations for a story. The first showed a young woman with cropped blonde hair leaning forwards over a pool of water, looking back at her own reflection; the next was of the same woman, now dressed in classical hunting robes, holding a spear, surrounded by hunting dogs that looked like Bosse. In the next she appeared again, now sitting playing a harp amid a crowd. In another she was standing before a large, full sun; in yet another by a pool of water in the moonlight. In another she appeared twice, once in sunlight, the other in moonlight. In the final image the woman was standing by one of the statues of a lion in Trafalgar Square, wearing a contemporary summer dress and holding a handbag, looking alarmed; her hair cut as mine used to be, before I met Lars and Kalle, before I came here. In all the images the woman had my face. Of course I knew immediately that these images were not just images of me, but referenced all of those Artemis and Apollo myths we'd retold on our countless forest walks. And yet, tellingly, Lars had chosen to depict both of the ancient gods as women. Clare must have told him about Polly. It was self-evident. And if Lars knew about Polly and Will, then maybe so did Kalle. I remembered his words on the boat, earlier, about Lars producing a special series of drawings. Maybe he knew about them, knew all about me. If so, why didn't he say anything? Why was he pretending not to know? What was he waiting for? Evidently he wanted to hear everything direct from me.

Suddenly I knew the answer to Kalle's challenge all those months ago; try to work out what you've lost and what you need to find. I'd known what I'd lost before I came here; I'd lost a sense of myself. I'd lost the ability to give myself, to love, to share my deepest thoughts. Dad had not loved Mum and maybe she had not loved him but had simply waited patiently for him to give her up; she had never been able to talk to him about how she really felt. Maybe that was what Kalle was waiting for. I recognized her malaise in myself, a sickly patience, an inertia, an inability to bring things to a head. Suddenly I felt very tired. There was a bed in the corner of the room made up with sheets and big, heavy blankets. I crawled inside, and as a semi-darkness fell I found myself drifting to sleep.

Hours later a scrabbling sound woke me and I sat up, disoriented. The light was bright again, shining directly on to me through the studio window. Something was scuffling around outside. Tentatively, I looked out. A pale young fawn was eating berries from the undergrowth, directly below me. As I watched, it looked up; our eyes fixed and it surveyed me, curiously. Then a buzzard called out in the sky above, startling it, and the fawn turned and darted away into the small forest on the edge of the island. I watched as it leapt into the water and began to swim back, then scrambled up on to the granite beach the other side and fled into the trees, its wet coat gleaming.

I wandered down towards the water and the boat, and spied another figure in the sea, this time swimming towards me. Presently Kalle climbed out and strode up the steps towards me, the sunlight glistening in his wet hair.

'I'm sorry for frightening you yesterday,' he said. 'But please don't run away like that again, Emi. I was worried.'

'I want you to see the other side of me,' I found myself replying, 'but I'm afraid to show it to you. I think it would change everything.'

He held out his arms and gathered me in.

'You need to trust me, to tell me what you want, what you need, or we'll never have anything worth keeping.'

'I want to leave the past behind,' I said. 'But it's creeping up on me, just as you and Clare both said it would. Even you can't let it go.'

Kalle sat down on the warm jetty and looked out over the water as his skin began to dry in the sunshine.

'You know, you're right. I was devastated when Stephanie left me,' he said. 'I had understood our commitment to be for life. I would still be there, with her and Lotta, if she wanted me to be. When you walked into my life it took me by surprise: the way I immediately felt, as you sat in that restaurant in London, watchful and uncertain. However fond I was of Stephanie it made me realize that she had never made me feel this instinctive love that I feel for you.'

I looked down at him, startled by his frank words. He laughed and pulled me down next to him, then held my face in his wet hands.

'Emi, I want to open my mouth and swallow you whole,' he said. 'Stephanie's well and truly left me, at last. Our shared history, it's beginning to cement itself into my past. I'm sorry it's taken so long.'

'We are our past,' I whispered. 'That's the whole problem.'

A tear trickled down my face. He took a finger

and stopped it, then raised it slowly and put it into his mouth.

Now it's unleashed, our love seems to know no bounds, and when finally we sleep I feel as if I'm sleeping right next to the ocean, Kalle's breath rising and falling gently over me, like the waves.

I keep thinking of his words all those months ago, asking me first to work out what it was I thought I'd lost, and then what I needed to find. There are so many ways to answer his question. Perhaps that was always the point. I know now that I had needed to find a route back to the time before anyone in my life had died, to learn how to live with those deaths, to allow them their place, but not to let them overshadow my living, to suffocate my breathing any more. For years now, I realize, negativity had held me in its steely grip, had paralysed me, stopped me from touching the raw nerves that existed at my core, those endings that needed to be felt, to hurt and to find amusement in things again, to feel unburdened, passionate. When I thought of Will and my marriage, of my inability ever to feel emotionally or physically satisfied by our relationship, I understood that I had lost the ability to release myself into the moment – until now. Everything in my life had been tinged by a lingering, residual sadness. I had marked my life out by negative punctuation points. In some of Kalle's notes I had read the metaphor of a black and a white horse running a race. In the negative person's mind the black horse always wins, the white horse is always left behind. I knew that, like Mum, I had always backed the black horse until now, and that Polly had always backed the white. Everything that had followed had felt like an inevitable trail of misery. I had allowed Will to lead me like a sleepwalker through my twenties. It's only now that I've finally begun to wake up that I can see the white horse leaving the black one behind.

36

Since the note had arrived, Polly and Will had found themselves in new, unfamiliar territory. There seemed little point in searching for Emi any more, and they both felt but didn't voice the fact that her interjection had marred their affair, tainted it. This new stasis left Polly feeling ineffectual, and as the city temperatures crept ever higher, her mood dipped low. Most days London hit the nineties.

'It's global fucking warming. We all need to reduce our carbon emissions,' Will scorned and Polly laughed. He looked at her enquiringly.

'Your next crusade,' she teased. 'After you've sorted out the Middle East, you're going to resolve climate change single-handed, I can feel it coming.'

For a moment Will looked hurt, then he laughed.

'Be a lot easier than looking for Emi,' he replied.

It was really too hot to work, to think, even, and Polly found herself going about her reports like a sleepwalker, filing bland stories on the effects of the rising temperatures on the city's workers, on summer festivals and the Queen's eightieth birthday, on World Cup fever and the first anniversary of the July the seventh suicide bombs. This day in particular brought Emi to the forefront of her mind. As she stood with her cameraman among the victims' families in Tavistock Square, her mind was cast back to the dreadful morning a year ago. She had called Emi as soon as she heard that bombs had gone off, but their lines were both jammed. Polly had been sent to report from Russell Square as the firemen began to bring the injured out. She had not dared look, was terrified that one of them would be Emi. When, finally, her sister had called, Polly had burst into tears of relief. Emi had seemed surprised by Polly's uncharacteristically effusive outpouring. 'Hey,' she had said. 'It wasn't very likely, really, that it would be me, there are millions of us in this town.' Polly had felt oddly foolish and exposed. Now, a year later, it was hard to believe that she really had gone and lost Emi, among those very same hordes.

Since Emi's note had arrived, Will had taken to working with a new ferocity that disturbed Polly. Term was out, but all his energies were focused on the facts and figures in the Middle East. The war in Iraq rumbled on, but now Israel was fighting Hezbollah in the south of Lebanon, too, and the region seemed set for a period of even greater instability, of civilian carnage. Will followed the news eagerly, seemed energized by the escalation of violence and spent countless hours with Ralph, discussing the latest attacks, calculating their impact, economically, environmentally and, most significantly, from a humanitarian perspective. He was tipping up at Polly's place later and later at night and she noticed that he was drinking more. Many days could go by when he no longer mentioned Emi.

Meanwhile, with increasing regularity Polly found herself wondering about the identity of the man she had met in Trafalgar Square. It occurred to her one evening, as she sat alone at the window in her flat coaxing a subtle breeze off the humid city, that perhaps he was the link with King's Cross. That perhaps it was he who had made that first call to Emi on the Sunday night before she went away. She decided that she would go and look for him there. It was at least something tangible she could do.

Soon after their affair began she had confessed to Will about her chance meeting with the prostitute, Kaz, at the station back in February and what Polly had told her, too.

'Promise me that you won't go there again,' Will had implored.

At the time, the idea of not seeing Kaz again, or any of the other characters she'd encountered around the station, had felt like a failing, which she knew didn't make sense, but inadvertently they'd come to be part of Emi's story for Polly. Kaz's implicit disappointment had felt familiar: there was an absent look in her eyes, as if she were always, to some degree, still engaged in another story of herself that was taking place elsewhere. It was a look Polly recognized, one she realized Emi had always had, ever since, well, ever since she could remember; it was a permanent part of who she was. Sarah had had it too.

'What frightens me most,' she had confessed, 'is that if I don't have King's Cross, I don't have a destination to fix on that's just about her.'

'It's not about Emi, that's the whole point,' Will had replied. 'It's about you.'

Polly had kept her promise, and had not been back. But

now, tonight, sitting there in the sticky heat, she felt a strong urge to go to the station, to see if she could spot the stranger. Will had called to say that he and Ralph were going to a meeting 'about a new humanitarian aid pro-gramme to the Lebanon'. She knew that meant they'd be heading to the pub afterwards. It was still only seven thirty. He wouldn't be back for hours. She pulled herself up, grabbed her bag and left the flat.

A blood-orange-coloured sun was still high in the sky and the heat was muggy and intense. She took a taxi to the station and got it to drop her at the front. Dishevelled people with nowhere to go were sitting on the dirty, dusty pavements, arms hanging low from their knees, faces glistening with sweat, watching commuters heading for the scorching tracks, heading home. The atmosphere was loaded and the traffic around the station was heavy, the air clogged with a grey haze of pollution from passing cars. Immediately Polly wondered why she was there. The heat was making her dizzy and she knew, instinctively, that she wasn't going to find her stranger; that there was nothing of Emi here, not tonight, perhaps not ever. It was all hopeless, it was all a waste of time. Emi had vanished and she wasn't coming back – until she decided that she was ready to. There was nothing Polly could do about it, nothing at all. She looked around once more, then decided to go into the café where she had drunk a coffee with Kaz all those months ago. She was standing at the counter when she heard a familiar voice.

'Have you found her?'

Swinging round, she spotted Kaz sitting at a corner table, smoking a cigarette and drinking tea. Her melancholic face shifted to a becoming smile. She looks even thinner, thought Polly, ashen and dirty.

Polly shook her head and moved towards her. 'No, no sign at all, I'm afraid. How've you been?'

'I was given a Chelsea smile,' Kaz responded, turning her face to one side and running a finger down her cheek. There was a raw, red scar stretching from the corner of her mouth to her ear. It made Polly feel nauseous.

'Now, tell me, what's up with Emi?'

Polly updated her, mentioning the stranger with the message.

'He's not one of ours,' Kaz replied definitively, once she'd heard Polly out. 'I've never seen someone like him, either as a client or a pimp.'

As they'd been talking, Polly had been watching Kaz's body movements. She was jittery and her legs were shaking.

'Do you need something?' she asked her, gently.

Kaz gazed at her through wide eyes and for a moment Polly wished she hadn't spoken.

'I need a fix,' she whispered, hoarsely. 'But I've been too ill to work.'

'How much?' Polly asked, quietly. 'How much do you normally charge, say, for two hours?'

Kaz looked surprised.

'A hundred,' she said, quickly.

'I'll get the money for you. On one condition.'

Kaz was looking eagerly at her. Her hands were shaking more dramatically now.

'Afterwards, you come back with me, to my place, take a shower, have an hour's sleep.'

Kaz hesitated, looked suspicious, then nodded.

'Wait here,' said Polly.

She went back out into the sweltering heat and crossed over the street to the cashpoint. She didn't care if she was heading into unsafe territory, she thought as she waited in the queue, she didn't care if she was putting herself at risk. She wanted to help Kaz. Just for a minute. She wanted to take her away from this. When she got back to the café, she handed Kaz fifty.

'I'll give you the rest later,' she promised.

Kaz was up and out of the café in a flash. Polly sat and waited. The heat was making her clothes damp. Moments later, Kaz returned and they left together, taking a cab back to Bermondsey. Kaz had had her fix and was immediately calmer; her face was a touch glazed and she didn't speak. When they arrived Polly let her in, took her to the bathroom and turned on the shower. She left Kaz there and went into the sitting-room, switched on a fan and stared out over the Thames. When Kaz finally reappeared, half an hour later, she'd wrapped herself up in one white towel, and tied up her hair in another, like a turban. Without make-up she looked painfully young and vulnerable. Still, she didn't speak. Instead, she smiled abstractedly, curled up like a stray cat on the sofa and closed her eyes. The next thing Polly knew, she'd fallen asleep.

More than an hour later, Will entered the scene. Polly hadn't moved; she'd just sat watching Kaz, hoping that somewhere else, someone else was being this kind to Emi, wherever she might be.

'Who is she?' he whispered.

Polly hadn't invited any friends home for months. She'd become increasingly reclusive, electing to spend time alone or with Will.

'An old friend,' she replied enigmatically. 'Having a rough time.'

He looked quizzical, gesturing at her scarred face with a grimace.

Suddenly, Kaz stirred and looked up at them.

'Hi,' she said, then pulled herself upright. 'Are you Will?'

He nodded as she smiled knowingly at Polly.

'What's the time?'

'It's gone ten,' Polly told her.

'Time up,' Kaz said, then, pulling her towel tightly around her, she headed for the bathroom.

'What does she mean by that?' said Will.

Polly didn't reply; just watched as he rolled a cigarette on the coffee table and headed for the open window to start smoking it. She could smell lager in his clothes.

At that moment Kaz reappeared, dressed in her lime green top and hot pants. Will looked incredulous but said nothing.

'I'll see you out,' said Polly, reaching for her bag.

Kaz took the money Polly now proffered, thanked her, and took off into the night.

'It's her, isn't it? That hooker from the station?'

Polly nodded. 'I just wanted to do something for someone else. I gave her some money, for drugs, let her take a shower, have a sleep. She was in a mess.'

'Are you going completely insane? Fuck knows what

347

she's taken, when she'll be back for more. You're crazy, Pol, fucking crazy.'

Polly couldn't answer. She couldn't stand it, losing Emi, she couldn't stand it any more. She turned from him, headed for her room, closed the door, lay down and switched out the light, trying to block it all out. Moments later she heard her front door open and close and knew that Will had gone.

The next day he called to ask how she was. The conversation was superficially light, but beneath their dialogue a new tension was prowling.

'Someone at college mentioned a flat going, over in Bayswater,' he told her casually.

'For whom?' Polly asked, feigning confusion.

'With Tom coming back next month, I'm going to need my own place,' he reasoned. 'And it might be good for us to have somewhere to go that doesn't hold any memories.'

She felt queasy, didn't trust herself to speak. It was the start of the inevitable end, she knew it, and she knew he wouldn't voice it, that he didn't need to, but that there was no point in them dabbling in false commitments. She didn't blame Will, it was really too hard, and she knew as well as he did that it couldn't go on for much longer. And yet at the same time she wasn't ready, not yet, to let him go. She'd only really be able to do it, she realized, once Emi came home.

'Oh, and there's something else,' he added, even more casually.

Polly braced herself.

'I'm definitely going on that field trip to Damascus. Confirmation came through this morning.'

Panic began to mount in her insides.

'It's a war zone,' she said.

'That's right,' said Will. 'That's the whole fucking point.'

37

Once Sarah and Peter's divorce is finalized, Peter takes a large payout and early retirement. Then he goes to live with Brigitte, just outside Montpellier. The distance negates regular visits from his daughters. When he's in England, Sarah knows that he calls them, that he sees them for lunch, or dinner, but the girls barely mention their meetings and his trips over seem to be growing increasingly rare. Polly and Emi are frequently absent from London, too, especially now that they have reached their third year of university and live in flats with friends, off-campus. They stay throughout the holidays in their prospective university towns and only pop back to London for parties, or to see her for special occasions. Will is always at Emi's side, but her daughter remains emphatic that they are 'just good friends'. Sarah misses her daughters, but she knows that the course between her and them is a natural one, that this is an inevitable loosening, not severing, of the family ties. Oddly, with her marriage over, her daughters away, Sarah realizes that she feels more confident, more certain, and capable of managing on her own.

Sarah has only seen Peter twice since their separation and he looks more relaxed than she's ever known him. On the second occasion, she tells him so.

'I'm happy,' he says, with apparent nonchalance, while fixing her, a touch accusingly, she feels, in the eye.

'At last,' she replies, speaking his thoughts aloud.

Sarah feels nothing for Peter, other than affection for him with regard to their daughters. Even so, his life-shattering heart attack six months later comes as a shock. He is only fifty when it happens – hardly any age at all. Her first thoughts are for the well-being of the girls. They arrive pale-faced and dejected from their respective universities. The atmosphere is tense and quiet and she hears them murmuring together in low tones long after they retire to bed for the night. The following morning, Emi and Polly appear at breakfast as if they are one unit and, for the first time in years, for a moment even Sarah can't tell them apart. They are both dressed in black, have their hair scraped back from their make-up-free faces in tight ponytails; and each has pooling grey circles under their father's blue eyes. They sit opposite her in the sitting-room and Polly informs her, in low but decisive tones, 'We'd like to go to the funeral on our own.'

Sarah feels as if her daughters are landing her a body blow; nevertheless she acquiesces without complaint. But before they leave Polly calls Carol to tell her the news. She arrives within moments, brandishing her own passport, her eyes crimson from crying. The girls move towards her in unison and the three of them hug, in a circle. Sarah feels separate, on the outside. She drives them to Heathrow and

351

watches as their Air France flight takes to the skies. Then she drives home and goes to bed for three days.

When they get back, Carol heads straight home in the cab that drops the twins, without stopping to see Sarah. Emi and Polly stay for a night, but remain distant and uncommunicative. In the morning they head back to their universities on early trains. It is spring. Neither returns to London again until the summer break. While she waits for them, Sarah throws herself into completing her diploma and applies to study for an MA in medieval tapestry design.

38

With the summer break over, Kalle and I headed back to
Stockholm. August was a quiet time in the city, many of
the workers still not back at their desks, the traffic light
and the air still warm. Kalle didn't need to go back to the
university hospital until the end of the month, so he
worked from home and we spent a lot of time in bed.
Without Lotta to entertain, I put all my energies into
focusing on Kalle, on learning to trust in my own voice.
Little by little, I began to talk about my life; in teaspoon-
fuls, one morsel at a time. I talked more about Sarah and
Peter than about Polly and me, and I had still to mention
the fact that we were twins. I also failed to tell him that
Polly and Will had fallen in love. There would be time; it
would all work its way out. I felt confident of that now.
And I had begun to trust that Kalle was patient enough to
wait, until I was truly ready.

At the end of August we drove back out to Solgläntan
with a large crate of iced crayfish on the back seat,
purchased from the finest supplier in Stockholm. Lars had
returned from America. But he wasn't alone. Clare had
come back from the US with him and the idea of her

presence made me uneasy. When we arrived, however, she and Lars were evidently so absorbed in each other that our previous encounter seemed rapidly to dissolve into insignificance. She smiled knowingly at me when we greeted one another, and at the first opportunity she had to speak to me alone she informed me that she had delivered my missive, but that she had not seen Polly or Will, or even James for that matter, that she had had to curtail her visit and head back to the US early. And that seemed to be that; there appeared to be nothing else between us that Clare felt she needed to discuss. Lars was jubilant around Clare and strangely I found their eagerness for one another uncomfortable, and wondered if I weren't a touch jealous of Clare. I wasn't used to sharing Kalle and Lars with anyone but Lotta: perhaps that was it. And yet the more I wondered about it the more uncertain I was that this really was the reason for my slight unease. I was concerned that for Clare, Lars was a mere plaything, a colourful, complex character to explore, a personality inevitably bound for her fiction. In short I didn't trust her motivation and I found her enthusiasm insincere. I didn't reveal my views to Kalle. I worried that he would confuse them with jealousy, or resentment at having to share them, as I had initially done.

After lunch, Lars took us all out into the forest in search of chanterelles, 'the royals of the wild mushroom world', as he triumphantly described them. In all, over a few hours hunting, we found only a couple of handfuls of these delicate trumpet-shaped fungi, but they were worth the search. We ate them on little toasts this evening, a subtle appetizer, and they were sweet and fresh and delicious.

354

Then the crayfish ritual began. First Lars took one of the bright pink specimens from the bowl and lifted it towards his mouth.

'First you suck the juices from the belly,' he advised, slurping noisily. 'It is seasoned with salt, dill and garlic – delicious! Now, here's how you pull out the claws.'

Clare was rocking backwards and forwards on her chair and let out a shriek at the sound of the shell cracking. Lars smiled affectionately towards her.

'And then you suck the flesh from each one, like this. Next, you crack one claw, then the other, and eat the flesh inside. Now concentrate, everyone.' He turned the crayfish on to its front and lifted off its shell to show us its insides. 'This is the very best bit, the caviar.'

He turned the half-excavated shell over once again. I observed with quiet concentration and Clare got up from her chair and went to stand behind to get a better view as he demonstrated how to peel away the crayfish's under-belly and extract the white fillet embedded inside, then how to peel back the top layer to remove its fine grey thread of intestine, and finally, how to devour it whole.

'Everyone got it?' he asked, looking gaily up at her, one claw in each hand, like his own pincer extensions. Clare laughed and hugged him, over-effusively, around his neck, then came and sat back down. Now we all reached for our own crayfish. It was time to have a go.

While Lars had been demonstrating, Kalle had poured each of us a glass of ice-cold aquavit and now, as I was fast learning was customary for all Swedish rituals, he began to sing. Lars immediately joined in.

*   *   *

Helan går
Sjung hopp fallerallan rallan lej,
Helan går
Sjung hopp fallerallan lej.
Och den som inte helan tar
Han heller inte halvan får.
Helan går!
Sjung hopp fallerallan lej.

Next they raised their shot glasses and knocked back the ice-cold liquid. Clare and I cheered, then followed suit.

'Now, at last, let's eat!' exclaimed Lars.

I woke early this morning. My dreams had been filled with images of Christa, of his voyage out to the island, and of his tragic end, but in my surreal version it had been Kalle, not his grandfather, drowning in that scarlet sea. I felt gloomy and anxious, as if a new, impending tragedy was awaiting us all, somewhere out there, just beyond the horizon, just out of reach, just out of control. I slipped out of Kalle's sleeping embrace and went downstairs, put on boots and a raincoat and headed for the woods, carrying a small basket. It was mild and overcast outside, the intense green tones of the forest intensified by the heavy grey sky above it. It was the last weekend of August, and already our summer here felt like a distant memory. The forest smelt damp, fecund and autumnal. I wandered slowly through the trees, eyes down, hoping to find some more chanterelles for Kalle and me to share at breakfast. After dinner last night, Lars and Clare had rowed out to sleep in the studio, so we had had Solgläntan to ourselves. I thought about the progress of our quiet relationship as I wandered, aimlessly, between the trees. In recent days I had almost succeeded in sweeping Polly and Will from my mind, but now, as I walked, their spirits seemed to be nagging at me, demanding I concentrate on them once more, on finding us a way towards a shared future. Clare's presence, I realized, felt like a mild threat. She held the knowledge, the key to my recent past, and I wondered how much of it she had now shared with Lars and he, therefore, with Kalle. So much time had passed now that I wasn't sure if I could ever go back. The problem, I knew realistically, was that if I didn't, they would eventually find me. I had to decide if I could bear to be hunted for much longer, or whether it would be less painful to confront them before they tracked me down. As for Lars, so far there hadn't yet been time for me to discuss with him the drawings I had seen in his studio, but I knew that I would have to find the strength to raise the issue. I wanted to find out how much he knew about Polly and Will and me, and I wanted to understand the significance of the contemporary drawing he had made of me in Trafalgar Square.

Just then I spied him wandering through the forest towards me, head down, evidently searching, too, for fungi.

'Ah, Emi, here you are, just when I needed you to be,' he exclaimed, looking up at me with a broad smile.

'I'm trying to find more chanterelles,' I explained.

'This way,' he said conspiratorially. 'I think I may have just spotted some.'

Together we picked the delicacies and laid them carefully in my basket, before wandering on together, talking of small things, looking for more, while I tried to find a way to raise the issue of the pictures. But I need not have worried, because Lars readily took me to the subject himself.

'I promised in the spring that I would show you my work,' he remarked, with affected casualness, 'but I didn't want to because I was busy making a series based on your mythical namesake. I didn't want you to see them until I felt they were ready. But now, if you like, you can come to the studio and take a look.'

I hesitated. 'I've already seen them,' I confessed. 'I'm so sorry but in the summer Kalle and I had a fight of sorts, and I rowed over to your island, to get some time to myself.'

Lars paused and put a hand on a tree trunk. He looked troubled.

'Did Clare tell you about Polly?' I asked.

Lars nodded. 'Everyone in London is so worried, Emi,' he said. 'They're searching for you.'

'I know, but I don't know how to get back to them now,' I replied. 'Polly's got a whole life to share with Will and I feel that just maybe I have a whole life here, beginning to shape with Kalle. When I came here I was sick, a shadow, and now my spirit's filling back up, with Kalle, and Lotta, and with you. For the first time in my life I think I might be finding what it is to be happy.'

He put his arm around my shoulders and I leant my head against him.

'I know how important that can be,' he said.

I knew I should ask him how things were with Clare, but I couldn't, I was worried that he would recognize my lack of conviction.

358

'Have you talked to Kalle about it?' I asked.

Lars paused, took a chanterelle from the basket and rolled it between his fingers.

'I wanted to, but Clare made me promise not to,' he said. 'She said it had to be your story to tell.'

I didn't reply.

Together we headed out of the forest, back towards the jetty.

'When you're ready to bring all the pieces back together,' he said as he set himself adrift in his rowing boat, 'I'll be there to help you.'

I found myself smiling. I knew that he would. Then I watched him rowing away from me, before I turned with my basket of mushrooms and headed back to Solgläntan to wake Kalle up.

39

Will left London with Ralph on the first of August. To begin with he emailed Polly daily reports about their arrival in Damascus, their meetings with local academics at the university, their planned trip to the south of the country, to witness first-hand the effect of the Israeli bombings. Their intention was to try to gain an overview of the humanitarian disaster that was unfolding, statistics-based knowledge to bring back to London and feed out to the news agencies. In his emails and on the phone he sounded like his old self, his self before Emi had disappeared; passionate and engaged by everything that he was witnessing. He promised Polly that he was safe, that he was doing fine, that the experience was invaluable; that it would form the basis of a new course he wanted to teach in the spring. Polly tried to remain calm and enthusiastic for him, to focus on her own work. After all, he would be back in under six weeks. She would survive. In London the weather had broken and now an unseasonal, autumnal breeze had eclipsed the record-busting heat of July, pulling wet weather in its wake.

* * *

On 10 August Polly woke to her mobile ringing.

'There's been a foiled terrorist attack,' she was told. 'Quick, we need you to go to Heathrow.'

The target had been transatlantic jets out of Heathrow Airport and the country was set on high alert. The tension was palpable. Fourteen thwarted suicide bombers had been arrested around the capital and thousands of business people and holidaymakers were stranded at airports across the UK. Generally, Polly would have risen to such an occasion, would have enjoyed the sense of drama that accompanied such high-level breaking news. She was known for her ability to remain calm and objective even in the midst of chaos. Instead, today, the mayhem around her triggered a rising anxiety. The threat she faced at the airport was close to home, yet still intangible. No bomb had actually gone off. Out there in the Lebanon, however, Will was in the thick of it. Every day someone was being blown up, and any minute now, she thought with panic, it could be him.

When she finally headed back to the office, Polly made a decision. She was owed holiday. She went to see Nick and requested two weeks off. He appraised her slowly, then ordered her not to come back before the start of September.

'Go away, take a break,' he advised kindly. 'Leave the city, go to the sea. You've always got your phone – in case anyone calls.'

She knew he was referring to Emi, not to her work, and she appreciated his sensitivity, nodded and left, headed straight back to her flat, shut the door and crawled into her bed. She felt paralysed by fear and grief, hardly able to function at all.

As if to reinforce her anxieties, for the following two weeks she heard nothing from Will. And as the days passed she found herself disconnecting, mentally, from the world around her. She slept and watched television and stared out of her window at the Thames. She began to believe that she might have just lost Will, just as she'd lost Emi, had lost everyone else.

Eventually she had nothing left to eat in the flat and forced herself out to the supermarket on Southwark Street. As she wandered along the road in a warm, dirty drizzle, the world outside seemed big and oppressive and for the first time she found that she felt afraid of the capital, of all the people, the noise, the city's brutal energy. It made her feel . . . agoraphobic, she supposed. When she arrived at the store, the idea of the crowds and the queues caused her to hesitate, but she knew she had to eat something and forced herself to go inside. She selected food almost at random: tropical fruit, pre-washed summer salad, sun-ripened cherry tomatoes – and coffee, she must buy coffee. She was reaching for a rich Kenyan blend, direct from the growers, when she got the impulse to look to the end of the aisle and was just in time to see a figure that could almost – in fact definitely – have been Emi, moving swiftly from view. Dropping her basket, she ran after the person, colliding with a shelf-filler as she turned the corner, scattering his eggs across the floor. 'Watch where you're going, lady,' he seethed, but Polly didn't respond, she was too busy searching the gathering faces attracted by the commotion for the one that could be her sister. Sure enough, Emi was standing next to the chest freezers, watching curiously. At least, the woman Polly had mistaken for her was there. But she was at least twenty years their senior, had mad eyes and a scar across her arching nose. The only characteristic she shared with Polly or her twin was angularity, a slight awkwardness caused, perhaps, by being so tall. The woman caught Polly's eye and began to laugh like a hyena, as if aware that she had been the cause of the drama and was happy to be the main spectacle in the scene.

Polly turned her head and made for the exit, her breath short and sharp, then leant against the wall outside. False sightings of Emi had been habitual in the early months, but she'd thought that recently she'd learnt to control them. Shoppers trudged past in both directions, plastic bags filled to splitting with their groceries. Some looked at her curiously, but no one offered to help, or asked if she was OK. Either they assumed that she was insane or they simply didn't care, would rather not get involved. Eventually she made her way home, went straight to bed and fell asleep with her clothes on.

Polly woke in the dark to the sound of knocking on her front door and her heart lurched into her mouth. It was after 2 a.m. She half opened the door with the chain on to find Will standing before her, swarthy from the sun. She released the chain and allowed the door to swing open, wondering for a moment if she was dreaming. She noticed Will hesitate as he looked at her, evidently shocked by her weight loss, by the deep circles of sleeplessness around her eyes, her crumpled clothes, then he held open his arms and pulled her in, towards him, back to safety.

'I'm so sorry, Polly – we couldn't call. It all got a bit messy. We had to come back early,' he murmured. 'It got too dangerous. You were right to be afraid.'

40

'Coffee?'

Sarah looks up from the library desk and surveys the whisperer, hesitates and then smiles. It's Louis, the man from the summer course all those years ago. Curiously he appears younger, as if the weight of the world has been lifted from his shoulders.

Without speaking, she puts down her pen and stands up, reaches for her coat. He helps her on with it, his hands resting a few moments too long on her shoulders. They leave the library and walk along the corridor towards the V & A café.

'How've you been, Sarah?' he asks, quietly.

'Never better,' she replies.

Sarah feels as if Louis could have made 'that' phone call to her yesterday. The difference is, now that five years have passed, Louis is retired and she is divorced – or is it widowed? – and they are both approaching the final stages of their studies.

'It seems we're in the same boat,' he says as they catch up on one another's lives in the café. 'Or almost,' he adds. 'I haven't mentioned Sasha, I don't exactly live alone.'

For a moment Sarah feels a jolt of disappointment.

'I'm a bit soft on her,' he adds. 'I even let her sleep in my bed – well, at the end of it, in fact. You couldn't ask for a kinder companion than a dog.'

Sarah laughs, failing to hide her relief.

'I'd like to introduce you,' he adds. 'We tend to take an early-evening walk, around the great pond, after I finish here. My flat's on the other side of Hyde Park, just off the Bayswater Road. She gets a bit fed up if I'm too late.'

He glances at his watch, and she at hers. It is a quarter to five.

'Ready when you are,' she says. 'I can't wait to meet her.'

Sarah is amazed to discover that with Louis holding her arm, she can walk freely, breathe easily, even in such wide open spaces. They often return to his flat in the early evenings now, to collect Sasha and take her out for her walk, through Kensington Gardens, then on, past the wooden ship erected in the Diana, Princess of Wales, gardens for children to play on, and then further, all the way around the pond. Sasha is a lovely golden retriever with a gleaming coat. It is as easy to fall in love with her as with Louis, who is so kind and patient with Sarah, never overstepping the mark. Slowly but surely, Sarah talks him through, around and over her life with Peter and the twins, until it feels as if he knows it all. It takes weeks before he kisses her and another month before they first go to bed. When finally she gives in to her feelings, it is as if all her nerve endings are alive. Louis is an experienced lover and for Sarah the affair is revitalizing, invigorating; with it she is awoken from her mid-life malaise. And yet, however much she enjoys every second of every day, from the moment she wakes until the moment she closes her eyes again at night, she can't help but feel a touch . . . guilty. She was married to Peter for ever, and on a very deep, very private level she still finds the affair deceitful, dishonest. She knows it's insane; he divorced her, married someone else, even died; the ties weren't just loosened, they had been severed for years. And yet . . . she hasn't quite got over it, not quite yet.

She decides not to mention Louis to the twins, not for a while at least, not until she's sure.

41

'I think, when Lotta gets back, we should sleep apart – just for now – until I've told her,' Kalle suggested. We were lying, locked together, looking up from the high windows at the softening blue sky above the city. It was our last day without her. With Stephanie so far away I realized that it had been psychological 'time out' for Kalle. We'd been immersed inside our own affair, disregarding the world and its worries outside. I knew his anxiety was not just about Lotta; I knew that part of him didn't want to tell Stephanie about us, didn't want to concede that she was right, that for him too their marriage had failed.

'It's fine,' I replied, gently, but my stomach twisted with anxiety.

When he went to work I went out walking. Although it was only mid-September the evening air already had an edge to it that forewarned of the imminent snows to come. Second winter around, I recognized the signs, the whip of the wind on my cheeks as I crossed the walkway at Katarinahissen, the weakening rays of the sun that failed to warm my skin. The leaves are falling fast; they scuttle crisped and papery along the cobbles, like discarded memories. I can't imagine being anywhere else, with anyone else – quite. Yet deep down guilt stirs my spirit, guilt at my lack of disclosure over Polly, guilt for not calling her and guilt over my feelings towards Lotta's return, too. I can't quite imagine sharing Kalle with her any more. I feel that symbolic black horse in my mind urging itself ahead of the white. It's still a furlong behind, but there's a way to go before the end of the race.

Today Lotta arrived back. As soon as I saw her my heartbeat quickened and when I held her in my arms I felt an overwhelming sense of belonging, a surge of happiness. She allowed me to hug her but to my surprise she didn't respond in kind, in fact she seemed guarded, uncertain of me and unsettled at the flat, too. She wouldn't talk about her holiday, either. I wondered if perhaps she had felt excluded by Stephanie and Marcus in the US, left on the outside. By contrast, when she dropped Lotta off this morning, I noticed a new aura of calm and contentment in Stephanie's disposition. If Kalle's theoretical studies are anything to go by, a mother's contentment should have a positive effect on a child's own emotional security – so long, I reasoned, as the child continued to feel involved. Unfortunately, in Lotta's case, that was the sticking point. Between Stephanie's aggressive workload and her love affair with Marcus, maybe Lotta was becoming aware that there was increasingly little space left for her.

Up and down the plastic slide, feet banging, slap, slap, slap. Lotta's tongue's curled above her lip and there's a storm brewing in her eyes. There's something wrong, something she can't explain. I'll wait and watch for a clue, wait for her to let me in. Her closure makes me think of Mum, in the early days. I can remember playing for hours on the carpet in her bedroom as she sat and embroidered or read, or stared at the ceiling, or out of the window. I had liked – or was it needed? – that sense of her physical proximity but often we didn't speak; just as Lotta and I often don't speak now. Although she was always physically there, mentally she was often absent, lost in her own contemplations, in her own malaise. Polly was often somewhere else, too, roaming around the house, looking for new distractions, playing with the latest au pair. She kept her distance from Sarah's room, as though, for her, it was out of bounds. Sometimes Sarah would pull me up on to the bed and read me stories through absent eyes, classical myths about Artemis and Apollo that took us to faraway places and times, places outside ourselves, times with no other reference to me but a shared name. Often, halfway through a tale, she'd allow the book to slip from her hands and apologize that she didn't have the energy, today, to reach the end.

Much later, in my teens, Mum would often come and join me in the study. Then we would work alongside one another for hours in a far easier silence. At that point I recall that something significant had changed in her. She'd become really alive – alert and outward-reaching. It had given me a certain confidence, the start of self-belief, but underlying it still lurked the knowledge of how things had been before, of how uncertain the future had then seemed. It was imprinted in me, that notion of her fragility, of her not being strong enough to cement things, to pin them down. Kalle's notes had informed me that emotional impacts in the early years stayed with you for life – perhaps that was why I had found it so hard to feel secure and why, in my twenties, I had so depended on Will to bolster me up. Now at last I feel a darkness that has been lodged inside me beginning to shift.

As I watch Lotta, rocking madly backwards and forwards on her swing, I wonder whether Stephanie's aware of what she's done.

One of the children Lotta had befriended before the summer tipped up in the park this afternoon and I watched with interest as she skipped over and sat down next to Lotta in the sandpit. To my amazement, Lotta immediately picked up a handful of sand and threw it into her face. The mother gave me a fierce look as she scooped up her squealing daughter and took her away to console. I headed for Lotta, who continued to play, sullenly, in the sand. I had rarely felt the need to reprimand her and had never seen her behave so aggressively before.

'Go and say sorry right now,' I scolded.

She eyed me defiantly and refused to budge. I bent down, took hold of her arm and tried to heave her up but Lotta twisted out of my grip, steadied herself.

'You're not my mom!' she shrieked, landing me a hefty kick on the shin.

As I bent down to rub my leg she was already running from the playground and before I knew it she was darting across the church gardens. I only caught up with her on the far side of the church. Her eyes were smarting with tears and her face was crimson.

'Don't tell Papa,' she said fiercely, clenching and un-clenching her fists, as if in preparation for another round.

I thought for a moment, said nothing. Instead I held out my hand. This was not the time for further confrontation.

'Come on,' I said. 'It's time to go back to Café String. Frank's missed you.'

Frank whooped with joy when he saw Lotta, scooped her up and swung her round and round, then produced an enormous hot chocolate for her with cream and jellied sweets studding its surface. I watched, fascinated, as her mood picked up a beat. She extracted the sweets one by one with her delicate fingers, and guzzled them quickly. She followed them with spooned hot chocolate and cream, chattering between mouthfuls to Frank. She appeared more than happy to tell him all about her trip to America, about the surprise barbecue party they had held for her grandmother's seventieth birthday, about their stay at the 'enormous house' by the ocean with her American cousins. I sat back and listened quietly. Evidently, after all, she had had a really good time. So what was the fuss about? Then, as suddenly as she had started, Lotta paused and her face took on a conspiratorial air. She glanced sideways at me, placed both elbows up on the table, her hands underneath her chocolate-smudged chin.

'And the biggest thing is,' she whispered, eyes wide, focusing on Frank alone, 'I'm going to have a baby brother or sister!'

Frank glanced momentarily at me and I raised my eyebrows. Now, at last, it was all fitting into place.

'Is your mom having a baby?' he asked her, encouragingly.

'Yep,' replied Lotta. 'With Marcus! They're going to get married.'

Her tone had suddenly become very grave, and her bottom lip was trembling.

'Are you going to be their flower girl?' Frank asked, enthusiastically.

Lotta shook her head sadly. 'No one asked me what I want and I don't want Marcus to be my daddy.'

Frank sat down and beckoned Lotta on to his lap with innate paternal ease. Her face suddenly appeared flushed and slightly damp again, and as she clambered on, she wiped her eyes with her sleeve. I wanted to lean forward, to reassure her, but she seemed to have forgotten I was there, had begun to take sugar crystals from the bowl on the table and to line them up on the table, one by one.

'But you already have a papa,' Frank reasoned. 'Kalle will always be your daddy.'

Lotta's eyes flickered across to me, then back down to the sugar crystals. 'Not if he marries Emi,' she mumbled.

Frank glanced at me and I shook my head.

'Who said that was going to happen?' he enquired.

'Nobody,' Lotta replied slowly, as she lined up a second row of the little caramel-coloured crystals along the table-top.

'Well, there you are then,' he said. 'Emi's not going to take your daddy away from you.'

As I watched them I thought about Peter's absences throughout our childhood, and then about Brigitte, and I knew that, in its own way, his leaving us had been as devastating for me as it had been for Polly – and how the idea of losing Kalle must be equally terrifying for Lotta. Peter's departure had happened so late in our childhood that I had expected its impact to be minor. Instead, I now saw, in a fundamental, quiet way, it had been catastrophic – both for Polly and for me. With his leaving, everything we had clung on to as true, the basis upon which we had lived out our childhood, felt like a fabrication. Mum's ensuing singularity had been terrifying to me, too. I thought about Polly's reticence to help her move into Blenheim Crescent, and understood it better. My first priority had been for Mum's well-being, but for Polly, Peter had been the security net. I felt a rush of panic. How must she be feeling now? And how on earth would I ever be able to repair the damage? It was too late. There seemed no way back.

'*Hej*, Emi, are you OK?'

Frank and Lotta were both eyeing me with concern. I held out my arms and at last Lotta climbed off Frank's knees and on to my own. I put my arms around her small, hot frame and squeezed.

'I'm sorry I kicked you,' she whispered, with genuine feeling. 'I love you even when I hate you.'

I tried to suppress a smile. 'And I promise, I'll never take your papa away from you, Lotta.'

As we wandered home, hand in hand, I felt remorseful. I remember how hard it had been to lose Dad, but I had always had Mum, constant, alone, there for us. If Lotta felt she was losing Kalle to me – and Stephanie to Marcus – where would that leave her?

*   *   *

By the time Kalle came home Lotta was already sleeping and he was tired. He held me to him and then we went upstairs to bed.

'I hate to ask, but will you switch to your own bed by morning?' he whispered into the darkness.

'Of course,' I replied.

I wanted to tell him about the baby, about Lotta's mood today, but something held me back. I didn't feel it was my tale to tell – and more, I feared his reaction.

42

Will had come back with renewed energy and focus on humanitarian aid to the Middle East. There was a programme in the south of the Lebanon he had visited in August and he spent hours of each day in email communication with its leaders, lobbying aid organizations for funding. He seemed increasingly preoccupied with the affairs of war-destroyed communities, of displaced people; victims, Polly reflected, that he could do something tangible to help. And although they talked about Emi, she recognized that Will had decided to compartmentalize her, to keep her active only in one part of his mind. For Polly that would have been an impossible feat, but she understood why he had done it, and in her most objective moments she was pleased that he had managed to do so, for both of their sakes. Meanwhile he slowly coaxed her out of her withdrawal. Tom had arrived back from New York, and without them really discussing it, Will had moved his stuff into Polly's spare room, 'just for now'. Although their affair was continuing, its pace seemed to be slowing and they would often sleep together now without making love.

*　　*　　*

September began warm and sunny. Before long Polly was back at work, putting in long hours, accepting overtime, trying to follow Will's model and not think too much about Emi. Sometimes it felt as if people were beginning to forget; there were days when no one mentioned her sister. There was no longer a slot on the news, there was nothing new to say – there'd been nothing new to say for months, and the police no longer called. Polly knew in her heart of hearts that Emi was OK, that she was alive. The letter, combined with the assurance of the man in Trafalgar Square had lodged itself inside her with a dull certitude. Nevertheless, a part of her – the Emi part – remained numb and vacuous, waiting.

A few weeks after his return, Will arrived home late one night to Bermondsey. He had been attending an evening lecture and when he embraced her Polly could smell the pub in his hair. He seemed sheepish, a touch nervous, and when he spoke he avoided looking her in the eye.

'Remember that flat I mentioned before I went to Damascus?' he began, tentatively. 'Well, I've rented it. I can move in tomorrow.'

The flat was high up in the eaves of a white, stucco-fronted Georgian terrace, overlooking Kensington Gardens. It was very small, little more than a studio; one large room with a separate shower and kitchenette. He moved in the following week and now Polly often came to stay. Will was right in one respect: it felt different, like a new stage between them, one that was just about them, an exclusive place where Emi had no hold. In the early evenings they often crossed the Bayswater Road and wandered over to the Round Pond, arm in arm. It was unseasonably warm and sometimes it felt as if the heat would never abate. Will encouraged Polly to breathe in the air, to enjoy the sense of space around her again. She thought about Carol's description of Sarah, walking around this park, and often watched single, late-middle-aged men walking alone with their dogs, wondering if one of them was Louis. Will and Polly talked about their days, about their work, about their worries, about Emi. But they never talked about the future. And they still searched for clues, for signs of her in every stranger's face. And at night, they continued to lose her and themselves inside one another's bodies. Somewhere, deep down, however, they both knew that inevitably their time was running out.

On a Saturday morning towards the end of October there was a ring on the buzzer while they were both still dozing. It was Will's brother, Tom. Will looked questioningly at Polly, lying in his bed. Traditionally, she would have leapt up, got dressed, to cover their tracks. Today, however, she lay back against the pillows.

'I just don't want to pretend any more,' she found herself saying.

Will hesitated, then pressed the intercom to let him in.

'Emi, when did you get back?' Tom shrieked when he saw her. Then he saw the expression on Polly's face as she began to shake her head, backwards and forwards. He stopped dead in his tracks, turned to look at Will, questioningly.

'Is this why she fucking left?' he mumbled, stumbling for the door.

'We need to talk, Tom,' Will replied, dressing hastily. He looked imploringly at Polly, then followed his brother out of the flat.

43

Sarah never spends the night at Louis's flat. A part of her would like to, but always, at the last moment, she decides to head back home, to the safety of Blenheim Crescent. She can't decide whether it's about retaining independence, or something to do with guilt, or even 'respectability', perhaps. Even though Antonio is only the porter, if she stayed out all night he would know, and other people who lived in her building might guess. She didn't feel ready for her affair to go public. And there was something else, too. However much Sarah enjoyed Louis's company, his sexual adventurousness and encouragements, she was beginning to worry that essentially she did not – or was it could not? – love him. She would feel she'd cheated him if she stayed, that it would suggest her feelings were more significant, more permanent. It would make letting him down later harder to do, if it ever came to that.

One thing makes her sure she is right to hold back; she still hasn't told the twins about Louis. He has begun to make suggestions – that they might holiday together in the summer – and Sarah finds herself becoming vague, retreating subtly. After they complete their dissertations there is no longer a reason for Sarah to go to the V & A, and their routine is no longer the same. And instead of going on holiday with Louis, she suggests spending a celebratory weekend in Rome, with Carol. She feels she owes her old friend something, an apology, at least, for the way she has discarded her in recent times. She feels so well now, she is ready to talk it through.

The Sistine Chapel blows her away and Sarah spends hours sitting at café tables in ancient squares sketching pattern designs into a drawing pad, with oil pastels. She feels carefree and, without Louis around, completely released from her marriage to Peter, at last. Somehow, perhaps, Louis has provided a route out of her past, she thinks, away from her paranoia, and now she finds that she is ready to live in the present tense, and even, perhaps, to dip her toe into grander future plans. But for now, at least, she needs to exist alone.

She perceives by contrast that Carol's stature, her self-assurance, seem to be on the wane. She seems less sure of herself than she used to be, more cautious of expressing her points of view. Sarah feels partly responsible, that she has let her old friend down. They eat every evening in a small *locante* where the young waiter flirts outrageously with them both and Sarah responds in kind. Carol affects disapproval but underneath it Sarah knows that she's pleased to see her so happy, so free of the depression that has plagued her. One evening they drink a litre of red wine with their meal and Sarah feels emboldened. At the end of the meal she looks earnestly at Carol across the table.

'I want to make an apology,' she begins. 'Over the past

few years I've had to retreat from our friendship; you were so close, to everything. And then I met Louis, and all I could think about was myself. I want you to know that I'm really, really sorry. You did so much for us all.'

To her surprise, Carol smiles, then looks away, as if experiencing a private agony.

'Oh, dear Sarah, you owe me nothing,' she whispers. 'Nothing at all, least of all an apology.'

On their last day, the two women wander through the city's market together and Sarah stops at a stall selling mohair shawls.

'I shall have this red one, to remember our weekend by,' she states brightly.

'Let me buy it for you, please,' urges Carol, rummaging in her bag for her purse. 'To say thank you, for inviting me, for forgiving me, for everything.'

Sarah looks at her curiously, does not understand.

'Thank you,' she says, quietly, as Carol places the shawl around her friend's shoulders, then turns to pay the man standing behind the market stall.

44

Amy and Louisa Crisp, thirty-two-year-old identical twins, seem to be exactly the same. They have the same thick, golden hair, the same high cheekbones, the same habit of rubbing their forefinger and thumb together during conversation. When Seinfeld is mentioned they respond with exactly the same intonation, 'Oh, I adore that show!' They live together, work one floor away from one another at an insurance firm, wear similar clothes, hang out with the same friends. They even confess to having the same dreams.

It appears the sisters are as alike as two people can be, but in many ways they are opposites. Amy's outgoing and confident; Louisa more introverted and shy. They share the same lovely face, but those cheekbones make quiet Louisa look enigmatic and contemplative while Amy glows with a healthy sweetness. Amy tends to speak for her sister: 'Louisa's always been more private, inhibited,' she explains, with a smile, and Louisa nods her serious head in agreement. They see themselves as a duo – but more like complementary photo negatives than duplicates of each other. 'I think we balance each other out,' says Amy. 'She's right,' Louisa agrees. Amy says, 'In every family photo,

I'm smiling, she's . . .' 'I'm not,' Louisa interjects with a defeated giggle.

It was when they lost their parents, in quick succession in their early twenties, that the deeper differences between the twins came to the surface. Theirs had been a strong, loving, stable family and the girls were both, understandably, devastated by their loss. But as Louisa sank into a depression, Amy picked herself up and the experience became a catalyst for change. She left the US for London, met and fell in love with her future husband. Meanwhile, Louisa stayed where she was, catatonic with grief. It was the first time the two had ever been apart.

After a year in England, Amy moved to Los Angeles. She and her now husband encouraged Louisa to join them there, and she did so, but even though she was now reunited with her sister, she seemed incapable of shaking off her depression.

In recent years, we've come to believe that genes influence character and personality more than anything else does. It's not just about height and hair colour. DNA seems to have its clutches on our very souls. But spend a few hours with identical twins who have exactly the same set of genes, and you'll find that this simplistic belief crumbles before your eyes. If DNA dictates all, how can two living, breathing clones of one another be so different?

To answer such questions, scientists have begun to think more broadly about how genes and life experience combine to shape us. The rigid idea that genes determine identity has been replaced with a more flexible and complex view, in which DNA and life experience conspire to mould our personalities. We now know that certain genes make people more or less susceptible to

384

traits like aggression and depression. But susceptibility is not inevitability.

'You're absorbed – what are you reading?' Kalle enquired, standing over me.

'Oh, just more of your fascinating studies,' I replied, casually placing my arm across the recent paragraph and turning to look up at him.

Kalle smiled but he was shaking his head. 'Sometimes I can't read you, not at all,' he mused.

'It must be something to do with my DNA,' I replied, trying to smile.

I thought about the report on those American twins for the rest of the day, and I thought about Polly. Susceptibility is not inevitability; destiny is not fate. Like Amy and Louisa, Polly and I may have the same basic make-up, but with variations caused perhaps by absorbing different levels of protein in the womb, by the different ways in which we were born and held, from the evolving variants in our relations with our parents, from the effects of our peers, from the loves and losses we have both experienced, from our natural inclinations and our learned patterns of behaviour. I'm also becoming aware of how very naïve I have been – how literally I have always absorbed the concept of self-determination, how self-obsessed I have been to believe that I could ever have had a real impact over other people's futures, or pasts. I cannot alter Polly's fate, my fate, or the fate of others. But I might alter my behaviour, and so alter my destiny. I have listened to the negative side of my brain for too long, the negative reasoning side, the side that has told me that

Polly is bad for me, that Will is bad for me – that I am bad for me.

Lotta is my shining example. A month has passed since she told Frank and me her news about Stephanie and she seems to feel better, back to her old positive ways. She renews with every new day, is being shaped right now by the world that touches her skin, by the experiences that she absorbs, by a subtle process of osmosis, through the air. She's fresh and new and exciting and hungry for stories and love and drama. With her eyes, I view the world as a sparkling place; a place to be happy. I must allow myself the privilege of self-forgiveness. I must learn to see the positive side, and I must learn to enjoy loving and being loved. I need to tell Kalle more; for the past year I have existed like an extended pause.

Kalle still hasn't mentioned Stephanie's pregnancy to me, and I have determined to wait, to let him find the right moment to tell me. It is his news to tell, not mine. I imagine that he is cogitating over the idea, trying to grasp the ramifications, none more so than the inevitable shift in the dynamic that will ensue with Lotta. I am surprised that he seems so calm and unperturbed by this development. I would have expected him to rage.

When Kalle got home from work tonight, he came straight to find me and informed me that he had been to his favourite deli and bought us some Swedish delicacies for supper. His mood was light, jubilant even, and I knew that he must have had some good news. When I came through to the kitchen, he was already reaching for the corkscrew to open a bottle of wine.

'My first draft's been accepted,' he exclaimed. 'I want to celebrate, and I want to apologize, for my unspeakably intense workload. It's been appalling. Please, Emi, forgive me.'

'I don't mind that,' I reassured him. Suddenly I could hold it in no longer. 'But I am upset that you haven't talked to me about Stephanie's pregnancy.'

'Her what?'

For a brief moment I wondered if Lotta might have made the story up, but instinctively I knew that what she had told me was true. Yet my words had stopped Kalle in his tracks – and I realized that I had been wrong all along. Evidently he hadn't heard.

'She's pregnant?' he asked, putting the bottle down.

'Lotta told me, at least a month ago,' I stuttered. 'I'm so, so sorry, Kalle. I assumed you knew. Lotta informed me that she's going to marry Marcus. She's terrified that she's going to lose her mommy – and she thinks he's going to take your place, become her dad. I get the feeling it hasn't been very sensitively explained.'

'She could have told me. She could have helped me prepare Lotta. It's just typical bloody-mindedness,' he raged now. 'Lotta will simply have to come and live with us.'

I watched with a sinking heart as he left the kitchen and headed into the rotunda. Rain was bucketing out of the sky, falling in cascades across the city; Kalle looked out upon it morosely, and I knew that I couldn't help him, not tonight. I had been the bearer of poisonous news. Quietly I put away our uneaten food and the bottle of wine, then slipped off to my room. Moments later I heard him use the phone, then leave the apartment.

387

*   *   *

When I woke up this morning Kalle wasn't back. I went out to buy groceries and when I arrived home he was there, sitting on the sofa, his daughter in his arms. They looked up at me vacantly.

'Jag kommer altid att vara din pappa,' he was murmuring.

I moved quickly to the kitchen and put away the food, then went to my room, closed the door and sat on my bed. Eventually I heard them move from the sofa to the kitchen, start preparing food. I listened as they continued to chatter in Swedish as they began to eat. I felt sick to the pit of me, as if a circle was closing up, with me on the outside. I felt truly alone; not a shadow of Polly, only me, Emi Leto. Polly had ceased to be my signifier, or me the signified. I was Emi; just Emi, nothing but me. It was all that I could be. I feared this new sensation, of being discarded by them, being left alone. I feared that Kalle would put Lotta's needs before his or my own – that I would have to go while he worked things through. What would I do? How could I go back?

Later, once she was asleep, Kalle knocked on my door.

'Come in,' I whispered, tentatively.

'We talked, it's a start,' he said, then affected a laugh. 'She was afraid that you were going to take me away from her, too.'

I tried to laugh, to appear unconcerned, but failed.

'I told her you could never do that,' he continued, moving towards me and sitting down next to me on the bed.

I fiddled with my fingers, chewing my bottom lip.

'I told her the way I love you is different from the way I love her. But I also told her I hoped that you'd never leave us, that you'd always be here.'

45

'We've got a new lead of sorts,' Officer Richardson said.

He was on his mobile and the line was crackling but, even so, Polly could tell from his deadpan tone that something was wrong. She hadn't heard from him for months, had assumed that the police had given up on Emi, had closed the file. She hadn't contacted him either, because she had nothing to say – and had decided to live by the premise that no news was good news; a touch ironic, she knew, considering that news was her daily trade. But with things the way they were between her and Will, she was loath to stir things up, to draw too much attention to their current circumstance. She knew that the press would have a field day if they found out; she could see the headlines now.

She called Will and by the time they got to the station Richardson was back behind his desk. He was still talking on the phone, however; he nodded towards the chairs opposite and they sat down to wait. Presently he hung up and in one swift move leant forward, hands clasped under his chin, and began, without greeting, to fill them in.

'I'm not saying it really makes any difference but, frankly, you guys haven't been completely honest with me,' he said. 'We got a call this morning from a security guard who works at Tate Modern. He's in charge of wheel-chair access; ground floor, front right, corner entrance. He'd spotted a piece about Emi and a photograph of the two of you in his paper and it had triggered a distant memory. The more he thought, the more he remembered what it was.'

Polly glanced at Will, confused and concerned. She felt a deep sense of foreboding. He leant over and put his hand on top of hers and squeezed as Richardson picked up a remote control and swivelled around in his chair to gaze up at a TV screen, hanging from the corner of the room. 'This helped him to remember what it was – as I'm sure it will you. In fact I think you'll agree that we've found the trigger for her leaving.'

As the CCTV footage flickered into life they were taken back. There was no mistaking the day; it was almost exactly a year ago, the Sunday morning after Helen's dinner party, to be precise; the day, of course, when Emi had disappeared. It was a day that no one had forgotten, that no one ever would forget.

Inside the frame, the CCTV camera had picked up on Polly and Will walking together in the winter sunshine along the South Bank, towards Tate Modern. Their heads were bent together and as they moved they were talking, laughing. They came into closer focus by the second. As she watched, Polly was immediately startled by how different their appearances were; how young and relaxed, how normal they both seemed. If she hadn't known whom she was observing, she would have assumed that this couple were in the first stages of a new love affair. They walked in unison, their heads cocked together, but their bodies maintaining a very slight distance, as if they were dancing either side of an invisible line. As they slowed, then stopped in front of the museum Richardson pointed the remote and froze the frame.

'There,' he stated, coldly.

If one looked carefully, as they all now did, behind Will and Polly you could see a third figure; in fact, you could almost be fooled that it was a double impression, a reflection or a shadow of Polly, because it was a female figure and she shared the same frame as Polly, the same features, and she walked in time with them, just a few paces behind. But if you looked carefully you could see that this woman's demeanour was less certain than Polly's, that her gait was more tentative, her disposition less sure. There was no mistaking Emi.

Will's grip on Polly's hand loosened as Richardson let out a half whistle, half sigh and switched the tape back on. Now they continued to watch themselves as they headed into the museum. Emi hesitated, then followed them in. Moments later, however, she reappeared and sat down on a bench opposite the entrance.

'Now wait,' Richardson said to them. 'As Emi did. At least, I'm assuming it's Emi, not you.'

The tape flickered as he pointed and pressed the remote to slow forward-wind. Now people buzzed back and forth across the frame, arriving at the museum, leaving it again, or simply wandering aimlessly, enjoying the winter sunshine. And all the while, in the background, Emi continued to sit, motionless, on her bench, her eyes fixed on the entrance, her expression glazed.

Finally, four hours later, Will and Polly reappeared. You could tell that Emi had spotted them because she sat up straighter before turning her head slowly to focus on their exchange, as Will leant forward and embraced Polly, then kissed her on the cheek. Now it seemed that they were arranging something; both looking at their watches, agreeing to a plan, before laughing and nodding. Finally Will hugged Polly again and she hugged him back. This was a more lingering embrace. As they separated once more Polly looked up into Will's eyes and beamed. Even on the grainy footage it was impossible to miss the fact that she looked elated. Then Will took off, up the river walk, towards the South Bank as Polly watched him go. He turned and grinned, waved at her, then disappeared from the frame. Now Polly turned and began to walk towards Emi. There was a moment when she moved directly in front of her twin, blocking out the camera's view of them both, but then, without pausing, she moved on again, past Emi – who was still sitting, static, on the bench – and on out of the frame. And now, at last, it was Emi's turn to move. The second twin got up and hurried away from the camera's lens, away from them all.

Polly's heart shuddered in her chest as she sat there, thinking of the last time she had seen Emi, the night before all of this; standing in Blenheim Crescent, pulling down the blind. The memory of what had happened next was tugging at her now, still distinct. Polly had told the cab driver to take her home and on the way she had pulled her mobile from her pocket and instinctively she had called Will. She had wanted to fill him in about the disastrous dinner, on Emi's words in the cab, on her continuing, thunderous mood. He had listened attentively and then he had confided that Tom was back from New York with his new girlfriend, that he felt he was intruding on their space.

'Do you want to come over?' Polly had enquired, instinctively.

Will had stayed before, that first night when Emi had asked him to leave, when he had had nowhere else to go, before Tom had given him the keys to his flat, but this time, when he arrived, it had felt subtly different, subtly like deceit; at the time Polly had convinced herself that this was because of Emi's irrational accusations, but now she concurred that perhaps it had more to do with the way she was beginning to feel. This time they had stayed up for a while, both confused, finding solace in their shared experience of Emi's wrath, becoming greater allies than before – and then she had got the spare duvet out and Will had spent the night on her sofa.

Before Emi disappeared, Polly had played her grandmother's cello in a casual quartet, once a month, and, despite her lack of sleep, the next day she had risen early to rehearse for her next concert. The instrument was her means of escape from the world – and her most prized possession, too. It felt like a link in the chain to a woman she had never really known, a woman whose hands had played this instrument so artfully for years. She had recordings by her grandmother from various public performances that she had given around the world. In fact, she had listened to her playing the very piece that Polly was now practising to perform herself, with far less panache but hopefully as much feeling. She always rehearsed on Sunday mornings; it was a ritual, a spiritual release, her Sunday worship, she often joked. But she had never practised to an audience before; it was a private activity, a meditation of sorts. However, this morning her playing had woken Will and he had appeared and perched on the side of the armchair to listen. She was attempting Dvořák's Cello Concerto in B Minor. It was a particularly emotive and difficult piece that required her full attention. Rather than distracting her from her endeavour, Polly found to her amazement that Will's presence actually improved her concentration, and another hour passed before she put down her bow. Afterwards Will had thanked her for the privilege of letting him listen and offered to take her out for brunch. They had left the flat and, as Polly looked back now, had taken the first of many walks to follow. That first time, of course, they had decided to head to Tate Modern where they had gone to the members' café on the fifth floor to eat brioches and drink cappuccinos while looking out across the glistening river towards St Paul's, rising majestically on the other side. Afterwards they had wandered through the galleries together, talking more than looking at the art, enjoying one another's quiet company, a shared moment outside the everyday. Finally, at around four, they had left the museum. She recalled now that she had been surprised by the emotion that stirred in her when Will embraced her, then kissed her very gently on the cheek. She could still remember how he had trapped her gaze inside his eyes for a moment before embracing her once more and telling her what a great time he had had, how she had helped him to push Emi totally from his mind. As Polly watched the screen now and reflected on the ensuing events, she knew that this very moment had been the start of something – the start of all of this. And not only had Emi been there to witness it; she had known it, too.

46

When she returns home from Rome, Sarah surveys the sketches she had made there and realizes that she wants to turn her pictures into tapestries; she decides to buy herself a full-scale loom. She used to embroider, when the children were young, and the desire to create, on a grander scale, is becoming stronger by the day. She's received a commendation for her MA and it is to be published in a journal, but now she knows that what she really wants to do is to become a practitioner of this ancient art. Sarah doesn't return Louis's increasingly irregular calls. Instead she blocks him out, puts all of her emotional energy into her newfound craft. There's something gratifying, soul-lifting, in the process of taking the thread, of weaving it in and out, of pressing the treadle with her foot, of seeing an image emerge, so slowly, yet resolutely, from between the threads. It suits her temperament; this slow, methodical manner of working, and she determines to make it her vocation.

When Polly next comes to see her, she remarks on the beauty of the loom, then sits before it and raises her fingers while her mother shows her how it works.

'It reminds me of sitting playing my cello,' Polly says, and Sarah suddenly feels her own mother's presence near them, recalls for the first time in years the comforting presence of her sitting, playing the very cello that now belongs to her own daughter. The loom takes up a similar amount of space in the room, and when she sits at it and works, there is a certain meditative, rhythmic concentration required. It is as if, with it, she has found her own 'music'. A gap in her invisible circle seems to be closing up. Perhaps, she contemplates, she has a natural place inside her family history, after all.

When the call comes from America it is a shock for Sarah. As she picks up the phone, she expects to hear her father berating Bush's post-9/11 policies, a year on. Even since her mother's death, already thirteen years ago, her father still calls each week, still has an opinion to share, about the state of the British economy, US–UK relations, the economic inequalities in the world and his latest concern, global warming. Sometimes she thinks she should hand the calls directly to Will, when he comes to stay with Emi; for both he and her father seem to share a common sense of the injustices meted out by the superpowers, the global injustices that make the world such a precarious planet to inhabit. But this week, when she picks up the phone, it is not the voice of her father calling from Maine at all, but of a woman called Carys, a friend of her parents whom Sarah has never met but about whom in recent years her father has spoken with greater frequency. She has wondered if their friendship has become something more, but would never have known how to ask. In a trembling tone Carys pronounces that Sarah's father has had a stroke and that, sadly, he has died.

Sarah feels bereft. She is surprised to find herself wishing, for a moment, that Peter were there to talk to about it; at least he had known her father, would have been able to share, albeit superficially, perhaps, in her grief. The twins had hardly known him – indeed either of her parents – and she knows that his passing would really mean very little to them. In the end she calls Louis. He sounds surprised to hear from her. It has been nine months since she went to Rome with Carol, and she hasn't been in touch with him, had needed to be alone. She still couldn't explain why. For a moment he seems reticent when she asks if he would mind meeting her for tea.

'I'd rather we walked,' he said. 'Like old times.'

She sees Sasha first, the large retriever galloping around the pond, with the slim, slightly gauche figure of Louis following on behind, swinging her blue lead in rhythm with his step. As soon as Sarah sees him, she feels her melancholy lift in the breeze. Sasha reaches her first, leaps up barking repeatedly with excitement. Sarah can't help but laugh, and when Louis now approaches he, too, cannot suppress a wary smile. Sarah falls into step beside him, and by the time they have walked the perimeter of the pond twice, she has told him all about her father.

He pauses and turns to her.

'Would you like me to come?' he asks her gently. 'To the funeral?'

'It will be in America,' she explains.

'I know,' he says. 'But that's OK.'

'What about Sasha?'

'I'm sure I can think of something.'

He puts an arm very gently around her shoulders and they begin to walk, together again now, slowly, quietly, once more round the pond. Sarah feels she could continue walking with him, round and round, for ever, and then she feels the sensation of tears brimming behind her eyes. The offer is so kind, and to her surprise she doesn't want to rebuff him. In fact, she realizes that she really wants him there, next to her, for ever now. She wonders what it was about Louis, before, that she had run away from – was it the very kindness she now sees that she craves, that she needs from him? She doesn't trust herself to speak, simply allows the afternoon to ease the gap between them, and later, the evening to close it back up.

47

It's the last day of November. When December comes I will have been here for a whole year. I keep returning to Kalle's notes on mother-love; on its significance, its influence on our genes, our make-up, the way we are made, and the people we become. I can't see how I saw her before, now I think I see her for who she really was, to me and to Polly. And at last I think that I've stepped aside from Polly's shadow. Now I have to learn to fall into step beside her – and ahead of Sarah.

While Kalle was putting Lotta to bed, I went into the rotunda and, without hesitating, I picked up the phone and called Polly's number. It rang once, then twice, and for the first time I held my nerve. Will and Polly, their growing intimacy before I left, I finally understood, was simply the culmination of things, not the starting point, but the final trigger in a long line of disappointments, displacements, retractions – all on my part. It wasn't Polly's fault. It wasn't anyone's fault. There was no point in trying to point a finger of blame. But how to overcome it? I couldn't rely on Kalle to be my solution. If my love for him became dependency, as it had done with

Will, I knew it would lead to disaster, to a trailing off, to my inevitable departure. My former sense of duality, this year, had not evaporated, it had simply evolved into a cruel duplicity. It was time to face Polly and Will, it was time to try to explain, and it was time to say sorry to them all.

The phone rang again. Then Will picked up.

'Hello?' he said.

His voice was so familiar I almost laughed. He had just stirred. I knew him too well to be mistaken, even after all this time.

'Hi, Will,' I answered. 'How are you?'

'Pol?' he replied, anxiously. 'Where the hell are you?'

'It's not Polly, Will, it's me, it's Emi.'

There was a pause.

'Where are you, Emi?' he asked finally, his voice no more than a murmur, I couldn't tell if from anger or sadness.

'I'm a long way away,' I said.

'Goddamit, Emi, stop playing with us like this.'

'Are you OK? Is Polly OK?'

The words spilled from my lips, I couldn't stop them, but I was unsure if they made any sense. He remained silent.

'Are you together? It's all right – you should be – I understand it now.'

'You can't influence our lives like this,' he seethed.

I heard a sound and turned. Kalle was standing in the doorway, watching me, curiously. He raised his eyebrows, more with a look of concern than enquiry. Immediately I hung up.

'Are you OK?' he asked. 'You look pale.'

'I was just calling home,' I said.

He nodded, trying to imply disinterest, and then he grinned.

'That's great,' he said.

48

When Polly woke on the first of December she knew that something was different, that something inside Will was absent, even before he woke, and instinctively she knew that he was ready to leave her again.

They had intended to have dinner together the previous evening. Will had said he wanted to 'talk things over'. But at the last minute Polly had been asked to run a late report and by the time she'd arrived home Will had already been sleeping. She'd crept in beside him, curled herself around his body and slept fitfully. Now for no apparent reason she found that she was weeping. She couldn't bear the way she was feeling, vulnerable and out of control, but Polly was certain this time that there was nothing she could do, that this next break with Will was going to be a permanent one. She was caught between a rock and a hard place. She needed Will to stay but she also needed Emi to come home; and she was beginning to wonder if it would take his going for her twin to find a way back. It was nearly a year. Perhaps, she thought, Will's mind was also fixed on the impending anniversary. Her tears woke him. He rolled over and held her, then gently wiped them away, but he didn't ask her what had caused them. He suggested that, once they were up, they take a walk along the river and go into town.

Will's eyes were as cloud-filled as the day and he shoved his hands deep into his trenchcoat pockets, collar turned up against the cold. For a moment Polly could imagine how he would look at sixty and hoped, somewhat fatuously, that she would still be there, next to him, to share in his ageing. Otherwise the progress of time seemed to carry no value for her any more. But he was absent from her for now, alone with his own brooding thoughts. His arm didn't stretch out to place itself around her shoulders and he walked at his natural pace, a stride faster than her own. She felt tightness in her throat, the slight burn of acid there and struggled to keep up.

They headed west around Southwark Cathedral, along the medieval cobbled lanes and out on to the river walk that curved past the Globe, on past Tate Modern and its haunting memories, then under Blackfriars Bridge. They moved on towards the elephantine building blocks that comprised the South Bank. When they got to Westminster Bridge they crossed over to avoid the permanent police cordons, the crowds of tourists and the beleaguered protesters outside the Houses of Parliament, all the time in silence. It wasn't until they reached St James's Park that Will slowed at last. They circled the lake, dotted with throat-puffed pelicans and dipping eider ducks. He paused on the small iron bridge arching itself over the water that snaked its way from Buckingham Palace to Horse Guards Parade and smoked a cigarette unearthed from his pocket. Leaving him there, Polly moved to a bench. The rain had ceased and a milky sun was making its presence known as a faint, sickly glow from behind the clouds. She thought she understood what Will was doing. He was trying to separate himself from her so he could look independently at their predicament. He'd talked about this before, in fact they both had, about how hard it was for either of them to see the situation objectively because it was not just about Emi, it was about them all. Part of her wanted to flee, to return to her flat, get back into bed and close herself down under the covers, but she feared that if she did, Will would be lost to her, that there would be no way to retrieve him. But if she stayed what was there left to say? She couldn't answer her own question, so she did nothing, just watched him standing there, smoking and gazing into the water as she wrapped her arms around one another in a vain attempt to keep out the cold. Eventually he finished his cigarette and tossed the tiny white tip into the water, before turning to come and join her. He sat down, then leant forwards, elbows on his knees.

'She rang,' he said.

'Who?'

'Emi. She rang last night when you were at work.'

Polly thought she might faint.

'She said you and I should be together, that she was a long way away and then she hung up. I'm sorry, Polly, I tried, but there was no trace on the call.'

'Are you sure it was her?'

'Oh, yes, it was Emi all right. For a moment, I thought it was you.'

'But I'm not her, am I? I can't replace her, Will, can I? I never will be able to.'

The words tumbled from Polly's mouth before she could stop them. They made her feel like retching.

'There isn't a way to replace her,' he said, unemotionally. 'You're someone else. Someone entirely different.'

'Am I? Really?' she asked, and she really meant it. Where did Emi end and she begin? Where was there ever a clear dividing line between them?

'You used to be all light and music, Pol,' he mused. 'Emi was always hunting for something intangible that I now think she was never going to find. I fear that trait's rubbing off on you. We need to find a way to get you back to who you were before.'

Polly felt the sensation of tears brimming in her eyes again but this time they remained dry. So Emi really truly was safe. There was no longer any room for doubt. The moment should have felt like a huge relief, a celebration, so why didn't she feel elated? What did Emi mean, that she and Will should be together? Polly knew that her reiterated 'sanctioning' of their relationship worked in reverse; that it was like the final nail in its coffin. Her mind travelled down the dark tunnel of the past year, flicking back through the fictions – or should she say mis-interpretations? – that she had found in Emi's diaries, all the old stories her sister had twisted, the things she hadn't even told Will, the things he thought he already knew. And then she thought about how utterly, desperately she loved Will. Was he talking about that? Did Will love her? He had confessed to so doing. But now she was no longer sure.

'I've been changed,' she said quietly, 'maybe irrevocably. There is no going back to how I was, or to how things were. It's all over now.'

'Now I know, for sure, that she really is OK, I really do think I need to go away for a while,' he replied. It was a subtle form of agreement. He was talking quickly now, desperate to impart the information before Polly had a chance to stop his flow. 'There's another trip on offer, after Christmas, but longer this time, a sabbatical. I'm due one.'

For her part, Polly could no longer think straight.

'I need some distance,' he added, resolutely.

'If I let go I'm going to feel guilty,' Polly answered, distractedly. 'As if I've given up on her. She has to come home, even just for a moment, so we can start again.'

'We don't have to give up, maybe just take a more long-term view. Evidently, she really is OK. We should feel happy about that. It's a good thing, for everyone.'

'Let's go,' she said, rising abruptly and stamping her feet.

Will didn't protest. Together they trudged back towards the river, Will's arm now around her.

'I think we should take a cab,' she blurted out suddenly. 'I need to get ready for work.'

They stood apart by the roadside in Parliament Square and waited for a taxi in silence, and when one approached Will said that, after all, he thought he'd walk into Soho for a while, then head on home. Polly jumped into the cab without saying goodbye and turned her face from him as it began to drive away.

49

'Thank you,' says Sarah as she takes the butter-coloured roses from the florist, then makes her way back up Holland Park Avenue. Next she picks up a fresh strawberries and cream cake she's pre-ordered from Maison Blanc and two bottles of good champagne from Oddbins. It's mid-May and the light dances and sparkles in the sky. She wants her fiftieth birthday to be perfect – for them all. She's so lucky, to have all this, to have the moment, she thinks, as she wanders home, heavily laden with her packages, regardless of the recent loss of her father.

Antonio, the porter, helps her upstairs – thankfully he's always ready and willing to sort out domestic problems, to help her up with shopping, to make living alone feel all right. It means she hasn't had to burden Louis with her domestic affairs either. In some ways separating him from all of this has helped to keep their relationship fresh. She thanks Antonio profusely and once he's gone she shuts the door, puts the champagne in the fridge to cool, then goes to lie down. The girls will be here in an hour and she needs a moment to collect herself. Emi's promised to bring Will for the tea, which is, of course, no surprise. Sarah asked Polly if there was anyone she'd like to come along, but as usual Polly was elusive, said she might bring 'a new friend'. It worries Sarah that her daughter has so many short-term relationships, that she seems so emotionally restless, so ruthlessly ambitious. She'd like to talk to her about it, about the way she feels Polly is desperately searching for someone to replace Peter, about how she never will, and how she needs to find a way to reconcile herself with his death and move on. She needs to do this before . . . before it's too late. Oddly, she sees in Will a passion for politics, for current affairs, that Polly shares. But when she thinks of Emi's more ephemeral nature, she wonders why she and Will are still trying to make something of their friendship. Where Polly is restless, it seems Emi is utterly disinterested in searching for something *wonderful*. She and Will have been close friends for so long now, it must be more than six years, but still Emi asserts that their relationship is platonic, that their intimacy is purely cerebral – that Will is simply her 'best friend'. Sarah sees in Emi an extraordinary imprint of herself, of her emotional paralysis with Peter, and she feels to blame, desperately wishes that her daughter would take the plunge, whether with the wonderful Will, or elsewhere – and try falling in love. She fears, alas, that her daughter is more likely to follow her own pattern and allow herself to be looked after, to be secure, inside a relationship lacking in desire.

Sarah has contemplated asking Louis to tea but after her visit to the doctor she knew that this was no time for new introductions. He's taking her out for dinner, later, instead. She'll tell him first. Now she slips off her cotton cardigan and lies down on the bed. The windows are open and a light, kind breeze lifts the muslin curtains, then allows them to fall again. Sarah takes her right hand and moves it across to the curve between her left armpit and her breast and feels, gently, for the lump, just to be sure she hasn't been dreaming, that it really is there. Now the doctors have prodded and felt it, she finds it immediately. She knows there's no mistaking what she has found. They've recommended that they operate immediately. She'll tell the twins after today – tomorrow, perhaps. But for now she wants to live in the present tense. After all, it is her fiftieth birthday, the sun is shining, the breeze is soothing and her two lovely daughters, as well as Carol and Will, will all soon be here to help her to celebrate. Ironically, after all the years of misery, Sarah realizes that the last five years have been the best of her life. Nothing, she thinks, that happens in the future can change that – or take any of it away from her.

Will arrives first, clutching a bunch of peonies. He's become like a surrogate son to Sarah, is so much part of the family now – as, again, is Carol. She thinks of them now as she lies there, and of her ability to draw people in, lost people, she thinks suddenly, who need a sense of home, of family, a place and a way to belong – as does she. Although she knows Emi should leave Will, selfishly she can't bear to think of them ever losing him. If only there were a way to shift him to the other side, over to Polly, she thinks, briefly. He'd be strong enough for her: she would learn through him, occasionally, to acquiesce. But immediately she brushes the thought away.

411

*　　*　　*

'You don't look a day over forty,' Will teases, thrusting the flowers forwards at Sarah and unzipping his camera bag.

He's promised to record the birthday as her present and he's now focusing on her through the lens of his Nikon camera. Sarah laughs, quietly pleased by the flattery. Soon Polly shows up alone. She seems febrile and slightly flushed, bustles about arranging the glasses, the cake, chattering all the while to Will in an over-exuberant fashion. Sarah tries to discover what's upset her daughter but to no avail. Polly makes no mention of the 'friend' she said she was going to bring and Sarah assumes, sadly, that there has been some kind of break-up before they've even had a chance to meet him. Next Carol arrives, armed with another bunch of peonies, which makes them all laugh. Emi gets there last, in a well-cut grey suit, looking serious and slightly dishevelled from her tube ride. 'I'm so sorry to be late,' she exclaims, hugging her mother tightly. 'James got stuck in court, we overran.'

Now they're here Sarah finds it hard to hide her tears. They may be an odd, unconventional 'family' but it's all they've got and when they're back together like this, it feels like home. Instinctively she knows that she can't introduce Louis into it, that it is already too late, it would be too hard to explain, and she thinks Polly, particularly, might take the news of him very badly. Also, she knows in her heart that her prognosis is going to be bad. It's not that she's a pessimist any more, but there's something certain in her mind about her condition and she knows that this is the last time she's going to share her birthday with the people she loves. Tears swim in her eyes as she hears the pop of the first cork and they begin to sing 'Happy Birthday' to her. She blinks them away and looks out over the communal gardens. There's a small child running barefoot across it, chasing a lemon yellow butterfly, and she turns towards her 'family' and smiles.

50

I heard the sound of Kalle opening the outer porch door and looked up from my diary. He'd been out chopping wood for the stove and looked invigorated by the cold, healthy and euphoric. He was humming tunelessly under his breath as he lowered the heavy basket down on to the doormat, then shook the snow from his ski boots, unlaced them and left them outside. Next he pulled the door to and hung up his coat and scarf in the small white hallway. Only then did he catch my observing eye.

'It's a beautiful day to finish a book,' he exclaimed, with a sky-wide grin.

'If this is what it does to you, I understand why you keep writing,' I replied, trying to sound light-hearted.

'And you too,' he answered.

I stopped writing mid-sentence.

'I'm nearly there,' I said. 'A whole year nearly recorded, a whole year of "us".'

Kalle's shoulders shook with a long, resonant laugh whose echoes seemed to reach deep beneath his feet into the very foundations of this old wooden house. I love him. I would not wish to be anywhere else. And yet something was nagging at my insides, urging me to hurry, urging me to get home.

He carried the logs past me and on into the sitting-room. It was true, my last remark. I'd never seen him quite like this before, so even-tempered, so unencumbered. He always sounds different when he's here – his tone is richer, rarer – but this time his contentment seemed to run deeper. When we're in Stockholm the wilderness is stripped from his voice, it adopts an analytic crispness; his laughter never reaches so deep, and his reserve is raised far higher. I noted this loosening of Kalle's guard the first time we came, in January, all those months ago, for Lars's birthday dinner, but I didn't understand it as well as I think I might do now.

He came back into the kitchen and took an ice-blue cup from one of the wooden cupboards, moving towards the Aga. Battered old copper pots and pans hung in a row from hooks in the ceiling above it. He pulled the steam kettle back across to the hotplate to boil.

'We might as well just leave it on there all the time,' I remarked, clasping my hands around my own cup, still half full of warm peppermint tea.

'But I'll never manage to make you a cup of tea here that tastes like England, Emi,' he answered.

'Ah, England, my England,' I murmured, hugging the new green mohair shawl that I had recently bought in Stockholm around my shoulders.

'You'll never get used to it here, your blood's too warm,' he teased.

I love his knowingness of me. It's one of the many small details he's learned; that once the cold's seeped into my bones there's really no getting rid of it – other than by having a sauna, of course. I'd been sitting by the radiator, and now I've moved to the Aga where it's toasty but the air in between still retains a hint of ice. In midwinter it takes a whole week before the cottage completely thaws; I remember the first time we came, how Lars had already been there a week, and how even then, my sheets in the blue room had felt damp and cold. This time, it was just Kalle and me and at night our intertwined bodies kept us warm.

'Conversely, I think the ice warms my blood,' he added.

'Haven't you ever wondered why you Swedes call these places summer houses?' I chided.

'Ah, but by coming back in the darkest month we've turned our story full circle,' he replied, reaching for a loaf of nutty rye bread, brought with us by boat, all the way from the city. 'And, anyway, you know I needed somewhere quiet to read through my last draft.'

He took four slices, cut them into triangles and arranged them on two butter-yellow plates. As I watched him I felt warmth seeping back into the base of my spine. I held up my cup for a refill. He added scalding water. The steam rose into the cool air.

'Are you going to let me read it?' I asked.

'Who knows? If it never gets translated, maybe you'll never be able to.'

He handed me a plate with a surreptitious smile. He'd placed a perfect slice of his own, home-cured gravadlax on top of each slice and its pinkness glowed.

'And me your diary?' he added, as we moved together to the sitting-room and sat down on the sofa to eat the food and to drink our tea in front of the fire. The thought of Kalle reading my innermost thoughts sent shivers down my spine.

'One day, maybe, when I've gone,' I replied.

'Never, then, I hope,' he said.

I smiled but didn't answer. Instead I determined, for now, to sit there, next to him, listening to him talk, to savour the moment, without an eye on the future, or an ear towards the past.

It was the first food we'd had all day and we ate hungrily. The cured salmon was so soft and cool it dissolved imperceptibly on our tongues. When it was gone, we lay back, shoulder to shoulder, and watched the fire. It was only two o'clock but already dusk was falling. Outside, snow illuminated the low-lying meadow but behind us the forest was already turning black. It was the darkest day of the year. The room was receding into semi-darkness and the heat from the fire was making me woozy, but I forced myself up.

'I'll get some more logs,' I said, 'before we lose the light.'

Kalle didn't respond; he had drifted to sleep, long legs stretched out wide in front of him. I left him there, put on my boots and his coat. It was still warm and as I breathed in I could smell his sweet scent in its collar.

The air was hard with ice and the outcrop of slick black granite beneath my feet was slippery, but the moon was rising round and full and clear and the surrounding forest was already darker than the sky. Something rustled beyond the sloe bushes and startled me. I glanced up just in time to spot a white snow owl swooping out of sight behind the rust-coloured barn, like a spirit. When I came back inside

Kalle stirred and rose to help me. We placed the logs in a neat pile and added two to the fire.

'I have a Crystal Night present, to say thank you for helping with Lotta this year, for helping with the making of my book,' he announced, retrieving two packages hidden behind the chair. They were wrapped beautifully in silver paper etched with blue cornflowers and tied with silver bows. Inside the first was a long silver dress made from the softest satin. I laughed as I held it against me.

'Has this anything to do with my namesake?' I asked, delighted.

'Maybe,' he answered.

The second box contained a smooth, heavy, silver bangle.

'Thank you so much, Kalle, but where shall I wear these party clothes? Here, in the middle of the archipelago, with nowhere to go?' I said, bending over to kiss him.

'We'll have guests tonight,' he reassured me. 'Just you wait and see.'

He handed me a third and final parcel. Inside were a thick white fur wrap and a hat.

'I think you'll need these. It is a little cold for the dress alone,' he said.

51

Polly idled on the escalator, embracing its slow, regular whir and clunk. Since Will had told her he was leaving again there seemed to be nothing left to accelerate towards. Emi had become an incomplete tale that had run out of steam. The media was too busy keeping ahead of itself to allow stories to find their endings – even her own – and Will's mind was fixed on a future without either of them. All those threads, left hanging, left untied, she contemplated – and she was as much to blame as the rest of them. Inevitably, since the Tate tapes, the police had given up, too. Who could blame them? There was a call pending to the police station that she didn't want to make. She knew that if she told them Emi had phoned they would close the file. And yet, as far as Polly was concerned, until Emi physically came back she was still missing. The thought made her breath tight as she reached the surface and headed out along the Finchley Road to Scissors. It was time to cut her hair.

Her pace quickened a touch; she was keen to get inside, out of the rain, falling meanly now, cutting through her too-thin coat like shards of ice. She pushed open the fogged-up door, trying to ignore the Missing poster of her sister that she had stuck there almost a year ago. As ever, she failed and her eyes stuck to the fixed grin like glue. It was beginning to fade, the corners curling where the tape had dried out. The left side of Emi's face was peppered with small white spots where drops of condensation had seeped through and blotched her skin. Polly blinked past the picture and allowed the door to swing shut behind her. The salon was busy and the bustle helped to shift her attention away from the ghastly truth of it – that in the image Emi was starting to look ghostly.

A couple of women were sitting on the reception's too-shiny leather sofa between a glitzy pink Christmas tree, erected since her last visit, and the old, over-varnished umbrella stand that had been there for ever. They glanced up at Polly dully as she closed her dripping umbrella and moved forwards to place it next to theirs, then they stiffened in recognition, and allowed their gaze to slide away. She was relieved to avoid their eyes. Linda jounced towards her like a bantam hen with a fox after her feathers and pecked the wet coat from her star client's back.

'You look like you could do with a massage,' she murmured, chivvying Polly to her usual spot. She got her seated and caped in a single choreographed move, then ran her fingers lightly through Polly's hair.

'How about a new look?' she asked, doing her best to sound nonchalant. 'It might be time, you know, for a change.'

'Cut it all off,' Polly replied slowly, avoiding Linda's all-knowing eyes. 'Blonde, dye it, short, cropped, completely new.'

Linda said nothing, just gestured towards one of the girls to mix the dye.

'Must have been a bit disappointing for you this week,' she stated maternally, as she slipped surgical gloves over her ring-bedecked fingers. Linda was one of the few people she could still really talk to about Emi – yet she couldn't help but feel sorry, too, for her own continuing sense of the tragedy.

'I went round to Mum's flat,' she found herself confessing. 'I was so sure Emi would, you know, just walk back in.'

'I understand why you might imagine that,' Linda agreed emphatically, her stirrer pausing momentarily in the mix. 'Got to hope, haven't you?'

They both looked up and their eyes met in the mirror. Polly nodded and looked down at her hands. Kindness, she'd found over recent months, readily provoked a combination of self-pity and shame. Linda got the message, didn't urge her on. And as she turned her attention back to dyeing single strands of her client's hair, Polly realized that when she had these chats with Linda it was Sarah, not Emi, that she missed the most.

While Linda worked Polly shut her eyes and thought about the previous few days. She had dreaded the first anniversary but only now that Linda had mentioned it did she realize she was still reeling from her disappointment at Emi's no-show. Her mind travelled back again to the previous Tuesday night. After work she had gone home and paced around restlessly for a while. Will had left a message to say he wasn't coming over – again. They hadn't spent a night together since Emi had called and he had informed her that he was leaving. Instinctively, at around

421

11 p.m. Polly had got in the car and driven over to Blenheim Crescent. Just as she had that night exactly a year ago, the night Will called to tell her that Emi had vanished. She had curled up in their mother's old floral armchair, a rug wrapped over her legs, to wait. At some point she had finally drifted off to sleep, distant memories churning and clotting her dreams.

Finally her hair colour was set and Linda reappeared to rinse out the dye.

'You look Scandinavian, with all that blonde hair,' she beamed. 'It brings out the colour of your eyes.'

It was true, Polly felt renewed – on the outside at least. But inside, nothing had changed. She felt utterly emptied out. It had gone five and the earlier rain had turned to a steady December drizzle. She thanked Linda, reluctantly wrapped a scarf around her newly-coloured hair, and took the Jubilee Line back to London Bridge.

The idea of Will going away had turned the void Emi had left into an ocean of emptiness, and Polly knew at last that she was really experiencing Emi's terror: the terror of being alone and raftless. For his part Will was affecting a positive attitude but behind his stoic air she was sure that he was suffering, too. But uncharacteristically she couldn't raise the issue; her words were stuck inside her, a blur of emotion without a clear narrative. There were only two weeks before he was due to take his plane and they still had no idea where Emi had gone. The man in Trafalgar Square was the only real link. Polly had taken to wearing Emi's ruby ring, turning it round and round on her finger as she searched his gentle face in her mind for clues. Where had he come from? She couldn't place his accent; it had been European, eastern European, perhaps. There had been something spiritually uplifting about the man, there was a certitude about him, he had a reassuring demeanour and his aura had stayed with her ever since. But it didn't make her feel any closer to Emi, or any more certain that her sister would come back.

52

Sarah lies in her bedroom in Blenheim Crescent with the light fading behind her eyes and thinks about Peter. He had been such a thick smokescreen, so certain and selfish, that throughout her marriage she could never really see past him. When he had finally left her life, she had felt surprisingly elated. Her singularity had felt like a release. She had dips, but never back into the bleak periods she had experienced inside their marriage. When Louis first entered her life she had not known how to share. She had spent too many years hiding from her emotions, hiding from herself. She could see now that it wasn't until after her father's death that her guard had lifted and her fear of the unknown had gone away.

She's managed an extra six months, far more than the consultant estimated; she's done well. But now she knows it's near. Louis steals in to see her in the night, when no one else is there, and understands that he will have to say goodbye before the end, to avoid any confusion or upset with her daughters beside the hospital bed. The time is coming soon. She can no longer feel any weight in her body; the doctors have prescribed such heavy doses of morphine that she feels as light as air, semi-conscious, a touch delirious. It's not a bad feeling, but it's a hopeless one, a giving in, and one she accepts that she has no choice but to embrace.

And then, of course, she thinks, there are the girls. They had been so all-encompassing, such towers of strength. Her absorption in their lives, their coming into being, had also provided her with a certain, valid method of self-avoidance. But they were young adults themselves now – already twenty-seven years old, four years older than she had been when they were born. Since separating from Peter, she thinks she's been able to read Polly better. Her daughter covers a deep fragility with a bold optimism, a rash ambition. She's always been such a warm, loving person, with so much to give. But for Polly, emotional bonds have proved hard to form. She has flitted from boyfriend to boyfriend, never allowing anyone to get close enough really to touch her spirit. It's partly because of Peter, Sarah thinks. He adored her and she him with an uncritical commitment, a total immersion, and Sarah knows that Polly won't be able to settle with anyone new until she discovers that same deep bond again.

Conversely, Emi has been afraid to test her emotional boundaries, has depended on Will to keep her secure. Recently, she's been conscious of Emi and Will becoming more intimate and, although she wouldn't tell Emi, their growing involvement alarms her. There's something missing between them, something that her parents shared – and that, in a non-sexual way, she realizes, Polly did with Peter; something that, recently, in her own quiet way, she has found with Louis; something shimmering – an emotional flame. For a moment she can see her own parents, standing close together, looking down at her, a small child with the future open wide. They are smiling gently and holding each other by the hand. There was something about them that she now knows she recognized but was incapable of articulating in her childhood, something exclusive, all-immersing. Their shared passion for music was a bond that went deep into their cores, right into their souls. That was it, she suddenly knows, that was when her own sense of isolation began. Her parents had been soulmates. And she had always been on the outside – made by them, but not part of them. They had not needed her – not in the way that she had needed her own children. Because they had had one another, there was no real place for Sarah; she was the by-product of their love, not the heart of the thing. When she thinks now of her own life, of her relationship with Peter, she knows it was nothing more than an arrangement, like a floor plan, for them all to inhabit, as a family inhabits a house, coming together at the centre, for food, for leisure, but, essentially, living out their emotional lives in separate rooms. As children, Polly and Emi were inseparable, their bond so inherent as to be enviable. But in adolescence they had retreated behind their own separate closed doors. Now they seemed streets, even cities, apart. Even after Peter's death, when she thought they might find solace in one another, Sarah was surprised to see how little of their grief either of the twins was willing to share with the other. Of course, Emi had always had Will. She can see it clearly now, how they have both followed in their parents' patterns, inevitably, she supposes; Emi looking for security,

Polly searching endlessly for the new, for something Sarah worries that she is never going to find.

Sarah's aware that her current circumstance has forced her daughters back into one another's worlds – and she hopes that it will be the one positive result to come out of her death, that it will be a new beginning for them, a time for affirmation, of something implicit, and strong, something essential and unbreakable.

She hears the door open, then close again, gently. She assumes it must be Louis returned. Now someone has approached the bed, is sitting down next to her, quietly. Sarah wants to open her eyes, but the effort is too great.

'Louis?' she murmurs.

Presently she feels her hand being lifted and she knows that it is not him, but Emi, sitting there, stroking her palm. Her daughter's fingers are characteristically cool. As they move to tighten themselves around her own, she feels Emi's strength flood through her, giving her just enough energy to reciprocate with a smile.

53

After we woke we dressed and left the house in the darkness. I felt like a wrapped gift in my silver dress and furs; wandering through gleaming snow in the bright moonlight.

'Look!' he exclaimed. 'Here they come.'

Kalle raised a hand and pointed to the sea. Twinkling lights were bobbing across the surface of the black water, moving slowly but surely towards the island. We trod carefully down the dark path towards the harbour as four small boats came into focus.

'Listen!' he whispered.

Suddenly I heard it, a low, sweet sound, the sound of singing, a fine, pure choral chant. Under his breath, translating for me as he went, Kalle joined in.

> *Nightly, go heavy hearts*
> *Round farm and steading*
> *On earth, where sun departs,*
> *Shadows are spreading.*
> *Then on our darkest night,*
> *Comes with her shining light*

Sankta Lucia! Sankta Lucia!
Then on our darkest night,
Comes with her shining light
Sankta Lucia, Sankta Lucia.

As we arrived, the seafarers were already alighting; lights flickering from candle-lamps held in their hands. There were around two dozen of them, adults and children, all dressed from head to toe in white, the boys and men with peaked white hats covered with silver stars, the women and girls with garlands of ivy and white flowers in their hair. One little girl with ivory hair had a crown of candles on her head and as they continued to sing, a woman lit them with a long taper. In my mind I heard Lotta's words from the summer:

'One of the girls dresses as Sankta Lucia. I hope one day it will be me.'

I wished it were her, here, tonight, wearing the crown, with her pale skin, her lopsided fringe, holding on tightly to her rag doll, tipping her tongue out above her lip at the world around her, the confusing, big, wide adult world, and I missed her with a sharp jolt, wanted to be back with her again. I thought of Stephanie, of the future she was busy creating for Lotta with Marcus and the baby, within the folds of her new family unit, a unit that didn't contain Kalle. I held his hand tighter.

The lanterns and candles sent an ephemeral, closed light around the group. They drew us into their circle and continued to sing. Kalle's arm now moved around my shoulders. Then one of the men poured steaming liquid from a flask into tiny shot glasses and passed them around.

I took a sip. Inevitably it was alcoholic, warm and strong. Meanwhile one of the women handed out ginger cookies and saffron bread. In the candlelight I could now make out the faces; these were the same islanders who had come to our midsummer celebrations. We exchanged greetings and raised our glasses to the moon, shimmering in fine silver seams across the water. Only moments later, it seemed, the group was already bidding us farewell. Then they took back to their boats. We watched as the lights and the singing got increasingly faint, then they disappeared and the sea became silent.

In the middle of the night, something startled me and I woke. The moon had been swallowed by clouds and the darkness was as thick as velvet. I could hear another tune. For a moment I thought it was coming from outside, from the seafarers, returning, or singing far out at sea, but then I realized that it was playing inside my mind.

'Raindrops falling, falling down on me, rivers flowing, flowing to the sea.'

The words were familiar yet their root was out of reach. I allowed them to drift through me, round and round, over and over again; they were soothing, calming words. But beneath them there was something else, something tugging, then tightening around my heart: call it an instinct, a threat. Something was wrong with Polly, something had happened. I had to get home.

This morning we drove back to Stockholm, Kalle in high spirits, humming all the way, his manuscript sitting bound and ready for delivery on the back seat.

'Are you going to take it by hand?' I asked.

'Absolutely, I want to make sure it gets there on time,' he replied, earnestly.

When we got back to the apartment we lay on the bed, intending to have a nap. Instead we made love, then Kalle got up and headed off to his publishers. After he'd gone I called a taxi. I had wanted to explain everything to Kalle, everything I could find to tell him about Polly and Will. I knew that I had to, and that it was time, but until I'd seen Polly I realized I had only an incomplete tale to tell. Until I saw her I didn't feel I could promise anything more to Kalle, not even that I would be back. I left my diary open at the first page on the kitchen table, then I took my passport and money and headed for the airport.

54

There was only one place left for Polly to return to, a place she'd avoided for months now, ever since she'd invited Kaz home that hazy summer night when she had been going completely off the rails. When she got to King's Cross this time she realized it was nearly a whole year on from the day she'd first seen Kaz, but there was no sign of her, there were no faces Polly recognized at all. Everything around the station had changed and there was major commotion going on. All the roads around it were in the process of being 'rewritten' to make way for new, emerging lines connecting King's Cross to the sea and its new super-fast track to France, to Europe, to the beyond. It was mayhem, 5 p.m., and getting dark. The traffic was at gridlock. Everyone was trying to get to somewhere else, away from this urban nightmare. Sweat prickled at the back of her neck and Polly feared the onset of another panic attack. Since Will's announcement that he was leaving, they'd been coming with greater regularity. She feared she might be becoming agoraphobic again. And to make matters worse, she couldn't seem to find a way to get across the traffic, to the phone-box on the other side. Eventually she left the pavement and boldly wended her way between the cars, avoiding the insults hurled at her for adding to the inconvenience of the moment. At last, to a certain relief, she found herself back in the shadowy world of York Way.

But where the phone-box had been there was now only a pile of rubble and an ugly gash in the pavement. A digger was parked on the kerb and a sign saying 'Pavement closed, use other side' blocked her from pursuing her course. Polly found herself being directed back across the street, right round the corner from the station, and on to the main road leading to Islington. This was not the way she wanted to go but she couldn't work out how to get back across, to go in the opposite direction. She saw a bus queue and decided to join it. She didn't really care where it would take her, so long as it was away from there. A couple of primary-school kids were squabbling over a GameBoy in the queue in front of her and their mother was bent down, calmly reprimanding them for their bad behaviour. For a moment she envied them for the bland, ordinary domesticity with which they began their day. The kids could have been no older than five or six, a boy and a girl; they could have been non-identical twins, she mused. They were both clean-faced and tightly buttoned up in their green uniforms, school bags between their knees. As they noticed Polly's attention one glanced up at her, followed furtively by the other. They both had unsmiling, feline eyes. Meanwhile their mother was rifling in her faded leather handbag and unearthed a packet of cigarettes. She lit one, then followed her children's gaze. It was only then that Polly realized she was looking at Kaz. She was dressed in jeans and a denim jacket, her hair pulled back in a mother-of-pearl clip, her face scrubbed clean of the night's warpaint, her scar now a fine red line; just as she had been that summer night at Polly's flat. Instinctively Polly smiled in recognition but, to her shock, in response Kaz's face hardened. She took a deep drag of her cigarette, gaze still flint-cold on Polly. Then she blew the smoke out hard from the left side of her mouth, dropped the butt and turned back to her kids, grabbing one by each hand, roughly.

'Come on,' she told them. 'Let's walk.'

As the kids grumbled and complained Polly looked away, her cheeks smarting. When she glanced back Kaz was already hoicking them off up the street, school bags dragging behind.

Polly turned and started to walk, faster and faster, away from Kaz and her kids, away from the station, up the road towards Angel. Polly respected Kaz for her fierce protection of her children from her night-time activities, but felt sad and fearful, too, for Kaz and her kids' future – and also, most acutely, and suddenly, for Emi. Kaz was capable of reinventing herself, every day and again at night. Her two appearances couldn't be more dissimilar, her day and night-time preoccupations more contrasting, but it was too late for her to go back to wherever it was she came from now. There was no escaping from her current reality. Polly suddenly feared that the same may have become true for Emi, that she might have gone too far ever to find her way home.

She looked down a side street, spotted a small Italian café there, dived in and sat down at one of the red-clothed tables. A sullen-looking young waitress soon appeared, menu in hand. She couldn't have been more than nine-teen years old, thought Polly, with long, oily black hair and thin red lips. As she handed Polly the menu, her mouth turned upwards into a smile and Polly saw her eyes flicker in recognition. Her heart sank. This was no time for small chat about what it was like to be a news reporter on TV.

'Hi there,' said the waitress, enthusiastically.

'Hello,' Polly replied, guardedly.

'I had given up on you returning,' the girl continued, with growing familiarity. 'I was almost tempted to wear it myself.'

'I beg your pardon?'

'The shawl,' she said. 'Your beautiful shawl. You may have changed your hair, but I'd never forget your face.'

Polly knew, in an instant, that this young girl thought she was talking to Emi. She suddenly heard that her accent carried in it the promise of faraway places, warm breezes, the bitter-sweet taste of olives, the smooth silkiness of good Chianti. And as Polly looked up at her properly she also saw that the waitress was extremely pretty when she smiled.

'It's so beautiful, but, you know, something made me hold on to it for you, for a whole year. I always knew you'd come back in the end, come looking.'

Polly didn't speak – didn't dare to, didn't want to break this moment, to find that she'd been hiding inside another unbearable dream of finding Emi.

'One moment,' the girl said, and turned on her heel, more hurriedly now she had a mission to fulfil. She reappeared with her offering: Sarah's red mohair shawl.

'It was my mother's,' Polly told her, as she handed it over. 'Thank you so much for hanging on to it.'

She held the shawl up to her face and breathed in as deeply as she dared. She was still there, still in it; Emi's perfume, her inimitable scent, just detectable among the fibres now overlaid with the headier smell of Italian herbs, olive oil, cigar smoke and coffee. Sarah had bought the shawl in Rome, a year before she was diagnosed with breast cancer. She'd gone there on a 'field trip', as she called it with innocent pleasure, with Carol. She had wanted to see the Sistine Chapel first-hand. After she had died Emi had taken to wearing it. The colour suited her, or should Polly say their, Snow White complexion. She remembered Emi saying that she wore it when she was feeling nervous; it was like a security blanket that protected her.

'Only it wasn't me,' she informed the waitress slowly.

The girl cocked her head to one side and looked confused.

'Who left it here, I mean, it wasn't me. It was my twin sister, Emi. And since then, no one's seen her. She vanished, you see, that night, after she left here.'

The waitress sat down opposite her and pulled her chair in.

'My God,' she said. 'I'm so sorry.'

'What do you remember of her,' Polly asked. 'Was she here alone?'

The waitress shook her head vigorously.

'Oh no, no, no. She was with a man. I remember it clearly, you know, even though it was so long ago now, because it was a Sunday evening and they were our only customers. And she didn't eat a thing.'

'What was he like?'

She looked pensively at Polly, searching her mind for a description.

'Like a sailor,' she replied eventually.

'A sailor? In uniform?'

The girl shook her head vehemently.

'No, not that kind of sailor, not a serviceman. But there was something about him. He looked like he came from the sea.'

Twenty minutes later Richardson and Will showed up. They interviewed Rosa and she gave them all she had. Now she was in tears, this disconsolate young girl in a pair of Pepe jeans and a pink T-shirt with 'Ted Baker' on the front, and now the whole family had appeared to hear the story. They sat round the table, elbows crooked, faces cupped in hands, entranced: two small, wide-eyed infants with creamy cappuccino skin, and Mama, Rosa's double yet twenty years her elder – with twenty extra kilos to carry around. She, too, wore her emotions close to the surface, and as Rosa spoke she snivelled into a hankie and occasionally patted her daughter's hand. They felt for them all, for Will and for Polly, and for Emi, too, the girl they never knew but whom Rosa had so regularly dreamed would come back.

'The bill was paid in cash,' she informed them, with a determined passion; of that she was quite sure. Her memory seemed extraordinarily clear. 'The woman was a little nervous, I think,' she recalled. 'She drank red wine, ordered lasagne but ate nothing, not even a grissini. She kept this shawl around her shoulders all the time, until, just before she left, when she used the Ladies it fell to the floor, under her chair. I think she may have been a little tipsy. This was why I know they paid in cash,' she reaffirmed. 'Because I checked to see if I could trace her from the bill. The man, he was in middle years, with pale hair, a big smile, maybe blue or green eyes. He looked like someone who lived in the open air, definitely not a Londoner.'

Richardson flicked through a file of photographs for Rosa to see and the children gathered round to watch. Polly and Will had created it in the early days, pictures of everyone Emi was known to have seen in the weeks leading up to her disappearance, photos of all her friends. Rosa tried hard, but in the end, she said, she couldn't find the one they were all looking for. But Polly thought she might know who he was – the description was familiar, if skewed. Evidently Emi had been with the man she, Polly, had met in Trafalgar Square.

'It doesn't sound like she was being coerced,' Richardson said, as he drove them back to Polly's place in his smoke-screened car. Neither Will nor Polly replied but she was feeling buoyed up by the sighting. This was a real clue, something tangible to digest – with a subtly sweet after-taste. Recently, she had recognized a dulling of her emotions towards Emi's disappearance, and a greater pre-occupation with Will's imminent departure, too. She had felt guilty at the shift and feared what it signified: that her mind was drifting, that she was learning to live without her twin, as she'd already learned to live without her parents, that the agony at Emi's loss was already being replaced by

438

something less unworldly, a regular yet more slight emotional pain, coupled with a dull acceptance of a new status quo. But with this new concrete sighting, she felt the pain of her twin's absence picking up a beat. She glanced across at Will in the back seat but his expression was inscrutable, his self-immersion complete. The revelation had come as a shock and she guessed that he, too, was trying to figure out where it would take them next. Maybe he was even reconsidering the future, not going away.

When they got back home she went to make them all a cup of tea. Richardson was speaking on his phone in the sitting-room. She could hear urgency in his practised low tones, but none of the words. Presumably, she thought, he was recounting Rosa's story to someone back at the station, rallying the troops. Then she heard Will speaking to Richardson. Presently he appeared and stood watching her silently from the kitchen doorway. She switched on the radio; a Mozart piece was on air. She knew it, her old music group had played the quintet a couple of years previously, with an invited clarinettist called Ed Levi, a visiting lecturer over from America, who had been working at the Royal College for a term. She and Ed had had a brief fling. She thought about him momentarily. He had a diagonal scar across his flat stomach, a fine silver line, like a stream, from a motorbike accident in his teens, and his skin smelt sweet, like honeycomb. She'd never wanted anything more from Ed, nor he from her. Oddly, until now, she realized, she'd never wanted anything permanent from any of her relationships, had never looked to the future, or anticipated fully sharing it with anyone else. She'd always assumed that she was destined to live her life alone, with Emi on the sidelines, like a security blanket, like the shawl that was still around her shoulders, and had thought she felt at ease with the way things were. Until now, that was, until there was Will. Even if she couldn't have a future with him, this last year he had taught her that she wanted what he and she could, in another time and place, have possibly shared; a whole life made from two halves, a shared life that had nothing to do with her twindom.

While the kettle was boiling she filled the washing-up bowl and now plunged a used wineglass into the warm bubbly water, humming along to the Allegro. Her blood felt close to the surface of her skin and her fingers tingled in the steaming water. She took the quintet as a good omen and looked up to share her mood, to smile across at Will, but he didn't notice, his eyes gazing past her, to his usual place, out across the river.

'What are you thinking?' she asked.

Her voice had become gay, as if she were a touch inebriated, and when she caught sight of her face in the kitchen mirror she saw that she looked flushed. Her eyes were sparkling, an outward display of a newfound inner optimism, and a sense of expectation was brewing within her. They were definitely on to something. Emi was closer now.

'Pol, I don't want you to get your hopes up too much,' Will murmured. She looked back at him, surprised, but his eyes were now scrutinizing the floor. 'It doesn't get us much further,' he said, then paused. 'It was a year ago, after all. In fact, I'd go as far as to say the revelation's a bit sinister.'

Polly's optimism flipped and lurched inside her like an eel. 'It's the first real lead we've had since the summer. Surely that's got to be reason to celebrate?' she said weakly.

'She was with that fucking jerk you saw in Trafalgar Square, Pol, in the fucking back streets of King's Cross.'

Will's aggression hit her like a slap in the face. But Polly found herself toughening to the onslaught. She wouldn't let him spoil the moment. It was hers to cherish, for now, if only for this minute.

'There's no need to shout,' she replied coolly, staring at his bowed head.

Will looked up at her, challengingly. 'Get real, Pol,' he replied, his voice rising further. 'Emi's fucked off with no intention of ever coming back. And her selfish fucking act has destroyed any chance we might have had of a future. Can't you understand? It's all over. All of it. And no one wins, apart from Emi.'

Before she had a chance to respond Will had turned abruptly on his heel. She heard him say something to Richardson before her front door slammed. With his words she had felt something inside her snap and now she felt dizzy, a spiralling downwards. There was an insistent, sharp pain in her left wrist, too. Distractedly, she looked back down into the water. It was beginning to flush red, a viscose fluid spreading like tendrils of dogweed under the surface of the bubbly water. She was holding the stem of the wineglass in one hand, its goblet in the other. As it had broken in her grip, the cut glass had sliced through her skin. She watched the blood spreading for a moment, then took the jagged glass and rammed it through her other wrist. The blood spurted like crimson water from a fountain. Then she felt her face drain of colour, its heat turn to a clammy cold, and she fainted.

When she came round there were bright lights above her and a young man in a white nurse's uniform was leaning across the bed, checking a drip filled with a clear liquid. Polly's head hurt and she had no feeling left in her arms. But wait, yes, she did, after all. A fine, stinging pain crossed each wrist, both held tightly under thick, heavy bandaging. Slowly Polly began to recall what she had done, why she was here. She glanced to her side and saw Will sitting by her bed with his head bent low.

'I'm sorry,' she said and he looked up at her, searched inside her eyes for a reason.

'I've got to where Emi was,' she told him. 'Now I know how she felt. She was desperate, she was lost. She panicked, and then she left. Now I understand. And I forgive her.'

'Is that what you think she wanted? For you to understand? For you to react like this?' Will asked.

Polly's mouth was very dry. 'No,' she said. 'But I didn't have a choice. I'm following a pattern, it's pre-set, I can't explain it any other way. And Sarah, too, I know now how she felt, where she had got to, with Dad. But even right here, right now, I know I can get past this moment – Sarah did, finally.'

'Jesus Christ,' said Will. 'So now it's your turn to get all fatalistic, is it? You sound exactly like her. I can't take it.'

'Maybe Emi's changed. Maybe she's learnt to be strong?' Polly replied.

'Excuse me, but you need to sleep,' interrupted the nurse.

'Of course,' said Will, dispassionately. 'I'll go now.'

He got up abruptly and seemed relieved to have an excuse to leave.

'You'll come back, won't you?' Polly said weakly. She could hear the desperation entering her tone and despised herself for it, but she couldn't bear it, the idea of Will going, she really couldn't stand it. He hesitated and looked back at her. He seemed tired and unkempt, she thought. Evidently he hadn't slept; it must be another day.

'Sure, tomorrow,' he replied defeatedly, leaning forward to kiss her lightly, too coolly, on the cheek.

'Wait, please,' pleaded Polly, in a whisper, but it was already too late, the ward door was swinging shut.

The next day the doctor discharged Polly. She sat on the hospital bed and waited for Will but he didn't show up. Instead Carol appeared with a false, bright smile on her face.

'I said I'd come and take you home,' she said.

Polly didn't ask any questions. She signed herself out, took the plastic bag full of her bloodied clothes and together they left the hospital.

'Would you take me to Blenheim Crescent, please?' asked Polly. 'I don't think I can face being in my flat.'

'Of course, dear,' Carol replied.

When they arrived, Carol offered to come upstairs with her, but Polly refused. She desperately needed to be alone.

'Where is he?' Polly asked her, as they were saying goodbye.

Carol hesitated.

'He's gone, hasn't he?' Polly asked, more urgently now. She didn't really need confirmation, she already knew the answer.

'He thought it might be best,' Carol said. 'He brought his flight forward. He went this morning. He says he needs some time away, to try to get some perspective.'

Polly nodded, but didn't trust herself to speak.

'You're not going to do anything silly, now, are you, Polly?' Carol added, anxiously.

'What – like Mum and Emi did? Like I tried yesterday? No, Carol, I promise, I'm not.'

She almost felt sorry for the older woman, standing there so anxious and uncertain, but she hadn't forgotten what Hera had told her – and this was no time for false intimacy.

'I've got to go now,' Polly said to her, plainly. 'Thank you for bringing me home.'

55

Sarah keeps thinking of the yellow butterfly, trapped inside the frame of Will's photograph of her with her daughters, and of the child she had glanced at just moments before, chasing it through the communal gardens below them all in that bright spring sunshine. It's a strange feeling, this half-in, half-out state. She's lying, paralysed and closed-eyed to the world around her, tipped right on the edge of things, of her own life and, somehow, of life itself. She has so little time left, so little time to put the pieces of her jigsaw back together, and yet Sarah feels no anxiety, none at all.

Curiously, over the past few hours she's started to see her whole history in snapshots, like a pack of cards, shuffled indiscriminately. One by one the pictures flick over, each bearing a memory, and the really surprising thing is that all the images are of happy times, each one depicting just one tiny aspect of the wonderful, amazing, inconsequential moments of her being – and suddenly, all together, they make it feel substantial, worthwhile. Strangely, in the back of her mind a tune is replaying itself endlessly. She used to sing it, she realizes now, over and over again, a pre-natal lullaby she had learnt from her own mother, something she had reworked to suit her circumstances, had repeated like a mantra when the girls were still growing inside her. It's melodic, repetitive, circular, reassuring. It's strange how it's come back to her, insistently, urgently, now that she's so close to the end.

babies sleeping
deep inside me
sun rays shining
shining on to me
wind blowing
blowing through the trees
water rushing
rushing down the stream
waves rolling
rolling to the beach
raindrops falling
falling over me
darkness drifting
drifting down on me
moonlight shining
lighting up the sea
babies waking
wake outside of me

As she slips in and out of consciousness Sarah can see it all spread out before her: her past, her present and her daughters' futures too, and inwardly she is filled with love.

I want to go back, back to the start, she thinks. I want to sing to them now. I want to say sorry and I want to try again. I want them to start, not me to end, with this knowledge of what it is to be happy.

56

Emi turns her key in the door. It swings open without a sound and she feels intuitively for the hall light. It's strange to be back here in Blenheim Crescent, inside her old skin; she feels as if she is walking on to a staged set, a place that only exists inside her mind. Her coats are still hanging in a line along the hooks on the corridor wall where she left them over a year ago, her old, street-worn shoes in a row beneath them. She catches her face in the mirror – and there she sees the one thing that has changed. Her face is fuller, her eyes quick and bright; she no longer looks haunted. She had to come home, to see Polly, to try to explain. Now, seeing her own reflection, she knows that at last she's strong enough, that she's ready.

She moves deftly towards the sitting-room. The flat feels stale and cold. Sarah and she had always filled it with cut flowers. The curtains are open and the room is illuminated by the light of the moon. She doesn't switch on the light, heads for the mantelpiece, for the photograph of Polly and Sarah and herself, traces the three profiles with a finger. And as she surveys their bewitchingly similar faces she shivers; for a moment she has the sense of a presence, of her mother's spirit, perhaps lurking, somewhere just behind her. But no, she realizes, the presence isn't ethereal but real; someone is actually there, curled up and sleeping on her mother's floral chair, underneath her lost red mohair shawl. And now the figure is moving, stirred by her arrival, and suddenly it is conscious, sitting bolt upright and staring at her, wide-eyed. Emi's startled. It's as if she is seeing herself, with her short blonde hair – and yet also with that wan, haunted look around her eyes, that look she has lost; the look that has been erased by her year in Stockholm, by her relationship with Kalle, with Lotta, with Lars, with the island and the sea.

'Where've you been?' the apparition snarls.

Emi can't speak. She moves forwards and as she does so Polly springs from the chair, pounces at her, like a cat. Emi falls backwards as her sister lands on top of her, her fingernails tearing at her, pulling her hair. Emi tries to twist and turn herself out of Polly's arms and as she does so she smells her sister's warm, sleepy, sweet scent and she remembers how they were before, as children, how their physical bodies had been as one, and how at adolescence everything had seemed to change and they'd begun to fall apart, even sometimes to fight fiercely – like this. She remembers a green dress, a tussle on the stairs, not being able to breathe, or to push Polly away, not having the physical or emotional strength to do so, being afraid of Polly and of her own physical strength, too, of not wanting to test it, and then Peter appearing and wrenching them apart, and her mother, standing behind him, pale and passive and dismayed.

All these years later, at last, Emi now finds the strength

to fight back. She turns her sister over, twists Polly's arm around her back so she can't move, and straddles her, looking down into her sister's face, hot and fiery now, her eyes smarting with angry tears. As Emi's hold weakens, Polly manages to pull her arms forward again, but just as she's about to wriggle free, Emi grabs hold of her wrists. Each is bound with white gauze bandages.

'How could you do it?' Polly spits upwards into her eyes. 'How could you leave me like that?'

Suddenly the rage has turned to hysteria and her anger has evaporated. And once Polly starts crying she can't stop. Then Emi is crying too, and now they're holding one another, tightly, and there's no one else, just them, back together, back at the beginning, back before it all. Emi feels something at her core absorbing Polly's emotion, easing the gap, closing it back up.

'I need to try to explain,' she mumbles, eventually.

Polly says nothing, just sits back and wipes her eyes.

'You see, I saw you and Will, that Sunday morning,' Emi perseveres, even though her mouth is dry and her breath rasping. 'After Helen's. I'd come to say sorry, for getting it wrong. You were leaving your flat; it was early, too early for Will to have called by. Immediately I knew he had stayed over the night before. I began to follow you, along the river, towards the Tate. The sun was shining and the gulls were swooping over the Thames but I don't think either of you was aware of anything outside yourselves. It was like watching Will and me, as we used to be, before Mum died, before everything went wrong, but as I followed you I realized that it was different, too. Will's head was close to yours and even though you weren't touching there was something fused about the air between you – it was almost as if it didn't exist.'

'Please,' Polly whines. 'Please stop, I already know.'

Emi shakes her head. 'You and Will, you went inside the museum and then I lost you. I lost track of time, too, but it must have been hours later when I saw you both again because the light was starting to fade and my hands were freezing on my lap. You were back outside now, still talking intensely, and then he moved forwards and scooped you up, then he kissed you, very slowly, very lightly. Then you were saying goodbye, and then he turned to leave and you turned and walked, straight towards me. Your face was glowing, your eyes sparkling, ever so brightly – you looked happier than I had ever seen you, in your entire life. Happier, I knew, than I had ever felt. And at that moment I knew that I'd lost you to Will and him to you. I ran home, and decided to . . . erase myself.'

'Erase?' Polly's voice is a whisper.

'I took a bottle of sleeping pills and went to bed, intent on swallowing the lot.'

'So what stopped you?'

'Kalle.'

'Kalle?'

'Yes.'

'The man from King's Cross?'

'He rescued me, took me away. Forgive me, Polly, I felt I had no choice. I needed to leave you and Will together, to let you find a way to make it work, without me there.'

Polly pulled the mohair shawl tighter around her

shoulders. 'It didn't help,' she tells Emi forlornly. 'He's left me.'

By four o'clock in the morning Polly's heard it all. The night is still pitch dark and they're huddled together on the sofa, under the mohair shawl, their mother's armchair opposite them, empty.

'Come with me,' Emi is urging. 'Come back with me. I want you to meet him.'

'I don't want to go where you've been,' Polly says.

To her surprise, Emi senses that for once her sister is afraid.

'Anyway,' Polly adds, slowly, 'didn't Kalle tell you, we've already met?'

Finally, it's Emi's turn to be startled.

'He came to find me. He followed me from work to Trafalgar Square. He reassured me that you were all right.'

Emi looks increasingly confused.

'Proof,' Polly adds, holding out her finger for Emi to appraise her ring.

Emi stares at it for a moment, and then she remembers and it all fits into place, the picture, and Lars's words, in the woods, when she met him, in the summer, collecting the chanterelles.

'I left it on the island at midsummer,' she says. 'It wasn't Kalle you met, it was his brother, Lars.'

'He was a gentle man,' Polly replies. 'Once I'd spoken to him I knew you were OK, and then I got your letter. After that the searching for you became a personal crusade, one that was no longer based on fear that you were in any real danger. What I feared was that you might have become trapped, in another world, that you would find impossible to leave.'

'I nearly was,' Emi concedes. 'But without you in my life I realized that I have no future anywhere, with anyone else. I'm just sorry that for a while I thought it was the other way around.'

The next morning Emi and Polly head for the airport. Neither has slept. They take a plane and a car and then, suddenly, they are in Stockholm. Polly looks out of the car window at the waterlogged city, shimmering in a bright winter light just as snowflakes are beginning to swirl and scurry in the sky. When the cab gets to Soder, Emi asks the driver to leave them in MosebackeTorg.

'We'll walk from here,' she says.

As they cross the square Emi pauses and her sister stops next to her.

'It's the first thing I saw, when I arrived,' she says, appraising the statue. 'It made me think of us, of how desperate I felt to get away from you and from Will. I'd become an empty shell. But standing here now I know I've been refilled.'

'And I've been emptied out,' replies Polly, her voice trailing off.

She hasn't spoken to Will since she left the hospital. And she knows that whatever it was, whatever it might have been, already there's no future for them. She shivers uncontrollably. She misses him with a pain that bites like the ice now shredding the Stockholm air.

*   *   *

453

Emi uses her key to let them into the flat. Kalle is not there. Polly stands and looks out of the rotunda windows at the city in silence. Emi knows she's marvelling at the space, at the beauty, at the view. The snow is flurrying, thicker now.

'It's very late this year, the first storm of winter,' she informs her twin. 'Everyone's been waiting. At last Stockholm's dressing up in white; once it settles, hopefully it will stay like this for months.'

It's only now that she notices her diary sitting on the table where she left it, but it's closed now. On top is a piece of paper, folded in half, with her name on the front. She opens it and reads.

'Clare left Lars. Have gone to the island to console him. If you're back before me, come, my love. Kalle x'

Polly has moved away from the view, towards her, and is looking over her shoulder, reading the note too.

'So he was pretty clear you'd come back then,' she surmises.

Despite herself, Emi smiles. 'I guess we'd better get out there,' she replies.

'How?' asks Polly, glancing pointedly back out at the snow, falling even more heavily now.

'We'd better hire a car. The boats won't be going so far out in this weather.'

Three hours later Emi and Polly are heading out of Stockholm in a four-wheel-drive, wipers steadily pushing the snow from the windscreen, the roads whitening more with every kilometre they put between themselves and the city. The car is warm and fugged up but outside the weather is worsening. Emi knows instinctively that Polly's silence denotes her growing fear and for a moment she wants to reassure her, but then she thinks again. The journey towards Linanas is a significant one, one that she wants Polly to experience without her intervention. Maybe it's the final test, she contemplates – for their genes. Because Emi knows how being here makes her feel and although, to a degree, her love of the island has been shaped by her love for Kalle, for Lars and for Lotta, more significantly it has been shaped by her instinctive affinity with the place. She needs to know if Polly feels it, too. She takes a CD from her bag and slips it into the player. It's a copy of the one Kalle played for her the first time they drove here, themselves, the clean, cool sound of the key harpist and the deep melancholy of the cello.

'What is this? It's beautiful,' Polly asks after a while.

Emi feels the start of something and remains silent. She has never felt so determined to get anywhere in her life and she drives with an ever-increasing, fierce focus. There is no time left to waste, they must get there before the roads become impassable.

'When Marie died,' Polly says presently, 'you thought we were to blame, didn't you? You thought we willed it to happen.'

The wipers clear the windscreen, then again it is covered with snow, then it clears, over and over, backwards and forwards, clear, blurred, clear, blurred, in time, it seems, with the music. Emi doesn't reply.

'And when Dad left, you thought it was because of the row over the necklace, because of Hera.'

Still Emi doesn't speak, just presses her foot down harder on the accelerator. It's getting later, harder to see.

'You know, you were so wrong about that. You've always believed you could impose your emotions, your desires, on other people's lives – you think you know what you saw, but you were wrong. When you left, Will and I weren't having an affair. And Dad, well, he never had an affair with Hera, either. You were looking in the wrong direction – it was Carol, all the time.'

'Carol?' Emi feels sick, uncertain whether Polly is playing tricks, being cruel; the idea of Carol and her father together is inconceivable, disgusting to her. She can't speak, just drives on, trying to concentrate on the road ahead.

'Why did you tell Will you were born first? And when you went away, it was because you thought it would mean you were off the hook with Will, that I would pick up the pieces, that I could take your place, didn't you?'

Emi remains silent. She glances briefly across at Polly, who's feeling her wrists between her hands. She knows she deserves all of this. She knows Polly has a right to cut into her like this. And she also knows that what Polly is saying, on the whole, is fair, is true.

'Why did you slit your wrists?' she murmurs.

'Will left me and I couldn't cope with losing you both. Did you really need to push me to Sarah's edge? Was that really what she would have wanted?'

'I didn't mean to, I never thought you'd go that far down. I'm sorry, Polly, so very sorry. I thought it was only me who could feel like Mum.'

'The problem was, you were always at the heart of Will

and me. Even in your absence, your soul was between us. This year I've thought so many times, what if we'd met first, without you, if I'd been the one at Sussex, you at Edinburgh . . . or maybe that's just me being crazy. Back then I would never have been interested in Will – I was only interested in myself.'

'And now?'

'You know I love him. You knew it first, even before I did. But it's not enough. We can't be together. You'll always be there, between us. And it's no one's fault. But he made me feel something I've never felt before. Maybe one day, with someone else, I'll be able to feel it again.'

'Feel what?'

Polly watches the snow thickening on the windscreen, the wipers pushing it away.

'What, Pol, feel what?' Emi urges. The words are on the tip of her own tongue.

'Something I think Mum found with Louis, Dad with Brigitte, and you, I guess, may be finding with Kalle. Whole, I guess,' she says, weakly. 'Or almost whole, even without you, or Mum or Dad.'

Emi knows what she means because it's how she feels here, out here, right out on the physical edge of things. And it's to do with Kalle, of course, but more so, it's to do with herself. That's the bit that Polly hasn't yet found and she knows it and she wonders, just wonders, if, here, Polly might feel it too. Because even after this year of physical separation, and after all Emi's learnt, it seems that their emotional maps could still have been traced on top of one another; their feelings of love, of paralysis, of melancholy, of missing; they are all essentially the same.

'We're going so far out, Pol, you won't believe it,' she tells her, gently now. 'We're going to the edge, a place where you have to be yourself. It's a place I needed to get to in my life and now I've found it I know I'll never be able to give it up. I want you to get there too, I want us to experience it together.'

As the music comes to an end the sky begins to clear and the blizzard subsides. Suddenly, out of the darkness, there's that guiding light yet again, as if it is Emi's very own skimmed-milk moon, shining so brightly that it even illuminates the snow glimmering along their route. She finds her spirit rising and starts to sing, very quietly, that lullaby; it's come back to her again.

'*Raindrops falling, falling down on me, rivers flowing, flowing to the sea . . .*' and then Polly's joining in and they're singing it together. When they're done Emi notes that Polly is smiling at last.

'That was Mum's song. Do you remember? She used to sing it to us, when we were small,' says Polly.

Suddenly Emi knew where she had last heard it: it was on Sarah's last day. Polly and Carol had just finished their night vigil and she had come to the hospital to take over. The sun was pushing its way through the curtains and had settled in a peach glow over her mother, like a gentle balm. Emi had sat, trembling, holding Sarah's weakening hand. For a moment she'd seemed on the edge of consciousness, agitated, mumbling under her failing breath something about 'waves rolling to the beach'; the words at the time odd yet deeply resonant, something implicitly familiar and yet, at that time, out of reach. They had slowed, then finally ceased, and then Sarah's breathing had become more rasping, intermittent, her grip had loosened, and finally, imperceptibly, she had become quiet and still.

'In the weeks after Mum died, I felt a certain guilty relief,' she confesses to Polly now. 'There was something shackling about my relationship with her that began to lift as soon as she'd gone. Without her I discovered that I felt a little more bold in the face of risk – for example, in my decision to marry Will – or in my coming here, even. In both instances I had felt fearless to the consequences. But now I understand that this newfound "braveness" was really nothing more than an attempt at self-destruction. Something had broken inside me and I was determined to push my relationship with Will over the edge, to ensure that, in the end, it failed. I knew that she loved him like a son, that she would have been devastated by the idea of me parting from him. He had become family and she was not one to give up on such relationships readily. I threw myself into the marriage with him, knowing from the outset that it could only fail – false logic, perhaps, but accurate. What I hadn't anticipated was the effect it would all have on you, that in the end you would be the one who would find it hardest to let him go.'

They're going over a small bridge and now Polly finds she can't speak; she's in awe at the stillness, the beauty of it all, the shimmering, opalescent light reflected on the black water, and the whiteness, the brightness, of the snow above the thick, dark forest on either side of the tiny, winding lane. And now in the distance she sees a lamplight shining, and then another, and then she knows they are torches and they are moving up and down, in the hands of two dark figures, moving carefully together, towards them.

Finally, Emi stops the car and looks over at Polly.

'We've arrived,' she says, as she opens her door and clambers out.

Polly feels fresh, icy clean air flood over her as she watches Emi being embraced by a man who looks familiar to Polly; but Emi's right – it's not the man she saw in London, after all, it is someone else, someone who looks like him but different, someone slightly taller, with a finer frame. He looks past Emi now and into the car, and then he sees Polly sitting there in the passenger seat. He falters, his eyes widening, and then his face breaks into a delighted smile.

'Herre gud!' he breathes. 'You must be Polly.'

At that moment, Polly feels her own car door opening and as she turns she sees a face that she definitely has seen before, so far away and suddenly such a very long time ago, the face of a stranger, on that summer evening, in the middle of the crowds, in the heart of London, standing by the lions; a kind soul, reassuring her that Emi was OK.

'Hello, again,' she says.

'Hi, Polly,' says Lars, with a grin. 'We've been waiting for you. Welcome, at last.'

THE END

MASTERPIECE
Miranda Glover

Art, fashion, fame and sex – artist Esther Glass has it all.
That is, until a ghost from her past threatens to destroy her
perfect life. Trying to cover her tracks, Esther goes for
ultimate sensation, selling herself as a living work of art.
She takes the international art scene by storm, performing
as the female sitters inside seven great paintings.
But underneath the surface the cracks start to show as
Esther is forced to reconcile a very private history
with a very public life.

Fast-paced, smart and scintillating, *Masterpiece* gives the
reader a rare glimpse into a closed world.

'Gorgeous . . . Glover is an art-world insider and she looks
behind the glitter with great assurance'
THE TIMES

'Sumptuous, sensuous and thought-provoking'
MARGARET DRABBLE

'This novel is the ultimate comment on our obsession with
fame, celebrity and surface beauty . . . A superbly
thought-provoking read'
GLAMOUR

9780553817126

BANTAM BOOKS

THE LOLLIPOP SHOES
Joanne Harris

'Who died?' I said. 'Or is it a secret?'
'My mother, Vianne Rocher.'

Seeling refuge and anonymity in the cobbled streets of
Montmarte, Yanne and her daughters, Rosette and Annie,
live peacefully, if not happily, above their little chocolate
shop. Nothing unusual marks them out; no red sachets hang
by the door. The wind has stopped – at least for a while.
Then into their lives blows Zozie de l'Alba, the lady with
the lollipop shoes, and everything begins to change . . .

But this new friendship is not what it seems. Ruthless,
devious and seductive, Zozie de l'Alba has plans of her own
– plans that will sheke their world to pieces. And with
everything she loves at stake, Yanne must face a difficult
choice; to flee, as she has done so many times before, or to
confront her most dangerous enemy . . .

Herself.

'ONE OF BRITAIN'S MOST POPULAR NOVELISTS'
Daily Mail

'SHE IS SO TERRIFIC, SHE CAN WRITE ABOUT
ANYWHERE, ANYTHING, ANYONE'
Daily Telegraph

9780552773157

BLACK SWAN

THE TIME OF OUR LIVES
Imogen Parker

'A heartbreaking love story and a sweeping narrative
that captivates from first page to last.
Destined to become a classic'
Kate Mosse, author of *Labyrinth*

It is 1953. At the Coronation party at the Palace Hotel,
two lives are about to change forever.

Claudia – 16, beautiful, fragile and an outsider in this small
seaside town – finds herself talking to Michael, also a
newcomer, who is struggling with a rocky marriage. Their
instant, irresistible attraction to one another will have
consequences which stretch far into the future.

Against the ever-changing backdrop of events ranging
from grey post-war austerity to technicolour rock and
roll, from Suez to the summer of love, from Bill Haley to
The Beatles, from the buttoned-up glamour of the 50s
to the rebellious freedom of the 60s, *The Time of Our Lives*
is an intensely passionate love story and a
captivating chronicle of the times.

'As addictive as a good soap opera . . . A perfect beach read'
Sunday Times

'Divinely readable . . . I wish I'd saved it for my hols'
The Times

9780552151535

CORGI BOOKS

HE LOVES ME NOT . . . HE LOVES ME
Claudia Carroll

In the heart of County Kildare is Davenport Hall, the crumbling ancestral home of Portia Davenport, her beautiful younger sister Daisy and their dotty, eccentric mother, Lucasta. Disaster strikes when their father abandons the family, cleaning them out of the little cash they had managed to hold on to. But a ray of hope appears when the hall is picked as the location for a major new movie.

Do Davenport Hall is taken over by the *crème de la crème*, including the self-centred Montana Jones, fresh out of rehab and anxious to kick-start her career, and Guy van der Post, a major sex symbol with an eye for Daisy. Throw in Ella Hepburn, Hollywood royalty and living legend, and soon there's more sex, romance and drama off-camera than on!

'It bubbles and sparkles like pink champagne.
A hugely entertaining read'
PATRICIA SCANLAN

'A fab tale!'
OK! Magazine

'Heartwarming and witty. A wonderful début from Ireland's new answer to Jilly Cooper'
MORAG PRUNTY

'It made me laugh out loud'
ANITA NOTARO

'Fabulous fun – a sparkling début'
KATE THOMPSON

9780553816648

BANTAM BOOKS